"DANCE with me again." She stood and held out her hand. When he took it, she pulled him to his feet and draped an arm around his neck. She moved in close to him and he had no choice but to hold her. When she began to sway, he swayed with her. They danced in silence, but this time, when the song ended, she did not step away.

"I'm sorry that you lost so much," she told him.

Jason shrugged. "A lot of people have lost more than I did. A lot of people have it worse than . . ."

She drew his face down to hers and kissed his mouth to stop the words. His lips were softer than she'd expected, hesitant, as if surprised to find themselves pressed to hers. But if there'd been some confusion on his part, it passed. His arms tightened around her and his tongue teased the corner of her mouth. When he started to release her, she pulled him back to her. It had been a long time since she'd been kissed like this, and she wasn't ready to let him go.

BY MARIAH STEWART

At the River's Edge
The Long Way Home
Home for the Summer
Hometown Girl
Almost Home
Home Again
Coming Home

Acts of Mercy
Cry Mercy
Mercy Street

Last Breath
Last Words
Last Look

Final Truth
Dark Truth
Hard Truth
Cold Truth

Dead End
Dead Even
Dead Certain
Dead Wrong

Forgotten
Until Dark
The President's Daughter

AT THE RIVER'S EDGE

THE CHESAPEAKE DIARIES BOOK 7

MARIAH STEWART

BALLANTINE BOOKS • NEW YORK

A Ballantine Books Mass Market Original

Copyright © 2014 by Marti Robb
Excerpt from *On Sunset Beach* by Mariah Stewart copyright © 2014 by Marti Robb

Published in the United States by Ballantine Books, an imprint of Random House, a division of Random House LLC, a Penguin Random House Company, New York.

BALLANTINE and the HOUSE colophon are registered trademarks of Random House LLC.

This book contains an excerpt from the forthcoming book *On Sunset Beach* by Mariah Stewart. This excerpt has been set for this edition only and may not reflect the final content of the forthcoming edition.

ISBN 978-0-345-53842-0
eBook ISBN 978-0-345-54559-6

Cover design: Scott Biel
Cover image: Britt Erlanson/Cultura/Getty Images

Printed in the United States of America

www.ballantinebooks.com

9 8 7 6 5 4 3 2 1

Ballantine Books mass market edition: February 2014

For those adorable Maybaum boys

ACKNOWLEDGMENTS

Many thanks to Jim Delvescovo for walking me through the renovation of my fictional restaurant. I also have to thank Jim for letting me occupy space in his restaurant (Aurora Pizza and Pasta Kitchen in West Grove, PA) while I wrestled with dialogue, untangled plots, and bullied uncooperative characters—not to mention his amazing fig pizza and butternut squash agnolotti, and his terrific staff, who never fail to greet me with a smile and a glass of unsweetened iced tea.

To Helen Egner, for many, many years of friendship and for handing over several of her prized recipes for inclusion in this book.

At the River's Edge represents a crossroads in my career. For thirty of my last thirty-two books, I had the joy and privilege of working with Senior Editor Kate Collins. For almost twenty years we discussed, dissected, chopped and diced characters, plots, motivations, and career direction. Kate, I miss you and will always remember how you strived to make my books better, and wish you all the best.

As always, when one door closes, another opens.

With Kate's retirement, the editing of my books passed into the extremely capable hands of Senior Editor Junessa Viloria. *At the River's Edge* is the first book we've worked on together, and I can say with complete honesty that it's been a total pleasure. Every comment, every suggestion, was spot on, and I am grateful for her thoughtful and insightful editing. I can't thank her enough for making this a painless transition.

Thanks to the incredible team at Ballantine Books for their part in getting this book—and all my books—off the ground and into the hands of readers.

And lastly, thanks to my Facebook friends for making me laugh and smile every day.

Diary ~

I keep thinking about that expression, "bucket list." It seems that, these days, everyone has one—present company excluded. My, the things people want to do before they die . . . well, let's just say, to each his own.

Now, I have to admit that I've never really thought about it—my life is full and I've done pretty much everything I've wanted to do. I married my soul mate, had three terrific kids, and raised them in this wonderful town surrounded by love and family and friends in abundance. I have my work—my newspaper, passed down through several generations and entrusted to my care. I've been to Paris and Rome, and Dan and I celebrated our twentieth anniversary in Egypt, before travel there became so dicey. I've seen pretty much what I wanted to see and done most of what I wanted to do. So no bungee jumping from the Eiffel Tower or scuba diving with sharks for me, thank you. Someone in my circle of friends actually has those two on her list—not for me to say who, of course, but it's got me wondering if that person wishes to meet her maker sooner rather than later. If she passes anytime soon, you can be sure I'll be asking those who have already passed if Bungee Jumper a/k/a Swims with Sharks arrived banged and bruised or missing a limb or two.

That Ouija board does come in handy at times.

It would be nice if the weather this year would make up its mind—winter or spring? Cold enough to freeze your Winnebago one day, melting all over the place the next. At the risk of sounding like an old fogey (someone called me that just the other day. Cheeky little bugger!), I miss the old days when winter meant three months of cold weather that gradually gave way to spring. This warm-cold-warm-cold nonsense has the trees and the spring bulbs not knowing if they're coming or going. Clay—that would be my son-in-law—said last week he's covering his peach trees at night because he's afraid the buds will pop too soon and he'll end up losing his entire crop to a freeze. Some say it's global warming; others insist it's just nature following an age-old pattern. Either way, it's annoying the devil out of me. Now, I'm not one to wish away my life, but I could happily skip right through February and March and get right to April.

And of course, this year spring will bring a wedding many of us have been looking forward to. Jesse Enright and Brooke Bowers are tying the knot in April. Poor Brooke was widowed far too young—these recent wars have been devastating to our young generation. For her to have found love again—and with such a wonderful young man—well,

I couldn't be happier for them. Our invitation arrived yesterday and I was delighted to be included in their big day. Of course, I will cover the wedding for the newspaper. Some think it's old-fashioned, but the St. Dennis Gazette has been covering weddings in this town for over one hundred years, and I'm going to keep that tradition alive for as long as I own the paper. Which will be until I leave this world, because I'll never sell it. I was hoping that one of my children would take it over someday, but I'm not holding my breath. Daniel is perfectly happy running the inn, and Lucy's event planning business is going great guns. Yes, of course, there's always Ford, but I can't see my youngest settling down to run a small-town newspaper. I'll even go out on a limb here and predict that, after years spent living in all manner of places as a UN Peacekeeper, chances are that running the St. Dennis Gazette is not on Ford's bucket list.

~ Grace ~

Chapter 1 ⌁

SOPHIE Enright stared at the two flat tires on the driver's side of her car and wondered if she'd ever had a worse day in all her thirty-two years.

It started when both the victim and the star witnesses for the assault case she was prosecuting failed to appear in court and were nowhere to be found. The judge had given her until four o'clock to produce them, and when she couldn't, he dismissed the case.

It was never a good day when that happened.

She opened the trunk of her car and peered inside. One spare, two flats. She slammed the lid, got into the car, called her boyfriend, Christopher, and listened while the phone rang, then went to voice mail.

"I'm on the fourth level of the parking garage with not one, but two flat tires. My case went into the tank after my victim and my witnesses failed to show and I was forced to endure a blistering tirade from Judge Palmer. I'm parked in my usual spot. Bring food."

She disconnected the call, then dialed for roadside assistance.

"I'll need your guy to bring a spare," she said after

being told that they had someone on the road in her area.

"Not a problem," the dispatcher assured her. "Hang tight right there and we'll have you fixed up in no time."

Sophie sighed and searched her bag for the paperback novel she'd started over the weekend, grateful that she had enough gas in the tank to keep the heater running. She opened one window for a little fresh air, then settled back into her heated seat to read. After twenty minutes, she tried Christopher again. Still no answer. Thirty more minutes passed, and she called the dispatcher once more.

"He's on his way," she was promised. "He'll be there any minute."

"Any minute" turned out to be fifteen, but once help arrived, both spares—hers and the one the driver brought with him—were changed and she was free to go.

She glanced at her watch: seven twenty. Cursing softly under her breath, Sophie turned the key in the ignition and started out of the parking lot. She drove down to the second level, which was now empty except for a black BMW sedan off by itself on the far side of the garage.

A black BMW sedan that looked uncannily like Christopher's.

She drove slowly around one concrete post, then another, and stopped in front of the car. How many black BMW sedans—complete with a UPenn sticker on the right rear bumper—could there be in the courthouse lot at this hour?

Sophie figured that Christopher—also an assistant

district attorney—must be working late. She started to dial his number once again, then decided to surprise him in the office. She parked next to him and got out, slammed her car door, and had taken three steps in the direction of the stairwell when she heard voices coming from the BMW. Without thinking, she walked around the car and looked into the backseat.

"Oh, crap." Christopher's voice.

"What?" a woman asked. "What is it? Chris, where are you going?"

The back passenger-side door opened and Christopher—*her* Christopher—emerged, his shirt unbuttoned, one hand zipping his pants and the other slamming the door to keep whoever was inside, inside.

"Sophie, I . . . I can explain . . . ," he stammered.

"No, actually, you can't." Sophie's stomach knotted and her mind went blank. She took several steps back, then got into her car and poked the key into the ignition with shaking hands.

"Sophie, wait . . . wait . . ." Christopher's voice trailed behind her as she pulled away.

"You asshole!" Tears rolling down her face, she yelled as loudly as she could, even though he couldn't have heard. "You are a total and complete *asshole*."

She slammed a hand on her steering wheel for emphasis. Her phone began to ring and she knew who it was without looking at the caller ID.

"I'm only answering because I want you to know what a dickweed I think you are."

He sighed heavily as if exasperated. "Dickwad."

"What?"

"I think the word you want is dick*wad*."

Funny, but that professorial tone that she used to think made him sound intellectual suddenly seemed obnoxious.

"Whatever," she snapped.

"Sophie—"

"Can it. We are so done."

She hung up.

She blew the red light at the corner and felt a momentary touch of relief when she realized there were no cars coming from the opposite direction and no police officers to flag her down. Since starting at the DA's office seven years ago, she'd been careful not to do anything that might cause her embarrassment when she had to face the cops in court. Getting stopped for running a red light would be one of those things . . . especially at that moment when she knew her mascara was running and her face was a blotchy mess from crying. Hardly the professional image she'd worked so hard to create.

The street in front of her condo was slick with the cold rain that had been falling since early afternoon, and she was lucky to find a parking spot close to her door. She hopped out and dodged puddles. Water splashed up on her legs and her skirt anyway, but she barely noticed.

The red message light was flashing on her phone, but she ignored it. She dropped her briefcase near the door and kicked her shoes halfway across the room. Then she went straight into the bathroom, turned on the shower, peeled off her clothes, and tossed them back into her bedroom, where they landed on the floor.

"Bastard!" She stepped into the steam and cursed softly under her breath as the hot water stung her back, stood under the steady stream until her skin began to pucker.

Reluctantly, she got out, dried off, and pulled on her oldest sweats—gray fleece washed so thin the fabric was almost see-through in places—and an oversized navy tee. She went into the spare bedroom, where she stored things she either had no immediate use for or didn't have time to deal with, and found a large box that had delivered a down comforter back in November. She'd been filling the box with clothes she planned on taking to a thrift shop, clothes which she now dumped unceremoniously onto the floor.

She dragged the box into her bedroom and tossed in all of Christopher's belongings that he'd left at her place. She opened her closet and tossed in his robe along with a few extra shirts, then added clothes from the dresser drawer she'd been happy to empty to make room for his jeans, underwear, and a few sweaters. She spied a book that rested on the table next to his side of the bed—a political thriller—and tossed it in. It landed spine out, the pages splayed atop his jeans. She hesitated, fighting the urge to smooth the creases and close the book, but she resisted after reminding herself that she'd been the one to recommend it to him.

She was tempted to remove a few key pages so he'd never know who the bad guy was and how he'd set up the hero, but even her wrath wouldn't permit her to deface a book.

"You're lucky I have a conscience," she muttered.

She tossed in a pair of sneakers she found under the bed, then returned to the bathroom for his toothbrush, shaving stuff, and the body wash he preferred over hers. Her apartment stripped of everything that was his, she pushed the box into the back hall, then dragged it down one flight of steps. She opened the back door and shoved the box out, positioning it so that it sat directly in front of the trash cans.

Sophie trotted back up the steps, phone in hand, texting as she climbed:

Your stuff is in a box behind my building. The trash men come at nine.

She hit *send* just as she arrived at her door.

She'd hoped that the purging of her apartment would make her feel a little better, but she still had that huge lump in her throat and that gnawing pain in the pit of her stomach. She considered calling a friend, thinking that maybe some sympathy would make her feel better, but she stopped midway through dialing the number. She couldn't face the actual telling of what happened, couldn't bring herself to speak the words. It hurt too damned bad.

I caught Chris with someone . . .

She frowned. She'd been so focused on *him* that she'd ignored his partner. Now she found herself wondering who that someone might have been. Was it someone she knew?

She tried to recall the voice she'd heard coming from the backseat—had it been familiar?—but in her shock, she hadn't paid close enough attention. Though she gave it her best effort, she couldn't make the voice play back in her head.

The phone rang again, and Christopher's voice filled the apartment for the fourth time. This time she sat and listened. This was the man who only two nights ago had declared his undying love for her. The man she thought she was in love with. The man she might even have built a life with.

She listened to his words of apology—at one point she even thought he might be shedding a few tears—and his sworn oath that "she" meant nothing to him. That it hadn't been planned, that it had just happened.

"The way your car 'just happened' to be parked in the darkest, most remote part of the garage?"

She rolled her eyes in disgust and left the room before he finished his message. She had reports to write explaining that day's debacle in the courtroom. Her heart might be burning and her insides in an uproar, but there was still work to be done.

It had been a long, rough night, and the morning found Sophie feeling almost as angry and hurt as she had the night before. She awoke with a massive headache, killer circles under her eyes, and a grumbling stomach. She scrambled an egg and forced herself to eat it, then popped a few Advils.

"This is no day to spare the concealer," she murmured as she applied her makeup in front of the bathroom mirror.

She put on a red cashmere sweater under her gray suit, and while ordinarily red heels would have been frowned upon in her ultraconservative office, today she felt they were a necessity. She brushed her black hair from her forehead and popped gold discs into her ears. She might feel like crap, but she was determined to look like a million dollars.

There was something about looking good that always made her feel better. And she did. Right up until the minute that she walked into the conference room for an early morning meeting and saw the smirk on the face of one of her co-workers.

The smirk was like a shot to Sophie's gut.

Anita Hayes. I should have known.

Sophie glanced away as if she hadn't noticed, and she kept her gaze on the memo she'd been handed even when Christopher entered the room and Anita moved over to give him a place to stand next to her. Sophie continued to act the professional, listening attentively though an ocean's roar of pain filled her head and she could feel Chris's eyes on her the entire time. Finally—mercifully—the meeting ended, and though she wanted nothing more than to bolt from the room, she walked leisurely to her office and closed the door, pretending not to notice the looks of sympathy from several others as she passed. But once the door was closed behind her, Sophie leaned back against it, squeezed her eyes tightly shut, and wished that the roof would fall on her head.

It took less than two minutes for her desk phone to buzz. She debated the possibility of ignoring it, but it could have been someone important. Like her boss.

"Soph, it's Gwen." Sophie's best friend in the office apparently hadn't been blind to what was going on. "What the hell?"

"I'll tell you at lunch."

"It's my day in district court," Gwen reminded her. "I won't be here. Tell me now."

"Christopher and Anita were . . ." Sophie sighed. "I caught them together in the backseat of his car. In the parking garage."

"In the *parking garage*? Chris and *Anita Hayes*?"

Gwen all but gasped. "Is he nuts? She's the office skank."

"Apparently he didn't get that memo."

"What are you going to do?"

"I'm going to pretend I don't know either one of them. What else can I do?"

"You've got more balls than I do. If George did that to me, I'd be off and running for some nice quiet corner where I could nurse my broken heart and suck my thumb in peace. Right after I sent him screaming into the night with a fork in his eye."

"Running away doesn't solve anything, and while I do love the image of Chris with something sharp painfully protruding from his face, I've prosecuted enough domestic violence cases to know I don't want to go where they send you."

"There is that," Gwen agreed. "But either way—running or incarcerated—at least you wouldn't have to look at him or her every day."

Gwen had a point, Sophie considered, one that was driven home when she left the confines of her office around eleven and saw Christopher go into the library, followed within seconds by Anita, who closed the door behind her.

Yeah, Gwen definitely had a point.

⌒⌒

"Of course you can come for a visit. Stay as long as you want." Sophie's brother, Jesse, had sounded pleased when she called to ask if the following week would be convenient for her to visit. "We never get to spend time together since I moved." Jesse paused. "But is everything all right?"

"Everything's fine." Sophie swallowed hard. "Well, except that Christopher and I did break up."

"I thought the two of you were getting serious."

"Apparently that was only one of us."

"What happened?" Jesse asked.

"I don't feel like going into it right now, if that's okay."

"Sure, but if you ever feel like talking . . ."

"I know. Thanks, Jess. I'll see you on Saturday."

"Can't wait, kiddo."

Jesse was three years older than Sophie, and he was now making his home in St. Dennis, Maryland, a small town on the Eastern Shore of the Chesapeake Bay. He'd gone there to join their grandfather's law firm and had found the love of his life. Jesse and his Brooke would be married in a few months, and Sophie thought their love story had "happily ever after" written all over it. She couldn't be more pleased for her brother—he'd always been a good guy and if anyone deserved to be happy, it was Jesse. She smiled, recalling how he'd always taken his role as big brother very seriously. On the phone, she downplayed the situation with Chris because she could imagine Jesse's reaction and she didn't want to deal with any more drama this week. She just wanted to put Christopher out of sight. With any luck, out of mind would eventually follow.

When Sophie asked Joe, the district attorney, for the week's vacation she'd been floating, he'd readily agreed. That she had no trials on the docket for the next several weeks made it easy for him to say yes. Somehow she made it to the end of the week without breaking down in the office or losing it in court. If anyone in the office—including Chris and Anita—thought she was running away, well, let them. It might very well have been the truth.

On the other hand, Sophie decided she'd rather think of this trip as *running to* than *running from*. After all, who wouldn't love a week away in an idyllic little Bay town with nothing to do but relax, visit with a favorite relative, and eat glorious food? If at the same time a broken heart began to mend, so much the better.

Chapter 2 ᔗ

JASON BOWERS sat in his pickup outside the chain-link fence that surrounded the vacant lot, engine idling, a container of steaming coffee in one hand and a pair of binoculars in the other. Through the lenses he could see across the open space to the bare trees at the back of the property and clear on down to the river that ambled along till it met up with the Chesapeake a few miles to the west. He'd taken to making this a regular stop on his way to work every day since he first saw the "For Sale" sign posted on the gate back in November. The single acre was so overgrown with weeds that the Realtor had been forced to hire someone to come in to cut them down and clean up the lot so that prospective buyers could get a decent look at the grounds. The *someone* the Realtor hired had been Jason, and for him, it had been love at first sight.

For the past two months, he'd found himself drawn back over and over, not yet tired of imagining the way his nursery would look when he finally got it up and running. He'd blacktop the area from the road down to the trees so he could store his heavy equipment—the Bobcat, backhoes and riding mowers, his dump truck, and the extra pickup—and still have room for the piles of mulch and soil he'd need for his landscaping business. Not to mention parking places. He was planning on needing lots of parking because he was already envisioning lots of customers.

Jason wanted it all so much he could taste it.

Eighteen months ago, he'd sold his Florida landscaping business. It had been a tough decision: he and his late brother, Eric, had started building it before Jason had even graduated from high school. Eric had put up half the money that had gone into making Bowers for Landscape a success, and Jason felt obligated to return that money to his brother's widow, Brooke, after Eric was killed in Iraq. That obligation had brought him to St. Dennis with no intention of staying, but the opportunity to spend some time with his nephew, Logan—Eric's only child—had kept him around longer than he'd planned. The longer Jason stayed, the harder it was to think about leaving.

For one thing, Logan was the image of his father, and that alone tugged at Jason's heart. The fact that Logan was Jason's only living relative made it even more difficult to move on. Once he'd made the decision to stay in St. Dennis, Jason knew he was doing the right thing. Family connections had opened prominent doors—Brooke's brother, Clay, was married to the daughter of the owner of the town's most popular inn, and Brooke was marrying the grandson of St. Dennis's most prominent resident—but Jason knew it was his hard work that kept his phone ringing.

When he first arrived in St. Dennis, Jason had struggled to establish himself in a town where everyone seemed to belong but him. Thanks to a few influential people, like the Sinclairs and Jesse's grandfather, Curtis Enright, Jason was slowly building up his business. But in order to prosper, he needed to expand. And in order to expand, he needed more equipment, along with property on which he could park it all, and he'd need to branch into retail sales of garden supplies. The long-neglected field on River Road was exactly what he'd been looking for. After a week's worth of haggling with the owner, his offer had been accepted, and settlement was now only a week away.

He could hardly believe his good fortune, but he had the owner's signature on the agreement of sale and had an appointment tomorrow to look at some equipment that was being sold by a retiring landscaper from a neighboring town. There were times—such as right now—when he felt like pinching himself.

Jason took one last sip of coffee before returning the cup to the holder, replaced the lens caps on his binoculars, and tucked them back into their case. He made a U-turn and eased past the old cyclone fence that separated his property from the one next door, where a square stone building stood. Boarded up and covered with vines, it looked every bit as neglected as the lot he was buying, but once cleaned up and renovated, it would make a sweet little shop for the retail business he'd open as soon as he got the nursery going. He'd already had his Realtor contact the owner to see if they could work out a deal, but the owner wasn't interested in selling right then. Jason would just have to bide his time, maybe have the Realtor try again in the spring.

Of course, he'd have to hire someone to run the shop because he'd always been an outside guy, but he was a smart enough businessman to recognize a void in the marketplace when he saw it, and Jason planned on being the person to fill it. The closest big-box store that carried garden supplies was sixteen miles from St. Dennis and carried plants that were grown who-knew-where across the country in factory-sized, warehouse-style greenhouses. Jason's perennials would be field grown right there in St. Dennis.

Jason sighed. He'd had all that and more in Florida, and it had killed him to sell it, but it had to be done. That was all behind him now, and there was nothing to be gained by looking back. He told himself that things had all worked out for the best, and there were times when he really believed that. Except for the fact of Eric dying, he wouldn't change much about his life these days.

Jason wondered what Eric would have thought about living in St. Dennis.

It was a nice enough place, with pretty streets, a lot of old houses, and fabulous views of the Chesapeake Bay. St. Dennis was a town that was fat with history. There were homes several centuries old and families that had lived there almost as long. And all things considered, *here* was better than most places. Here he could be a part of Logan's life, and he knew he had Jesse to thank for that as much as Brooke. Even though Jesse would soon be Logan's stepfather, he never seemed to resent the place that Jason played in the child's life. In fact, it had been Jesse's idea that Jason share coaching duties of Logan's basketball and soft-ball teams, and he never failed to let Jason know when there were school plays and concerts. All in all, St. Dennis was a pretty good place to have landed, especially when he considered the fact that he didn't have any real ties to anywhere else.

That was okay, too. For the most part, he kept himself too busy to think about it. Most days he worked from dawn to dusk building up his clientele. Time off was mostly devoted to Logan or joining a few of the guys he'd made friends with—Jesse, Clay, and Cameron O'Connor, the local contractor—for a beer or two. He'd had a few dates since moving here, but he hadn't met anyone who'd interested him enough to spend much time with and he'd never been one for casual dating. Small talk always seemed like a waste of time to him. He knew some people were pretty good at it, but he wasn't one of them. If he occasionally felt pangs of loneliness, well, everyone got lonely from time to time, right? As far as he could see, one-night stands in a small town like St. Dennis could only lead to trouble. If the right woman came along, one that turned his heart as well as his head, he wouldn't walk away. That just hadn't happened yet, and Jason wasn't one to use up valuable time worrying about something he couldn't control.

The important thing right now was that his business was growing. Those few months between selling his old business and establishing the new had been torture. He'd been focused on work since he was fifteen, and without that focus to give him an anchor, he'd felt adrift. He loved what he did and he was really good at it. Back in Florida, his landscape designs had won competitions. He was looking forward to building Bowers for Landscape into an award-winning firm on the Eastern Shore as well.

All in good time, he reminded himself as he turned

the truck around on the broken concrete that he'd replace once he held the deed in his hand. Right now, he had a crew to get working and later this morning, a meeting with old Curtis Enright, who'd asked him to stop by this morning to go over a special project.

Jason smiled as he headed back out River Road. He had a full day ahead of him, dreams that were becoming reality, and a feeling that something . . . *something* was on its way.

Life was good.

Chapter 3 ~

"FOR some reason, I always think the drive to St. Dennis takes less time than it does." Sophie took a seat at her brother's kitchen table and sipped the coffee he'd just poured for her. After leaving her home before dawn, it felt good to finally have arrived at her destination.

"Why didn't you fly instead of exhausting yourself driving all that way?" Jesse leaned back against the counter.

Sophie shrugged. "I guess I just wanted some time alone."

"You live by yourself." He'd pointed out the obvious.

"Not the same as having hours alone in the car. When I'm home, I'm either working on a case or sleeping." Or snuggling with Chris, but there was no reason to mention that, now that *that* chapter had ended. "It was good for me to have some uninterrupted time to think. You know, put things into perspective."

"Things like what?"

"Just stuff."

"What kind of stuff?" he persisted.

"I don't think you'd like it."

"Try me."

"I've been thinking about making some changes in my life." *None of which you'd approve.*

When she hesitated, he gestured for her to continue. "Such as . . ."

"Such as maybe exploring other career options."

"Other career options?" He frowned. "What other options? I thought you liked your job. I thought you enjoyed being a prosecutor, bringing the bad guys to justice and all that."

"Well, yeah, I do like that part," she admitted. Choosing her words carefully, she added, "I'm just not sure that law is the right field for me, at least, not forever."

"This has something to do with you breaking up with what's-his-name, doesn't it?"

"Maybe. Probably." Time to fess up. "To be honest, yeah. But this isn't something that hasn't occurred to me before. It just seems that now might be the best time to consider other possibilities. You know, maybe see if there isn't something else I'd rather do."

"That sounds to me like a bunch of rationalized b.s." Jesse was still frowning. "And why the rush? Why now?"

Sophie sighed. "When you get totally entrenched in something, it's harder to move away from it. The longer you do it, the more difficult it is to give it up and try something else." She averted her eyes. "I just feel that if I don't do something now, I never will. I'll be a lawyer forever."

"And that would be bad because . . . ?"

"Because maybe I'd be happier doing something else. Maybe law really isn't the right thing for me."

"Like I said, rationalized b.s."

"Jess, I need a change."

"This guy really did a number on you, didn't he."

"Yeah. He did. But the situation has also made me think about some things that I've been avoiding."

Brother and sister stared at each other for a long moment.

"Look, the truth is, I went to law school because I thought that was what was expected of me. You, Dad, Mom . . . everyone in the family is a lawyer. Okay, Dad's might not be the footsteps either of us wants to follow, what with the scandal and him having been disbarred and all, but there's you and Mom. Not to mention our grandfather and uncle and several cousins. The law is like the family business, Jess. I never thought I'd have a choice."

"Okay. I get that part." Jesse nodded. "Sure. But what's the alternative? What else would you do? You've never done anything else."

"Not true." Sophie smiled. "You're forgetting about all those summers when I worked at Shelby's. Every year, college right through law school."

"The diner?" Jesse choked on his coffee. "You were a short-order cook."

"I loved it," she confessed. "That was the best job I ever had."

"Oh, come on . . ."

"Nope. I loved it. *Loved* it."

"Well, hey, there's a little dive over on River Road that might be for sale. You could always give up law and live out your short-order fantasies right here in St. Dennis."

She set her cup down on the table and met his eyes.

"Where," she asked, "is River Road?"

Jesse groaned. "Forget I mentioned it."

"No. Really. Where's River Road?"

"I can't believe I let you talk me into bringing you here," Jesse grumbled when, fifteen minutes later, he parked in front of the old square stone building that sat in the middle of an untended lot.

"Humor me." Sophie got out of the car the second it stopped.

"I'm trying to." Jesse turned off the ignition. "Wait up. You don't know what might be living around this place."

"Like what?"

"Raccoons, rats . . ."

"Oooh, not raccoons! Anything but raccoons!" She feigned horror, rolling her eyes, and kept walking.

The building was perfectly square, the front door smack in the center, with big double windows on either side, both of which were boarded up. Dead vines clung to the stone as far as the second floor, and the entire front was flanked by an impressive growth of dead weeds that must have been formidable last summer. A large sign hung crookedly from the side of the building. The name of the restaurant was painted in faded green letters on what had been a white background, but dirt and debris made the sign illegible.

Sophie pointed to the sign and asked, "Can you read the name?"

"Let me see." Jesse pretended to look from several angles. "Yeah. I think it says D.I.V.E."

Ignoring his sarcasm, Sophie took a few steps back and to the right, trying to get a different perspective.

"I think it says 'Walsh's.' "

"Maybe the people who owned the place." Jesse appeared unimpressed.

"How long do you suppose it's been boarded up?"

Jesse shrugged. "No idea. I only noticed the place the other day when I drove by on my way to drop off some papers at Dallas MacGregor's office."

"It still blows my mind that an A-list movie star like Dallas MacGregor lives in St. Dennis."

"Not only lives here, but she's got her own production company here now. She bought some old warehouses just down the road and is renovating them. She wants to make her own films here."

"I heard about the studio." Sophie stopped in midstride. "It's going to be right down the road?"

"Yeah, about a half mile. Maybe a little less."

"Hmmm . . ." She tucked away the information.

Her inspection took her around the right side of the building, where she found more boarded-up windows and a staircase that led to the second floor.

"I don't know how stable those steps are," Jesse cautioned when she started up the stairs.

"I just want to peek. I bet there's an apartment up here."

"If there is, it's locked up, so you're wasting your time." Jesse looked at his watch. "And mine."

At the top of the stairs, Sophie tried to peer through the windows, but the tissue she found in her bag was woefully inadequate to remove the amount of dirt that had built up on the glass. "I can't see much," she called down to Jesse, "but it looks like it's totally empty. What do you suppose is the story on this place?"

"I don't know. Violet might, though."

"Violet who works in your office?"

"She's lived in St. Dennis forever. If there's a story, chances are she'd know it."

"Good point." Sophie descended the steps and walked around to the back of the building. More windows, another door, all boarded up.

"Seen enough?" Jesse joined.

"Almost. Any idea where the property lines are?"

"Well, you've got the river down there, so it could go all the way down to the river through the woods."

She could see through the labyrinth of shrubs and bare-limbed trees all the way down to the riverbank. When summer came and the trees leafed out, that view would be obscured. The dense leafless overgrowth continued as far as the gravel driveway that belonged to the boat rental place a stone's throw down the road to the left.

"And I'd guess that the end of the parking lot out front is the right-side line," Jesse said, pointing toward the macadam lot.

"That cyclone fence your first clue?" She frowned at the ugly fence that ran the length of the property on the right side. "I wonder who owns that hot mess."

Jesse shrugged. "I've no idea."

"That fence has to go."

"Good luck with that."

Sophie stood with her hands on her hips, surveying the tangle of vines and brush that surrounded the building, mentally removing it. Except for a few of the large trees that could give shade to outside diners, most of what grew there was haphazard and unsightly.

"What are you thinking?" Jesse asked.

"I'm thinking how cool this place could be if it was all cleaned up." She turned and pointed toward the jungle that grew around them. "Clear away all that stuff and you have a great space here. You could see all the way down to the river. A patio would be perfect out here for alfresco dining. And if that fence was replaced with something that was less of an eyesore, over there I could . . ."

"Don't." Jesse covered his face with his hands and begged, "Don't go there, Soph."

"Why not?"

"Because this place is a mess on the outside and it's probably even worse inside. Because you'd have to spend a fortune to make it look like anything." He paused. "Do you have a fortune I don't know about?"

"I have some savings and some equity in my condo, but nope. No fortune."

"There you go, then. Look, it's okay to dream, but some dreams shouldn't be acted on. This is one of them. It wouldn't be practical, sis. You know nothing about running a restaurant. And your experience cooking on the grill at Shelby's aside, you're really not a cook, and let's face it, that alone isn't enough to run a restaurant. If you want a change in your professional life, come to work with me." He took her arm and guided her through the brush to the front of the building. "I need another attorney in the office now that Uncle Mike has retired for good. I'd actually thought about calling you, but I was under the impression that you were happy where you were, doing what you were doing. If you're serious about making a big-time change in your life, why not move down here and help me out?"

"Jess, you couldn't possibly have enough work for both of us."

"Are you kidding? There's more than enough. Ask Brooke how many nights and weekends I've had to work these past few months just to keep up with my own cases while I'm taking over Uncle Mike's."

"I don't know, Jess . . ."

"Just think it over." He glanced at his watch again. "Right now, I have to pick up Logan. He has basketball today and I'm one of the coaches."

"Can I tag along? I'd love to see my soon-to-be nephew."

"I'm sure he'll be happy to see you, too. And you know the boy loves an audience."

Sophie got into Jesse's car and snapped on her seat belt with some reluctance. She'd have loved to explore the property a little more, would have loved to test the lock on that back door to see if she could get a look inside. She was only half listening to Jesse as he pulled away from the building and headed to Brooke's family farm, where she and Logan lived in a house on the property. Sophie's imagination went into overdrive. If all that ground to the left of the front of the building was part of that parcel, she could have a garden. Flowers for the tables and herbs and vegetables for the dishes she could serve. Contrary to her brother's opinion, she *was* an accomplished cook. Granted, she'd never cooked full-time for a living, but her summers at Shelby's had taught her a thing or two.

She shook her head in an attempt to dispel the picture of that square stone building dressed up with window boxes spilling over with petunias and verbena, and fresh paint on the door, on both sides of which she'd plant hollyhocks and Shasta daisies and Knock Out roses.

She must be mad to even consider it.

Well, she'd be mad to consider it with the limited knowledge she had about the property, but she knew where to go to get the information she needed. Jesse wouldn't like it, but really, would it hurt to ask?

After a cheery reunion with her soon-to-be nephew and two long periods watching seven- and eight-year-olds play their version of hoops, Sophie wandered over to the bench where Jesse and the three other coaches were trying to send the team's next group of players onto the court.

"Jess," she said, waving to him. "When you get a minute . . ."

"What's up?"

"I think I'm going to walk over to see how Pop's doing." It had been a month since Sophie had seen their grandfather, and while he always appeared to be in good health, he was well into his eighties.

"Great idea." Jesse reached into his pocket and pulled out a set of keys. "Here, take my car. I'll get a ride with Jason." He gestured over his shoulder in the direction of the bench. "You remember Jason Bowers, right?"

Sophie glanced at the tall guy leaning over to speak with one of the boys.

"Eric's brother. Logan's uncle." The guy she'd mentally nicknamed *Uncle Hottie*. "Sure. We met at Pop's birthday party."

Jesse nodded. "Right. I'm sure he won't mind dropping me off."

"Thanks, but I think I'd like to walk. I spent so much time sitting on my butt already today, it'll feel great to move around. The weather is mild and sunny, much nicer than what we've had in Ohio this winter. I'm pretty sure I remember how to get to Pop's. Across the field to the dirt road, to Charles Street, then left on Charles until I get to Old St. Mary's Church Road, then straight on down to the end?"

Jesse nodded, his eyes on the player who was just coming up to the foul line. "Take your time, Brandon," he called. "Don't rush the shot."

"I'll see you back at your place later on." Sophie tapped Logan on the back to say goodbye, then headed toward the exit. Once outside, she walked across the baseball field onto the dirt road leading to St. Dennis's main street.

It *was* a great day, and it felt good to stretch her legs and breathe in the cool, fresh air tinged with the scent of salt. St. Dennis was a pretty town, with a picturesque marina and a row of shops that sold everything from souvenirs to antiques. Sophie passed a flower shop where pansies spilled over the sides of pots lining the front window, a reminder to passersby that spring was coming. Next door was Cuppachino, where the locals met for coffee and gossip, and across the street was Sips, where hot or cold drinks to go could be purchased along with the local newspaper, the *St. Dennis Gazette*. Sophie crossed at the light and stepped inside, where she bought a bottle of water and picked up a calendar of events that the St. Dennis Chamber of Commerce made available in the local shops. She stuck the calendar into her bag to look at later, then took a long drink from the bottle before tucking it into her bag with the calendar.

Next to Sips, the windows of the shop appropriately named Bling were filled with trendy fashions that caught her eye. On her last trip to St. Dennis, Sophie had dropped a bundle there on several sweaters, a bag, and some costume jewelry. She momentarily toyed with the idea of stopping now. She'd met the owner, Vanessa Keaton Shields, and was tempted to pop in and say hi. On the other hand, she was on a mission. Reluctantly, she walked past Bling—slowly enough to take in the lovely displays—and reminded herself to fit in a visit to the shop before the week was over. After Bling there was a bookstore, an antiques dealer, and a food market. Foot traffic in the center of town was light, but Sophie knew that once the tourist season began in the spring, the sidewalks would be crowded.

Had it been only a month or so ago that she'd fantasized about bringing Chris here to meet her grandfather? She banished the memory as quickly as it came. It was a beautiful day and she was here to put that unfaithful S.O.B. as far from her mind as she could. That so far she'd been unable to do that—that the pain beneath her ribs was still as sharp—was no reason to stop trying.

Sophie hesitated outside Brooke's bakery with its pink-and-white striped awning and the hand-painted sign announcing the shop's name—Cupcake—which hung in the window. Courtesy dictated that she stop and say hi to her brother's fiancée, but the day was passing quickly. Besides, she'd most likely see Brooke at dinner. She walked the few remaining blocks to Old St. Mary's Church Road and turned right onto one of the town's original streets.

Sophie reached the block where the old town square began. The magnolias and azaleas, which were yet to bloom, lined the brick walkways leading to the square's center. From her grandfather, she'd learned that the townspeople had gathered here for centuries to discuss whatever currently concerned them, from preparing a strategy against the British to escape destruction during the War of 1812 to hearing the local candidates for town council square off.

Across the street from the square, a modest sign identified the handsome red brick building on the corner as the offices of Enright & Enright, Attorneys at Law. Sophie had heard but lost track of how many generations of her family had practiced law beneath the slate roof. If she were to take Jesse up on his offer, she'd be part of that chain that stretched back many years. She paused on the sidewalk out front, contemplating the possibility. She'd been dreaming of leaving her current situation, of a life that offered something new and different. Joining Jesse at the firm would be a compromise that she wasn't sure she wanted to make. Was only half the dream worth pursuing?

Still, it would put distance between her and the source of her heartache, and that could only be a good thing, right?

The front door opened and an elderly woman stepped onto the porch. She held a grocery bag in one arm and her handbag in the other, and she appeared to be struggling with the door. Sophie hurried up the walk to offer a hand.

"Here, let me help with that."

The woman turned sharply, a guarded expression on her face.

"Oh, Sophie!" she exclaimed, her expression softening. "You startled me."

"I'm sorry, Violet. I should have called out to you. May I take that bag for you?" Sophie reached for the groceries.

"That's very kind, dear." Violet Finneran handed the bag over without protest. "I don't know what possessed me to load up that bag the way I did. I left the car at home this morning because it was such a nice day—I just love a warm day in January, don't you? I stopped here to bring in the mail and of course one thing led to another, and here it is, the afternoon passing . . ."

"It happens to the best of us." Sophie waited while Violet successfully locked the door. "Did you say you left your car at home?"

"I did." She hoisted her shoulder bag a little higher and reached for the bag of groceries.

"I have them," Sophie told her. "I'll walk with you. You're just a few blocks down and one street over, is that right?"

"What an excellent memory you have!" Violet nodded. "But I don't want to take you out of your way . . ."

Sophie shook her head and slowed her pace so that the older woman could keep up. "I'm going to visit my grandfather's, so I'm going your way."

"Well, then, I'd love for you to keep me company,"

Violet said. "Are you in town for the weekend? Jesse hadn't mentioned you were coming."

"I just decided on the spur of the moment to come for the week. It's been a while since I've had time to spend with Jesse, and with his wedding coming up, this might be my last opportunity to see him for a while."

"It's nice that you're so close, dear. I'm sure he's delighted to have you visit. Just don't let him put you to work unless he puts you on the payroll. That poor boy is working his behind off, now that your uncle Mike has left the firm and turned over all his files. It's too much for one person to handle."

"Is there really that much work here?"

"Oh, yes. Enright and Enright handles legal matters for most of the people in town—has for years. Now that Curtis and Mike have retired, it's all falling on Jesse. I keep telling him he should advertise for another lawyer, but he's reluctant to do that."

Sophie walked along in silence. Her brother wouldn't bring in someone outside the family to the firm, because it would no longer be Enright & Enright. She was beginning to feel the weight of his offer with each step she took.

On a whim, she asked, "Violet, do you know who owns that boarded-up restaurant over on River Road?"

"Yes, of course. It belongs to Enid Walsh, poor soul."

"Why 'poor soul'?"

"Enid's family owned that restaurant for more years than I can remember. It may not look like much now, but in its day, it was quite nice. They did a respectable business before the new highway was put in and directed traffic into the center of town. Her father died when Enid and her twin brother, Leon, were toddlers. They worked in that place alongside their mother from the time they were able to stand, till Ida—that's the mother—passed about eight years ago. Then Enid and Leon ran the place—ran it into the ground, some might say, but I try not to judge. When Leon died a few years back, Enid boarded up the place and hasn't set foot in it since."

"How many years are 'a few'?"

"Oh, let's see now. Might have been five or six. I hear she's had offers to sell it, but so far she hasn't been inclined to let it go. Don't know why she's holding on to it. I saw her at church a couple of weeks ago and if you ask me, she isn't long for this world."

"Maybe she just hasn't gotten the right offer." What, Sophie wondered, might be the right offer?

"What are you thinking, child?" Violet slowed her already snail-like pace.

Sophie shrugged. "It just looks like a place that could be really special in the right hands, that's all."

They walked in silence for an entire block. When they arrived at Violet's corner, they paused.

"I had an aunt and uncle who owned a restaurant up in Chestertown," Violet said. "It's terribly hard work."

"It is a tough way to make a living," Sophie agreed. "I spent seven summers working in a diner. It was hard, but I enjoyed it."

Violet started down the street and Sophie fell in step until they reached their destination, the third house from the corner. It was a handsome American four-square that sat back a bit from the street, had a wide front porch, and was shaded by an enormous red oak in the middle of the front lawn.

"I should call Enid and see if she needs a ride to church in the morning," Violet said somewhat absently as she searched in her bag for her house keys. "She hasn't been getting around too well lately."

"If you do see her, would you ask her if she's interested in selling the place?" Sophie tried to sound nonchalant, but she could tell by the look on Violet's face that she wasn't fooling anyone.

"I'll try to remember to do that."

"I'd appreciate it. I'd even be happy if she just let me have a key to wander around inside a bit."

"Oh, she doesn't have the key anymore." Violet pushed open her front door. "We have the key."

"We? Who's 'we'?"

"We at the office. Curtis—your grandfather, that is—handled all the legal work for the Walsh family. Enid gave us a key so that Mike could check it from time to time, you know. Keep an eye on the place. Said since her whole family was gone she couldn't bear to go inside herself."

"So Uncle Mike has the key?"

Violet shook her head. "No, no. Mike brought all the files back to the office. Jesse might have the key . . ."

Chapter 4 ❧

JESSE *has the key?*

Sophie's stride lengthened and her pace picked up with every step. *Jesse has the key?*

Walking briskly, her feet keeping time with her growing annoyance, she dug out her phone from her bag and speed-dialed her brother. The call went to voice mail.

"Call me, bro. You've got some 'splaining to do."

She dropped the phone into her pocket and kept up the pace all the way to her grandfather's home. But once there, she slowed her step, stretching out the trip to the front door, the better to take in the beauty of the old structure. Built of brick in the 1850s, styled after a Carolina manor house, it had been purchased by Sophie's great-great-grandfather after the Civil War, and for almost 150 years, Enrights had called it home. It was the largest and grandest house in St. Dennis, and its inclusion in the previous year's Christmas House Tour had had the town buzzing for weeks. Curtis Enright, her grandfather, hadn't entertained since his wife, Rose, died almost twenty years ago. People had lined up to buy tickets once it was announced that the Enright mansion, as the locals referred to it, would be on the tour.

It was an imposing sight, and it never failed to impress Sophie. Both the grounds and the house itself were beautifully maintained, and she couldn't help but wonder what it might have been like to grow up here. She could, of course, ask her father. If she were speaking to him, which she was not. Having managed to screw up almost every area of his life, Craig Enright was reportedly now on his fourth wife. It had been years since he'd made any effort to contact any of his children from his previous marriages.

How could someone grow up with all this—not just the grand home, but the love and support, which from all accounts had always been there for Craig and his brother, Mike—and still have his life go so far off the rails? Sophie shook her head as she rang the doorbell.

"Well, well. Look who's here!" Curtis Enright opened the door, a huge smile on his face when he recognized his granddaughter. "I didn't know you were in town, Sophie. Please, come in."

"Hi, Pop." She stepped into the cavernous front hall and his embrace at the same time. She hugged him once, then once more before closing the door behind her. Did he seem just slightly thinner, perhaps a little more fragile than she'd noticed when she was here in December? "How are you feeling these days?"

"Fine, fine. Never better. Here, now, let me take that jacket."

She slid off her peacoat and handed it over, then followed him toward the living room off to the left.

"Now, what can I offer you? Coffee? Some tea, perhaps?" He paused in the doorway, her jacket still over his arm.

"Nothing, thank you." She paused to look around, then smiled. "I like that nothing ever changes in this room." She pointed to the wall of family portraits. "I like that they all seem to be watching out for you."

Her grandfather laughed as he hung the jacket on the coatrack, then gestured for her to take a seat on the sofa. "As long as your grandmother is looking out for me, I don't need the likes of them. They're a nosy bunch. They keep an eye on everything, like they must know what's happening at all times."

"Think Gramma Rose is still hanging around?"

"Now what do you think?" Curtis's smile was indulgent. It was obvious what he thought.

Sophie, not so much.

"Oh, Pop, you know I have a problem believing in things I can't see."

"You hear that, Rose? Sophie can't see you, so she doesn't think you're here." He took a seat next to her on the sofa and turned toward the windows as if addressing someone. "What do you have to say to that?"

Rose Enright had been gone for decades, but to hear Curtis tell it, his wife had never really left, her presence made manifest by the occasional whiff of gardenia that had been her favorite fragrance when she was alive. Sophie had never believed in ghosts, though she had to admit that from time to time, she did, in fact, catch a sudden floral scent when she was in the house.

Like now.

"How did you do that?" Sophie's eyes narrowed

and scanned the room, searching for a vase of flowers but finding none.

Curtis laughed. "You know it isn't anything I've done. You just don't want to accept what your senses are telling you."

"I don't know what my senses are telling me, Pop." She dismissed what he considered the obvious.

"Well, let's just say I know what I know, and we'll leave it at that. Now, when did you arrive in St. Dennis and why didn't I know you were coming?"

"It was pretty much spur of the moment. Jesse's wedding is in a few months, and I got to thinking about how little I've seen him since he moved to St. Dennis, so I thought I'd take a week off and spend some time with him. I just arrived a few hours ago."

"Nice that your boss let you take a whole week off with such short notice."

"I have a lot of time accrued, and I was between trials," she explained. "I wouldn't have asked for the time if there was something going on next week."

"Well, then." Curtis leaned back into the sofa cushions. "Tell me about the most interesting case you tried in the past six months . . ."

An attorney who'd practiced for more than sixty years, Curtis had retired with some reluctance. He loved the law and made no effort to hide the fact that he missed his work terribly. Sophie was more than happy to share her courtroom experiences with him. For more than an hour, they discussed first one, then another case, him commenting from time to time ("Hmmm. Doesn't seem the defendant was very well prepared for your cross. Good for you, keeping one step ahead of 'em." Or, "Had a case like that one time . . .") and her occasionally stopping to ask him what he'd have done with the same case and set of facts.

"I'm certainly proud of you and the way you've taken to the law, Sophie. It's a shame you're tied to the DA's office back in Ohio. We could use you down here in St. Dennis." He eyed her carefully. "Any chance you'd be willing to think about joining Jess at Enright and Enright?" Before she could respond, he noted, "You know, with your uncle Mike and I both retiring last year, the firm is really only *Enright* now."

"I think Jesse can handle it on his own, Pop."

"I'm not so sure."

"Jesse's a good attorney." Sophie was taken aback slightly. Was her grandfather implying that he didn't think Jesse was up to his professional standards?

"Of course he is. He's a fine lawyer. I wouldn't have turned the firm over to him if I'd had any doubts about his ability. I couldn't be more proud of the boy. But even the best of us can't be in two places at the same time, nor do two things at once. Enright and Enright has always been the go-to law firm in St. Dennis. I need to be able to count on the next generation—*your* generation—to make sure it stays that way."

"Pop, I'm sure Jesse is doing his best."

"You're missing my point. Since your uncle Mike retired and turned over his files to Jesse, the workload is more than one lawyer can realistically handle if he wants to have a life. I'm assuming Jess wants a life, since he's getting married soon. I'd hate to see him start his marriage working an eighty-hour week."

"What about Mike's kids? Didn't one of them grad-uate from law school?" Because her father and his brother had been estranged for many years, Sophie had met her cousins only twice. She tried to recall what they'd told her about their career plans.

Curtis dismissed the comment with a wave of the hand. "Lightweight."

"Do you really think Jess is having a problem?" Jesse *had* mentioned a burgeoning caseload, but she assumed he was just throwing her a lifeline.

"If he isn't now, he will be before too much longer. Give it some thought. That's all I'm asking."

"All right." *Scratch Pop as a potential advocate for my big career change.*

"How are you feeling nowadays?"

"Fit as a fiddle. Just a bit of a lingering cough from time to time, but otherwise, couldn't be better." He cleared his throat.

"Pop, do you think you should be living here alone in this big house?"

"Now, you know I'm not alone," he replied softly.

"I hope you're not referring to Gram. Because if you fell in the middle of the night, I doubt she'd be calling 911."

"If I need 911, I'm capable of calling them myself."

"Not if you aren't near a phone."

"I have a cell phone, and believe it or not, I do know how to use it."

"You take it to the bathroom with you if you get up at night? You have pockets in your pj's or your robe?"

"Don't get smart with me, young lady."

"I worry about you. Jesse worries about you, too."

"Well, thank you very much, but I don't need anyone fussing after me."

"But Pop . . . if you fell . . . if you got sick . . ."

"And what's the worst thing that could happen if I do? I die?" He snorted. "You think I'm afraid of dying?"

"But . . ."

"Listen, missy, I'm more afraid of living another ten years than I am of dying before this one is over." He reached over and patted her hand. "This will be hard for you to understand, because you're so young, but I look forward to the day when my Rose and I are together again in the same dimension. Yes, she's here with me—more and more all the time, so I'm thinking maybe my time is drawing closer—but we're in two different spheres, she and I."

"Pop, is there something you're not telling me? Has your doctor . . . ?"

"No, no, nothing like that. Not to worry."

"Are you taking medication for anything?"

"I have a few prescriptions for some meds for my heart."

"Are you taking them?"

"When I remember."

"Did your doctor tell you to take them every day?"

"I suppose."

"And you wonder why I'm worried about you living by yourself, being alone all day?"

"I'm not alone all day every day. I have Mrs. Anderson—she's the housekeeper, cook, Jill-of-all-trades. She comes in around eight thirty, makes my breakfast, runs errands some days, does the laundry, keeps the house clean, makes lunch, cleans a little more, makes dinner before she leaves." He recited the list of chores as if from rote.

"She comes in all seven days?"

He nodded. "Most weeks."

"Well, at least there's someone who could help you up if you hit the floor."

Curtis laughed heartily. "I'm steady as a rock, Sophie. I'm not worried about taking a fall. Besides, I do have visitors. Mike stops in, Violet Finneran stops in, Jesse's over here every other day, old friends come by, though there are fewer of them around these days. Why, there's any number of people who can help me up if I 'hit the floor.'"

It would be impossible to miss the note of sarcasm in his voice.

"I'm hardly a recluse." Curtis's voice softened. "I appreciate your concern, but there's no need for it. I'm well, but if the good Lord decided to call me home tonight, I'd be just fine with that. I'm just waiting to go, Sophie, and I'm not one bit afraid."

"I really don't want to think about that." She thought about all the years she and Jesse had been estranged from their grandparents. "It seems like we've just found each other again."

"In that case, we should be smart enough not to waste any of the time we might have together talking about foolish things." Curtis slapped his hands on his thighs, then stood. "Want to see my latest project?"

"Your latest project?" Her eyebrows rose.

"Indeed." He reached for her hand. "Let's get our coats and take a walk."

Sophie slipped back into her jacket while her grandfather retrieved his coat from the front hall closet. Then he led her into the wide hall toward the back of the house, through the kitchen, and into a glassed-in area he referred to as his conservatory. Off to one side was an arched doorway, through which she could see the greenhouse.

"Are you growing something new?" Sophie started toward the greenhouse door when he tugged on her hand.

"I left all that to your grandmother. It's all I can do to keep her old favorites alive. Easier now, though, that I have help. You can wander through here later if you like." He steered her to the door that opened onto the backyard. "My project is out here. I'm very excited about it."

She followed her grandfather down three stairs to a path that looked new.

Sophie stood, hands on her hips, surveying the scene. "Well, it looks as if you've been busy."

"Wait till you see it all when it's done." He walked in the direction of the carriage house. "It's going to be restored to look just the way it did in the old photos we have. It's taking a while, but it's going to be worth it in the end."

"That's some project," she agreed.

"Oh, this isn't the project I was talking about." He paused midway to the structure. "That's over here." He took her elbow. "Over where the lawn's been dug up six ways to Sunday. It's quite the mess now, but it's going to be glorious when it's finished."

They followed the path to a spot where sections of the lawn were outlined with what appeared to be spray paint.

"What's going on out here?" she asked.

"This," he pointed beyond them, "is where the formal garden used to be. I'm having it restored."

"From which era?"

"Good question. I wasn't sure myself there for a while, but I've been working with a landscaper who has experience with this sort of thing. It's been quite exciting, actually. Rose would have loved it." His eyes were beginning to twinkle. "The most clearly defined garden we've been able to find is a layout consistent with gardens which would have been popular in the 1880s, and since we do have photos from that time period, that's the one we're going with." He pointed to the far end of the proposed garden. "And there, we're planning a rose garden."

"For Gramma Rose."

"Yes. She had a rose garden years ago, tended it like it was one of the kids. Unfortunately, most of the canes couldn't survive the terrible neglect I inflicted on them after she passed, but a few managed to survive. We'll be moving them so they'll be part of a permanent garden."

"That's a lovely idea."

"Whatever happens to me, I want to leave the house and the gardens in mint condition."

"This renovation . . . I'm guessing it's going to take a long time."

"It won't happen overnight," he agreed.

"Good." She hooked her arm through his. "That means you're going to have to stick around until it's finished. That could take years. You wouldn't want to have half a garden out here."

"I'm not a necessary part of the project at this point. My landscaper has his plans drawn up and the money has been set aside to complete the job. So regardless of what happens, the gardens will be completed. I don't have to be around to see it through."

His words had an ominous ring.

"Pop, are you sure there isn't something wrong, something I should know about?"

"Not a thing. I just like to cover my bases."

When she started to question him further, he squeezed her hand and made it clear he was finished with the conversation. "Now, how about we get your brother on the phone and see if we can arrange to meet him and Brooke for dinner tonight at Captain Walt's. I have a craving for rockfish, and I hear they're running this week . . ."

Chapter 5 ◡

"So what's with playing dumb about the restaurant on River Road?" Sophie was waiting for Jesse when he stepped through his front door. "Why didn't you tell me you had the key all along?"

"What are you talking about?" He dropped his gym bag in the hall. "What makes you think I have a key to that old place? And if I did, why wouldn't I have said so?"

"Because you think me running a restaurant is a stupid idea."

"Whoa, girl. Back up. Who told you I had a key?"

"Violet. She said the owner is a client and there's a key in the office."

"Well, Violet would know. The owner could be one of Pop's or Uncle Mike's clients. I haven't had time to go through all the old client files. I think I may have mentioned that fact." He went past her into the kitchen and turned on the cold water faucet. "But do I think it would be stupid for you to quit your job and open a restaurant when you have no clue how to run one and no game plan? Let's just say it probably wouldn't be your finest moment, kiddo."

He got a glass from the cabinet and filled it with water, then took a long drink.

"Well, what if I had a plan?" She knew she sounded pissy but couldn't help herself.

"Do you?"

"Not yet," she admitted. "But if I were serious about opening a restaurant, I most certainly would have a plan before I moved on it."

"That's reassuring."

"Sometimes you make me feel as if I'm ten again and you're fourteen, and it makes me want to stick my tongue out at you."

"Hey, if it makes you feel better . . ." He drained the glass and set it on the counter.

"What's going to make me feel better is taking a peek inside that building."

Jesse glanced at his watch.

"It's getting late and I need to take a shower. Pop called about dinner, and you know he likes to eat early. Brooke will be here in about an hour, and we need to pick up Pop by six."

"We could have time if we hurried."

He shook his head. "We'd have to go to the office and look for the key, and that could take hours."

"Violet might know where it is," she persisted.

"She probably does," he agreed. "Why don't you call her while I'm in the shower, and if she knows exactly where it is, and if there's time before we have to pick up Pop, we'll stop and get the key tonight. Otherwise, we'll get it in the morning, which is a better idea anyway, since I'm sure the electricity has long been shut off in that old place and you won't be able to see a damned thing anyway." He took his phone from his pocket and handed it to his sister. "Violet's number is programmed in. Go ahead and give her a call."

Jesse started out of the room.

"And between now and the time she answers, you think about how you're going to get approval from the owner for entering her property."

Sophie frowned. "If she gave you a key, doesn't that assume that she's okay with you going in?"

"I don't know the owner, therefore I do not know the circumstances of how we came by that key."

His voice trailed off as he climbed the steps.

"Violet will know," Sophie called back even as she heard his bedroom door close. "Violet knows everything."

She searched through the directory on his phone until she found Violet's number, then pushed *call*. Moments later, voice mail picked up, and a disappointed Sophie left a message for Violet to call back as soon as she could.

"Nuts," she grumbled as she started up the steps to get ready to go out to dinner. Once in the guest room, she opted for a quick siesta, just a few moments with her eyes closed against the fatigue of the long drive from Ohio.

The next thing she knew, Brooke was standing over her.

"Sophie, wake up," Brooke said softly. "Wake up."

"What?" Sophie opened her eyes. "Brooke . . . oh, crap, what time is it?" She shot up.

"Time to get up and get ready if you're going to dinner."

"Damn, I just thought I'd rest for a minute . . ."

Sophie sat up and shook off the dream she'd been lost in—one in which she and Chris were still together and happier than they'd ever been in real life. It had left a sour feeling in the pit of her stomach and a pain behind her eyes. She swung her legs over the side of the bed.

"Happens to the best of us. Hey, love your hair." Brooke reached out to touch the strands that fell past Sophie's shoulder. "I like it longer."

"Thanks. I hadn't planned on growing it out, but I never seemed to be able to find time to get it cut. I've had it short for so many years that it still looks a little strange to me."

"It looks great."

"Thanks." Sophie smothered a yawn.

"Jesse tells me you're here for the week."

Sophie nodded as she stood and stretched. "I thought I'd take a little time to hang out with Jess and spend some time in St. Dennis before the wedding."

"We're glad you're here." Brooke went to the door. "I'll tell you all about the wedding plans over dinner, but right now, you'd better get moving unless you want your brother bellowing about how late you're making everyone else."

"Hmmmm . . . sounds as if you've been there."

"Too many times to count." Brooke laughed.

"I'll be down in ten minutes," Sophie told her. "Well, maybe fifteen."

"I'll see if I can get Logan to distract Jesse, buy you a little more time."

"I just need fifteen . . ."

She'd actually needed that and then some. By the time she made it downstairs, she found Brooke and

Jesse milling about in the front hall, obviously waiting for her.

"I thought Logan was here," Sophie said.

"He is, but he's not coming with us. He's having dinner with Jason," Brooke told her.

As if on cue, Logan and his uncle came into the foyer from the kitchen.

"You guys know each other, right?" Jesse looked from Sophie to Jason as he slid his arms into a tweed sport jacket. "Be right back—forgot to lock the back door . . ." Jesse disappeared down the hall.

"Of course. How are you, Jason?" Sophie offered her hand.

"Great. Good to see you again, Sophie." He took her hand and held it for just a few seconds longer than might have been necessary.

God, but his eyes were blue, she thought as she met his gaze. Blue blue blue . . .

She reminded herself that a response from her was anticipated. "Ah . . . good to see you, as well."

"Hair's different," he noted. "Longer."

"Ahh, yeah." She self-consciously touched the strands that fell over her shoulder. "Seemed like a good idea at the time."

"Doesn't she look gorgeous?" Brooke smiled.

"Couldn't have said it better myself." Jason nodded.

Sophie felt the color begin to rise from her chest to her cheeks under that ice-blue gaze.

"Thanks." She turned from the unexpected compliment to her soon-to-be nephew. "Nice game today."

"I did good, but my team lost." Logan made a face.

"I saw you shoot a few times when I was there. You made a couple of nice baskets," she added.

Logan nodded proudly. "I'm real good at free throws."

"Remember what I told you," Jason prodded him.

"It's important to play your best, but it's more important for your team to win."

"Close enough. It's a team sport, Sport."

"Jace, are you sure you don't want to join us for dinner?" Jesse called from the kitchen.

"Uncle Jason is taking me and Cody for pizza," Logan called back. "And we're going to watch some movies."

"Uncle Jason sure does know how to do Saturday night," Jesse said as he returned to the foyer. "He likes to live large."

"I appreciate the offer," Jason told him, "but we already made plans."

"Yeah, we get ice cream after we have pizza." Logan obviously had planned the menu.

"Sounds like your evening's all mapped out," Sophie said.

"Uh-huh." Logan nodded. "Then we go back to Uncle Jason's and we eat popcorn and watch movies, and me and Cody sleep in our sleeping bags."

"Their Saturday night routine," Brooke explained to Sophie. "Gives Jesse and me a night out."

Sophie turned to Jason. "That's nice of you."

"Hey, there's nothing like being out on the town with your buds, right? Rolling with your posse?" Jason cracked a half smile and ruffled his nephew's dark hair.

Logan nodded. "Right. It's guys' night."

"So, you just here for the weekend?" Jason turned

back to Sophie, and she had to fight back a sigh that threatened to embarrass her.

"The week, actually," she managed to say.

"You've come at a good time," he told her. "We're having a warm spell. At least, they tell me this is a warm spell. I'm from Florida, so I'm still not convinced."

"I'm from Ohio, and after the winter we've been having, trust me, this is a warm spell."

"I'll have to take your word for it."

Logan tugged impatiently on Jason's sleeve.

"Right, buddy." Jason acknowledged the nudge. "We need to get going if we're going to pick up Cody and have time for a few other stops before the movie." Jason turned Logan in the direction of the front door.

"Behave yourself, now," Brooke told her son. "Don't you and Cody be giving Uncle Jason a hard time."

"We won't," Logan promised.

"And don't even think about going through that door without giving your mama a hug." Brooke stopped Logan the second his hand grabbed the knob. Logan turned back to hug her neck and sighed heavily.

"And button your jacket," Brooke called after her son, who fled out the door. "It's getting a little breezy." She turned to Jason. "Thanks, Jace."

"No problem," Jason assured her. "Jesse, Sophie— I'll be seeing you."

" 'Night, Jason." Sophie made a point of not watching him walk away, but there was something about him that drew her eye. She hoped it wasn't obvious, though she knew there was no harm in looking. She just didn't want her brother teasing her about some imagined interest in Jason Bowers. She just liked the way he walked.

"Sophie, you ready?" Jesse stood in the doorway. "We need to get moving. I told Pop we'd pick him up five minutes ago."

"How did he look to you the last time you saw him?" Sophie followed Brooke outside and waited on the walk for her brother. "Did he seem well to you?"

"For the most part, yes. Why?" Jesse opened the back driver's-side door and Sophie slid in while Brooke got into the front passenger seat. "Didn't he seem okay today?"

"He just seemed very philosophical about life and death and . . . I don't know. It was just a few comments he made, like looking forward to being with Gramma Rose again."

"He talks like that all the time. You know he thinks she's still there, in the house, right?" Jesse got behind the wheel and started the engine.

"What do *you* think? About Gramma Rose, I mean. There were times today when I could almost smell the flowers. I'm sure it was just the power of suggestion," she hastened to add, "but still . . ."

"You mean the gardenias?" Jesse nodded as he pulled away from the curb. "I smell them all the time when I'm there. I've stopped wondering why or how when there are no flowers in the house. It's just always there."

"I've smelled it, too," Brooke turned in her seat to face Sophie. "Even before I knew that your grandfather thinks his wife is still around, I smelled gardenias in that house. So who's to say? And does it matter?"

"I guess not."

"Did Pop show you the plans he has for the back of the property?" Jesse asked.

"You mean the historic garden re-creation and the rose garden and the carriage house? Yes, he showed me. Impressive." Sophie shifted in her seat. "He was very proud of his 'project,' as he called it. I just hope this landscaper knows what he's doing. I'm sure it's costing a fortune. I'd hate to see Pop scammed."

"Oh, I can vouch for the landscaper," Brooke told her. "It's Jason."

"Jason's a landscaper?" Sophie frowned. Had she known that and forgotten? "He does historic garden restorations?"

"Back in Florida, his company specialized in them. Gardens that were popular in Florida in 1880 probably didn't look like the ones here back then, climates and architectural styles being different and all that, but I'm sure he knows what he's doing. I've seen the sketches and I was really impressed. It's going to be gorgeous. I wish it could be done in time for the wedding. It would be a perfect spot for a garden reception, but it wouldn't be possible."

"You're having the reception at Sinclair's inn, right?"

Brooke nodded. "Jason designed the gardens there as well."

"That's how Pop came to hire Jason to work on his gardens. He saw the work Jace did there and was impressed. He's been really happy with the progress they're making at the house, and that's what matters." Jesse pulled up in front of their grandfather's stately home and got out of the car. "Pop's been talking about this project for as long as I've been in St. Dennis, and if it gives him pleasure—gives him something to focus on and look forward to—I say more power to him."

The front door of the big house opened and Curtis Enright appeared on the top step, carrying an overcoat.

"You're seven minutes late," he called to Jesse. "I'm an old man. I don't have time to waste sitting around waiting on other people . . ."

"Don't try to pull that 'old man' stuff on me," Jesse called back. "You're going to outlive us all."

Jesse leaned back into the car, smiling in spite of the scolding he was receiving. "Pop's in fine spirits, so buckle up," he told his sister. "This could be a long night . . ."

∼∽

Another Saturday night, another bowl of popcorn, another hour and fifty-four minutes of watching *The Goonies* followed by *Toy Story*.

Jason leaned back on the sofa, his long legs stretched out between the two sleeping bags where Logan and his buddy Cody were camped out on his living room floor.

"I wish we could find a treasure map like the kids in the movie did," Logan said while he loaded the DVD.

"Me, too." Cody sat up. "Or maybe we could find one of those underground tunnels. I'll bet there are lots of them around here. St. Dennis is really *old*."

"Yeah." Logan said, his voice rushed with sudden excitement. "There used to be pirates that came here. Everybody knows that. Maybe we could find their ship in one of those tunnels . . ."

"First we have to find the tunnels," Cody reminded him. "I wouldn't want to find one that had all those bats in it, though."

"First you have to find the treasure map," Jason told them both.

"Oh. Yeah." Cody sank back down into his sleeping bag as the video began.

They watched for few minutes before Cody asked, "Who would you be in the movie? I want to be Mikey."

"I want to be Luke Skywalker," Logan replied without hesitation.

"Luke Skywalker isn't in *The Goonies*," Cody told him. "He's in *Star Wars*."

"I know, but if I have to be a movie person, that's who I'm going to be." Logan turned around and tapped Jason on the knee. "Who would you be?"

"Chewbacca," Jason replied, and the two boys dissolved into laughter.

"Fleur should be Chewbacca." Cody picked up his little dog, Fleur, and held her up to Jason. "She's furry enough to be a wookie."

Fleur jumped from Cody's arms to the sofa and curled up next to Jason as if appalled by the very thought of being anything but a bichon frise.

"I think Fleur likes being a dog," Jason told them.

"Shhhh," Logan commanded. "I like this part . . ."

The boys fell under the movie's spell and Jason watched for a few minutes before leaning his head back against the sofa. Usually he tried to keep awake when the boys were watching movies, but the week's activities were beginning to catch up with him tonight and he was having a hard time keeping his eyes open. He'd been up by four thirty every morning and hadn't gotten to bed before one A.M. even once. There'd been sketches to be made, plants to be ordered, and résumés for prospective new hires to review, not to mention the physical labor he still did in addition to running the business. Between work and his Saturdays with his nephew, he had precious little time for a social life, but for now, that was okay. He'd always been a hard worker, but having to establish a new business in a new town made him even more conscious of doing what he had to do to be a success.

He thought back to those early days in Florida, after the car crash that took his parents' lives and shattered his and his brother's. He rubbed his left leg above the knee, where the pins that had been inserted to hold his leg together seemed to burn every time he remembered that night and that time. After the dust settled and Jason had recovered from his injuries, Eric figured out that the only way they could keep a roof over their heads and food on the table was to find some sort of work that they, as fifteen- and eighteen-year-olds, could do. While their maternal grandmother had been granted official custody of Jason until he turned eighteen, her love of gambling often won out over her love for her grandsons. For the most part, she was content to let Eric raise his younger brother. Those times when the boys found they needed something that resembled parental guidance, their next-door neighbor, Mrs. Hilton, was always more than happy to step in when Grandma was out of state visiting the casinos. Mrs. Hilton might have clucked her tongue at their guardian's behavior, but she'd never dreamed of alerting child services. She knew how important it was for the boys to stay together, especially after the terrible accident that had changed their world forever.

Seeing Logan and Cody curled up on the floor, laughing and giggling at the movie, shouting out the familiar dialogue at the appropriate times, reminded Jason of nights long ago when he was about Logan's age. He and Eric would pull the blankets off their beds and drag them into the small living room, make nests for themselves, then slip a video into the VCR. They'd pop corn and set the bowl between them, and settle into the latest movie they'd picked up at the Blockbuster two blocks away. Favorites would be played over and over again, until they knew all the dialogue by heart.

Jason could still recite lines from *Ghostbusters* at the drop of a hat.

The boys' shrieks of terror brought him back to the present and the film on his TV. The shrieks turned to laughter, then total silliness. Eight-year-old boys were eight-year-old boys, no matter the era. In that, Jason took comfort, even as the pain of missing his brother once again washed through him. He'd never stop missing Eric—Jason knew that, but sometimes the renewed awareness of his death came suddenly, and overwhelmed him. No matter how much time had passed, the reality of it could smack him in the chest, just as it had when it was still new. The loss had never grown old, and he doubted it ever would.

Jason knew he was lucky to have reconnected with Eric's son, lucky to be given the gift of being part of Logan's life. It wasn't the same as having his brother back, but Jason's ties to the boy were strong, and growing stronger, and he was grateful for that.

Jason opened his eyes and looked down on the boy, who was totally immersed in the drama playing out on the screen. Logan had inherited Eric's smile and his laugh, his sense of logic, his habit of rubbing one foot against the other when he was tired—like now, Jason noted—and Eric's way of tilting his head just slightly to one side when he was about to question your facts, your opinion, or your authority. It amazed him, when he thought about it, that little things like that could be passed on from father to son. Because of Eric's deployments, he'd spent precious little time with his toddler son, who had been far too young to have observed his father's behavior closely enough to memorize and imitate it. And yet there was Eric's smile, his laugh, the subtle habits that only someone who had known Eric well over a long period of time could have recognized.

"That girl looks like my stepsister." Cody pointed to the screen. "Paige, I mean. My mom says that Paige is just my sister now since my mom married her dad."

"I'm going to have a stepfather," Logan said softly. "When my mom marries Jesse, he's going to be my stepfather."

"I have a stepfather," Cody reminded him. "'Cause my mom married Grant."

"My real father's dead." Logan's voice was soft.

"My real father's a jerk," Cody countered. "He did bad things with ladies who were not my mom and made a video that lots of people saw." He hunkered down a little more into his pillow. "Kids from my old school saw it."

"If it was a bad video, why were kids allowed to watch it?" Logan asked.

Good question, Jason thought. *Eric's logic again . . .*

"Maybe not the kids, but their moms and dads saw it and talked about it. That's why we came to St. Dennis. My mom wanted to get away 'cause everyone was talking about it on the TV."

"That's 'cause your mom is famous and everyone knows her," Logan pointed out. It seemed that everyone knew that Cody's mother was Dallas MacGregor, a very famous movie star.

"Everyone here knows her, too, but no one's mean about it."

"Shhh, here's my favorite part." Logan effectively ended the conversation.

The popcorn bowl was empty, and Cody's dog was at the back door waiting to go out, so Jason picked up Fleur's leash and set the bowl on the kitchen counter. He stepped out into the cool air and wished he'd had the sense to grab a jacket. His southern sensibilities had yet to acclimate themselves to the northern winter. He followed the dog down the darkened street, pausing when she did. The scent of the Bay carried on the night wind, and he wondered how different the evening might have been if he'd joined the Enright crew at dinner. He hadn't known Sophie was in town, and her appearance at the basketball court that afternoon had taken him slightly off guard. He'd always sensed something special about her, beyond her pretty face and trim body, had always hoped that someday he'd have a chance to get to know her a little better. Maybe this time the opportunity would present itself, he thought as he turned from a gust of wind. And if not, he'd just have to make sure that it did.

Chapter 6 ⌒

SOPHIE stared out Jesse's kitchen window onto the fenced-in yard while she waited for her first cup of morning coffee to finish brewing in her brother's ancient coffeemaker. She wished he had one like the one that sat on her own kitchen counter, the one that brewed one fresh cup at a time. Hearing Jesse's machine gurgle and burp painfully, what to give him and Brooke for a wedding gift was no longer a question. Even the coffeemaker they had in the DA's office was better than this one.

She wondered if Christopher was fixing Anita's morning coffee the way he used to fix hers. Was he, right at that moment, picking up two Danishes from the coffee truck that always parked in front of the courthouse regardless of the weather? The coffee was terrible, but somehow Sis, the woman who owned the truck, managed to snag the best Danishes in town. On mornings when neither of them had court, she and Chris would meet first thing in his office. The thought of Anita sitting in *her* chair, drinking coffee he'd brewed, eating *her* Danish, made Sophie see red.

She squeezed her eyes closed as tightly as she could, willing the image to vanish.

Think of something else, she demanded. *Focus on something else. It's a beautiful day,* she reminded herself. *Don't let Christopher spoil this, too.*

She took a deep breath and stared out the window.

The yard was quite nice, Sophie told herself, forcing her attention outside. The small brick patio was surrounded by beds covered with dried leaves. She wondered when those beds had last been planted. If she were living here, she'd put in a garden. She'd do flowers around the patio and lots of herbs and some vegetables out there in the center of the yard, where it was nice and sunny. If she had a restaurant, she'd want to serve really fresh salads and a vegetarian dish or two. And maybe she'd plant some red peppers to roast with garlic and olive oil. Mint for iced tea to be served on hot summer days . . .

Stop stop stop! She tried to shake the thoughts from her head but they did not go gently. It had been easier to ban Christopher, it occurred to her. She wasn't quite sure what that meant.

The machine had just given up its dark brew when Sophie heard the front door slam.

"Jess?" she called.

"Yeah." He tossed his jacket over the back of a chair. "Hey, you made coffee. Thanks."

"Didn't Brooke make coffee this morning?"

"Yes, but she got up early to bake for the shop, and by the time I got up, it was sludge."

Sophie reached overhead into the cabinet and grabbed a cup, which she filled, and held out to her brother. When he reached for it, she pulled it back.

"First, the key."

"What key?"

"You know what key."

"Oh, you mean this one?" He pulled a braided green string from his pocket and dangled its lone brass key in front of her. "Could I interest you in a trade?"

She passed the cup over and he tossed the key into her outstretched hand.

"This is really it?"

"No, actually, that's my garage key."

"Jesse, you . . ."

He laughed. "Yes, it's really 'the key.' I stopped by the office on my way back from Brooke's and called Violet. She was just leaving for church, but she knew exactly where it was, as you suspected."

"Did she say why you had it? Did she think it would be okay if we went in?" Sophie asked eagerly.

"The owner gave the key to Uncle Mike so that he could check up on the property periodically. Make sure there'd been no break-ins and that the roof wasn't leaking, that sort of thing."

"When was the last time someone went in?"

"I couldn't tell. There was nothing in the file to indicate that anyone from the firm had made a visit."

"Then I'd say we were due."

"Well, *I'm* due." He smirked. "*A member of the firm* is due."

"Now that's just plain mean. If—and it's a big fat if—I ever decided to come to work with you, it would be because I wanted to and because I felt it was the right move for me, and not because you goaded or bribed me. That's a big decision to make, Jess."

"True. So I won't goad—but that doesn't mean I've given up. There are other ways . . ."

Sophie tucked the key into the pocket of her jeans. "I just need to grab my bag and put my shoes on. I can't wait to see what this place looks like inside."

"Don't get your hopes up," he called after her as she hustled toward the steps. "It's bound to be a mess."

Sophie drove her car because she wanted to see what it felt like to drive onto that lot and park near the door, though the reason she gave Jesse for wanting to drive was so that he couldn't rush her and threaten to leave before she was ready to go.

"This place is really off the beaten path," Jesse said as he got out of the car. "They probably didn't do much business here before they closed."

"Maybe not," Sophie agreed, "but the new movie studio should bring a lot of traffic down this way, once it's up and running. So not being in the center of town could be an advantage."

"How do you figure?"

"No competition." She fitted the key into the lock and it turned reluctantly. "Plus you heard that talk last night at Walt's about the bait shop next door filing for a permit to dredge the river to make it deep enough for larger boats to dock there, right?"

Jesse nodded.

"And that they might even build a marina right there so that visitors to the studio could come by boat?" Sophie pushed open the door. "People could fly into Baltimore, charter a boat, and just come right across the Bay." She paused in the doorway. "Boy, it's dark in here."

"Have a flashlight." He handed her one of the two he'd grabbed before they left the house.

"Thanks." She turned on the flashlight and scanned the room with its beam. "Maybe if we left the door open it would help."

Jesse pushed the door back as far as it would go.

"Not much better," he noted. "Dark and wow, really dusty. You sure know how to pick 'em."

She took her time walking around the room, shining the light on the four big windows in the front and the two smaller ones on each side, all of which were covered with boards. There was just enough light to see the ancient cash register that sat atop the L-shaped counter with its eight stools lined up along the left side of the room.

"It's not very big." Jesse sneezed. "Eight tables for two, five tables for four." With the beam he scanned the upturned chairs that sat atop the tables, their legs pointing toward the ceiling.

"Plenty big enough." She flipped the light switch on the wall. "Just checking," she said when the lights failed.

"The electricity's been off for a few years." Jesse sneezed again. "There was a note in the file that all the utilities were turned off."

"Allergies acting up?" Without waiting for an answer, she added, "Want to wait for me in the car?"

"What, and miss all the fun?"

Sophie pushed through a door behind the counter and stepped into the kitchen. It seemed even darker than the front room, but she could see two ranges, a double sink, a large refrigeration unit, and a couple of metal shelving units on wheels. She went to the back door, pushed aside the slide lock and a dead bolt, and pulled the door open. The cool air rushed in with the light, as if it had been waiting for a chance to enter.

"There's some nasty-looking stuff in here," Jess noted. "Wonder how long those dishes have been sitting on the drain board." He held the light over the windowsills. "Nice selection of dead flies, bees, and wasps here, if you know anyone who collects. Oh, and one damned fine cobweb. Might be the biggest one I've ever seen."

"Ugh! Mice droppings on top of the stoves." Sophie made a face and peered into an open cabinet. "Not to mention on the shelves."

"And the counters." The light from Jesse's flashlight skimmed along the countertop. "I wouldn't even think about opening that old refrigerator or looking inside either of those ovens. This place is pretty disgusting, Soph."

"Needs a good cleaning, that's for sure." Sophie sneezed three times in rapid succession.

"Needs to be razed. This place has 'biohazard' written all over it."

"It's not that bad. It's just . . . neglected. And dirty." She took a look around the room. "Very, very dirty. But there's nothing here that can't be fixed."

"You have got to be kidding." Jesse snorted. "Everything in this place needs to be tossed. It's all Dumpster fodder, if you ask me."

"Which I did not, but that's okay. You're entitled." Sophie closed the back door and relocked it. "Let's go look upstairs."

"Why?"

"Because I'm curious, that's why. And because I don't know when I'll get another chance."

Jesse sighed and followed his sister back through the dining area and waited outside while she locked the front door.

"It's probably as big a mess up there as it is down here," he muttered.

"Maybe," she nodded. "But you have a responsibility to your client. She's depending on you to keep an eye on her property. What if there was an electrical fire . . ."

"The electricity has been turned off."

"Lightning," she said as she rounded the corner of the building. "Could always be lightning, this close to the water."

"You're grabbing at straws."

Jesse followed her up the stairs that led to the second floor and brushed her aside when her attempts to unlock the door failed.

"Let me try." He jiggled the key and pushed, and the door opened.

"Thanks." Sophie walked past him into a large room that had windows on three sides. "Wow. Living room–dining room combo. I like it."

"You have to be kidding. This place is pathetic."

"It's a great space and it has great light," she pointed out. "And the kitchen . . . well, it's okay, I guess." She fixed the beam of light on the fridge and the stove, opening, then closing the doors. "Of course, there *is* a restaurant right downstairs."

She opened one of two closed doors and glanced inside.

"Bathroom. Shower and a tub."

On to the other closed room. "Oh, this would make a really nice bedroom. Big windows on the side and across the back, lots of light. Great view of the river."

"And like the first floor, probably infested with all sorts of living things you wouldn't want to share your space with."

Sophie laughed. "Oh, c'mon, Jess, it's a really good apartment. Spacious, airy, high ceilings . . ."

"Old everything here—pipes, wiring. I'll bet nothing in this building is up to code. And it's filthy, and I'll bet there's mold and that everything in the kitchen needs to be replaced."

"Exterminators. Plumber. Electrician. Lots of water and household cleaners." She counted them off one by one.

"Sophie, this is silly. Unless you're ready to quit your job and move to St. Dennis, this is a waste of time."

He leaned against the door that opened to the stairwell. "Are you ready to move to St. Dennis?"

She shook her head no.

"Then what's the point?"

"I wanted to see what was here. I wanted to see if it was a place I could make work for me, *if* I decided that was what I wanted to do. And *if* it ever came up for sale."

She pulled the key from her pocket and walked outside. From the top of the stairs, she looked around. The lot next door was completely surrounded by a chain-link fence and was even bigger than she'd originally thought, the parcel being not only longer, but wider as well.

"What do you suppose that's being used for?" Sophie pointed to the adjacent property.

"Doesn't look like it's being used for anything," he noted. "Just like everything else out this way. Except for the bait shop on the other side. You might get some business from the fishermen in the morning—assuming you're up at four when the boats head out on their first run."

Through the bare trees across the road, she could see almost as far as the Madison farm.

"You can almost see Brooke's family farm from here." She pointed toward the barely visible barn roof.

Jesse leaned on the railing that surrounded the landing and followed her sight line, then nodded. "Yeah, I think that's the old barn."

Sophie turned and locked the door.

"This place is pretty isolated, though. Not much traffic, no neighbors at night. I doubt the bait shop stays open too late. And next door, that fenced-in place." Jesse shrugged. "I don't know what that is."

"But as I mentioned, Dallas will be bringing in a lot of people this summer, and if the bait shops gets its permits and dredges for a marina, there will be boats coming and going. And besides, you and Brooke will be living at the farm, so you'll be right through those trees. Why, we'd practically be neighbors."

"Please tell me you're not serious about all this." He waved a hand to take in the building.

"I'm not serious." She finished locking the door, then handed him the key before taking off down the steps.

"Why don't I believe you?"

"Because you have a suspicious mind."

"The only thing that's suspicious is the fact that you are barely reacting."

She smiled and got into the car. He got into the passenger seat and turned to her. "So is your silence your way of conceding that this place is good for nothing but a bulldozer?"

"I am not conceding anything." She started the car and turned around in the parking lot.

"That's what I was afraid of."

"I won't do anything stupid, Jess. Right now, I just want to feel as if I have some options." She stopped the car at the edge of the road. "I want to feel as if I can change my life if I decide that's what I want to do."

He nodded. "Got it."

"So don't waste any more time badgering this witness, okay?"

"I'm not trying to badger you. I want you to think about what you'd be giving up in Ohio. I just want you to be happy."

"I know."

"I want you to find as much happiness as I have. If it's here in St. Dennis for you, as it is for me, so much the better. It would be nice to have you around more, especially since I'm getting married, and Brooke and I are going to want to start a family. I'd like you to be a bigger part of that."

"Thanks, Jess." She started to pull out onto the road but paused to allow a pickup pulling a trailer to pass. When the road was clear, she eased onto the macadam and headed back toward Jesse's house. "I know there are a lot of things to consider. I have a lot to think about."

For the rest of the day and through the night, it seemed Sophie could think of little else but the way the restaurant would look all cleaned up. If she bought it, the name wouldn't be Walsh's anymore, though she really had no idea what she'd rename the place. The dingy walls and furniture could be painted, the counter and floor refinished, the windows scrubbed clean. The kitchen would need a major overhaul; there was no getting around that. Of course, maybe in the light, things would look better.

Then again, they could look worse.

The one thing Jesse was right about was the need for an exterminator. No way was Sophie going to deal with rodents on her own. Who knew how many generations of mice had taken up residence in the walls? She wasn't going to be the one to evict them.

One thing she hadn't shared with her brother was that while the appliances were old, they were top quality from what she could see. With any luck, the fact that they'd sat unused for a few years might not spell doom. Those two old Vulcan ranges could have a lot of miles left on them.

"Top of the line, Vulcan is," Thomas, the old cook at Shelby's, often said. "Still good fifty, sixty years, if you don't abuse them."

Of course, who was to say the ranges at Walsh's hadn't been abused?

And the big refrigeration unit—she'd bet just about anything it was a True. She'd know for sure when she could see it in the light. It might need a new compressor, but there was a good chance it could be revived.

Not that she'd share any of this with her brother. At least not until she had a game plan, which right now, she did not have. She'd been honest with him about that. She wasn't about to resign from her job without giving it much thought. It would be a big move, to pull up stakes in Ohio and move here to start something new. She liked thinking about the possibility, but she wasn't sure that in reality she was ready to take such a leap of faith. No, Jesse needn't worry that she was going to pull up stakes and leave her law career in Ohio.

At least, not yet.

Chapter 7 ⌐

"So what's on your agenda for today?" Jesse packed a stack of yellow pads into his briefcase, which lay open on the coffee table in his sparsely furnished living room. "Where did I put that file . . . must have left it up on my desk. 'Scuse me . . ."

He blew past his sister, who stood in the doorway trying to decide whether she had an agenda, and if not, whether she should. One of the nice things about taking time off from your job was that you didn't have to *have* an agenda if you didn't want one. For Sophie, a Monday morning that didn't find her racing out the door with a twenty-pound briefcase in one hand and a pair of shoes in the other had all the makings of a good day.

"Gotta run." Jesse reappeared, stuffed some folders into the briefcase, closed the lid, and headed for the front door. "Stop in at the office later. I should be back from court by noon."

"Maybe," she called after him as he closed the front door behind him.

Sophie sat on the bottom step of the staircase and contemplated the free morning—the free day—that awaited her. The house was so quiet, she could hear herself breathe. She got up and went into the living room and turned on the television just to hear something other than the exhaling of her lungs. She flipped from one channel to the next until she hit on one of the morning shows, where a well-known, bestselling author was talking about her new book and the movie deal that had just been cemented. The conversation held Sophie's attention for about three minutes before her mind began to wander and she started to think about what might be going on back at the office.

She pulled out her phone and sent a text to Gwen:

Miss me? What's hot?

Sophie's joy at having a free morning began to fade into guilt. She probably should be at work today. She shouldn't have let her emotions force her into leaving town, tail between her legs, to hide out until the office chatter died down. There were other things she should be doing besides sitting on the arm of her brother's sofa in his little rented house in this pretty bay town, watching morning television and wondering how to spend a Monday for which she had no plans.

Her phone alerted her to an incoming text.

Damn right. C. & A. are the talk of the office. Everyone's appalled. Having fun?

Great. The entire office now knew that she'd been dumped for Anita.

A. can have him. Fun abounds here. Miss you 2.

She turned off the TV and went upstairs to change out of her pj's and robe. It was cooler this morning, so she pulled a heavy sweater over her jeans and zipped up her ankle boots. After grabbing her bag from the dresser and her jacket from the chair onto which she'd tossed it yesterday afternoon, she ran down the front steps and into the morning air.

The walk to Charles Street was invigorating, if without destination, and she paused at the corner of Cherry and Charles, debating which way to go. The door to the coffee shop across the street opened and a small group went in. Cuppachino, the town's coffee shop, drew the locals like a magnet every morning by seven. The best coffee in town, she recalled, so she crossed the street when the light changed and pushed open the red door.

From past visits, Sophie knew to place her order at the counter. While her coffee was being prepared, she glanced around the room. A lively discussion was taking place at the table next to the front window, and Sophie recognized several of the participants, who were too deeply engaged in their conversation to notice her arrival. She knew the white-haired woman seated with her back to the room would be Grace Sinclair, owner of the town's only newspaper, the *St. Dennis Gazette*. The family of Grace's late husband had built and still owned the Inn at Sinclair's Point, the town's most celebrated inn and destination wedding venue. Next to Grace, Steffie Wyler MacGregor leaned on the back of a chair as she chatted. Steffie was the town's well-known ice-cream maker whose shop, One Scoop or Two, sat down near the Bay and drew visitors all year long. Next to Steffie was Brooke, and Clay Madison, Brooke's brother, sat next to her. A woman with black hair pulled into a severe bun sat across from Clay. Sophie couldn't hear what was being said, but it was obvious that several differences of opinion were being voiced.

The door opened and another customer came in just as Sophie's coffee was placed on the counter.

"Hey, Sophie. Good morning."

She turned as Jason Bowers approached the counter.

"Oh, Jason. Hi." She opened her bag and drew out her wallet.

"I've got this one, Josh," he said to the young man behind the counter.

"Oh," she said, surprised. "You don't have to . . ."

"Hey, it isn't every morning I get to buy coffee for a beautiful woman. Especially one who appreciates the chaos of an eight-year-old's basketball game."

"How can I refuse when you put it that way?" She smiled up at him. "Thank you."

"You're welcome." He leaned one elbow on the counter, his body half-turned in her direction. "You're up and out early. Aren't you supposed to be on vacation?"

"I needed some good coffee. The stuff my brother has is barely two levels above swill."

"Best coffee anywhere, right here," he agreed and placed his order.

Josh reached for a ceramic mug from the array that lined the shelf behind the counter.

"I need it to go," Jason told the young man. "Sorry. I should have told you."

"What are those mugs?" Sophie pointed to the shelf.

"Special mugs." Josh grinned. "For our special customers."

"How do you get to be a special customer?" she wondered aloud.

Josh grabbed several mugs and placed them on the counter so she could read the names on them.

"Bling. Book 'Em. Petals and Posies," she read aloud.

"For the regulars who have businesses in town," Josh elaborated as he rung up Jason's order.

"Jesse's is the fifth one in," Jason pointed out. "Guess he hasn't been in yet."

"He has court in Ballard," Sophie told him. She turned to Josh. "Could I see Jesse Enright's mug, please?"

He held up the mug that read ENRIGHT & ENRIGHT in black script on one side, and J.C. ENRIGHT on the other. She was tempted to reach for it, to pour her own coffee from its plain white mug into her brother's, but felt it would have been the mug equivalent of cheating. She didn't work for the firm, and she wasn't a regular, though she might be this week.

Josh handed Jason his change, then showed Sophie the mug he'd returned to the shelf moments earlier: BOWERS FOR LANDSCAPE in green block print.

"Very nice touch," Sophie noted.

"The mugs were the owner, Carlo's, idea," Josh told her. "His wife makes pottery, so every time a new business opens, she makes the owner a mug. It encourages them to become regular customers if they aren't already."

"Any of them ever sit unused?" she asked.

"Nope." Josh grinned.

"Clever idea." Sophie nodded.

"People seem to like it. Keeps 'em coming back." Josh added, "And the coffee, of course." He pointed to a table near the back wall and told Sophie, "Creamer, sugar, over there."

"Right." She picked up her coffee and moved to the table. She'd just finished adding half-and-half when she sensed Jason behind her, not touching, but there. The awareness went up her spine in a slow tickle.

"So how are you spending your vacation week?" He set his large Styrofoam cup next to her mug on the table. "Any special plans?"

"None." She added sweetener to the coffee, then stepped out of the way to give him room, which also gave her space between herself and Jason. The man was imposing, tall and broad-shouldered, and needed the space to fix his coffee, she told herself, ignoring the fact that being close to him was causing an embarrassing albeit involuntary flush to spread from her neck clear up to her hairline.

"Everyone needs a little downtime."

"I'm not used to downtime," she admitted. "I feel as if I should be doing something."

"You *are* doing something." He turned those blue eyes on her. "You're having a great cup of coffee on a Monday morning, maybe even sitting a while and chatting with some friends who are happy to see you." Jason gestured toward the front of the room.

Brooke was waving to get Sophie's attention, and the others at the table had turned to wave as well.

"Sophie! Come join us," Brooke called.

"So, there you go. You've got something to do." Jason smiled and touched the small of her back.

She felt that light, brief touch all the way to her toes. It was unexpected, but definitely not unpleasant.

"Grab a chair, Sophie." Brooke motioned to the chairs that stood around the table behind her.

"Take mine," Steffie told her. "I was just leaving.

Stop in at the shop while you're in town. I'm playing with new ice-cream flavors this week."

"Count on it." A number of articles had been written about Steffie's ice cream, which had been selected as Best of the Bay by several publications. Sophie never visited St. Dennis without making at least one trip to Scoop, as the locals referred to the ice-cream shop.

"Well, this is a nice surprise," Grace Sinclair greeted her.

"It's a nice surprise for me, too." Sophie took the chair Steffie had vacated.

Grace nodded in the direction of the woman with the dark hair. "You've met Nita Perry? She owns Past Times, the antiques shop a few doors down from Bling."

"We haven't met, but I've passed by your shop several times and have admired your window displays." Sophie smiled across the table at the antiques dealer.

"Come in next time. I've all sorts of wonderful things besides what you see in the windows," Nita told her.

Drawn into conversation about how long she'd be in St. Dennis, and what she should not miss while she was there, Sophie was still aware of Jason's presence at the table, though he and Clay stood off to the side and were involved in a quiet discussion. She'd been hoping to ask him about his plans for her grandfather's property, but one minute he was there, just at the periphery of her vision, and the next he was leaving.

"Thanks again for the coffee," Sophie told him.

"Anytime, Sophie. Good seeing everyone this morning. Miss Grace." He patted the older woman on the shoulder as he turned from the table. "Sophie. I guess I'll see you at Logan's school on Wednesday."

"You will," Brooke nodded. "Sophie just doesn't know it yet."

"What about Logan's school?" Sophie tried hard not to watch as Jason left the shop and crossed the street directly in front of the window, where she had full view as he walked to his pickup.

"Science fair at Logan's school on Wednesday. There's a sort of meet-and-greet the teachers and cookies and punch, that sort of thing," Brooke explained. "Logan asked me to ask you if you'd come."

"Of course I'll come. I imagine Jesse is going, too." Sophie took a sip of her coffee. It was every bit as good as she remembered from her last visit. "This leaves Jesse's stuff in the dust."

Brooke laughed. "Tell me about it. Sometimes I wonder if he actually has taste buds. We're hoping he'll be able to make it on Wednesday. He said he'd try his best to be there."

"Why wouldn't he be?" Sophie asked. "I'd think he'd be happy to go. The annual science fair was a big thing when we were growing up. Jesse always took one of the top prizes. He loved science."

"That's what he told Logan. He's just been so jammed with work lately. Most nights he's at the office until seven or eight, and he brings work home."

"Okay, I get it." Sophie put her mug down. "Really. I do. You can stop."

Brooke looked at her blankly. "Stop what?"

"Stop trying to convince me that I should go into

practice with Jesse because he's so overworked. Jesse put you up to it, right?"

"Jesse is overworked, but I didn't know there was a possibility that you'd be coming to work with him."

"I'm not."

"Then why are we talking about it?"

"Because Jesse only brings it up every chance he gets."

"It's no secret that since your uncle retired, Jesse's plate is overflowing. And now with the paralegal having left . . ."

"Liz is gone?" Sophie frowned. "Jess didn't mention that."

"She left last week. Went back to Jacksonville so her kids could be closer to her family. Friday a week ago was her last day."

"So Jesse really is the only person in the office now?"

"Jesse and Violet, who's had to come back to work full time until he can find someone to take her place, and I'm sure you know that Violet is irreplaceable."

"So he's really three people down in the office," Sophie murmured. "Liz, my granddad, Uncle Mike."

"Has he considered one of those temp services?" Grace joined the conversation.

"I don't think he's had time to, well, time to think," Brooke told her.

"My granddaughter might be able to help out," Nita said as she rose, her PAST TIMES mug in hand. "She's been working for a lawyer over in Annapolis for the past couple of years, but she might be looking to make a change."

"I'll mention it to Jess," Brooke said.

"He can call me at the shop. Which is where I need to be." Nita glanced at her watch. "I like to have a few hours in the morning to putter, move things around, before I open."

"I need to get going, too." Clay stood. "I'm supposed to pick up Wade and go look at some equipment that a brewery over near Rehoboth is selling."

"I guess I should get going as well." Brooke drained her mug—pink with white letters that spelled out CUPCAKE. "Monday is my big baking day. I was in extra early this morning, so I convinced myself that I could take a break, but break's over."

Grace sighed. "I'm afraid I'm going to have to be off now, too. I'm meeting with the new president of the historical society to discuss this year's project for an article to run in this week's paper, assuming I can write it fast enough." She stood, one hand on the table to give her leverage. "Seems everything takes me longer these days. My fingers don't move as quickly on the keyboard and my right hip is giving me trouble this week. Getting older can be so tedious at times."

"Thanks for letting me join you this morning, Miss Grace." Sophie rose, her mug in her hand. She reached for Grace's mug, which had been left on the table. "I'll take this up to the counter for you."

"Oh, thank you, dear. Well, I hope I see you again while you're visiting." Grace patted Sophie on the arm.

"Maybe I'll stop back in another morning."

"Oh, do. We're here every day. Sometimes the group is larger, sometimes smaller. It all depends on

who shows up on any given day, but all are welcome.
I hope you feel welcome, too."

"I do, thanks." Sophie carried the mugs—her plain
white one, Grace's with THE ST. DENNIS GAZETTE written in white on marine blue—to the counter, where
she handed them over to Josh. He nodded his thanks
as he whipped up a cappuccino for a woman who
watched him intently.

"Did I hear you say you walked, dear?" Grace appeared to be waiting for Sophie on the sidewalk outside the coffee shop.

"I did."

"Would you like me to drop you off somewhere?"

"Oh, no, thank you. I'm enjoying the freedom of
just taking off and walking wherever this morning.
It's such a nice day."

"A bit chilly for me, but at least the sun is toasty."
Grace drew gloves and her car keys from her bag. "If
you're sure . . ."

"I'm sure, but thanks." Sophie gave a quick wave,
then buttoned her jacket against the breeze as she
crossed the street. She really hadn't given much thought
to her destination, but now that she was out and about,
and fueled by caffeine, she headed toward Old St.
Mary's Church Road and the law offices of Enright &
Enright. Jesse wouldn't be back from court, but Violet
would be there, and Violet was the person Sophie
really wanted to see.

At the sound of the opening door, Violet turned
sharply to peer into the hall.

"Oh, Sophie. It's you." Violet sounded relieved.

"Were you expecting someone else?" Sophie came

into the reception area, and as always, felt an urge to lower her voice. The dark hardwood floor was covered with an ancient Oriental carpet, and the paintings on the walls were of early St. Dennis street scenes and early Enright ancestors. The walls were wainscoted below richly colored wallpaper, and the furniture was all well-polished mahogany. The room was quietly elegant and well appointed, and bespoke of decades of legal matters resolved calmly with expertise and civility.

"Jesse's not back from court yet." Violet returned to her desk, where a large stack of paper awaited her. "I was just trying to sort the mail."

"I thought he'd probably be out most of the morning. Actually, I thought I'd stop in and see you for a few minutes."

"That's lovely, dear, but I don't have much time to socialize." Violet rested one hand on the pile of envelopes on the right side of her desk. "The mail is just overwhelming these days. Since Liz left last week, it's been all I can do to keep up with it."

"I heard that Liz left."

Violet nodded. "We put an ad in the paper as soon as we found out she was going to leave, but Jesse hasn't had time to go through the résumés we've gotten in response. I've tried to sort them, weed out the ones that obviously won't work—you know, the ones with all the misspellings, including the name of the firm, and the ones without experience. But even that's getting away from me these days." Violet heaved a heavy sigh. "I'm just too old for this."

"Maybe I can help." Sophie pulled a chair over to

Violet's desk. "Pass the résumés over here and I'll see if I can get that pile down for you."

"I'd appreciate that." Violet slid the entire pile of envelopes across the desk. "There's another stack on Jesse's desk. I left them there with the hope that he'd have time to look them over during the weekend, but apparently not. It doesn't look as if they've been touched."

"My fault. I insisted on making him take me to see that boarded-up restaurant on River Road." Sophie opened an envelope and glanced at the cover letter. No experience. Into the trash it went. She looked up at Violet and grinned. "No point in wasting anyone's time with applicants who clearly aren't qualified."

"I suppose I could have done that myself, but I didn't feel right making that decision for Jesse."

"You're as much a part of this firm as Jess is," Sophie told her. "Didn't you work for my grandfather for, like, forever?"

Violet laughed. "It does seem that way. I did try to retire when he did, but then along came Jesse, and while I admit I was skeptical about him for a time, he did win me over."

"Skeptical because of our dad." Sophie nodded. She knew the story.

"Yes." Violet met Sophie's eyes without apology. "Your father was a scoundrel. I suppose he still is and always will be, though God knows why he should have been. He was always loved and he was raised right, and he still turned out to be a scoundrel. Your grandmother was my best friend, and he broke her heart. Some things you don't forget. Some you can't forgive."

"I have a hard time understanding him, too." Sophie started to open another envelope, and Violet passed her a letter opener with a silver handle. "Actually, I don't understand him at all."

"He was always a handful, that boy, but once he hit high school, he became worse. Always in trouble of one sort or another. Made it through college somehow, though he was bounced out of the first school he went to. Law school, he barely graduated, but he did pass the bar. Then he met and married that lovely Delia and had those three sweet children . . ." Violet shook her head. "Whatever possessed him to leave her—and them—I'll never know. Your grandmother Rose told me that he had no contact with Delia and the children after he left. He just walked away from that family, and she never did know why. Oh, I understand he did pay some child support, but still, what kind of a man does a thing like that?"

"No answers here." Sophie shrugged. "He met my mom after he left Delia, and they had Jesse and then me. Then he met someone else and he left us as well. Now he's onto his fourth wife—at least I think she's his wife, but I'm not sure that they're actually married. I don't know if his divorce from Pam—she was wife number three—is final. I think the new woman is a lot younger than he."

"I'd say she was a gold digger, but since he was disbarred, I don't suppose he's making as good a living as he could have."

"I don't know her—don't know anything about her—and I haven't seen him, so there's not much I can say."

"It has to weigh on you, though." Violet's hands rested atop the letter she had yet to begin to read.

"Oh, it does. At least, it used to. These days, I guess I just feel that he's made his bed—literally—and he's going to have to live with the choices he's made."

"How is your mother? I haven't seen her in years."

"My mother is great. Terrific. She has a successful career—she's made partner in the firm she works for—and she has what looks like a solid relationship with a very nice man. I don't think she has a lot of complaints about her life these days." Sophie balled up another résumé—no legal experience—and sent it overhand to the trash can. "I'd say all of us have weathered the storm that was Dad and we all came out okay. Of course, Judd's still really young, so the jury's still out on him. Then again, with Pammie for a mother, who knows how he'll turn out."

Sophie was aware that there was an edge to her voice every time she spoke of or thought about her father, and she knew that Violet had picked up on it, because the older woman fell silent. It was hard to talk about him, harder than she ever liked to admit. The years after he'd left them for Pam had been painful for all of them. But in the end, things had worked out well enough. Her mother had been forced to take out loans to go back to law school, but after a few low-level jobs, she'd landed one she loved and had excelled. Craig hadn't yet been accused of siphoning funds from a client's account—charges he vehemently denied even as he was disbarred—so the Enright name hadn't yet carried the stain it would later bear. Jesse and Sophie had gotten through college and law school on student loans, which they were both still paying off, but the end was in sight on that score. So while they'd been down for a while after Craig left them, they were never really out, thanks to their mother's strength and smarts and her no-excuses approach to life.

Funny, Sophie thought—her father's first wife, Delia, had managed pretty well, too. After Craig had dumped her and their children, Delia started writing mystery stories—at first to amuse herself at night after her kids, Nick, Zoey, and Georgia, had gone to bed. She'd found she was good at it, and eventually found the nerve to submit her writings to a literary agent, who found a publisher for the first three of what would become dozens of bestselling mysteries. Delia Enright was to this day one of the top-selling writers in the country. Her latest book sat on the coffee table in Sophie's living room.

"Funny how both your mother and Delia blossomed after Craig," Violet said.

"Funnier yet that I was just thinking the same thing." The lesson wasn't lost on Sophie. Could she rise above her failed relationship and flourish, as her mother and Delia had?

Perhaps, but maybe not while she remained in the DA's office.

"Well, I guess a lot of women find themselves once they're on the other side of a bad relationship," Violet went on. "I'm not sure why, but a lot of women really come into their own. Maybe it's because they want a new direction in life, and that makes them focus on what's important to them. Some women find strengths they never knew they had—strengths they might never have found if they'd stayed in a relationship that proved to be bad for them. Sometimes all we need to grow into the person we were meant to be is a little push, however painful that push might feel at the time."

"Not everyone has that kind of strength. Not everyone can find their way out, or see beyond where they are." Could she?

"True," Violet agreed. "But we've handled our share of divorces in the years I've been here, and I've seen a lot of women who changed their lives for the better when they had to."

"Change is harder for some people than it is for others. It's not always easy, knowing what's the best course to take." Sophie could attest to that.

"No doubt. But all of life's a challenge, you know, and eventually, it all comes back to the choices we make. Sometimes the choices that are the hardest are the ones that, in the end, lead us to where we're supposed to be." A small smile played at the corner of Violet's mouth. "Sometimes we have to go out on a limb to find what makes us happy, what makes our lives complete." She looked up at Sophie and added, "Choices, don't you know," before focusing her attention on the piece of mail she'd just opened. "Everything comes back to the choices we make."

Sophie narrowed her eyes and stared across the desk at Violet. Had Jesse told her about Sophie's current dilemma, about her cheating boyfriend and her infatuation with the boarded-up restaurant on River Road?

The phone rang and Violet answered it, taking a message for Jesse, and after a brief, cordial chat with the caller, hung up.

"I know that voice mail is all the thing these days," Violet said as she jotted down the message, "but it goes against my grain to make a client go through the motions. I'd just as soon talk to whoever calls myself. It's the only way to find out what people really want when they call." She rose and took the message into Jesse's office, where, Sophie assumed, she'd leave the note on his desk.

"Oh, by the way, I saw Enid Walsh on Sunday. She's younger than I, but she's had her problems over the years and doesn't get around very well these days. Anyway, after you brought up her name on Saturday, I kept thinking I should call and see if she needed anything. That would be the charitable thing to do." Violet sat back down at the desk and rolled her chair forward. "She said it had been ages since she'd been to church—can't drive anymore because the arthritis in her legs is so bad and her vision isn't what it used to be—so of course, I offered to pick her up. I think she's looking poorly these days. I saw her back in the fall, and I can see where she's failing. Poor dear. It must be so lonely for her, having her whole family gone."

Sophie had to bite her tongue to keep from urging Violet to get to the point—the point being the status of the restaurant. She knew that once that thought was in Violet's head, the woman wasn't going to rest until she knew what was going on with the property.

"She's thinking about going into a home, Enid is. There's a new one out on the highway going toward Ballard that's supposed to be very nice. I believe she's looking into it, though I hear it's very expensive. She said she'd probably have to sell her house in order to afford it."

"That's too bad." *No, no, the restaurant,* Sophie thought. *She ought to sell the restaurant.*

"She'd be much better off in a home, really, with people to look after her. She said she fell around Christmas and if her neighbor hadn't come over to bring her a plate of cookies, she'd probably still be there on the floor. Then again, that house was built by her grandfather and it's going to break the poor woman's heart to part with it."

Get to the point. Please. Get to the part where she's going to sell the restaurant.

"So I asked her what other properties she owns— the Walsh family had some holdings here in town— but she said that everything had been sold over the years. Except, of course, the place out on River Road." Violet looked up at Sophie. "She said she just couldn't sell that place. Too many happy memories there, you see."

Damn. Sophie's heart sank.

"But I pointed out that she should probably have the property appraised," Violet went on. "Because you never know, really, what lies ahead. Better to have one's affairs in order, you know. I said, 'Perhaps the better option might be to sell the old restaurant'— which really is of no use to her, after all—'and keep the house.' As I pointed out to her, with the nursing home being so pricy, why, she could stay in her own house and have someone live in for much less money." She glanced up at Sophie again and added, "I believe she may be taking that into consideration."

"That would seem like a smart thing to do." Sophie tried to hide the surge of hope that sped through her.

"I'm sure I'll hear either way."

"You think she'll call you when she makes up her mind?"

"I'm sure I'll hear about it when I pick her up on Sunday mornings for church. I told her I'd drive her whenever she wants to go." Violet smiled again. "It's the charitable thing to do . . ."

Diary ~

Well, what a nice surprise I had at Cuppachino this morning! Sophie Enright is in town visiting her brother for a week. She's a lovely girl, and I know that her grandfather is tickled that she's going to be around for a few days. He'd never admit it—not in a million years—but he must miss his son, Craig—her father—terribly. Whatever happened between father and son, between mother and son, it's not mine to say. I do know that being separated from your children for a long period of time can break your heart. To have your children stay away because you've sent them away, well, I cannot imagine. I know that my son stays away because he's chosen a life that sends him into other parts of the world where maybe he can do some good. Keeping the peace, he says, even when I know that some of the places he goes to are in a state of civil war. And yet he'll call whenever he can, he writes when the spirit moves him, and I know that if I ever truly needed him, he'd come home. Ford knows that he is loved, and we are confident that he loves us in return. I cannot bear to think of a time when we would not speak or communicate in some way. I don't know how Curtis has lived these last . . . dear me, could it be twenty or more years already? Yes, I believe it has been. How could he stand to not see the face of his child in all that time? Yes, of course, I've heard the stories of Craig's failed marriages and the families he's abandoned, of the scandals and the allegations of fraud committed against a client. Still, when it's your flesh and blood, do you not still love even when the actions may have been unlovable?

I'm thanking my creator tonight that I've never had to make that choice, and I pray that I never will.

~ Grace ~

Chapter 8 ⌒

Jason drove his pickup to the end of Curtis Enright's driveway and parked in front of the old stone carriage house. He'd barely gotten out of the cab when he heard his name called.

"Jason!" Curtis came toward him across the uneven lawn, a weathered walking stick in his right hand.

I'm going to level off that section, Jason thought as he saw the old man wobble slightly and pause to steady himself on the bumpy terrain. *After we get rid of the moles.*

"Hey, chief." Jason walked to meet him so that his client wouldn't have to navigate over the increasingly lumpy ground. "I was just about to come up to the house. You didn't have to walk all the way down here."

"Nonsense. A man has to get his exercise somehow." The old man's eyes sparkled.

"Seems like moles are tearing up the lawn down here. It looks like they have a series of condos that reach almost to the river." Jason bent down to inspect the ruts in the ground.

"I'm afraid I've been remiss in taking care of the far-back portion of the property," Curtis admitted. "Other than having the grass mowed and the trees pruned from time to time, I haven't paid as much attention as I might have. Guess I'm paying for that now. So how do we get rid of them?"

"I can have someone come in and take care of the problem."

"Good, good. Whatever you need to do. I'd hate to see someone trip and break an ankle."

That would most likely be you, Jason thought. Aloud, he said, "I'll have someone out by the end of the week. In the meantime, let me show you what we're going to be doing in the big garden starting next week."

They started toward the house, Jason slowing his pace to match Curtis's, though he didn't mind that it took a few minutes longer to reach the other side of the yard. He enjoyed the company of the older man— looked forward to it, actually. Jason had never known either of his own grandfathers, but he thought he would have liked one of them to be a little like Curtis Enright. It wasn't so much about the fact that Curtis was prosperous as it was about his spirit. Jason had been comfortable in his company since the first time they'd met to talk about possible refurbishing of the grounds. There was something about the old guy that clicked with Jason, something that made being around him a pleasure.

"Let's go on inside." Curtis pointed his walking stick toward the back door. "Bring your plans in and we'll take a look."

"I'll grab the folder from the truck and meet you in the house."

Jason waited until Curtis safely reached the flat part of the yard before grabbing his work folder from the front seat. Curtis was already inside by the time Jason caught up with him.

Curtis glanced at the clock on the wall.

"Four o'clock," he muttered. "Well, it's six o'clock somewhere. How 'bout a beer while we go over those drawings of yours?"

When Jason hesitated, Curtis added, "Unless you have another client this late in the day . . ."

"Done for the day after this. A beer would be great, thanks."

Curtis went to the refrigerator and removed two bottles. "Jesse dropped off some of that new beer Clay and Wade are working on. Blueberry honey beer. Sounds more like one of Steffie's ice-cream flavors than beer, you ask me. But no. Beer." He shook his head. "Blueberry honey *beer*."

"I had some the other night. It's pretty good, actually."

"I remember when beer's flavor was beer." Curtis went into the butler's pantry and returned with two pilsner glasses. "You may not remember, but beer didn't used to come in flavors."

"I remember." Jason felt mildly amused. "I'm not *that* young."

"It's all relative, my boy." Curtis opened one of the bottles, poured the beer down the side of the glass, and handed both glass and bottle to Jason, then repeated the process for himself. When his own glass had been poured, he gestured toward one of the doors leading from the kitchen. "Let's take these into the library. You can spread your plans on the table in there and we can take a look."

Jason followed Curtis through one of the doors and into the grand entry hall. A table held a lamp, a large painted vase filled with branching arms of forsythia, and a pair of silver candleholders. Jason thought he detected the faintest hint of gardenia in the air.

"Mrs. Anderson's touch." Curtis pointed at the vase as they passed by. "She thought the house looked dreary last week, so she cut some bare branches and brought them in to force them into bloom. Looks like it worked. Flowers popped out over yesterday afternoon. Does look brighter."

He continued walking as he spoke, pausing only to open a door on their left, then stood aside for Jason to enter.

"Feel a little chilly in here?" Curtis asked Jason.

"Maybe a little." Jason pointed to the fireplace. "I could build you a fire."

"That would be nice." Curtis nodded and looked pleased by the offer. "Thank you."

"You chop all this wood yourself?" Jason asked as he selected a few lengths of wood from the black iron cauldron where they were stacked and piled them on the hearth.

Curtis chuckled. "Ah, it's been years since I so much as carried the stuff into the house. Jesse had someone cut it from some branches that fell from an old oak last year."

"I bet you're glad Jesse lives so close." Jason crumpled some newspaper and placed it under the rack upon which he'd stacked several pieces of wood.

"Couldn't be happier. He's the future of Enright and Enright, and he's grown into a good man. I'm delighted to have him around. Wish I could convince his sister to come aboard." Curtis eased himself into a seat at the table facing the fireplace. "Matches are in the box on the mantel."

I wouldn't mind having Jesse's sister around full time, either.

Jason struck a match and held the flame to the newspaper, allowing the fledgling fire to crackle for a moment or two before using the bellows to gently urge it upward to the logs. When the logs caught and the fire began to settle into the wood, he replaced the bellows onto the iron rack that had held it.

"Very nice." Curtis nodded. "Thank you. You get old, you can't be too warm."

"This really is quite the library." Jason took in the entire sweep of walls that were lined with shelves almost to the ceiling. He'd seen pictures of rooms like this but he wasn't certain such rooms existed these days. "That's some collection of books you've got there."

"Enrights have all been readers, apparently. There are books there that ancestors of mine had decades ago. Every subject you can imagine. Go ahead, take a look if you'd like." Curtis pointed to the wall of shelves.

Jason pushed back from the table and walked around it, approaching the shelves with a sort of wonder. He'd never seen so many books in a private home.

"Quite an assortment." He glanced from bookshelf to bookshelf. "*The Complete Works of Ellery Queen.* My dad had those."

"Your dad a mystery fan?"

"He was. He's been gone for a long time." Jason turned back to the shelves. "I like that you have modern mystery writers on the same shelf. Harlan Coben and James Lee Burke, P.D. James alongside Sir Arthur Conan Doyle. Nice."

"All my favorites. If you see something you like, feel free to borrow it."

"Thanks. I'm afraid I don't have much time for reading these days." Jason's gaze rested on a large volume. "Frank J. Scott's *Victorian Gardens,*" he read aloud. *"The Art of Beautifying Suburban Home Grounds."*

"You know the book?"

"I paid eight dollars for a used copy years ago. It's a classic. First published in 1870." He touched the spine reverently. "This was the major style book of the Victorian period. He was one of the first to propose that gardens were supposed to enhance the house they were built around."

"What was the previous thought?" Curtis asked. "What else would they enhance?"

"Nature. The naturalists believed that gardens should enhance their natural surroundings. Scott— and a few others—thought the landscape should add beauty to the house. That you should see something beautiful when you looked out of every window."

Jason's eyes lingered for a long moment on the Scott, his fingers itching to pull the book from its place and open it to check the copyright date. He'd bet everything he had that it was a first edition from 1870. He'd never been that close to one before. He had his secondhand copy, a reissue, and he'd seen the original reproduced online, but there was nothing like seeing a first edition. He sighed, then went back to the table.

Jason put the coveted book from his mind and got back to the business at hand. "Did I tell you I bought some property out on River Road for my business?"

"No, you didn't. What do you have in mind?"

Jason took a seat and one long swig of beer, then described his plans.

"It sounds ambitious," Curtis noted.

"It's pretty much what I had back in Florida."

"So you already have a business plan."

"I do. Now, as far as your project is concerned, I have several tons of mulch on order—different types, so you let me know what you prefer for out back and I'll order that now. There will be a lot of topsoil coming in another month or so, and I'm buying some equipment from a local guy who's retiring, so I'll have my own Bobcat."

"Sounds like you're going to have quite an operation." Curtis smiled approvingly. "Good for you. I like to see initiative."

"I've got plenty of that." Jason took another sip before opening the folder he'd brought with him. "Now, if you want to take a look at the revised plan for the garden, I've got it right here . . ."

An hour later, Curtis stood at the end of the drive and waved as Jason drove off. He'd drawn out their meeting for as long as he could, and finally had to let the young man go. He enjoyed his company a great deal, and his protestations to Sophie aside, he really didn't have that many people to talk to these days. Oh, he loved having Jesse around, but Jesse was overworked and trying his best to keep his head above water at the office and balance work with his relationship with Brooke and the plans for their upcoming wedding. He did have dinner once or twice each week with Violet, but that still left him with at least five dinners he'd eat alone.

He walked back to the house and returned to the library, where Jason had stacked more wood before he left. *Thoughtful of him,* Curtis nodded to himself. But then, Jason was a thoughtful young man. And smart—that was obvious. Good sense of humor. Ambitious. He liked to see a young person with ambition who was willing to work for what he wanted. There was something about him that Curtis just flat-out liked, something about the young man's company that put him in an easy frame of mind.

Which was why his ears had perked up when Jason mentioned he'd bought that property out on River Road. That would certainly imply that he was setting down permanent roots in St. Dennis.

Interesting, Curtis thought. Jason was just the sort of young man that Sophie should be looking for.

Curtis lowered himself into a wide leather chair near the fire, nursing his beer and thinking. They were going to have to find a way to persuade Sophie into joining her brother at Enright & Enright. She'd be around, and Jason would be around . . . and who knew where that could lead?

When the scent of gardenia began to fill the room, he looked up and smiled.

"Ahhh, Rosie. There you are. We had company today."

He rested his head against the back of the chair.

"Nice boy, that Jason Bowers. You'd like him." He paused, then nodded. "I think you'll be very happy with the plans we have for the gardens." Curtis closed his eyes for a moment, breathing in the scent that surrounded him, taking comfort in it. "I was just thinking that he's just the type of young man I'd like to see Sophie settled with.

"Of course, I'm not thinking of playing matchmaker. Have you ever known me to interfere in someone else's life?

"Now, you know you'd like to see our girl settled here as much as I would. The firm needs her. And if you know of a finer young man in town for the girl, you just let me know and I'll be sure to introduce him to her."

He closed his eyes, and warmed by the fire and comforted by the love that surrounded him, he drifted off to sleep, thinking how good it would be for Sophie if she were to move to St. Dennis like her brother had. And if she happened to find the right guy and decided to stay, well, what was wrong with that?

Chapter 9 ⌒

SOPHIE drove her rental car to the St. Dennis Elementary School on Memorial Drive and parked in the almost filled-to-capacity parking lot. Jesse was still at the office with a client, but he'd promised Logan and Brooke that he'd meet them there as soon as he could.

After having gone through a second batch of résumés yesterday, Sophie had to admit that her brother was not exaggerating when he'd claimed he was swamped with work and that his offer for her to join the firm wasn't simply an attempt to lure her to St. Dennis under false pretenses. He really did need another attorney, and in all fairness to Violet—who should be permitted to return to her well-deserved retirement—he had to start looking for another office manager as well as a paralegal. Since he hadn't had time to go over the résumés she'd left on his desk, Sophie had brought them home with her. After reviewing them a second time, she'd written notes on each one and left them on the kitchen counter next to Jesse's coffeemaker, stacked in order of her ranking of one through eleven, with one being her recommended hire. He'd written a note on the top one, *Ask Violet to arrange interview.* Sophie had done that herself, scheduling the interview for Friday morning. She had mentioned Nita's granddaughter to Violet, who'd merely sniffed her disapproval. Sophie wasn't sure what the problem was but knew better than to ask, lest Violet think that Sophie was questioning her judgment.

She entered the school through the big double doors out front and followed the signs for the science fair, which took her down one short hall and then another. A bulletin board announced upcoming events on a giant calendar that highlighted OUR WINTER HOLIDAYS and showcased students' artwork depicting such notable dates as Groundhog Day, Valentine's Day, Presidents' Day, and St. Patrick's Day. A corresponding bulletin board heralded the anticipated arrival of spring, with April Fools' Day apparently the favorite holiday in that month, there being several drawings to illustrate the day.

"Cookie?" someone asked.

"What?" She turned, frowning.

Jason stood behind her, his outstretched hand holding a napkin in which rested several chocolate chip cookies.

"I thought the punch-and-cookie thing was after the science fair," she said.

"It is."

"So how'd you rate cookies now?"

He shrugged. "Came in the back door looking hungry."

"Nice of you to share." She took one and bit into it. "Homemade. Nice. Thanks."

"I think it's a rule at these school things that if you bring cookies, they have to be homemade. At least, that's been my experience here."

"You've been before?"

Jason nodded. "School play, awards ceremony, last day of school, art show, winter band concert." He rolled his eyes at the last.

"I think Jesse mentioned that. He said it was pretty rough."

" 'Rough' is kind. You haven't heard 'Santa Claus Is Coming to Town' until you've heard it played by an elementary school band.

"You going in?" He gestured in the direction of the auditorium, where the exhibits were set up.

"I am. Have you seen Logan and Brooke?" she asked.

He fell in step next to her. "Logan's already in there with his project. Brooke's wandering around somewhere, no doubt socializing. She grew up in St. Dennis, so I guess she pretty much knows everyone in town."

"That's what Jesse said." Sophie smiled and added, "Hard to believe she was once the town mean girl, or at least to hear her tell it, she was. She's such a sweetheart now."

"She's told me that, too, but I don't see it either. Though she did say that when they were in school, she and Dallas MacGregor were both hot for Grant Wyler."

"Well, we know how that turned out, right? Grant married Dallas—eventually, anyway—and Brooke . . ." Sophie stopped in midsentence and looked away.

"Yeah, Brooke married my brother and had Logan."

His face was unreadable. "And then Eric went to Iraq and didn't come back."

"I'm sorry." Sophie turned to face him. "It's never come up in conversation between us before, but I did hear about your brother, and I'm sorry for your loss. Brooke told me you were very close."

He nodded. "Thanks." He met her eyes for a moment, then looked past her to the table where a student was displaying her project. "Ant farms. I had one of those when I was a kid. Did you?"

"Jesse had one." She followed him to the table, where he spoke to the girl.

"I had one of these when I was your age," he was saying. "What do you feed yours?"

For one moment, when Sophie had looked into Jason's eyes, she felt a connection—a sort of *zing*—but the moment had passed quickly. It was obviously painful for him to talk about his late brother, and he'd shut down the dialogue before it could turn into a conversation.

"Sophie!" Logan waved from several tables down. "Come see what I made!"

"Wow, that's . . . that's really complicated." Sophie studied the charts that stood on Logan's table and tried to keep from frowning. She had no idea of what she was looking at. "What's your project about?"

"It's about how exercise helps your brain," he explained. "Like how when you exercise, you can remember things better." He led her from one piece of poster board to the next. "These are the kids who played a game at the table . . ."

"A board game?" she asked.

"Uh-huh. And these are the kids who played dodgeball." He pointed to a second chart. "Then I showed everybody some stuff and they had to write down what they remembered. The kids who played dodge-ball remembered more of the things than the kids who played Chutes and Ladders."

"Proving what?" Jason asked from over Sophie's shoulder.

"That your brain can do more things if you play dodgeball?"

"Close enough." Jason nodded.

"I'm impressed," Sophie said.

"You gotta see Cody's." Logan pointed to his friend several tables away. "He cloned a cabbage."

"Don't want to miss that one." Sophie glanced in the general direction in which Logan was pointing and noticed that Cody's mother, Dallas, was standing in front of her son's display. "I think I'll go on over and check out that cabbage."

"It's pretty cool," Logan told her.

Sophie passed an exhibit of molds that a student had grown on various food substances, a display of rock crystals, and some poster boards charting the speed of sound through different mediums.

"Pretty sophisticated stuff," Dallas said when Sophie approached Cody's table.

"Nothing like what I made when *I* was in second grade. I think I was still growing sweet potatoes over jars filled with colored water," Sophie replied.

"That was about my speed, too." Dallas smiled. "Looks like the whole family has shown up for Logan tonight."

"Well, Jason's the only other person I've seen. It's

rumored that Brooke is around here somewhere, and Jesse hasn't arrived yet."

"I saw Brooke and her mother about five minutes ago when I dropped off cookies, and I could swear I saw Jesse talking to someone in the lobby a few minutes ago."

"Well, then, I guess we are all here. Just not in the same place." Sophie turned to Cody. "I hear you have a cloned cabbage."

He pointed to the vegetable that appeared to be growing out of the side of a cabbage stalk. "Cool, huh?"

"Very cool," she agreed as a giggling pack of girls stepped up to the table.

Sophie took a step back just as Christina Pratt, the mayor of St. Dennis, stopped to chat with Dallas.

"Dallas, I just want to tell you again how much everyone is looking forward to the opening of your new studio," the mayor gushed. "You just can't imagine what this will do for the town, what it will do for the merchants."

"Actually, I have an idea," Dallas replied with a faint smile.

"Well, we're just all so excited. This will put our little town on the map."

Dallas's smile remained fixed, and after a brief exchange, Mayor Pratt went on to the next display.

"As if I don't know that a major studio would give the town a boost." Dallas shook her head, the smile fading.

"I'm sure she's just grateful and wants to express that."

"She's already done that about twenty times. Like

every time she sees me. I don't need to be patted on the back constantly. This is my home, and I want to work where I live and where we're raising Cody, but yes, I'd be a fool if I didn't realize how much revenue this venture will bring into St. Dennis."

"How is the studio coming along?" Sophie asked.

"The renovations on the building are coming along very nicely. The offices are all finished, so I can go to work every day and function quite well. I've hired some key people to work in my production company, and some of them are looking for temporary housing in and around the community already."

"At the risk of sounding like the mayor"—Sophie lowered her voice—"it really is kind of exciting."

"No one's more excited than I am," Dallas admitted. "I love the idea of having my business right here in town. There's no way I could go back to California for more than a weekend with Grant here, and Cody having settled in so well, and my aunt Berry ready to tackle what will most likely be her last screen role."

Dallas's great-aunt, Berry Eberle, as Beryl Townsend, had been, in her day, every bit the major movie star that Dallas currently was. Now in her eighties, Berry hadn't made a film in years, but she was coming out of retirement to play a lead role in Dallas's first production.

"I read the book," Sophie said. "*Pretty Maids*. It's going to make an incredible movie."

"Thank you." Dallas beamed. "I've finished the screenplay and we've started casting. That's going quite well—I expect to have some announcements to make very soon, though so far we've only signed

Aunt Berry and Laura Fielding as her granddaughter."

"They're going to be perfect. Your aunt is totally Rosemarie, and Laura will be amazing as Charlotte. I can't wait till it's finished."

"There's a long way to go before we can put this baby in the can, but I appreciate your enthusiasm. Everyone agrees that Berry is going to be radiant in the role, but not everyone's on board as far as Laura is concerned."

"Oh, you know that everyone's a critic. I think Laura will be wonderful and the movie will win all sorts of awards."

"Thank you so much, Sophie. It's nice to get support from the hometown crowd."

Sophie could have reminded Dallas that she wasn't exactly hometown, but she let it go. Instead, she asked as casually as she could, "So when do you think you'll be up and running?"

"By the summer, definitely. I expect to have the cast firmed up and the crew hired on by April, May at the latest. I want to be shooting by the summer." Dallas smiled. "You interested in an audition?"

"Me?" Sophie laughed. "I couldn't act to save my life, but it's nice of you to ask."

Grace Sinclair appeared at her elbow, camera in hand. "Ladies, may I take your picture for the paper? The *St. Dennis Gazette* has covered this event for the past forty years or so, you know. Always had the money shot on the front page."

"I think Dallas is the very definition of money shot," Sophie said. "I think this is my cue to find my brother." She turned to Dallas. "Good seeing you again."

"Likewise. And if you change your mind about auditioning, you give me a call."

"Not going to happen, but thanks." Sophie drifted off into the crowd, scanning the room for Jesse or Brooke. She did catch a glimpse of Jason, his arms folded, head bent as he appeared to be listening to a pretty dark-haired woman who was looking up at him as if he were a big, yummy slice of chocolate cake and she couldn't wait to take a bite. A shot of something hot suddenly stung Sophie right around her midsection.

Ridiculous, she chastised herself. *Jason and I have nothing in common except Logan.* She turned her back, the hot little nugget in her gut still sizzling.

"There you are." Jesse, still dressed in a three-piece suit, motioned to her from about ten feet away. "I've been looking for you. I wanted to thank you again for going through those résumés. You did a great job. I'm going to ask Violet to call your number one and set up an appointment."

"I already did. She'll be in on Friday morning. I cleared it with Violet. She said you were free."

"Thanks, Soph. I don't know when I would have gotten to it."

"If you had a good paralegal, you might be able to have dinner with your fiancée one or two nights a week."

Jesse nodded. "Don't think I'm happy about the way things are."

"Look, I'm sorry that I didn't really believe you,

about you being so jammed with work. I thought you were just trying to get me to move to St. Dennis."

"Well, there is that."

"You can hire another lawyer, Jess. I don't know how you're going to avoid it if the firm is going to maintain its reputation."

"I didn't want to be the one to change the name of the firm from Enright and Enright to Enright and someone else." Jessie's expression said it all. "But I guess you're right. The reputation is more important than the name of the firm. I guess I'll talk to Pop, make sure he's okay with it."

"I think he'd rather see the name change than to see you work yourself into a divorce before you've even had time to enjoy a little married life."

"Brooke's a rock—don't kid yourself. And she works a lot of long hours, too. Runs her business, raises her son . . ."

"Yes, but you're going to have to be more involved with that now, too. You're going to be his father, Jess. You have to be there for something more than his sports teams on Saturdays."

Jesse nodded; it was clear to Sophie that he understood his responsibilities and wasn't happy feeling that he wasn't currently totally fulfilling them.

"Would it be tossing salt into the wound to tell you that you need to hire another office manager–receptionist?"

"Yeah, but go ahead," Jesse groaned. "Pile it on."

"Sorry."

"No, it's all right. It's true. Violet needs to be able to retire for real this time. Though I don't know if anything would keep her out of the office completely. I mean, that office is a big part of her life."

"I know, but if you hired a manager, Violet could just pick out the things she likes to do, and she could come in two or three times each week for a few hours here and a few hours there when she felt like it, do what she wanted to do, then go home."

"That's what she was doing when I first started here, but she came back full time pretty much because she didn't trust me."

Sophie nodded. Violet had admitted as much to her.

"She stayed on because she wanted to," he continued. "I think it makes her feel young, you know, like she did when Pop was just starting out and she came to work for him and his dad. I don't know if she'd trust anyone else to step into her job."

"I think if you found the right person, she'd be okay about turning over the desk and her keys."

"Well, the desk, maybe, but I don't see her giving up that key ring without a fight."

"So let her keep the keys for old times' sake."

"That could work." Jesse's eyes were drawn to something over his sister's shoulder. "Say, is that Pop? He said something about wanting to see Logan's project, but I didn't expect him to show."

Sophie turned in time to see Jason spot her grandfather at the same time she did. Turning away from the woman who was obviously trying to hold his attention, Jason greeted the old man with a pat on the back and a wide grin. The two men fell into what appeared to be an easy conversation. Funny, Sophie thought, that Jason seemed more interested in her grandfather than he had in the young woman, who was looking slightly miffed.

"Nice of Pop to stop by." Jesse raised a hand to get his grandfather's attention, but Curtis, accompanied by Jason, was on his way to Logan's table. "Let's catch up with them."

"You go on," Sophie told him. "I'll be over in a minute."

Jesse made his way through the growing crowd while Curtis made slow progress in the same direction. Jason's steady hand on the older man's elbow guided him safely to his destination. Once there, Jason stood slightly behind Curtis as if guarding him. Several times, he extended his arm protectively across Curtis's back. It didn't take long for Sophie to realize that Jason was shielding him from being jostled by people going by. The small gesture went straight to her heart.

She walked through the throng to Logan's display.

"Hey, Pop." She greeted him with a kiss on the cheek.

"Well, there's my girl." Curtis reached out for her hand. "Did you see Logan's project? Brilliant, don't you think?"

"I do," she agreed.

"Pop, look," a beaming Logan called to him.

"What's that you've got there, son?" Curtis stepped closer to the table.

"I got an honorable mention." Logan held up the ribbon.

"Thanks for watching out for him," Sophie whispered to Jason. "He should be using a walker—or at the very least, a cane in a crowd like this—but he's too proud."

"He's doing okay," Jason assured her, leaning in a little closer. "We just need to keep an eye on him."

"I appreciate that you've been doing that."

Jason shrugged, as if his vigilance were of no consequence. "He's a good man, your grandfather. I've been working with him for the last few months and I've grown very fond of him."

"It looked to me as if he's equally fond of you."

"We get along," Jason replied.

She took a few steps back so as to not be overheard. "I think he's slowed a bit since Christmas." She waited for his response. "Have you noticed any changes in him over the past month or so?"

"Maybe a few steps slower, but mentally, the man is as sharp as they come."

"I understand you're designing some gardens for him."

"We're working together on that. He wants to restore the formal garden that was behind the house at one time—probably a hundred years ago or so—and he wants to re-create his wife's rose garden. We found the remnants of a wall near the carriage house, and he'd like that rebuilt and some beds there refurbished." Jason looked down at her and smiled. His eyes held hers for a second or two.

There it was again. That *zing*.

"He's the best kind of client," Jason continued. "He knows what he wants, and he gets out of my way and lets me do it."

"Has he seemed . . . not sure how to say this . . . somewhat fatalistic to you lately?"

Jason frowned. "I'm not sure what you're asking me."

"Does he talk a lot about dying?" she blurted out.

"Sometimes. I guess at his age, the thought does cross your mind from time to time. He doesn't seem particularly concerned about it, though. If anything, he's pretty blunt about looking forward to being with your grandmother again."

"To hear him tell it, they're together all the time." Sophie made a face. "According to him, she's never left."

"Oh, right. The gardenia thing."

"You've smelled it? Gardenia?"

"Sure. At least, I think I have. But do I know where the scent's coming from?" Jason shook his head. "I thought I figured it out when he was showing me around his greenhouse. There's a huge old gardenia plant in there, but it wasn't in bloom. I even picked a leaf off and sniffed it to see if it gave off any fragrance, but it didn't."

"He swears it's her. My grandmother."

"Who's to say it isn't? And why does it bother you so much?"

"I'm a prosecutor. I deal strictly in facts. Are you telling me that you believe in ghosts? You believe she's really there?"

"It doesn't matter what I believe, only what he believes. Whether she's really there with him . . ." Jason shrugged.

"So in other words, it doesn't matter what I think, either."

"Not to sound rude, but no, actually, it doesn't. Your grandfather isn't a stupid man. He's one of the smartest men I've ever met. If he believes she's there, that they communicate with each other, that's good enough for me." Jason turned his attention for a moment to the man under discussion, watched his interaction with Logan.

"How did he get here?" it occurred to Sophie to ask. "God, I hope he didn't drive that big old Caddie of his . . ."

"He said one of his neighbors gave him a ride. I told him I'd drive him home, though."

"That's nice of you, but I can drive . . ." Her phone buzzed in her jacket pocket. She reached in and pulled it out, checked the number. Her office. "I should probably take this."

She answered the call, but the background noise in the auditorium was so loud, she couldn't hear. She made her way through the crowd as quickly as she could, passing through the double doors into the hallway.

"Hello?" she repeated when she reached the lobby.

"Sophie . . . it's Christopher." He added hastily, "Don't hang up, it's about work. One of your cases."

"Which one?" Her jaw set squarely. The sound of his voice went straight to her gut and made her stomach turn.

"*State versus Liston, Essex, and Crowley.*"

"My rape case? What about it?" She frowned. Why would he be calling about that?

"There was a hearing today, and . . ."

"What hearing? There was no hearing scheduled."

"Defense counsel for Essex filed a motion on Tuesday morning . . ."

"Why am I just hearing about this now?"

"I'm trying to tell you. Just . . . just listen, okay?" His exasperated sigh was unmistakable. "Counsel filed a motion to dismiss the charges for lack of evidence, and . . ."

"There were hairs from all three attackers on her clothing." She pushed the door open and went down the steps and onto the sidewalk, where she began to pace. A stiff breeze blew across the parking lot, and she shivered inside her wool blazer. She wished she'd paid more attention to the weather reports.

"They all admit to having been in her home on several occasions. They're claiming the hairs could have been transferred somehow, like from the sofa where they all sat to watch TV."

"There was a witness who saw them drag the girl into the alley."

"Past tense."

"What do you mean, 'past tense'?" Sophie's heart dropped.

"I'm saying there's no witness."

"No, there *is* a witness. Gloria Davis. I'm set up to interview her next Wednesday."

"Is there a written statement from her that I don't know about?"

"Not yet. She told me she was at her father's in Indiana but that she'd come back next week to give me a statement."

"Well, I'm afraid she's already given her statement. To the defense. And it probably isn't what you were looking for."

"Are you telling me that she's changed her story?"

"According to Davis, she met up with the three guys just after they'd left the vic a block from her house. Says she saw the girl walking alone. Says all three of the guys walked with her—with Davis—to a party on the other side of town. Lacking any other evidence against them, and given the other circumstances, Judge Winston dismissed the case. There was no DNA and they're all maintaining their collective innocence."

"They're lying and you know it. They raped that girl, Chris. You know it and I know it."

"Knowing and proving are two different things. You have a victim who was drunk and doesn't even remember the actual rape, so she can't identify her rapists . . ."

"They literally poured liquor down her throat, Chris. She was not a willing participant."

"So she says."

"Don't," she growled. "Don't even say that. That girl was innocent. She's a victim—she does not deserve this."

When he made no response, she asked, "Is it done?"

"It's done. At least for now. Maybe some evidence, some other witness will pop up at some point, but for now, it's over." He hesitated before adding, "I'm sorry. I know how you feel about this case. How passionate you are about the victim. I understand, Sophie. I really do." Another pause. "I miss that, you know? Your passion for finding the truth, for protecting the innocents. I miss *you*, Sophie. Look, I know I screwed up and I'm more sorry than I can say. If I could just go back to that day . . . it never would have happened."

He was on the verge of pleading. If she'd ever had a

thought about getting back together—of giving Chris another chance—this was her opportunity.

Her mind replayed the moment when he'd opened the back door of the BMW and stepped out with his zipper in his hands, of the flash of pain that had shot through her, of the pain that had stayed with her.

Just then, the lobby door opened and a figure emerged and paused on the top step. Backlit, the figure was in shadow, but there was no mistaking the form. Through the space that separated them, Sophie felt his gaze lock on hers, and the thought occurred to her that there were men who would cheat, and men who would not. The man on the phone had already proven which kind of man he was.

"Well, see, Chris, here's the thing about the past. There's no undoing it."

"Sophie . . ."

"Are you still seeing Anita?"

His silence spoke for him.

"That's what I thought."

"It's you I really want. If I could only make you see . . ."

He was starting to sound desperate. Funny how his desperation seemed to ease the pain she'd been feeling up until that moment. Funny how she was able to see him as he really was, once that veil of pain began to lift.

"I saw enough. In the parking garage."

"I said I was sorry. It never should have happened."

"Like I said, there's no undoing it." She blew out a long breath. Time to cut this conversation off before it went any further. "Anything else I should know about? In regards to the case?"

The pause was just a few beats too long.

"What? What else?"

"Joe reassigned the case."

"What? *What?* Reassigned it? Why? Who?"

There was an awkward silence.

"Why. And who," she demanded.

"Well, Joe thought it shouldn't be switched back and forth, so he decided that going forward, the case should stay with the ADA who handled the matter today."

"*You?* You took my case? Knowing how I feel about this case, you allowed him to take it from me and you took it yourself?" Her voice lowered to a growl. "You bastard."

"Ahhh, no." He cleared his throat. "No, it wasn't reassigned to me."

"Then why are you . . ."

All of a sudden, she got it.

"Who, Chris? Say it."

"Well . . . Anita didn't have a case on the docket this week, so . . ."

"Thanks for the call."

Sophie punched *end call* and stared helplessly at the ground. She'd lived and breathed this case for the past two months. The thirteen-year-old girl's story had broken her heart. She was a good kid living in a bad situation: divorced parents, her mother remarried, a seventeen-year-old stepbrother whose unsavory friends had been quick to notice the pretty, shy, studious eighth grader.

Sophie had been adamant that the victim pursue the criminal case, and to have it fall apart now felt to her that the girl was being assaulted all over again.

To have it fall apart in Anita Hayes's hands made the intolerable all the worse.

Her breath came in short, angry spurts, and she wondered why she didn't feel like screaming. Instead, she felt cold inside, helpless, sad, and stunned. She barely noticed the hot tears that ran down her face.

"Damn," she whispered to the cool night air, still in shock, not quite sure if she was damning Christopher, Anita Hayes, the three rapists, the DA, Judge Winston—or herself, for having left town when she did. *"Damn . . ."*

Jason had watched the door, wondering where Sophie had gotten to and if she was coming back. He'd been just about to ask her to meet him for a drink after he dropped off her grandfather when she disappeared, her phone in her hand, a solemn look on her face. He'd waited several minutes before following her into the lobby, but Sophie was nowhere to be seen. He was about to go back into the auditorium when he saw her on the sidewalk in front of the school. She stood ramrod straight, her arms crossed over her chest, staring at the night sky. He stepped outside and paused for a moment on the steps.

"Let me guess," he said as he began to close the distance between them. "Counting falling stars."

She turned to him, her expression unreadable.

"Hey, is something wrong?" He was close enough to see the tears that slid down her cheeks.

Uh-oh, he thought. Guy trouble, if he had to guess. *Figures. All the really great women seem to have a guy in the background somewhere.* Did he really think that a woman like Sophie would be unattached?

"I . . . yes, fine." She nodded, even though it was apparent to anyone with eyes that she wasn't fine at all. "I just needed some air. It's stuffy and crowded in there."

"Stuffy and crowded go with the territory," he agreed.

They stood in silence for a moment. It was obvious that she wanted to be alone—she'd come out here to be alone, and here he was, intruding on whatever it was she was wanting to be alone about. He felt awkward and uncertain of what to say or how to remove himself without sounding even more lame than he already felt.

"Could you do me a favor?" she asked. Before he could respond, she said, "Please tell Jesse I drove back to his place and I'll talk to him in the morning."

"I'll tell him, but are you sure you're okay?" Even though he knew she wasn't, even though he knew she'd deny it. Whatever happened had made her so sad that it was hard for Jason to meet her eyes. There was so much pain there. "Can I drive you . . ."

"I have my car, thanks."

"Is there something I can do?"

"No, no. But thank you." She tried to force a smile, but her lips were trembling.

"Aw, Sophie . . ." His arms reached out and drew her in. "Whatever it is, I'm sorry it's made you so sad."

"It's all right."

"If it were all right, you wouldn't be crying." He held her very gently, as if she were made of fine crystal and she'd shatter if he held her too tightly. But for a moment, it felt like she belonged there, that she was exactly where she was supposed to be. "I'm not going to ask, but whatever it is, if there's anything I can do . . ."

"You can't." She wiped her face with the back of her hand. "But thank you."

"Look, if you ever want to talk . . ." He tried to hold onto it, but the moment had passed, and he felt her begin to slip away from him. "How 'bout I drive you home? Or someplace where we can sit and talk until you feel a little better?"

"I'm fine. I'll be fine. Thanks, Jason, but I think I need to be alone right now. It's just something I have to work out for myself." Without looking at him, she took off for the parking lot, her back still straight, her pace clipped and steady though she'd looked anything but.

She looked like someone who was running away.

Yeah, guy trouble.

Jason didn't know who and he didn't know what, but he did know that whoever the guy was who'd caused such sadness was a total asshole who didn't deserve her.

He wished he could have found the right words to comfort her. Instead, she'd walked away with whatever pain she was feeling still tucked deep inside her and he'd been powerless to help.

Jason watched until she located her car, got in, and drove from the lot before going back inside to deliver her message.

Chapter 10 ~

SOPHIE sat in the dark on a chair in Jesse's living room, her knees pulled up to her chest and her arms wrapped around her legs, her thoughts a jumble. Hearing Chris's voice had been jarring. She'd been determined to put her relationship with him behind her, but like a bad penny, he'd come right back.

Oh, his apology had sounded sincere enough, but a little time, a little distance, and she saw him now in a totally different light. If not for having to break the news to her about the case, would he have called at all? Did he really think that he could talk her into giving him another chance, even while all systems were apparently still go with Anita? Was he crazy?

As far as Sophie was concerned, the import of his apology paled compared to the news he'd delivered about her case.

More accurately, that would be Anita's case now, she reminded herself.

God, but that frosted her!

She sought comfort in the knowledge that by dropping the charges at this juncture, there was always the possibility that if evidence was discovered in the future, the case could be revisited, but she knew how likely that was—and she knew she wouldn't be the one to refile the charges.

She heard Jesse's key turn in the front door lock, heard him in the foyer where she'd left the light on. He grew still for a moment, listening, she suspected, for sounds of life in the quiet house. There was a slight thunk, the sound of Jesse's briefcase on the hardwood floor when he dropped it near the stairwell, his customary spot. His footsteps trailed down the hall to the kitchen. A moment later, she heard the refrigerator open—Jesse on the hunt for a snack, no doubt, something more substantial than the cookies and punch they served at the school reception.

Sophie wondered what Jason told her brother when she didn't return to the science fair. She'd had such mixed emotions when she realized that Jason had followed her outside. She was totally embarrassed that he found her in such a state of turmoil, and yet, at the same time, she'd been grateful that he had. Just for a moment or two, the comfort he'd offered her had eased her heart, and just for a moment, there'd been that *zing* again.

When she heard Jesse in the hall, she sunk back into the chair, as if by doing so, she'd disappear inside the paisley fabric. As an attorney, Jesse would totally understand how she felt about her case. But she just wasn't ready to talk to anyone, not even Jess, about anything that had happened that night. He turned off the hall light and climbed the steps to the second floor. It wasn't until she heard his bedroom door open and close that she let out the breath she'd been holding.

She wondered who had told the thirteen-year-old girl that her rapists were going free.

She sat in the dark amidst the night sounds, a creak from something here, a squeak of something there, the wind whistling through the trees and slapping against the exterior brick walls, while she thought things through—Chris and her job and her future. Another hour passed before she tiptoed up the stairs to her room and, tossing her pants and sweater onto a chair, crawled into bed in her underwear.

When she awoke in the morning, Jesse was gone and fat, wet snowflakes were falling, catching on the trees and shrubs and covering the grass in the yard. She made coffee on Jesse's annoying machine and listened to it sputter as she sat at the kitchen table writing out her game plan on the small pad she always carried in her purse. When her thoughts were in place, she rinsed out her coffee cup, then went upstairs, changed, and drove to Jesse's office.

"Hi, Violet." Sophie poked her head into the reception area. "Jesse in?"

"Good morning, dear." Violet's face lit up when she saw Sophie in the doorway. "No, I'm afraid he had a meeting with a client this morning. I expect he'll be back by noon."

"Do you think it would be all right if I used his office for a few minutes?"

"I don't see why not."

"I promise not to move anything on his desk or otherwise upset your efforts to organize him," Sophie assured her.

"I'd appreciate that. Thank you."

Seated at Jesse's desk, Sophie turned on his computer and opened a Word document. She typed for several minutes; then, satisfied with her wording, she printed out the memo and read it over.

Jess — Something's come up at my office and I've had to leave. Thanks for the hospitality. See you at the wedding.

Sophie

P.S. Leave the "& Enright" on the letterhead.
P.P.S. Any chance I could sublet your house after you move in with Brooke?
P.P.P.S. And could you please clean out that little back office for me?

Sophie smiled. That ought to get his attention. She left the sheet of paper unfolded smack in the center of his blotter. She was just about to push away from the desk when a bit of braided green string caught her eye. She tugged it out from under a pile of papers. The key to Walsh's. She tossed it up and down in her open palm a few times before dropping it into her bag. Then she turned off the light and closed the door.

"I'm going to run out for a few, Violet. Could I bring you anything from town?" Sophie paused at the door.

"No, dear, but thank you."

"I'll be back."

Sophie fought the urge to skip as she walked to her car. The sporty little sedan had a luxury logo and she had loved every minute driving it, but this morning, all Sophie could see was its lack of cargo space, space she was going to need if she was going to pack in all her clothes. *Maybe an SUV,* she thought as she headed toward River Road. One of the new ones that got better gas mileage than the older ones did.

She parked in front of the old stone building and watched the falling snow, so soft and wet that the flakes seemed to drop in little bundles like cotton balls. The roads were too warm from the past week for the snow to stick, but it clung to the branches of the trees behind the restaurant and piled on top of the ugly fence separating Walsh's property from the one next door. She got out of the car and locked her bag inside, then went to the front door and unlocked it.

The old restaurant seemed even darker than it had been when she and Jesse had been there, but she'd seen everything she'd needed to see on her first visit. Right now, she just wanted to stand inside the open room and let her dreams build. This morning, her decisions having been made in the dark the night before, she needed her dreams, needed to feel that she was taking control of her life and moving forward in her own direction. Committing herself to Enright & Enright had been step one. Resigning from the DA's office would be step two. Buying this place—making it her own—would be the third and final step.

Starting right now, she was taking charge.

She walked around the big room, envisioning what she'd do there, how it would look. She'd paint the interior walls a soft, creamy yellow, the tables and chairs black. The countertop was a mess of scratches and chips, so that would have to go. Poured concrete, tinted something pretty, perhaps a soft gray, might be nice, if the wood was too far gone. The metal stools looked okay, but the seat cushions would need to be replaced. She'd probably have to do that herself, but she'd figure it out.

As for décor, she wasn't sure. She loved the Bay but didn't want her place to look too kitschy—no fake blue-claw crabs or fishing nets. She'd come up with something that reflected the true flavor of St. Dennis. Some valances at the windows—maybe a black-and-white toile—and some ceramic vases. Pale yellow maybe, like the walls, or blue, like the sky. She could grow the flowers herself from seeds, right outside the door and around the perimeter of the building, at least until she could get a proper garden going in that strip of ground between here and the bait shop. There was plenty of room for herbs and a cutting garden. Maybe after she got established, she'd plant some of her own produce.

She'd clear away some of the overgrowth outside and buy some flagstones to build a patio, buy a couple of tables and offer alfresco dining framed by views of the river. Of course, she'd have to plant something along the side to block out the ugly fence, but surely she could find shrubs or trees that would grow quickly.

She went into the kitchen, wishing she'd brought a flashlight as she opened each of the cabinets, took note of their contents, then closed the doors. The plain white dishes would be perfect if there were enough of them that were not chipped or cracked, but it was too dark to tell.

She glanced around one last time.

"I'll be back," she said aloud before she locked the door behind her. "I don't know when, but I will."

Back at the office, she slipped the key under the pile on Jesse's desk where she'd found it. Violet wasn't at her desk, but she could hear someone in the little kitchen at the end of the hall. She walked past the small room she'd asked Jesse to clean out for her. The odds were that he'd never get around to it, but Violet would make sure it got done. She went into the kitchen, where Violet stood at the sink washing a cup and saucer.

"Back so soon, dear?" Violet asked without turning around. "Did you do what you set out to do?"

"Yes. I only had one short errand." Sophie smiled. As if she could fool Violet. "Something's come up at home, something involving one of my cases, and I'm going to have to leave this morning. I left a note for Jesse on his desk. I don't want to wait for him since I don't know when he'll be back."

"Did you try calling him?"

"I don't want to disturb him if he's with a client."

"Oh, good point." Violet dried her hands on a bright blue towel as she turned to Sophie.

"I'm just going to run back to the house and grab my things so I can get on the road." Sophie rested a hand on the back of a chair, stalling while she tried to figure out the best way to approach the one thing she needed to say.

"I'll tell Jesse you waited for as long as you could."

"Thanks, Violet."

"You're welcome." Violet started toward the door, and when Sophie didn't immediately move out of the doorway, she asked, "Was there something else, dear?"

"I was just wondering . . . well, about your friend. The woman who owns that property out on River Road?"

"Enid Walsh."

"Yes, Enid Walsh. I was wondering if maybe she'd mentioned anything about selling the place anytime soon."

"What a coincidence! We had a discussion about that very thing just last night. I remembered that in her younger days, Enid loved to play bingo. Last night was bingo night at the grange hall, so I thought perhaps she'd like a night out. Of course she was delighted to go, and she seemed to enjoy herself. Won fifty dollars, too, so all in all, it was a very good night for her."

"That was nice of you to take her."

"One does what one can for one's fellow travelers in life, dear." Violet sighed. "Anyway, we did get talking on the way home about how she got to thinking about our conversation and how she's come to the conclusion that she needs assistance to safely stay in her house or she'll wind up in some sort of group home—a nursing home, that is—where she can be cared for. Now, Enid abhors that very idea—she's pretty much a loner, don't you know, never was one to socialize much, never married nor did she want to. When she worked at the restaurant, she stayed mostly in the kitchen, let her mother deal with the public. Went to church, and other than the occasional bingo game, she stayed pretty close to home. So the thought of having to sell her home to be able to afford to go someplace she doesn't want to be, well, that doesn't make sense. I said . . ."

Oh, please . . . get to the point. Is she going to sell it?

Violet bustled past Sophie when she heard the phone ring on her desk. Sophie stepped out of the way and followed in the older woman's wake, then forced herself not to tap her foot impatiently while Violet took the call.

"Let me just make a note for your brother," Violet said after she hung up. "There. Now, where was I . . . ?"

"You were talking to Enid Walsh."

"Yes, yes. She said she'd been thinking about what I'd suggested, about it making more sense to sell the restaurant and use the money to stay in her family home. She could hire someone to live in with her so she's not alone all the time, and she . . ."

"Do you think she'll do that? Sell the restaurant, I mean." Sophie's impatience got the best of her. She had to cut to the chase.

"I believe she is seriously considering it, yes."

"Do you think she'll let you know when she makes that decision?"

"I told her I could help her to find someone to appraise the property so she could ask a fair price for it. She said she'd call me when she's made a decision." Violet tapped a pen on her desktop. "She does need to get as much as she can for it, you know. If she can't make enough from the sale to enable her to stay in her home, there's no point in selling it, as far as she's concerned. She will need to get fair market value for it."

"Of course." Sophie wondered what the fair market price would be. "Could you . . . um, when she has a price, when she makes up her mind, do you think you could let me know? I mean, before she officially puts it up for sale?"

"You'll know when I know." Violet paused. "You seem to have quite an interest in the place."

"Oh, it's always been a dream of mine to own my own little café. I guess everyone has their little dreams, right?"

"Does Jesse know of your interest?"

"He knows, but he doesn't think much of it," she admitted. "So if you could maybe not mention this conversation to him." She added pointedly, "Or to anyone . . ."

"My lips are sealed."

"Thanks, Violet." Sophie gave the woman a quick hug. "I'll be back for the wedding, so I'll see you soon. In the meantime, if anything . . ."

"Of course, dear. I promise I'll call you."

Violet watched from the front window as Sophie drove away from the curb, then sighed deeply. She hated keeping things from Curtis—they'd been friends for seventy years, and his wife had been her dearest friend. These days, they'd say BFFs—best friends forever—and she and Rose Enright had certainly been that. So to keep something important from Curtis, something that he'd probably like to know—something he probably *should* know—just felt wrong.

On the other hand, she'd promised Sophie that she wouldn't say a word. Oh, of course, the idea was that she not mention anything to Jesse, but Violet felt pretty sure that Sophie's "or anyone" was a direct reference to her grandfather.

Violet had known, of course, where Sophie had gone earlier that morning. She'd taken the mail into Jesse's office and had started to place it in the center of his desk where she always did—lest he later claim to not have seen something—and seen the note Sophie had left there. Violet hadn't meant to pry, but she knew every piece of paper on Jesse's desk and hadn't recognized that one, so she had to investigate, didn't she? Her heart had skipped a beat when she read it—Curtis and Jesse would both be over the moon when they found out that Sophie was planning on moving to St. Dennis and would be joining the firm after all—but she'd also noticed that the key to Walsh's restaurant was no longer on the desk. She'd deliberately positioned that string to hang off the side of the pile that Jesse had left there the day before, lest the key be misplaced. If she'd had time to search for the Walsh file, she'd have returned the key herself. God only knew where he'd put it—it wasn't in the drawer where it belonged.

Of course, with his sister joining the firm, Violet suspected that Jesse would have more time to deal with those little details he so often overlooked these days. Then again, there was always the possibility that Jesse Enright was just not as detail-oriented as some.

Violet turned away from the window and went into the small office that Sophie had selected as her own. There were others upstairs, all unused at this point, but apparently there was something about this room that she liked. It had two nice windows that looked across Old St. Mary's Church Road, so it did have a view, but that was about all. Violet made a mental note to check upstairs for a few paintings to bring down and hang in what she already thought of as Sophie's room. Something told her that the young woman would appreciate a few of the older prints that had once hung in her grandfather's office. She seemed like someone who'd appreciate her roots, even if she was just discovering them.

A sigh escaped Violet's lips. If in fact Sophie was going to do something that was going to upset her family, she should be permitted to do so on her own terms and in her own time, and it wasn't Violet's place to interfere. And she of all people knew Curtis, knew how he could be when he wanted someone to do something—the word *manipulative* sprang to mind—whether or not others were inclined to go along with him. Lord knew she hated to judge, but it wasn't easy for Curtis to back off when he wanted something—and right now, what he wanted was for Sophie to be one of the Enrights in Enright & Enright. How badly he wanted that to happen, Violet couldn't know for certain, but perhaps it would be best not to get into the middle of all that.

Best to let things take their natural course.

Besides, there was always the chance that Enid would decide not to sell the property after all, and everyone would have gotten into a snit for no reason at all.

Satisfied that her chosen course was the correct one, Violet answered the ringing phone with a clear conscience and a cheery voice.

Jason picked up his set of documents from the settlement table and tucked them under his arm. He'd already said his goodbyes to the representative from the mortgage company and Paul, who'd handled the sale on behalf of both parties. Once outside, though, the new property owner broke into a huge grin, and mentally, he was jumping into the air, clicking his heels. Everything had gone smoothly, and he was in and out in less than an hour. He hopped into his truck and headed straight for River Road.

He stopped the pickup at the gate, and leaving the engine idling, he got out and unlocked the gate with the key he'd been given. He swung the gate wide open, then drove his truck through and across the cracked and broken macadam to the back of the lot where the tree line began. There he parked and got out again.

The wind had picked up, enough that he had to zip up his leather jacket almost to the neck, but he barely noticed. This was his place now. *His.* He walked every inch of it, clear down to the river, which effectively acted as the back property line. Once at the water's edge, he raised a hand to his forehead, using it as a visor to shield his eyes from the late afternoon sun, and looked downriver as far as he could. About a half mile away were the old warehouses that Dallas MacGregor had renovated and were now housing her start-up film company. A mile or so farther down was the start of the residential area, where several of the biggest and grandest homes in town were built in the nineteenth century. Dallas's great-aunt Berry lived in one of those. He'd been at a holiday party Dallas and her husband, Grant, had hosted there in December. It was the fanciest house he'd ever been in. If his property had come with a dock, he'd probably be able to see the back of Berry's property from here. He thought about the feasibility of putting a dock in, then dismissed the thought. It would serve no purpose but to amuse him if he ever decided to take up kayaking.

From here the river looked endless, but he knew that around a curve or two it met the Bay. He liked that his property had a connection to the Chesapeake, albeit a peripheral one. He'd been in town long enough to understand that here, on the Eastern Shore, the Chesapeake was everything. Waterfront property was highly desirable. That he'd been able to purchase an acre of it delighted him. The only thing that would have made this day better was if Eric had been here to share it.

Of course, if Eric were still alive, Jason most likely would never have come to St. Dennis. The plan was to continue to build the business in Florida once Eric left the military. There'd never been any thought of moving Bowers for Landscape north. It never occurred to him to wonder if he'd have been better off in Florida. He'd done what he'd needed to do, and there'd been no point in questioning the wisdom of selling the one business and starting up the next— though he knew all along he'd be rebuilding, he hadn't thought of staying in St. Dennis. But once he'd made the decision, he'd moved right ahead with it, buying his equipment one piece at a time and hustling for customers. Landing those two big jobs—the Inn at Sinclair's Point and the Enright property—had pretty much set him up.

And now here he stood, his hands on his hips, surveying the little bit of the Eastern Shore that he could call his.

He'd need to have a sign made for the gate, he thought as he walked through the wooded section to his truck. Mentally he tagged some hardwoods that he might be able to sell, maybe make a few dollars there—with luck, enough to have the front of the lot repaved.

The stone building next door was the last piece he needed to complete his vision.

He went to the fence and leaned on it. The sign over the door may have said Walsh's, but he could blink and see Bowers for Landscape in black script, just like on the side of his truck and on his business cards. Paul had assured him that he'd contacted the owner, who wasn't interested in selling at this time. Jason told him to try again in six weeks, feel her out, see if maybe the right offer would get her attention. In the meantime, Jason had plans for the lot he now owned. Right there, next to the fence, was the perfect spot for the mulch he'd be having delivered in the spring. The ground there was flat and the area was tucked off to the side, so the piles of the various kinds of mulches and soils he'd ordered wouldn't interfere with parking the equipment he'd bought. He could run truckloads of the stuff right down to the tree line. Right now, his deliveries were being made to a vacant lot he was renting from Hal Garrity, but once the new blacktop had been put down and cured, there'd be no need to rent space from anyone else.

A truck with a Bobcat on the bed pulled into the lot, and Jason stepped away from the fence to greet the driver. It gave him great satisfaction to see his equipment parked on his property, no doubt about it. He glanced over his shoulder for one last look at the old stone building and thought how great this was all going to be when his vision was complete.

Chapter 11

SOPHIE drove straight through to Ohio, but she was still up and out early on Saturday morning. Her first stop was the car dealership on Township Line Road. She'd never been particularly fussy about what she drove, as long as it served its purpose. Her pretty little sedan had been intended only to be pretty and comfortable and reasonably efficient when it came to mileage. The car she was looking for now only had to have decent mpg and cargo space, even if she had to forgo some of the comfort. She was going to need lots of room to transport her belongings to St. Dennis, since hiring a mover was out of the question.

She hit two more dealers before finding what she wanted. She ended up having to give up some of the mileage—and some of the comfort—for more cargo space, but the SUV was new and the dealer was offering great incentives, so with the trade-in on her sedan, her monthly payments were lower than what she'd been paying. She took this as a sign that things were going to fall into place. She'd have to go back on Monday to pick it up, but that was okay. She had one more trip to make this weekend, and it didn't matter to her which vehicle she drove to get there.

It was late afternoon when Sophie pulled into the parking lot at Shelby's Diner, where she'd spent many an early summer morning scrambling eggs and making pancakes, and just as many afternoons flipping burgers on the grill. She left her car around back in the employees' lot just for old times' sake and went in through the front door.

The interior hadn't changed in the eight years since she'd hung up her apron the day after she learned she'd passed the bar exam. The tiles on the floor were still black and white, and the faux leather on the counter stool seats and the benches in the booths were still red and frayed in spots. There was still a lot of chrome and glass, and the smell of cooking burgers still made her mouth water. She stood in front of the reception desk, closed her eyes, and took a deep breath. It took her back to the first time she walked through that door to apply for the advertised job.

When she opened her eyes, she found the hostess staring at her.

"Can I help you?" the woman asked warily from behind the desk. "Are you all right?"

Shelby herself appeared before Sophie could respond to the hostess. "Sophie! It's so good to see you!"

Shelby touched a hand to Sophie's shoulder-length hair. "I remember when your hair grew almost to your waist." Shelby then reached up to her head, where gray stubble grew. "Mine too."

Surprised by the woman's appearance, Sophie wordlessly hugged her old boss. For as long as she'd known her, Shelby's hair had been long, dark auburn streaked with gray. Now, except for the stubble, she was completely bald.

"Don't bother telling me how good I look." Shelby returned the hug. "They tell me it grows back, but it's taking its damned sweet time."

"Shelby, what . . . ?" Sophie sought words.

"Yeah, I probably should have mentioned it when you called, but I didn't want to scare you off."

"Why would I be scared off?"

"Some folks have a problem being around sick people and they don't know what to say. Yes, I have cancer, and yes, I'm having chemotherapy. The doctors all tell me I'm doing real good with the treatments and I'm not as sick as some people get with them, so it's all good, right?" Shelby ushered Sophie into the last booth.

"I'll take good, Shelby," Sophie replied. "As long as the doctor's are optimistic, I'll take it."

Shelby nodded. "It's only been a few months, but like I said, it's going well." She signaled for a waitress. "What can we get you? Coffee? Iced tea? A soda?"

"Water would be fine."

"That's it? You drove all this way for a glass of water?"

"I drove all this way to talk to you."

"Jean-Anne, bring my friend a glass of water. Throw some lemon in it." Shelby instructed the waitress she'd called to the table. "You can bring me a cup of my tea."

Shelby turned to Sophie and wrinkled her nose. "Herb tea. That's what I've been reduced to drinking. Herb tea."

"There are some very fine ones on the market," Sophie told her.

"I like my coffee. Strong and dark. But it makes me sick to my stomach these days. This herbal stuff . . ." She shrugged. "But whatcha gonna do?"

"How much longer will you be getting treatments?" Sophie asked, not sure what questions would be too personal, what might make Shelby uncomfortable.

"Till they tell me I can stop." She shrugged again. "Look, I'm fifty-seven years old and I have had one hell of a good ride in this life. I'll do what I have to do to keep it all going—I mean, I won't give up without a damned good fight—but I got nothing to complain about. Like I said, I've had a good life. That's more than a lot of folks can say."

Sophie nodded, grateful when the waitress served her water and Shelby's tea because it gave her a moment to swallow the lump in her throat.

"Now, what brings you back to Shelby's? You said you wanted to pick my brain about something?"

"I do." Sophie took a sip of water, then put the glass on the chipped tabletop. "I need your advice."

"About . . . ?"

"About running a restaurant."

Shelby raised an eyebrow. "Who wants to run a restaurant?"

"I do."

"You went to law school to be a lawyer, right?"

Sophie nodded. "I did. And I like being a lawyer. But the best job I ever had was right here."

"You were a short-order cook." Shelby was frowning. "You didn't need to go to law school to do that."

"I went to law school because everyone expected

me to. I became a lawyer because that's what people in my family do."

"They don't become short-order cooks."

"Not until now."

Shelby sighed. "So you want, what, to go back to cooking?"

"In my own restaurant."

"No offense, hon, but what do you know about owning a restaurant?"

"Very little. That's why I'm here." Sophie tucked her hair behind her ear. "The place I'm looking at is very small. Maybe a dozen tables. I'm thinking about a relatively limited and simple menu, breakfast and lunch only."

"How do you plan on making any money serving two meals a day?"

"The restaurant is in a small town that gets a lot of tourist trade, it's right next door to a bait shop that does a lot of business, and it's a stone's throw from Dallas MacGregor's new film studio."

"Dallas MacGregor, the movie star?"

When Sophie nodded, Shelby said, "She moved to some small town in Delaware or Jersey. I read about it in *People*."

"Maryland," Sophie told her. "St. Dennis, Maryland. My brother lives there, and soon, I will, too."

"This a done deal?"

"Not yet," Sophie admitted. "Right now it's still in the dream phase. But when the place comes up for sale, I want to be ready."

"So what is it that you think I can tell you?"

"You've been in the business for a long time . . ."

Shelby nodded. "Since I was twenty-two and my husband and I bought the place from his uncle. Scrapped together every penny we could get our hands on, but we did it."

"I figured you've learned a few things in all that time. Maybe you'd be willing to give me a few pointers."

Shelby played with her tea bag for a moment.

"Okay, so you want a crash course in making a go at it? You want to know what I've learned over the past thirty-five years?" When Sophie nodded, Shelby said, "You start taking notes, because I'm not going to repeat myself."

Sophie looked in her bag for her iPad, then decided to go old school with a pad and pen. She wasn't as fast a typist as Shelby was a talker.

"Okay," she told the older woman. "Shoot."

"First of all, you gotta know your place, every inch of it. First thing in the morning, you stand in the doorway and check it out. The floor and tables are clean and the flowers on every table are fresh. Did the kid who sat at the table near the window lick the glass and leave a smear? Make sure it's been wiped off." Shelby drummed a finger on the tabletop. "Most important thing: the customer is always right. Cliché, right? It's always true, no matter what. No one, but no one in your place argues with a customer. Something isn't making them happy? It's the job of every employee in your place to make them happy. That is rule number one. You cannot be a success if anyone leaves your restaurant unhappy with the food or the service or anything else. Without your customers, you have no business. Never forget that. Especially," she pointed at Sophie, "if your business is small. Your restaurant's success will depend on your repeat customers. Treat them like royalty."

"Okay." Sophie wrote furiously. "Got it."

"You might have real celebrities in your place from time to time, that close to the studio, but everyone who comes in wants to feel like a celebrity, like they are special. They want to be waited on and fussed over just a little. You know how good it feels to walk into an establishment—restaurant, bar, coffee shop, whatever—and people remember your name." She pointed her spoon at the pad on which Sophie took notes. "Write that down. Get to know your customers' names and call them by name."

Sophie nodded.

"Now, the food. What are you planning on offering?"

"Breakfast fare, the usual . . ."

"What's usual?" Shelby stopped her.

"Eggs, omelets, cereal . . ." Sophie realized Shelby was staring at her. "What?"

"Small place, small menu. Unless you're planning on hiring a staff the size of mine, you need to limit what you're going to put on that menu."

"What would you do?"

"I'd do just a few staple items—maybe eggs two or three ways, toast, potatoes, sausage, bacon. Forget the cold cereals and offer oatmeal. No guy going out on a boat at five in the morning wants to eat cold cereal, trust me, and most of them aren't looking for fruit and yogurt at that hour of the day. But, since hopefully you're also going to be bringing in the studio people, you have early-bird specials for the fishermen, then later in the morning, maybe around seven or eight or so, you start offering something lighter, like the fruit and yogurt, maybe a little homemade granola. But nothing fancy. You won't have time for fancy," Shelby warned. "You need to stick to the basics. But then, have a special on the menu—pancakes one day, waffles another, omelets, whatever. But make that the same day every week, follow?"

"Ham Omelet Monday. Pancake Wednesday."

"Right. Day-of-the-week specials. Now, lunch is a different thing, but basics. Burgers, BLTs, grilled cheese. But again, a special every day. Chili in the winter, a nice quiche in the spring. Some sort of comfort food every day. I want to say it again: you won't have time for fancy, so you have to make sure that everything you serve is worth coming back for. Everything has to be simple, but it has to be the best in its class, you follow? Burgers from the best beef you can get your hands on, applewood-smoked bacon, fresh salads. Everything homemade, Sophie. Find someone local who sells homegrown produce and you've got it made." Shelby winked. "Those film types will love it if you serve an heirloom tomato salad."

Sophie immediately thought of Clay Madison. "A friend of my brother's has an organic farm and I'm pretty sure he sells to restaurants in town."

"That's what you want, hon'."

"And I think they're selling eggs from their chickens now, too . . ."

"Perfect. But don't forget your desserts. If you don't have time to bake, find someone who can. You don't need to have more than two or three things on hand, but everyone likes a little sweet something now and then."

"The woman my brother is marrying has a little bakery in town. Cupcakes . . ."

"There you go, then. Pretty cupcakes would be perfect. Then maybe some fruit tarts or pies or something along that line in season. And something chocolate, like brownies, maybe. That's all you need to have." Shelby crossed her arms over her chest and leaned back against the booth. "You do those few things and your little restaurant might have a fighting chance. Not to discourage you, but you need to know that most of the new restaurants that open fail within twelve to thirty-six months."

"That won't be me." Sophie closed her notebook. "If I do this, it will not fail."

"Well, now, I'd bet some of my good, hard-earned money on that, Sophie Enright." Shelby smiled. "I surely would. But while we're on the subject of money, let's talk about how many employees you're going to need, and how you're going to pay them . . ."

Chapter 12 ⌒

Determined to make every minute count, Sophie gave her all to the job at hand. There were a lot of files to be passed on, some of which she'd handled from day one, and as eager as she may have been to leave, she felt a real responsibility to the victims whose cases had been assigned to her. Even though work was consuming much of her time, in the back of her mind the question was always there: what was Enid Walsh going to do with the property on River Road?

Down to less than two weeks till her last day, she was in the office early every morning and worked late every night. On her second-to-last Thursday, she was wrapping up a meeting with two other ADAs when she checked messages on her phone.

There was one.

"Sophie, this is Violet Finneran calling. I have some news regarding that project we talked about. If you could give me a call back before nine this evening, I'd like to chat with you."

It was almost six by the time the meeting ended and she was able to return the call. Hoping that Violet was still at the office, Sophie hit redial and waited impatiently for the call to be answered.

"Violet, hello. It's Sophie." She went for casual, hoping to mask the fact that she was all but hyperventilating.

"Hello, dear. I'm glad you were able to get back to me today. We may have a *situation* on our hands." Violet sounded rushed, excited even.

"What kind of situation?" Sophie frowned. She'd assumed that the call was about the vacant restaurant.

"Well, I told you I'd speak to Enid Walsh, and I did. She called me early in the week and told me that she'd decided that selling the River Road property was the right thing for her to do."

Sophie silently pumped the air. *Yes!* "Did she say how much she would be asking for it?"

"Let's not get ahead of ourselves, dear. The appraiser didn't get out there until yesterday and he didn't drop off his report until this morning." Violet gave Sophie the appraised value of the property.

"Ouch." Sophie grimaced. "That's more than I thought it would be."

"But it is fair value, and they are expecting the property's worth will increase over the next few years, what with Dallas's studio right up the road. Of course, it's hard to put a price on potential."

"True." Sophie's heart began to sink. There was no way she could raise that much money on her own.

"The asking price may be somewhat negotiable, but there is another situation that might interest you."

That word—*situation*—again. "What's that, Violet?"

"Someone else has expressed an interest in making an offer on the property."

"What?" That brought Sophie out of the funk she was starting to slide into. "Who?"

"A client of Paul Dunlap's." Violet went on to explain, "He's a relatively new Realtor in St. Dennis, so I'm thinking his client isn't local. All the locals use Hamilton Forbes for their real estate transactions."

Sophie felt blindsided, stunned. It had never occurred to her that someone else might be coveting that same piece of real estate.

"Sophie? Are you still there, dear?"

"I'm here, Violet. I'm just . . . surprised, I guess. I didn't think anyone else noticed the place. It's so overgrown and . . . well, that was naïve on my part, wasn't it?"

"I don't know that an actual offer has been made, and I don't know who the other interested party might be, but I wanted to give you the information so that if you wanted to make an offer, you could do so. Be first through the door, so to speak."

"I really appreciate the call, Violet." Sophie sighed. There was no way this was going to happen. "But there's no way I can make an offer right now. I won't have any cash for a down payment until my condo settles in May, and even then, I'll be short. I can make up the difference with my savings, but there won't be a dime left for the repairs and renovations and some new equipment. Without all that, there isn't going to be a restaurant."

"So you definitely intended to open a restaurant there," Violet said thoughtfully.

"Yes."

"With what experience, may I ask?"

Sophie told her about her summers working as a cook, and about her conversation with Shelby. "So I haven't owned a restaurant before, but I know what to do in the kitchen and I've gotten some good advice from someone who's been in business for many years. I believe I could have done this. I believe I would have been good at it."

"Tell me, what sort of restaurant did you have in mind?"

"Nothing very big, and nothing very fancy." *Not that it matters now,* Sophie thought, though it was nice of Violet to ask. "More of a café, just early breakfast and lunch."

"Why just the two?" Violet pressed.

"Early breakfast because the bait shop next door opens at five, so I figured there'd be fishermen coming out that way to pick up bait, so why not a quick stop for breakfast? I heard there's going to be a marina there next year as well, so that's additional traffic. Then figure in everyone on their way to and from Dallas's studio. There's nothing else in the neighborhood for a quick lunch, and we could deliver."

"And why not serve dinner?"

"One, because there won't be much traffic out there by five or six in the afternoon. The fishermen are in by then and if there are still people in the studio, chances are they'll be in the mood for fine dining rather than the casual fair I'll offer. They'll want Captain Walt's, or Lola's, or one of the other fancier places closer to the center of town and the B and Bs where they'll be staying. And two," Sophie continued, "I'll be working at the office for at least six hours or so every day after I leave the café. I can't help Jesse and serve dinner, too."

"I see you've given this a great deal of thought. I suppose you had the renovations and the décor all planned as well."

"I did." Sophie blinked back tears. "I was going to use as much of what's there as I could. The tables and chairs can be painted, and the walls . . . oh, it doesn't matter. I guess I'll just have to be a full-time lawyer for a while longer, until something else comes up."

"Unless, of course, you obtain financing."

"I don't know that the bank down there would be interested in loaning money for a restaurant when the borrower has no restaurant experience."

"Perhaps we could arrange private financing."

"Who would loan me money?"

"I would."

"Violet, that's very kind of you, but I couldn't ask you to . . ."

"You're not asking. I'm offering."

"It's speculative."

"Oh, so's the stock market, and that's not near as interesting."

"I think you should think this over, maybe talk to someone, ask your banker or advisor if they think this is a good move for you. You could end up losing your investment, and then I'd feel . . ."

"Really, Sophie, I'm not a babe in the woods and I don't appreciate being treated like one. I have been making my own investment decisions for years." Violet's indignation was frosty and just a little bit this side of scary. "I don't need someone else to tell me that it's a highly speculative venture."

"I'm sorry," Sophie apologized. "But I would feel terrible if you invested in me—in the restaurant—and it flopped."

"It isn't going to be a flop. I have total confidence in you. You're an Enright. You will make this work." Violet's voice softened. "Besides, it's nice to invest in something I can see. I'm excited about the prospect, actually. I think it will be . . . well, fun."

"Violet, I don't know what to say. What if . . ."

"Stop right there," Violet said sternly. "If you're going to do this, you're going to do it in a positive fashion. No negativity. No doubts."

When Sophie didn't respond, Violet said, "Sophie?"

"I heard you. I'm trying to think. This is so unexpected. When I heard the price, I started to shut it down in my head—the plans for the restaurant, that is—because it was out of reach for me. And now it might not be."

"Would you like to think it over and call me back?"

"I don't even know exactly how much money I need to borrow, Violet. I don't know how much it will take to renovate the place, and I don't know if I'll have to replace all the equipment or if some of it can be repaired. What's there is old, but it's good quality— and then there are dishes and oh, my God, Violet, we'll need an exterminator. There are bugs and . . . *vermin*. And then after all that's done, I'll have to hire people—waitstaff and another cook and a dishwasher." She paused. "I mean, *we'd* have to hire people."

"No, no. You were right the first time. I'm a silent partner here. No one is going to know I'm involved in this." Violet hesitated before adding firmly, "I would appreciate that you not tell anyone that I'm your investor."

"Really? I'd think you'd want . . ."

"No. I do not want." There was that stern voice again. "That's a condition of the deal, Sophie. I will loan you the money that you need, but no one's name is on the deed but yours. No one will know I've backed this venture. It's going to have to be our secret."

"All right. Let me think this through. It's not that I don't appreciate the offer. Oh, my God, it's unexpected and beyond anything I ever would have thought possible . . ." Sophie took a deep breath. "But it's a huge step for both of us, and I want to do the right thing."

"I understand, dear. Just don't take too long to make up your mind. Don't forget there's still another party out there, and we don't know how badly they want to buy that property."

"Good point." Sophie nodded to herself. "I'll call you first thing in the morning."

"See that you do, dear."

"And Violet . . . I don't even know how to adequately thank you for making such a kind and generous offer."

"You can thank me when the keys are put into your hand as the new owner of Walsh's. Wait, you can't keep calling it that. What will you call your restaurant?"

"I have no idea. I never got that far," Sophie told her. "I'm sure the right name will come to me."

The next week was a blur, but in the end, Sophie's offer to purchase the old Walsh's restaurant property had been accepted, and Violet had papers drawn up for the terms of the loan to finance the renovations.

"This was a tad tricky," Violet told her on the phone. "Normally, I'd have had my attorney take care of the paperwork, but that's out of the question for the obvious reason."

"Why didn't you just ask Jesse to do it?" Sophie asked.

"Did we not agree that no one would know that I was your investor?"

"Yes, but . . ."

"If Jesse knows, sooner or later, Curtis will find out. And if Curtis finds out that I went behind his back to help you do something we both know he wouldn't approve of . . . well, it smacks of disloyalty."

"How is helping me being disloyal to him?" Sophie sat in the nearest chair.

"Have you told him what you're doing yet?"

"Well, no . . ."

"Why not?" When Sophie didn't immediately respond, Violet added, "Because it isn't what he wants you to do, and he'll be a pain in the butt about it. You don't want to have that conversation with him."

"Not really." Sophie sighed.

"So what do you think your grandfather would do if he knew that I was the one who backed this business venture of yours? It's no secret that he wants you here, in this office."

"Would he be angry with you?"

"Probably. For a while, anyway. Mostly he'd think that I betrayed him."

"Why don't we both go talk to him, together?" Sophie suggested.

"Because he'll try to talk both of us out of it."

"You really think he would?"

Violet snorted. "This is Curtis Enright we're talking about here. He's used to getting his way. Some might even call him manipulative."

As much as she'd have liked to deny it, Sophie knew Violet was right. She certainly knew Curtis far better than Sophie did.

"So what did you do? Did you go to another firm?"

"Certainly not!" Violet bristled. Clearly the very thought was out of the question. "I wrote the documents myself and took them to Ballard to have them notarized. You'll receive your copy to sign via overnight mail in the morning. You'll have your signature notarized and return the copies to me. I'll sign them and send you back your copy."

"Not too late to change your mind, Violet. I'll understand if you do." Sophie wanted to give the woman an out if she felt she needed one.

"No second thoughts here. You?"

"None."

"Well, then." Violet sounded pleased. "I suppose we're partners. Silent partners, but partners nonetheless. Your grandmother would have approved of your initiative."

"Nice to think that someone in my family would have."

Sophie's time at the DA's office had eaten up an additional week she hadn't planned on, and it took another three for her to sort through her belongings—

clothes, books, kitchen items—and pack for her move. As soon as Sophie had shared her plans, Gwen had made a bid to buy her condo and the sofa, which was proving too large to move, and, at the last minute, decided she'd take the kitchen table and chairs as well. Sophie sold her bedroom furniture to one of the secretaries in the office, which left her with mostly clothes and boxes.

By the time the condo was cleaned out and everything that didn't fit in her SUV was stashed in a spare room at her mother's house in Pittsburgh, it was the first week of April. Sophie would make it to St. Dennis with but a few days to spare before Jesse's wedding.

Once the SUV was packed—with Gwen's help—Sophie was finally ready to leave Ohio behind.

"Are you sure you can see out your windows?" Gwen poked her head inside to see if the mirrors were blocked by boxes.

"I'm good. The mirrors adjust," Sophie assured her.

"They adjust that much?" Gwen was skeptical.

"I'll be fine."

"Well, hell." Gwen hugged Sophie. "I really will miss you. I wasn't kidding about not having anyone else to mouth off to. No one else in the office appreciates snark and sarcasm the way you do."

"I'll see you when we go to settlement for the condo. And there's the phone, Skype, text . . ."

"It's not the same."

"No, but it'll be fine. And we've already agreed that you'll come and visit."

"And you won't."

Sophie looked beyond her SUV to the building where she'd lived for the past four years.

"No, I probably won't." Sophie turned back to the SUV and opened the driver's-side door. "Not for a while, anyway. Except for you, there's not much for me here."

"So it looks like my vacation will be in St. Dennis this fall." Gwen nodded.

"Good. I'll look forward to that." Sophie slammed the car door. "Maybe I'll put you to work waiting tables, make you earn your keep."

"Maybe you'll introduce me to the hunky . . ." She paused. "What does the hunky guy do?"

"He's a landscaper."

"Nice." Gwen nodded. "I'll bet he's got some muscles."

"And some to spare." Sophie grinned and backed out of her parking spot, waved to Gwen one more time, then headed out of the lot, out of town, out of her old life, and into her future.

Chapter 13

SOPHIE had always thought that the drive *to* some-place seemed so unnecessarily longer than the drive *from,* but for some reason, the return trip to St. Dennis felt endless. Maybe, she reasoned, because she was so eager to get there, so stoked to get to work. Violet had assured her that the closing on the property would go through without a hitch, but it wasn't going to happen for another ten days. Of course, there was plenty to do between now and then. Jesse would be leaving on his honeymoon right after the reception on Saturday, so Sophie had only until Friday to acclimate herself to the workings of the office. There were files that needed to be reviewed and several situations he said he wanted to fill her in on, but there were no trials scheduled and nothing that had to be filed with the court in his absence, so she figured she'd be mostly fielding phone calls and researching case law for the few appeals he was leaving for her to write.

All of which was fine. She wanted to keep busy. It kept her mind off the many things that she feared could go wrong before the property went to closing.

It would be tough to keep the real estate deal under wraps, Violet had told her, but she'd do what she could to keep both Curtis and Jesse from finding out until Sophie could tell them herself, which she planned to do as soon as she hit town.

Jesse first, she decided, so she swung by the office before she did anything else.

"Hi," Sophie called into the reception area. When there was no response, she took a quick look into the room. No Violet.

She tapped on Jesse's half-closed door. He looked up from his desk, then smiled.

"What took you so long?" he asked.

"Traffic, mostly." She pushed the door open and went inside.

"I meant what kept you in Ohio for so long." He moved aside the pad on which he'd been writing and tossed the pen he'd been using onto the desktop.

"Don't you ever listen to your voice mail? I gave two weeks' notice but got roped into staying three, had to sell my condo, and had to drag everything I was keeping but couldn't bring with me to Mom's." Sophie plunked down in one of the guest chairs.

"How's Mom doing?" he asked.

"Fabulous as always. She's so psyched for the wedding. Showed me her dress, her shoes . . . she's going glam, Jess. Really planning on playing up the whole Mother of the Groom thing."

"She bringing Adam with her?"

"She invited him but as of yesterday, she wasn't sure if he'd make it. At best, he'll fly in on Saturday if he's back from his trip. She's planning on driving herself on Thursday."

"Why driving?"

"One, because she hates to fly; two, because she said having that brand-new and very sweet luxury drive that she finally broke down and bought for herself doesn't make any sense if she doesn't actually drive it anywhere; and three, that driving a distance is the only time she gets to catch up on the bestsellers she never has time to read. She's big on audio books these days," Sophie explained. "I am hoping that Adam can make it, though, so that we can get to know him a little better. I wouldn't be surprised if they decided to get married when things settle down."

"What things?" Jesse frowned.

"Her work, his work—he's been traveling a lot but she said they expected that would taper off by the fall, so I'm thinking within the next few months there might be some sort of announcement."

"You like him?" Jesse's face showed his concern.

"I really do. From what I've seen, he's a great guy with a great sense of humor, and he seems totally over the moon about Mom. And frankly, that's what I care most about."

"Me too." Jesse nodded. "Well, good. I want her to be happy."

"So do I." Sophie leaned back against the seat. "So are you ready for your big day?"

"Couldn't be more ready."

"I think it's so cool that you asked Pop to be your best man."

"He *is* my best man. I couldn't think of anyone else I wanted to have standing next to me when Brooke and I get married. And he's so tickled that he'll get to walk down the aisle with Dallas MacGregor after the ceremony." He wiggled his eyebrows. "I think the old man's got a crush."

"What man in his right mind wouldn't?" She could imagine her elderly grandfather offering his arm to the gorgeous film star who'd more than once been voted the most beautiful woman in the world. "She's Brooke's matron of honor, right?"

"Actually, she's the only attendant. Brooke wanted to keep the ceremony small since she was married before. Didn't want the big hoopla again."

"Did you?" She rested an elbow on his desk. "Want the big hoopla?"

"Nah. I just want to marry Brooke. We were trying for small, but between the two of us, it feels as if we know everyone in town, and everyone seemed to assume they'd be invited." He shrugged. "When you can't decide who to cut, you either cut everyone and just have your family, or you don't cut anyone. So we invited family and just our closest friends to the church, and everyone else to the reception. But we're keeping things simple, more like a big party than a fancy reception. It'll be fun."

"I'm glad you invited our sibs. I'm thinking less and less of them as half and more and more just as our brother and sisters."

"Me too. I've gotten to know Nick over the past year, and I was amazed to find how much alike we are." He hesitated. "I invited Delia, too. Do you think Mom will mind?"

"That you invited Dad's first wife?" She shook her head. "Mom is so over Dad, Jesse. *Totally* over Dad."

"I thought she'd be okay. I just wanted your opinion."

"What about Dad?" she asked. "Did you invite him?"

"I thought about it." Jesse ran a hand through his hair. "I went back and forth, should I or shouldn't I?"

"And you decided . . . ?"

"Not to invite him. It wasn't an easy decision, and I feel like a jerk for not calling him. I mean, he *is* our father, Soph."

"True, but what's your relationship with him?"

"Pretty much nonexistent," he conceded. "Which doesn't make me happy, but he is who he is, and I have a hard time dealing with that."

"Did you discuss this with Brooke?"

"Of course. She said I should do whatever made me most comfortable."

"And she's right. Dad's a loose cannon. We all know that. I think if you want to have a relationship with him at all . . ."

"I don't know if I do."

"Well, you need to decide that. And if you do, you should try to lay the groundwork at some time other than at your wedding." She bit her bottom lip, thinking of the havoc their father's presence could create. "There are other people to consider, Jess. It's not just us. There's Mom, and there's Delia and her kids. Mom's moved past it all and I suspect Delia has as well—Zoey said her mother was seriously considering marrying a man she's been dating for years now—but still. Let's face it. Dad dumped them both and moved on to marry someone else." She paused. "Actually, he'd dumped Delia and married Mom. That could get sticky."

"I thought about that."

"And then there's Pop. He hasn't spoken to Dad in I don't know how long. I don't think he'd appreciate being forced to deal with his wayward son in front of the entire town, when he hasn't been able to deal with him in private. And Uncle Mike . . ." Sophie shook her head. "It just gets more and more complicated."

Brother and sister sat in silence. Finally, Sophie said, "I think you did the right thing, Jess. Your wedding day isn't the day to try to reconnect with him, if that's what you want to do. If you wanted him at the wedding, you should have reached out a long time ago, and everyone should have been made aware that he was going to attend." She reached across the desk and tapped his arm gently. "I think that door has closed for now, but that's just my opinion. All that being said, it's your wedding so you should do what you want, either way, but I do think this is one of those times when you have to consider other people's feelings. It's just too touchy a situation."

"I think you're right. That's pretty much how I feel, too. If I wanted to . . ." He paused. "How do you feel about him? Do you think you'll ever contact him? You know, try to establish some sort of relationship?"

"I don't know. I guess at some point I might. Probably not on my wedding day, though." She smiled. "And on the subject of weddings, what all is going on this week before yours? Is there anything I can do to help? Anything you want me to do?"

"No, but thanks. Only prewedding event is the rehearsal dinner on Friday night. I've already moved most of my stuff over to Brooke's place. Not moving in till after the wedding, though. We both think it sets a better example for Logan. I left most of the furniture in the house, by the way. I didn't know what you had or what you were bringing or what you'd need. I figured we'd work it out when you got here. Anything you don't want, I can move out."

"I didn't bring any furniture with me, so I'm grateful for whatever leftovers you can spare. I imagine at some point I'll bring the stuff I left in Mom's basement, but for now, I just want to get settled into my new job."

"Which one?" Jesse leaned his chair all the way back.

"What?" Her eyes narrowed suspiciously.

"I asked which of your new jobs you wanted to get settled into."

They stared at each other for a long while.

"Sophie, this is a small town," he said softly. "Things get around."

"Like what things?" She squirmed.

"You're really going to make me say it? That I know you're buying the property on River Road?"

"How did you know? And I haven't technically bought it. We haven't closed yet. And does Pop know?"

"Ham Forbes, the Realtor handling the sale, is a client. He was in the other day on another matter and happened to ask me who Sophie Enright was in relation to me. And I don't think Pop's heard it yet. At least, he hasn't mentioned it to me, and I feel pretty sure he would if he knew. I did ask the Realtor to keep it under his hat until after settlement."

Sophie fell silent. Jesse added, "Is this," he asked, waving a hand around the room, "just a sham? An excuse to come to St. Dennis?"

"You're asking me if I'm going to work for you for real?" When he nodded, she said, "Of course I am. I wouldn't do that to you, Jess. I will help you as much as I can for as long as I can. And frankly, I'm a little put out that you'd even ask me that."

"Yeah, well, I was a little put out that you'd go ahead and buy that place without even mentioning it to me."

"I'm sorry. I should have told you. I kept thinking about it and thinking about how I would do things—what sort of food I'd have, how I'd budget, the menus—and all of a sudden, it was for sale, and I could buy it, and I had to decide quickly, so I went for it. It happened really fast, and I was so tied up trying to get my cases organized at the office. Things just moved very quickly. My head is still spinning. I planned on telling you when I got here."

"Who told you that it was for sale?"

Sophie shifted uneasily in her seat. "I'd rather not say."

Jesse laughed out loud. "Don't worry," he whispered. "Violet's secret is safe with me."

"She told you?"

"No, but you just did. I figured it had to be her. Who else is there?"

"She doesn't want anyone to know she was involved, Jess."

"You mean, she doesn't want Pop to know she's involved," he corrected her. "But Soph, you need to tell him before someone else—like Ham Forbes—tells him. He'll feel blindsided." He left out *like I did*, but she heard the words all the same.

"I know that you think this is folly on my part. But

it's something I've always wanted." When he started to speak, she held up a hand, then continued. "Let me finish, please. I think I can make this work. It's going to be a while before I'll be able to open for business, I realize that, and longer still before I can even think about working on that second-floor apartment, so I'm grateful to be able to sublet your place. I'm going to be working over there in the mornings—painting and whatever I can do on my own—but I'll be here in the office in the afternoons. I'm hoping that by the time the restaurant is up and running, I will have passed the Maryland bar and I'll be able to take on more responsibility for you. In the meantime, I'll write your appeals and I'll do as much of your research as you need me to do. I can interview clients and I can do a lot of the legwork for you."

"And once the restaurant is opened?"

"Same deal. I'll work there till two or so, then come in here and do whatever you need me to do. At least, for as long as I can. This year for sure. We'll see what next year brings."

"I don't see how you'll be able to pull it all off. You're talking about two full-time jobs, Soph. And what do you know about running a restaurant?"

"I can do it. You'll see. I spent some time while I was home picking Shelby's brain, and she gave me some excellent advice. And I have a plan. It's going to work."

"For your sake, I hope it does." He added, "I just hope it doesn't kill you."

"It won't."

"If you want my advice, you should call Cam O'Connor to take a look at the place, give you an idea what it's going to cost to fix it up. He's the best contractor in the area, and he's one of the most honest people I know."

"I'll call him. Maybe I'll even get him in there next week. I don't have any idea what it's going to cost to fix the place up."

"Maybe you should have called him before you came to an agreement with the owner."

"We had the property appraised and inspected. The structure is sound, the wiring and plumbing were updated about twelve years ago, and the roof's good."

"Still . . ." Jesse shrugged. "A pig in a poke, and all that."

"Are you angry with me for not telling you sooner?"

"Not angry. I just don't understand why you didn't."

"You so obviously disapproved of the idea, and I was so happy to finally have a chance to do something I've thought about doing for so long that I . . ."

"Didn't want anyone raining on your parade?" Jesse finished the thought for her.

"Something like that."

"I get it—and I'm sorry. I should have been more open-minded. I still don't know if it's the right thing for you to do, but it's your life and you have to do what you think will make you happiest."

"I'm glad we agree on that much. But I'm confident I can make this work." She smiled slowly. "Unless of course I start thinking too much about how much work and how much money this is going to take. Otherwise, I'm good."

"Good. Now, when can you start? We're still backed up. The new paralegal lasted exactly four weeks, then quit because she missed her fiancé in Hoboken." He stood. "We set you up in the little back office, just as you requested. Let's see if you approve." He held the door for her, and both went into the hallway.

"Oh, I love it!" she exclaimed as she stepped into the room that would serve as her new office. "It's perfect. I love the color of the walls."

"As much as I'd like to take the credit, I cannot tell a lie. Violet did all this. She said she had some ideas of what you might like, so I told her to do whatever."

"Where is she? I noticed she wasn't in the reception area when I came in."

"She took the afternoon off. Said she had some personal business to tend to."

"I can't wait to thank her." Sophie smiled as she took it all in: the palest of green on the walls, the shiny cherry desk and the dark green leather chair, the paintings. "That's Pop, right? The portrait on the left?"

"I thought so, too, but Violet told me it's actually Curtis's father. He died long before we came along." Jesse stood in front of the painting. "I was going to put some different paintings in here. You know, like, flowers or something, but Violet said no, you'd want these."

"I do want these." She glanced at the three paintings in the office, then pointed to the one that hung on the inside wall. "Is that Pop's house?"

"Yeah. He brought that one over after I told him you were joining the firm." Jesse stood in front of the landscape. "I think these are the gardens that Jason is re-creating."

She stepped closer to the painting for a better look.

The gardens depicted were lush and glorious, a riot of color and symmetry.

"I can't imagine that the back of Pop's place ever looked like that. Even harder to imagine that it could look that way again."

"Jason's really good. I saw his sketches. If you're nice to him, I bet he'll let you see them, too."

"I'll ask nicely." She stepped around behind the desk. "Computer?"

"You can use the one I bought for our now-you-see-her, now-you-don't paralegal. She barely used it."

"That's fine." Sophie sat in the chair. It was a little big for her, but it would do. "This is great, Jess. I'm looking forward to getting started."

"Me too." The phone in the reception area rang. "You can start right now by answering that phone . . ."

Jesse's right. I need to tell Pop what I'm doing before he hears it from someone else. Sophie sat in her car, her fingers drumming on the steering wheel. She sighed. No time like the present.

She'd stayed at the office later than she'd planned, and she was still feeling road-weary from the long drive from Ohio, but the longer she waited, the more difficult it would be. She glanced at her reflection in the rearview mirror and made a face. She looked every bit as beat as she felt, as if she wore every mile she'd driven that day. Makeup might have helped, but she doubted her grandfather would mind, nor would he care that she was wearing the same clothes she'd donned early that morning, clothes that were dusty from unpacking some boxes of files that Jesse had dragged down from the second floor, and whoops—

a cobweb she must have picked up in the process of looking through them for a client's will. She parked out front and practiced her opening line while walking to the front door.

Pop, I have something exciting to tell you. She shook her head. Pop wasn't going to be excited—at least, not in the same way she was.

Pop, you know how you always say follow your dream . . . Wait. He'd never actually said that. That had been her mother.

So Pop, you know how I've moved to St. Dennis and I'm going to be working with Jesse? Well, I'm going to be doing something else, too.

"Crap," she said aloud as she rang the doorbell.

When no one answered, she rang the bell again, then a third time. She was just a little concerned—of course he could be out to dinner with a friend. Or maybe napping. She glanced at her watch. Way too late for an afternoon nap.

Or he could have fallen and was hoping someone would come along to help him up.

Or he could be in the kitchen and hadn't heard the doorbell.

She walked around to the back of the house before her imagination had her dialing 911, then stopped at the edge of the back porch, wondering if she could flee quietly before anyone knew she'd been there.

"Well, look who's here. Hello, sweetheart." Curtis had turned at the exact moment she'd rounded the corner. "Jason, look who's stopped in. Checking up on our progress, no doubt."

She felt heat rise along her collar as blue eyes swept

over her. She hoped she'd at least gotten all the cobwebs brushed away. "Hi, Pop."

Trapped, she took another ten steps to kiss her
grandfather on the cheek.

"Jason." She forced a smile. The last time she'd
seen him—other than a few times over the past month
or so in her dreams—she'd been falling apart after
receiving Chris's phone call.

"Sophie. I heard you were coming back this week."
Jason's smile was warm, as always, and he politely
looked beyond her hair, lack of makeup, and the
clothes she'd been in since five that morning, dust and
road grime included.

"Wow, look at this!" Sophie's gaze was drawn to
the garden. "I can't believe what you've done here.
It's beautiful."

"Thanks, but it's still a work in progress," Jason
said. "We have a few more weeks till completion, but
it's coming along."

"It looks like the painting," she murmured.

"What painting?" Jason asked.

"A painting that's hanging in my office." She
pointed to the bank of trees that bordered the far end.
"Those trees are in the painting. And these shrubs.
And the irises . . . they're all in the painting."

"Oh, you like it, do you?" Curtis looked pleased. "I
thought you might."

"Jesse told me that you brought it in for me."

"At one time, it hung in my office on the second
floor. It came home with me when I retired, but when
Violet mentioned she was fixing up an office for you, I
suggested that she might consider that one for you.

She mentioned she was undertaking the décor of your new work space."

"Thank you, Pop. I love it." She turned back toward the garden. "I love that it looks like *this*."

"Many years ago, someone in the family commissioned several paintings of the house and the grounds from different angles," Curtis explained to both Sophie and Jason. "One hangs in the upstairs hall here, one in the conference room at the office, and the third—the painting of the garden—now hangs in Sophie's office. That one was always my favorite, so I'm glad you like it, too."

To Jason, she said, "I can't believe how much your garden looks like the one in the painting. It's uncanny. You must be psychic."

"That, or your grandfather showed me some photos that were taken when this place was in its heyday."

She rolled her eyes. "I should have known. Either way, you've done a remarkable job. It's a shame it won't be done by the weekend. It would have made the perfect spot for a romantic wedding."

"Jesse and Brooke have their spot all picked out and it's at the old church up the road," Curtis said. He turned to Jason and said, "I did mention that my granddaughter here has decided to join the firm?"

"I think you may have a time or ten, yes." Jason nodded. "Congratulations, Sophie. I know that Jesse and your granddad are both really happy."

"Very happy." Curtis beamed. "The name over the door will remain Enright and Enright, and I couldn't be more pleased or proud."

"Thanks, Pop. I'll try to live up to the firm's reputation."

"No doubt you will, my dear. No doubt at all."
Curtis patted her on the back. "Now, was there anything in particular . . . ?"

"Oh, no, no." Sophie shook her head. Curtis and
Jason had been deep in discussion over their landscape plans when she showed up, and her grandfather
was obviously interested in getting back to them. The
conversation she'd planned on having would have to
wait until another day. "I just wanted to let you know
I'd arrived."

"I appreciate that. Thank you."

"Look, I can see you're busy. I'll stop over again,
Pop."

"I don't want to run you off," Jason said.

"Oh, no. I have to get over to the house. Jesse's,
that is. I have a lot of unpacking to do."

"I'll see you on Saturday, if not before, then." Curtis kissed her on the cheek.

"Anything I can do to help?" Jason asked. "Carry
boxes, help empty the car?"

"Thanks, but no. I can do it, and Jesse's home
by now, so he can help. Besides, you have work . . ."
*And I need a shower, clean clothes, mascara, mouth-
wash . . .*

"Well, if you find you need an extra pair of hands,
give me a call."

"Thanks. Will do." *Looking like this? Not gonna
happen.*

She walked away self-consciously, acutely aware of
his eyes on the back of her dusty jeans.

"Probably have cobwebs hanging off my butt,"
she grumbled as she got into her car. "Figures. You

always run into the hot guy when you look like a hot mess."

Jesse's house was minutes away, and she pulled into the driveway behind his car. With his help, she had the car emptied of its boxes in less than thirty minutes. Unpacking would take a day or so, but at least everything was in the house. She shared a pizza with Jesse, put some of her clothes away, and took a shower. Once under the covers, she closed her eyes, exhausted. Her last thought of the day was to wonder how much more interesting the evening might have been had she taken up Jason on his offer to help.

Chapter 14 🖎

"You know, you could have stayed with me this weekend." Sophie hugged her mother in the lobby of the Inn at Sinclair's Point. "With Jesse and Brooke leaving right after the reception for their honeymoon, there's lots of room."

"What, and miss an opportunity to stay at this fabulous inn that I've heard so much about?" Olivia Enright returned her daughter's hug.

"Where'd you hear about the inn?"

"There was a feature about the Eastern Shore in one of those travel magazines last year. Several places on the Chesapeake were highlighted. Baltimore Harbor, Smith Island . . . several other locations, St. Dennis among them. They mentioned the inn—gave it four out of five stars, by the way—and some little ice-cream shop that's apparently quite well known."

"One Scoop or Two. The locals call it Scoop. All the ice cream is handmade by the owner right there in the shop. You'll meet her—Steffie MacGregor—at the wedding."

"MacGregor. Yes, I also read that Dallas MacGregor lives here and is building a film studio here."

"Steffie is married to Dallas's brother, Wade, who incidentally has started up a brewery with Brooke's brother, Clay. They brewed the beer that's being served at the reception."

"Really?" Olivia smiled. "Well, that makes you and Dallas practically related, in some twisted small-town sort of way."

Sophie laughed. "That sort of reasoning would make you practically Dallas's mother-in-law, since your future daughter-in-law's brother is partner to Dallas's brother."

"Ah, the bragging rights I'll have back home." Olivia grinned. "Now, have you had breakfast yet?"

"I did. I ate really early with Jesse. He has a meeting this morning, then he wanted to go into the office to finish up a few things there, but he said he'd see you tonight at the rehearsal dinner. How 'bout you?"

"I had a wonderful breakfast, thank you. They have an excellent chef here at the inn. So far, everything that article had to say about this place has been spot on."

"Good. I'm glad you enjoyed your first night here in town."

"I did. Now, what do you have planned for the day?"

"I thought I'd take you around, show you some of the sights. Nothing exciting to see, I'm afraid, but it's a charming town. I'm still discovering St. Dennis myself."

"I saw that very phrase on a mug on the reception desk. *Discover St. Dennis.* It must be the town motto."

"Well, then, let's do just that." Sophie took her mother's arm and headed through the lobby doors.

"It's so much warmer here than in Pittsburgh," Olivia noted as they walked across the parking lot. "The grounds here are just lovely, by the way. I had a walk after breakfast down to the Bay, and you can just tell that all those flower beds will be bursting with color come summer."

"They had a lot of landscaping done last year. There was a really high-profile wedding here. Maybe you read about it—Robert Magellan, the dot-com gazillionaire? The owners wanted the inn to really shine because they knew there'd be a lot of photos taken. They hired a landscape designer and had the whole back and side of the property down to the water redone with new gardens and paths."

"With all the daffodils and tulips and flowering trees in bloom, it's spectacular. Whoever they hired did a fabulous job."

"Oh, you'll meet him—Jason Bowers, the landscaper, that is—at the wedding." Sophie unlocked both of the car doors with her remote.

"Bowers . . . ," Olivia murmured as she opened the passenger door and got in. "Brooke's last name. Related?"

"Jason's brother, Eric, was Brooke's first husband."

"The war hero who died in Iraq. Logan's father," Olivia recalled.

"Yes." Sophie strapped into her seat belt and waited while her mother did the same before backing out of the parking spot.

"Interesting that she'd invite someone from her late husband's family to her wedding," Olivia said thoughtfully.

"Jason *was* Eric's family," Sophie replied. "Their

parents died when they were in high school. He and Logan are very close. Actually, he's Logan's only connection to his father. Brooke and Jesse both encouraged Jason to put down roots here for Logan's sake. He lives here now."

"He must be a nice guy if they want him to stick around for Logan's sake."

"He's a very nice guy, Mom."

"Oh?" Olivia raised an eyebrow.

"Don't give me that arched-brow look." Sophie waited for another car to pass before pulling out onto Charles Street. "I know what that means. All I'm saying is he's a nice guy."

"How old is he?"

"Early thirties, I guess."

"Single?" Olivia persisted.

"As far as I know."

"Good-looking?"

"Very," Sophie reluctantly admitted. Her mother was not going to let this go.

"What else?"

"Nothing 'else.' I don't know him all that well."

"What do you know about him?"

Sophie sighed in resignation. It had been years since her mother had interrogated her about a guy and she could see where this was leading. Olivia had never warmed to Chris and seemed to be taking his cheating on Sophie personally. For the past six weeks, she'd made it no secret that she was hoping her daughter would find someone "more deserving of you than Christopher."

"Jason's apparently very good at what he does.

He's restoring the gardens behind Pop's house, redoing the landscape there. It's going to be gorgeous."

"That's all you have to say about a thirty-something-year-old man who's good-looking and apparently hardworking."

Sophie smiled. When it came to desirable attributes in another human being, hardworking was right at the top of Olivia's list.

"What else do you know about him?"

Sophie thought about the gentle concern that Jason had shown to her grandfather at Logan's science fair, of his concern for her on that same night. She thought of his love for Logan, of the hours he spent coaching the boy's sports teams along with Jesse, of the Saturday nights he shared with his nephew instead of going out on the town with his friends.

She thought of the most amazing blue eyes she'd ever seen and a killer smile and a soft laugh. Of broad shoulders and long legs.

"Nothing else, really." Sophie shrugged nonchalantly. Jason would be at the wedding, and she didn't want to give her mother any reason to unduly focus on him and possibly embarrass the man. Nothing like an overeager mom to scare the bejesus out of a guy.

"Like I said, I don't really know him all that well."

"Pity."

"Mom . . ."

Olivia smiled and changed the subject. "Where are you taking me first?"

"Too early for ice cream or I'd take you to Scoop."

"We'll save that for after lunch. How 'bout if you take me to see your restaurant?"

"It isn't mine yet, and it's pretty much a mess."

"You told me that." Olivia waved a dismissive hand. "You're not the only person in the family with vision, you know."

"We'll have to stop in at the office to pick up the key."

"Good. It'll give me a chance to see Jesse before the rehearsal dinner tonight, and I haven't seen Violet in years." Olivia's gaze swept both sides of the street.

"Oh, look at that darling little shop!" she exclaimed when they stopped for the red light in the center of town, where a small crowd of tourists—day-trippers and weekenders—drawn to St. Dennis by the exceptionally warm weather waited to cross.

"That's Bling. Great clothes and accessories. Vanessa Shields owns it. I got my dress for the wedding there," Sophie explained.

"I'll have to make a point to stop in there before I leave. Slow down so I can see what's in the window." Olivia craned her neck to stare.

Sophie laughed, but rode the brake past the shop, where a display of leather bags in spring colors took center stage.

"I may have to go there today," Olivia said. "After lunch. There's a fabulous mustardy-colored bag . . ."

"Because you have so few bags."

Olivia waved her hand to dismiss her daughter's remarks. "We all have our vices. How much farther to the office?" Before Sophie could reply, Olivia rolled down the car window and leaned out slightly. "I love the architecture in this town. There's a lovely Federal-style house back there right next to a Victorian with a wide sweeping front porch and a huge bay window that goes three stories up." She turned back to Sophie. "And the trees! You're weeks ahead of us when it comes to the flowering trees. The town looks so pretty. No wonder you decided to come back to stay."

"I can't claim that the magnolias and the weeping cherries and all those other pretty trees had anything to do with my decision to move to St. Dennis. I've never been here in the spring. But I admit, it's pretty to look at."

She made a right turn onto Old St. Mary's Church Road, then another right when she arrived at the corner where the office was located.

"Enright and Enright." Olivia pointed to the sign. "I suppose it hasn't been lost on anyone that with you joining the firm, it's still . . ."

"Yes, Enright and Enright. I know. You're about the twentieth person who's mentioned that." Sophie blew out a long breath. "Sorry. Twenty might be an exaggeration. But it has been said that me agreeing to work here is keeping the tradition alive."

"I suppose it also hasn't been lost on you that if your father hadn't been such an ass, you'd be able to skip this step and concentrate on your restaurant."

"I can't say that it hasn't crossed my mind, but it is what it is, Mom. It may take me a while longer to get where I want to go, but I will get there."

"That's my girl." Olivia leaned across the console and patted her daughter's arm. "I wish . . . well, I wish that you could have skipped this step, that's all."

"It'll work out. I'll be fine." Sophie took the keys from the ignition. "You coming in?"

"Of course."

"I don't see Jesse's car," Sophie noted. "Maybe he's still at his meeting."

The office door was locked, Jesse apparently still out, and with Violet having the day off, the office was empty and quiet. Sophie grabbed the key from her desk drawer where she now kept it and tried to keep her excitement under wraps as she drove to River Road.

"Now, it's rough, like I said . . ." Sophie parked in front of the building.

Wordlessly, Olivia got out of the car as soon as it came to a stop. She stood, hands on her hips, staring first at the structure, then at the surrounding property.

"It'll look a lot better when the weeds are cut down and the doors painted," Sophie said somewhat weakly, trying to see the place through her mother's eyes.

"What's on the second floor?"

"There's an apartment."

"Are you going to live there?"

"Eventually. I need to get the restaurant up and running before I can start to work upstairs. I can sublet Jesse's place at least until the fall, when his lease expires."

"What's next door there? Behind that God-awful Cyclone fence?"

"I don't know." Sophie paused to take a better look. "Looks like a couple of trucks and some sort of heavy equipment."

"That could turn out to be an eyesore."

"I can always plant some evergreens, I suppose, to block the view."

Nodding, Olivia walked closer. "That would definitely help."

"I thought it would be pretty to have some flowers planted under the windows and next to the door." Sophie pointed to the flower beds that in her mind already existed.

"Some roses, yes." Olivia nodded as if she could see it, too. "Daylilies. And something else . . ."

"The door painted green, maybe. Or blue."

"Something light." Pointing upward at the sign, Olivia asked, "Name?"

"I haven't come up with one yet."

"There's time. Let's go inside . . ."

Sophie unlocked the door, this time grateful that she didn't have a flashlight with her. Maybe her mother wouldn't notice just how much work needed to be done.

She should have known better.

"Well, you do have your work cut out for you," Olivia said after having had the grand tour of both the restaurant and the apartment. "But I think it's going to be fabulous once you're done. I can hardly wait to see it."

"Thanks, Mom." Sophie swallowed a lump. Her mother was the first person in the family to give her venture wholehearted and optimistic support.

"I'll be here on opening day," Olivia assured her. "Now, tell me what you're going to have on the menu . . ."

"Mostly basics, with a special every day." Sophie reiterated her conversation with Shelby as they walked around the building.

"It sounds as if Shelby has given you good advice."

Olivia paused out back. "You'd have a lovely view of the river if you removed some of those trees. You could have some tables out here . . ."

Sophie grinned. "I'm planning on it. Maybe not this year . . ."

"Why not this year?"

"I don't think I'm going to be able to afford to have all the trees removed, a patio put down, and purchase the sort of tables that should be out here. So maybe next year."

"I wish we knew what was going on, on the other side of that fence." Olivia frowned disapprovingly at the sight. "Does the fence belong to you or to the property next door?"

"I'm pretty sure it's theirs. It goes all the way across the front and down the other side, and now that I'm looking at it more closely, there's a big double gate out front."

"It's really ugly. Well, maybe you can sweet-talk the owner into removing it."

"I don't know who owns it, and I doubt they're going to go to the expense of taking down a perfectly good fence—ugly though it may be—and then pay to put up something that's more aesthetically pleasing to me."

"Evergreens, definitely. And maybe you could plant some flowering vines on it," Olivia suggested. "At least along the section that faces your building."

"We'll see." They reached the bait shop side of the building and Sophie shared her plans for the garden.

"Yes, yes, I can see it. It's going to be beautiful. I applaud your good eye, Sophie. And I can see where this could be a success, given the amount of early morning traffic you can expect, and the opening of the studio down the road." She paused. "Now, if we're done here, why not show me where that new film studio is going to be. I read somewhere that they're casting their first movie. Then maybe we can stop in that little shop so I can take a closer look at that bag that was in the window. And after that, you can take me to that ice-cream place. I'm thinking this is a dessert-first kind of day . . ."

Jason rounded the bend in River Road just in time to see a dark SUV drive away from the parking lot of the building next to his property. The building he'd been coveting. The one where he'd planned on opening his retail business. The one that Paul Dunlap, his Realtor, had just told him had been sold.

"Sold!" he'd all but shouted into the phone. "How could it have been sold? You told me it wasn't even on the market!"

"It wasn't. At least, the owner told me that it wasn't. When I called this morning to check in with her again, just like you asked, she told me she'd had an offer and decided to take it."

"But she promised I'd have first shot at it."

"I don't remember a *promise,* Jason. I'd *asked* her to call if she wanted to sell the place, and she said she'd keep it in mind. There was no promise, nothing binding. She wasn't under any real obligation to call me."

"So it's done?" He couldn't believe it. His place. Sold out from under him . . .

"Not done as in gone to settlement. But she was pretty adamant."

"Can't you go back to the owner and see if we can make a better deal with her?"

"She's signed an agreement of sale. The only way it's going to be nullified is if the buyer found some way out of the contract, but I wouldn't hold my breath. I'm sure that whoever's buying it is taking it as is, no contingencies." The Realtor paused. "I'm sure that's the case, since it's such a fast settlement."

"How fast?"

"She said they go to closing week after next."

"Can we find out who bought the place? Maybe I can make them an offer."

"I'll ask around, see what I can find out . . . but you know, if someone went out of their way to buy that property that quickly, they must have some plans for it."

"Who was the Realtor?"

"Hamilton Forbes. Look, Jason, I'm sorry . . ."

"Yeah, thanks." Jason hung up, kicking himself for not going to Forbes himself when he first spied the property. Forbes was a lifelong resident of St. Dennis, his company had been around forever, and he knew everyone in town. Jason had gone with Paul because, even though he was new to St. Dennis himself, Paul had been the listing agent for the nursery property and had assured Jason that he'd keep an eye on the Walsh building, that he'd make certain that when it came up for sale, his would be the first offer.

So much for that. Jason blew out a long stream of agitation. He idled the engine and leaned on the steering wheel, watching the dark SUV disappear around the bend in the road, his earlier good mood growing fouler by the minute.

He'd counted on buying that building. He'd sketched it out fifty times—where he'd grow what, where he'd eventually build a greenhouse. He'd calculated how many people he'd have to hire right away, how many more he'd likely need next year and the year after, and how much income the business would have to generate in order to pay for it all. That property— that building—had played such an integral part of his overall long-term business plan that he felt momentarily stunned at the reality that it would belong to someone else.

He tried to remember if he'd ever before been too stunned to even curse, but was pretty sure that this was a first.

There was no way around it. He was going to have to come up with a Plan B, find another place for the retail shop. Unless, of course, he could convince the new owner to sell the property to him. Paul obviously thought that was a dead end, but hey, nothing ventured, nothing gained. Maybe the buyer picked it up on spec, thinking to hold it for a while, then sell at a profit. With Dallas's studio opening up soon, surely property values would increase along this stretch of River Road.

He finished his coffee and crushed the cardboard cup. He'd started the day on such an upbeat note and he hated that it had gone downhill in the time it took for him to answer his phone.

Good mood or bad, he still had a long day's work ahead of him. There was a new office building out on the highway that had contracted him to landscape, and his best crew was already on their way to the job site where he was to meet with them. He'd get them started, then spend the rest of the morning having sod laid in Curtis Enright's backyard.

"Got all the grandkids in town for Jesse's wedding this weekend," Curtis had told him. "I know the gardens can't be finished in time, but could we get some grass out there where the backhoe tore up the lawn when those big trees were brought in? I'd sure like it if I could walk the kids down there to show off what we're doing, maybe play a little horseshoes or badminton on Sunday afternoon."

"Not a problem." Jason tried to picture Curtis swinging at the birdie, but he couldn't quite manage it. "I'll take care of it."

They were cutting it close—Curtis's family was due to arrive in St. Dennis tomorrow—and the sod had taken longer to arrive than had been promised. It would need to be well watered today and with the weather forecast for tomorrow calling for temperatures in the 80s, Jason was pretty sure it would be dried off by the time Curtis's family descended on him.

All in all, no time to pout, Jason reminded himself as he turned the pickup around. Things were what they were. If he'd dwelt on hardship or misfortune every time something bad happened to him, he'd be in therapy right now. Tomorrow was bound to be better—his mother always told him that, that sun always followed the rain. She'd been an optimist, always looking for the bright side of things, always looking for the good in every situation and everyone she met. That was one of the things he best remembered about her, her little homilies about life and how everyone's life had hills and valleys. When things were not going so well and you felt like nothing was ever going to be good again, you were in the valley.

"When you're down, you have to look up," she'd tell him. "Watch the top of the hill, and see how much closer you get to it every day. Before you know it, you'll be at the top. Don't ever forget to appreciate your good fortune, hold on to how it feels when things are right, and be grateful. Then when someday you find yourself sliding back down to that valley, remind yourself that it's only a matter of time before you head on back to the top of the hill again. Peaks and valleys, Jace. That's what life is all about."

"Why can't we just stay at the top of the hill all the time?" he'd once asked her. "Why do we have to sit in the valley and feel bad? Why can't things just stay good?"

"If things were good all the time, you wouldn't appreciate it. Besides, no one's life is without some pain. Everyone goes through some bad times." She'd shrugged. "So when things are good, enjoy it. When things are not so good, make the best of it and re-member that it will get better." She'd ruffled his hair. "Life has lots of ups and downs in store for you. You ever want to talk about it—the good or the not so good—I'll always be here to listen."

And she was always there for him—until the day she wasn't.

Until the day his entire world went black and changed forever, and there'd been no one to blame but himself for the gut-wrenching loss that had, for a while, made time stand still. His left thigh began to throb at the memory, and the scars on his chest began to sear as if they'd been set on fire, fueled by guilt and pain and an emptiness he'd never get used to.

But there were times when he could swear he heard his mother's voice inside his head, times when he'd needed some strength that he couldn't find on his own. Whether memory or simply wishful thinking on his part, her words always seemed to come when he needed her guidance. Like the day they'd buried her and his father, and the day he got the call that Eric had been killed. Those were the darkest times, the worst times of his life, he reminded himself, life-changing moments that were real, the times that were seared into his soul. This—the news about the property being sold—this was nothing compared to those times, was meaningless in the scheme of his life. This was merely a minor setback of his business plan. There'd be another property, another opportunity.

He tried channeling his mother's optimism, her cheerfulness, but he was still really pissed.

"Sorry, Mom."

He thought of Curtis's insistence that his wife's spirit still inhabited the house they'd shared, and thought it probably wasn't much different from the way he felt when he thought he heard his mother's voice. He never thought he saw her, the way Curtis seemed to think he saw his wife; it was more a whisper inside his head. Real or imagined, it hardly made a difference, since whatever he thought he heard her say always seemed to be exactly what he needed to hear.

He drove along the winding two-lane road, the scent of magnolias wafting in through the open windows, the sun warming his arm that rested on the door frame, but the beauty of the day was lost on him. Losing the property without having a chance to purchase it didn't sit right with him, but apparently someone else wanted it and had had an in with the seller that he didn't. It irritated him to know that all along, someone else had had an eye on the same prize, and that someone had beaten him to the sale.

But who, he wondered? What were they planning on doing with the property? And more importantly, what might it take to get them to sell?

Chapter 15 ⌒

"WELL, I have to say, this is the first time I've been to a wedding where the color scheme was pink and *black*," Olivia whispered to Sophie from behind her program. They'd just been seated in the front row of the tiny church, where Jesse stood at the altar after having escorted his mother and sister to their pew.

"I like it." Sophie leaned closer to her mother's ear. "I like those black-and-white toile cones holding the pink roses at the ends of each row, and I like the way Brooke incorporated the pattern into the programs with the toile ribbon." She held up the program she'd been given when they entered the church. "Sophisticated and sweet at the same time."

"She said last night at the rehearsal that her dress was pink. Not pale pink, but a real pink-pink." Olivia turned to keep her eye on the back of the church, as if concerned that the bride might sneak in without her knowing it. "Have you seen it?"

"No, but Steffie has. She said it's gorgeous and very Brooke."

"My boy looks so handsome." Olivia nodded

toward Jesse, who stood at the altar awaiting his bride. "All the boys look handsome in their black suits."

"I'll bet it's been a long time since anyone referred to Pop as a boy," Sophie mused.

Olivia lightly swatted at Sophie's hand with her program. "You know what I mean. Logan and Clay and Delia's son."

"Nick. Delia's son's name is Nick. Jesse asked him if he'd act as an unofficial usher, since they wanted to keep the wedding party small but still wanted to have a few guys on hand to show guests to their seats. As you can see, the altar area is very small, so you really couldn't have a crowd up there. This is the oldest church in St. Dennis, and on the National Register of Historic Places."

"Well, it may be small but it's lovely. Simple but charming. I love the flowers growing in those big urns at the altar."

"Those were Lucy's idea. Spray paint the urns black and fill them with bulbs that would bloom in time for the wedding. She's ridiculously clever when it comes to things like that."

"And the flowering branches—the cherry and peach and pears—in those tall galvanized steel containers at either side of the entrance to the church . . . gorgeous. Who would think of something like that?"

"Lucy would. You know that she's a very well-known event planner, right?"

"Grace's daughter, yes. I met her when I arrived at the inn. Clay's wife."

"Right."

The string quartet that was set up at the side of the

altar began to play, and all heads turned to the back of the church where Clay began to walk his mother, Hannah Madison, down the aisle. Next came Dallas MacGregor in a sleeveless black silk sheath with a low drapey neckline and a huge bouquet of mixed pink flowers of every hue.

"Not sure I like the idea of black on the matron of honor." Olivia nodded in Dallas's direction. "I was afraid it would look more like a funeral than a wedding when I first heard what she was wearing, but I must say, she certainly can carry it off."

"Dallas can carry off anything. That figure and that platinum hair . . . she always looks stunning. Even when you see her in the grocery store."

"She does her own grocery shopping?"

"Of course. This is St. Dennis, not Beverly Hills. Though I wouldn't be surprised if she did it herself when she lived in California. She's pretty down to earth from what I can tell."

"Oh, look at Brooke!" Olivia wiped away a sudden tear. "Did you ever . . . ?"

On the arm of her brother, Clay, Brooke started down the aisle, the layers of her pink chiffon skirt flowing around her like billowing waves. She carried an all-white bouquet of roses, tulips, baby's breath, orchids, and ranunculus, and wore a tiny pink birdcage veil.

"That's so totally Brooke." Sophie grinned. "So girly and feminine and chic and, well, totally herself."

The bride passed their pew, and as Sophie began to turn toward the front of the church, her eyes met Jason's across the aisle. He winked. Smiling, she winked back.

"Well, I take back everything I said about the whole pink-and-black thing," Olivia whispered as the congregation took their seats and the brief service began. "The look is starting to grow on me."

"Ummmm." Sophie fought an urge to look back over her shoulder.

In consideration of the best man, who was in his mideighties, the ceremony was short and sweet. The vows were traditional—"Do you take this woman . . . in sickness and in health . . ."—even if the color scheme was not. Twenty minutes after the bride walked down the aisle as Brooke Bowers, she turned to the congregation as Brooke Enright, and those gathered in the church applauded as the happy couple made their way to the back of the church.

"Oh, that was lovely." Olivia dabbed at her eyes with a tissue. "Way too short a ceremony, but what there was, was just lovely."

"I think Brooke wanted it short because it wasn't her first marriage." Sophie gave a little finger wave at her grandfather, who looked proud as a peacock with Dallas on his arm. "And also because Pop can't stand forever."

"Surely there are chairs . . ."

"Where would you put a chair on that altar?" Sophie followed her mother out of the pew. "It's so narrow, there's no room."

"Good point." Olivia took Sophie's arm as they started toward the door.

On the opposite side of the aisle, Jason stood with his hands in the pockets of his dark suit jacket. Sophie had never seen him dressed in anything but jeans and a tee or a sweatshirt. Dressed up or dressed down, she decided as she passed by, he was one fine-looking man.

The wedding party and the family members made their way to the Inn at Sinclair's Point, where photos would be taken on the lawn and amidst the new garden paths, at the gazebo that had been erected the previous year, and in front of the small wooded area that was bursting with the color of a thousand daffodils and tulips. The sky was clear April blue, the Bay behind the lawn sparkling in the sun. It was a little over an hour before the photographer finally finished bossing them around for pictures.

"Now, Jesse, one with you and your mother and Sophie . . . and let's have your brother and Zoey and Georgia in there next to Sophie for the next shot . . .

"I think we'll have your grandfather join you . . . Now all of Mr. Enright's grandchildren with him in the middle. One with him and Brooke . . . Now, Jesse, you step into the shot right there next to Brooke . . ."

By the time the photographer had moved on to Brooke's side of the family, Sophie's head was spinning.

"Mom, I can't take any more. Want to join me for an adult beverage or three and some of those yummy hors d'oeuvres that are being passed around inside?"

"Not right now. I want a few more shots with Jesse and Brooke. But you go ahead. I'll meet up with you at the reception." Olivia's focus was on her son and his bride.

"The reception has been underway for . . ." Sophie checked her watch. "About forty minutes. Wait too long and you'll miss it."

"I'll take my chances."

"And I'll take that as permission to eat your share of coconut shrimp and teriyaki beef."

"Just save me a nibble." Olivia raised her camera and proceeded to photograph her daughter.

"Stop that." Sophie laughed and escaped into the inn.

She stood on the fringe of the crowd, taking in the sights and sounds. The string quartet played softly in the background, and waiters flowed through the room with silver trays to offer goodies to the guests. Sophie snagged a glass of champagne from one passing tray and a scallop wrapped in bacon from another.

The only thing I need right now is a comfy place to rest for a moment or two.

She glanced around the room, spied some empty chairs and started toward one, but was stopped so many times on her way across the room—"Lovely wedding, wasn't it?"—that she never did get to sit. Before she knew it, the wedding party made its way into the ballroom with all the attendant festivity, and in what seemed like the blink of an eye, she was seated with her mother and her siblings and their spouses and *their* mother and was being served a fancy salad.

She excused herself after the entrée and went to the ladies' room to freshen up. On her way back into the ballroom, she stopped to chat with Violet, who sat next to Curtis, who was in deep conversation with Cameron O'Connor about the renovations to the carriage house at the Enright homestead. Next to Cam sat his fiancée, Ellie Ryder Chapman, whom Sophie had met at Christmas.

"Ellie, how are you?" Sophie greeted her.

"I'm good. You?" Ellie turned in her seat so that she could face Sophie. "Great wedding. Everything is just perfect. The food, the music . . . and I love Brooke's dress. I doubt I'd have the nerve to wear it, but I love it on her."

"She does look amazing."

"Here, sit for a minute, why don't you?" Ellie moved her bag from the empty chair next to her and patted the seat. "You don't have any official duties right now, do you?"

"None. I'm home free." Sophie moved the chair slightly, then sat facing Ellie. "Actually, all I had to do today was show up, smile a few times for the camera, and sit with my mom."

"Your mother is the tall woman in the pale green suit?"

"Yes. That's our mom."

"I saw her in the church. She's very beautiful."

"Thanks. She is."

"And the woman seated to her left at the table . . ." Ellie nodded in Olivia's direction. "Who is she?"

"That's Delia Enright."

"The writer?" Ellie raised an eyebrow. When Sophie nodded, Ellie said, "I've read all her books. Obviously, I'm a huge fan. I didn't realize she was related to you and Jesse."

"Oh, she isn't. She's actually my dad's ex-wife." She smiled wryly. "Well, one of them, anyway."

"Oh. Is your father here?"

"No." Sophie signaled a waiter for a glass of wine. "Jesse didn't invite him, because . . ."

"Please. No explanation necessary. I know what it's

like to have a parent who isn't welcome in polite company."

Sophie nodded and took a sip of her wine. She knew the story—who didn't?—of how Ellie's father, a hugely successful investment broker, had bilked his clients out of multimillions of dollars, had been caught, confessed, and was now serving a very long prison term.

"Your grandfather looks good." Ellie changed the subject. "I see a lot of him now that we're working over at his place."

When Sophie raised a questioning eyebrow, Ellie explained, "We're renovating the carriage house."

"Oh. I did know that Pop was having some work done."

"I'm one of the contracting crew. I work for Cam. Right now, I'm scraping the old paint from the window sashes." She held up her hands with their very short fingernails. "Hardly enough nails left to polish."

"Nice that you work together."

"Sometimes good, sometimes not." Ellie shrugged. "But I am enjoying working at your grandfather's. It's kind of cool for me because my great-aunt and your grandmother were good friends."

"Oh, then your great-aunt must have known Violet as well. She and my gramma were the best of friends."

"Right." Ellie nodded. "The three blossoms."

"What?"

"That's what everyone called them. The blossoms. Rose, Violet, and Lilly—that was my great-aunt. Lilly Ryder was her maiden name. I found a whole bunch of photos of the three of them in my house, which once belonged to Lilly."

"Blossoms." Sophie mused, turning the name over in her head. "I'd love to see some of the photos. I only know of my grandmother through my grandfather. I'd love to see her with her girlfriends."

"I'll drop some copies off. You're going to be working with Jesse, right?"

"Starting Monday," Sophie explained. "I'll be holding down the fort while he's on his honeymoon."

"But you're staying in St. Dennis, right? At least, that's what I heard."

"I am staying." Sophie paused to think. She needed a contractor, someone to go into the building on River Road and tell her what she needed done and how much it was going to cost—and she was going to need that someone very soon. "Listen, Ellie . . . I want to discuss something with you and Cam, but I need the conversation to be confidential."

"Sure."

"I'm buying a piece of property on River Road—I close in just a little more than a week—and I need to hire a contractor to look over the place and then do whatever work I can afford to have done."

"We can help you with that. What's the property?"

"It's a boarded-up building, used to be a restaurant. Walsh's. It's been closed up for a number of years and it needs a lot, I'm afraid. I just don't know where to start with it."

"Just let me know when you want us to come in and look it over. We do a ton of renovations here in St. Dennis." Ellie smiled proudly. "Cam started this business on his own years ago and he's the go-to guy here in town."

"That's what I've heard. I have the key, so I can get

you in anytime you're free. The sooner the better, though."

"I'll check with Cam and get back to you. What are you planning on doing with the building? Did you buy it to flip?"

"I'm going to open a restaurant. It's been my dream forever, and now that I have the opportunity, I couldn't pass it up." Sophie paused. "There's just one thing. I'd appreciate it if you wouldn't mention this to anyone. Well, Cam of course, but other than that, I'm trying to keep it quiet until I can tell my grandfather. He's so happy that I'm joining the firm, I hate to upset him. I've been trying to find the right opportunity all week, but somehow, I just haven't had a chance to talk it over with him."

"I understand. My lips are sealed," Ellie assured her. "Now, what kind of restaurant is it going to be?"

For the next ten minutes, Sophie shared her plans with Ellie. When she finished, Ellie said, "It's going to be great. You can count on us to be at the opening."

"Thanks. I'm really excited, because . . ." Sophie looked up as Grace Sinclair approached the table. "Oh, hello, Grace."

"So nice to see all of your family here, Sophie. We have the privilege of having them staying with us at the inn. A lovely group, I must say."

"Thanks, Grace. I'm happy that everyone could make it."

"Now, what's this I'm hearing about you moving to St. Dennis to work with your brother?" Grace leaned on the back of Ellie's chair. "Is it true?"

Sophie nodded. "I'm now an official resident of St. Dennis."

"Well, then, I'm going to recruit you right here and now to work on our annual project for the historical society. This year we're taking on the restoration of Ellie's carriage house."

"Talk about the shoemaker's kids not having shoes." Ellie rolled her eyes. "I've never been inside the building. I don't know when it was last opened. I have no idea what's in there—there's one huge padlock and a heavy chain on the front doors, and we haven't found the key. The side door is nailed shut. Cam and I kept meaning to do something about it, but we haven't had the time." She laughed. "We haven't even had time to set a wedding date. This time of the year, everyone is sprucing up their properties to get ready for the rental season, which is right around the corner. We haven't had a weekend off in months."

"Well, it's a lovely building and we thought that since we do one property each year, this time around we should give Ellie a hand. Ellie's family was much loved in St. Dennis, and we know it would be a pricy project."

"And I appreciate it more than I can say." Ellie turned to Sophie. "We're going to do a grand opening of the building, and then we'll assess it for repairs and such. But there's been so much speculation in town about what is actually in there that the historical society is running a fundraiser. You buy a ticket and enter your guess of what's inside. When the doors are finally opened and we see inside, the people who guessed correctly will split half of what is raised. The other half goes to the group."

"Then, we'll split the committee into work groups and roll up our sleeves and bring the old place back to life," Grace added. "The tickets are already selling like gangbusters."

"Sounds like fun," Sophie said. "Sign me up."

"Consider it done. Thank you. We'll expect you at ten next Saturday morning at Ellie's." Grace looked pleased. "I'm happy to say that so far, no one has turned me down. Well, they're starting up the music, and it looks as if Jesse and Brooke are going to have their first dance, so I'm going to dash up to the bar and grab a glass of wine. Good to see you both."

"I think I'll move closer to the dance floor before they begin." Sophie stood. "I want to watch."

"I'll give you a call after I speak with Cam," Ellie told her.

"The sooner the better." Sophie stood. "And thanks for keeping my confidence, Ellie."

"Of course."

Sophie made her way through the crowd that was starting to gather to watch the bride and groom's first dance. The happy couple took the floor as the music began to play, and were obviously lost in each other's eyes.

Just like the morning a few months ago in Cuppachino, Sophie sensed Jason's presence even before he was standing next to her.

He held up a bright, shiny penny between his thumb and index finger. Sophie stared at it for a moment, then smiled. She put out her hand, palm up. When he placed the penny in the center, she closed her fingers over it.

"First," she said, "I was thinking how happy my brother looks, and how happy I am for him. He and

Brooke look like they were born for one another, like they were destined to . . ."

There was an awkward silence when she remembered that Brooke had previously been married to Jason's brother, who died in Iraq.

"Foot, meet mouth," she muttered. "Jason, I'm so sorry. I wasn't thinking . . ."

"Let it go," he said softly. Before she could finish her apology, he'd moved past the moment. "So, if there's a first, there must be a second. What's second?"

"My feet are killing me in these shoes."

He glanced down at her feet. "They are pretty hot-looking shoes, though."

"Yes, they are. But they're arch killers, and right now my arches are screaming for mercy."

Jason leaned over and whispered in her ear. "You could take them off. I'll bet no one would even notice. And I bet you won't be the only barefooted woman in the room before the night is over."

"Good point. I think I'll ditch them when I get back to my seat." She smiled and handed him back the penny. "Your turn."

"Well, I was thinking how beautiful you look in that dress. I like blue on you and I like your hair down like that." He stood as he had in the church, hands in his pockets, his stance casual. "Was that too politically incorrect? Is it okay to tell a woman she's beautiful these days, or is it frowned upon?"

"Ah, no. I do not frown when someone gives me a compliment. I say 'thank you.' Actually, I rather like it. I'm not used to it, of course," she explained, "having been a lawyer for the past eight years."

"A much maligned profession." He nodded knowingly.

"Often from within." She stepped aside to permit a couple to pass on their way to the dance floor. "How do you stop a lawyer from drowning?"

Jason shrugged.

"Shoot him before he hits the water. Where can you find a good lawyer?"

"I give up."

"In a cemetery. How do you get a lawyer to smile for a photo? Just say 'fees.'"

"Looks like I'm going to have to brush up on my lawyer jokes if I want to keep up."

"Just search the Internet. There are a million of them," she confided. "But enough about me. I believe you owe me one thought. You only gave me 'first.' What's the second?"

"I was wondering where your date is."

"My date?"

"Yeah. Don't women usually bring a date to a wedding?"

"Well, yes, if you're dating someone on a regular basis. Which I am not."

"And that answers the next question."

"So where's *your* date?"

He shrugged. "No one I wanted to bring."

"So we're even on that score."

"How fortunate for me."

Jason's smile brought a smile to her face as well. He definitely looked pleased, almost as pleased, she realized, as she was to find out that he was single and apparently available. Not that she was ready to admit that to her mother, who would read entirely too much into it.

"Now, for my bonus thought," he was saying, "I was wondering what this song was that they're dancing to."

" 'The Twelfth of Never.' "

"I don't know it."

"Johnny Mathis. Brooke's parents danced to it at their wedding. She thought it would be nice to have the same song. Besides, it's very romantic."

"Is it?"

"Definitely. One more thing to look up on the Internet."

"I just might do that."

More and more guests began to dance.

"Would you like to join them?" he asked, gesturing toward the dance floor.

"I would. Thanks."

He took her hand and they made their way through the crowd. At the fringe of the group, he took her in his arms and they began to move in time with the music.

"Small dance floor, many people," he noted. "Not much room to move around."

"It's okay. Dance floors at weddings are supposed to be crowded. You want a lot of people up to dance and have a good time," she said. "At least, that's what Brooke said."

Sophie was jostled slightly by a passing couple and Jason pulled her a little closer. His chin rested against her cheek and his fingers entwined with hers. With his breath soft against the side of her face, her heart began to race, and she wondered if he could hear it through the thin silk of her dress. His arms were strong and he smelled of an aftershave she'd once bought for Chris, who'd never worn it because he hadn't liked it. Ironic, she thought, because she'd been drawn to it then, and it was pulling her in now.

The song ended and she took a step back. Still holding on to her hand, Jason said, "It's really stuffy in here and the music is really loud. Want to grab a drink from the bar and find a place where we can talk without yelling over the band?"

"Sounds good." They wove their way around tables to the bar at the side of the room. Sophie waited while Jason ordered a beer for himself and a glass of wine for her.

"Let's head out to the lobby for a few minutes," Sophie suggested. "It's bound to be cooler and quieter out there."

The inn's lobby was cooler and it was quieter, but it was hardly more private. Groups of three and four guests congregated throughout the room.

"Apparently others have had the same idea," Jason noted. "I know where we can go."

He led her by the hand into the hall and through the side door, out onto the lawn, and down a flagstone path.

"How much farther? Are we walking all the way into town? Because if we are, I wish you'd told me. I'd have left my shoes under the table."

"We're here."

The path ended at a gazebo that overlooked the Bay. Jason opened the door and held it for her.

"Oh, this is lovely," Sophie told him.

"Cameron built it last year for a wedding that Lucy

was doing here at the inn. It was her idea to have the seats built in all the way around the sides."

"I like it. It's cozy. And you did all the landscaping here, I understand. I got to see a lot of it this afternoon when the photos were being taken. You did a beautiful job."

"Thank you. This was my first big job in town."

Sophie sat and peeled off her shoes and stretched her legs out in front of her. "Oh, God, that feels good."

"You have to wonder about the people who design shoes like that. I mean, what are they thinking when they make heels that high?"

"They're thinking that the shoe looks sexy, that if you wear them, your legs look sexy, you look sexy . . ."

"I don't know that they'd do much for me."

She laughed. "Most men like them."

"Liking them and wanting to wear them are two different things."

"So how's my pop's backyard coming along?"

"Great. He wanted to show it off to your family this weekend, so I had some sod laid yesterday and it looks good."

"He's having the out-of-towners over for brunch before they leave to go home. I thought it was pretty ambitious, but he's having it catered, so he really doesn't have to do anything." She thought of the look on her grandfather's face when he announced the brunch to the rehearsal dinner attendees. "He seems so happy to be hosting everyone. He even invited my mom and Delia."

"Who's Delia?"

Sophie explained.

"Let me get this straight. Your grandfather invited two of his former daughters-in-law."

"Right. It's okay. They like each other. At least, they appear to like each other. Probably because all of us—my dad's older kids, that is—we all get along. Finding them—my two half sisters and brother—has been one of the best things to happen to me in a long time. They're all terrific people and have wonderful spouses and kids."

"Your one sister looks just like you."

"Zoey." Sophie nodded. "We do look a lot alike. That was pretty freaky, the first time I met her."

"That's quite a complicated family tree you've got there," he said.

"You have no idea."

"But it's nice that all of your siblings—half or otherwise—are here for Jesse."

"Oh, not all of them. Pammie's son isn't here."

"Who is Pammie?"

"My dad's third wife. The one he left my mother for."

"Ouch."

"Right. But Judd's only nine, and since there was no way in hell that Jesse would invite Pammie, he wasn't about to invite her son. He may be a very nice little boy. I've only met him a few times and he was very quiet each time. Who knows what the kid thinks now that his father has left them?"

"Your father left them, too?"

"Last year. For Tish." Sophie rolled her eyes. "They might be married, but maybe not. No one knows for sure."

"Sounds like someone has commitment issues."

"Oh, he commits. He just can't stick. If that were the only issue my father had, we could deal with it," she said dryly. "How about you?"

"No errant branches that I know about. My parents only married one time—to each other—and Eric is—was—my only sibling."

"I'm so sorry."

"It happened to a lot of families. The war . . . well, it's been hard on a lot of people."

"Listen, Jason . . . what I said before, about Jesse and Brooke . . ."

"It's okay, Sophie." He seemed to be searching for words. "I don't know why things happen the way they do. Eric and Brooke did love each other very much. They should have been able to live out their lives together, maybe have a few more kids together, to live happily ever after, like in the fairy tales. But that wasn't in the cards for them. Sometimes life throws a curve when you least expect it and you have to deal with it. My parents dying when they did . . . Eric . . . I don't know why those things had to happen, but they did. I'm glad—really, I am—that Brooke found someone to love who loves her as much as Jesse does. I mean, it's obvious that he's totally shit-faced over her . . ."

Sophie smiled. "To put it mildly."

"They're happy together, and I'm happy for them. I wish my brother hadn't died so that she could have had that happy ending with Eric—I'm not going to lie. But I'm glad she's happy with someone and I'm glad it's Jesse. He's a good man and he's very good to Logan, and that means a lot to me." He looked up, and even in the dark she could see the sadness in his eyes.

"You love your nephew very much."

Jason nodded. "He's all I have left of my family."

"How old were you when your parents died?"

"I'd just turned fifteen. Eric was eighteen, old enough to qualify as my guardian, which means I didn't have to go into foster care. Our grandmother lived with us for a while, but Eric was more responsible than she, and we had a neighbor who was very good to both of us. We managed." He took a long sip of his beer. "I don't know where I'd be . . . what I'd be . . . if Eric hadn't been there for me." He paused, then added simply, "Things were really tough all the way around after the accident."

"It must have been very hard to lose both parents at the same time. I can't even imagine what it must have been like."

He turned his head and looked out toward the water. In the dark, the waves brushed quietly against the sand and for a long moment, there was no other sound.

"Yeah, it was rough," he said softly.

Music began to float across the lawn from the ballroom, where someone must have opened the French doors to bring in fresh air. Jason's grief seemed to float around him along with the music, and it saddened her.

"Dance with me again." She stood and held out her hand. When he took it, she pulled him to his feet and draped an arm around his neck. She moved in close to him and he had no choice but to hold her. When she began to sway, he swayed with her. They danced in silence, but this time, when the song ended, she did not step away.

"I'm sorry that you lost so much," she told him.

Jason shrugged. "A lot of people have lost more than I did. A lot of people have it worse than . . ."

She drew his face down to hers and kissed his mouth to stop the words. His lips were softer than she'd expected, hesitant, as if surprised to find themselves pressed to hers. But if there'd been some confusion on his part, it passed. His arms tightened around her and his tongue teased the corner of her mouth. When he started to release her, she pulled him back to her. It had been a long time since she'd been kissed like this, and she wasn't ready to let him go. Jason had reawakened something inside her that had died after her breakup with Christopher, and now that that spark was coming back to life, she wanted to see where it would lead. She kissed him again, letting herself feel the heat that was growing between them.

When the kiss ended, he touched his forehead to hers and said, "Was that a 'poor Jason' kiss?"

"No." Her hands slid to his lapels. "That was an 'I wanted you to kiss me and you didn't so I had to take matters into my own hands' kiss."

"Oh." He seemed to reflect on that for a moment. "How was it?"

"Pretty darned good."

"I thought so, too. Want to try it again?"

"Yes, but just a quick little one this time. I really need to get back inside before people start to worry about me."

The kiss was neither quick nor little, and it left

Sophie a little breathless and wishing she were somewhere other than a family wedding.

"To be continued." She pulled away and taking
him by the hand, started back along the path to the
inn.

The music grew louder the closer they got to the
building, but by the time they arrived at the ballroom,
it had all but ceased.

"Crap, they're cutting the cake already. Let's just
sort of drift into the room as if we'd never left."

"Good idea," he agreed.

Everyone at Sophie's table was standing and facing
the dance floor, where Brooke and Jesse were in the
process of cutting their wedding cake.

"I hope he doesn't do something dorky like smash
that into her face," Sophie said under her breath.

"Oh, there you are." Sophie's mother turned.
"We've all been wondering where you were."

"Oh, I've been around," Sophie replied.

"Where are your shoes?" Olivia looked down at
Sophie's feet.

"My shoes?" Sophie followed her mother's gaze.
"Oh, damn, my shoes. They were bothering me and I
took them off . . ."

"Ah, I think I saw them . . ." Jason pointed in the
general direction of the lobby. "I'll just go . . . I'll find
them."

" 'Oh, Mother, I hardly know the man.' " Olivia
whispered after Jason turned and headed for the door.
"If that isn't a direct quote, it's damned close."

"Close enough," Sophie muttered.

Olivia laughed. "You're such a poor actress, and

you're all flushed. Why, if I didn't know better, I'd think . . ."

"Don't think, Mom." Her mouth suddenly dry, Sophie reached for her water glass and took a long drink. "Spare us all, and don't think."

Olivia was still smiling when Jason returned with Sophie's shoes. Sophie was grateful that her mother turned her back when he handed them to her.

"Here you go, Cinderella," he said.

"Well, if I'm Cinderella, you must be Prince Charming." She tucked the shoes under her chair and made a mental note to remember they were there.

"I'm no prince." He stood with a hand on the back of her chair.

"Don't sell yourself short," she told him. "Now pull over that chair and let's see if we can carry on a conversation now that the music's starting again."

Talk was impossible when the band played a dance number and many of the guests took to the floor and sang along with the band.

"Now, do you . . ." Sophie pointed to the dance floor where bodies gyrated to "Moves Like Jagger."

"Uh-uh." Jason shook his head.

"Do you mind if I do? I see Mia and Steffie out there dancing with Brooke, and I could probably join them . . ."

"Go on. I'll stay here and talk to your mom."

She hesitated. Did she really want her mother talking to Jason after the way Olivia interrogated her?

"Go." Jason laughed. "I think I can handle it."

She went, and she danced three numbers back-to-back before nearing exhaustion. She made her way back to the table, where—Lord help her—Olivia was in deep conversation with Jason.

"What are you two talking about?" She maneuvered her chair so that she was between them.

"Just . . . things," Olivia told her with a wave of her hand.

"Oh." Sophie debated whether or not to ask what things they'd been talking about, especially since her mother appeared somewhat smug. She lost her chance when Logan appeared and hung over Jason's shoulder.

"What's up, buddy?" Jason reached an arm out to keep his nephew from falling into his lap. "Tired?"

"Uh-huh." Logan leaned but didn't fall.

"Past your bedtime by about . . . oh, almost two hours," Jason noted.

"Uh-huh."

"Everything okay?" Jason asked.

"I don't wanna stay at Gramma's house tonight. Can't I stay with you?" Before Jason could reply, Logan added, "It's Saturday night, and that's supposed to be guys' night."

"Why don't you want to stay at your grandmother's?"

Logan shrugged. "Just don't."

Jason's eyes met Sophie's, and she knew he'd been thinking the same thing she was. Their evening was ending too soon. If nothing else, she'd been hoping for another dance or two.

"Well . . ." Jason appeared momentarily torn. He stared down at Logan for a moment, then nodded. "Sure, as long as it's okay with your mom and your grandmother."

"Thanks, Uncle Jace. I'll be right back." Logan set off in search of his mother.

"Does he stay with you often?" Olivia turned to ask. "Your nephew?"

"Almost every Saturday night. 'Guys' night,'" he explained with a grin.

"I don't know many men your age who'd give up their Saturday nights to spend them with an eight-year-old," she continued.

"*Two* eight-year-olds," Sophie interjected. "Doesn't Logan's friend stay with you as well?"

"Yeah, they're kind of a package deal. I won't be surprised if Logan's roped Cody into coming along. It might do him good. I think the wedding—his mom remarrying—has rattled him a little, maybe more than any of us suspected. He and Jesse get along really well, and he knows Jesse cares about him, but even so, he might feel a little confused or insecure about the situation."

"Then it's good that he has you." Olivia reached over and squeezed his arm before turning to chat with Delia and Zoey.

"Sorry," he whispered to Sophie. "I was hoping we could spend a little more time together tonight. Maybe take a walk along the dock, take in a little moonlight."

"So was I. But you're right. Logan needs you in a way he doesn't need his grandmother." They both knew she meant that Logan's connection to Eric these days existed mostly through Jason.

"Thanks for understanding."

"Of course." She could see Logan—and as expected, Cody—dashing through the crowd toward them. "Here come your charges. Both of them . . ."

The boys were overtired and restless, and obviously had had far too much soda and cake.

"Mrs. Enright, it was a pleasure to meet you," he told Olivia.

"Please, it's Olivia." She extended her hand. "I enjoyed talking with you. Perhaps another time we'll continue that conversation . . ."

"I'd like that." Jason turned to Sophie, who'd risen from her seat. "So . . . well, I guess I'll see you . . . sometime."

"Yes, you will." She smiled when his fingers brushed against hers for just a brief second. "Bet on it . . ."

Diary ~

Well, what a week we've had around here! First—Jesse and Brooke's wedding was lovely. Such a beautiful couple. It was so nice to see their families gathered to celebrate their marriage—all present and accounted for except for the groom's father, but two of his ex-wives were there. One, of course, was Jesse and Sophie's mother—charming woman—and the other was—I still can barely believe this—my favorite author in the entire world, Delia Enright! Not only did I get to meet her—she was gracious enough to sign all of her books for me—but she stayed right here, in our inn. Well, I was beside myself, you can bet. Much to my delight, I found Delia—yes, we're on first-name basis—to be so nice and down to earth. She said she loved her stay here and would be booking at least a week this coming summer so that she could come back.

I'm just bubbling over with news tonight—I've learned that Sophie Enright has moved to St. Dennis to go into the family law firm. Curtis is simply beside himself—he's very fond of both Jesse and Sophie, Violet tells me. Sophie's already agreed to work on the carriage house restoration with us, so I'm pleased that she's interested in becoming a part of our little community. I know someone else who's happy that she's staying around. I noticed her walking into the reception on Saturday night, hand in hand with that nice Jason Bowers. Could there be another love story about to be written?

You know how I adore a good love story. I'm tempted to get out the Ouija and see what her grandmother thinks about this development. Rose always did love to gossip!

~ Grace ~

Chapter 16 ⬎

"IT was a lovely brunch, Pop. Everyone had a great time. Too bad Jesse and Brooke had to miss it."

Sophie and Curtis stood on the sidewalk in front of his house, waving goodbye to the rest of the family. The New Jersey group had made the trip together, in Nick's Escalade, and Mike and his kids had all driven separately and were now on their way back to wherever they'd come from. Sophie still couldn't keep her uncle Mike's boys straight. They were close in age and looked a lot alike.

"Jesse and Brooke have their own agenda. They should be arriving in London right about now." Curtis tucked Sophie's arm through his. Together they walked along the path to the front door, which Curtis had left standing open.

"Let's see how the caterer is doing with the cleanup," Sophie said once they were inside.

"Now, they know what they're doing," he told her. "No need to check up on them, or on me, for that matter. You don't have to hang around, Sophie. I can handle the caterer. This wasn't my first party, you know."

"I'm sure, but I'll stay till they're finished, all the same."

"You have a big week ahead of you." He ushered her into the living room. "You're going to be Enright and Enright for the next seven days. You might want to rest up."

"I'll be fine. Jesse and I went over all the big cases, so I know what to expect. He has nothing on the docket for another ten days, so no court appearances will be necessary. Mostly I'll be meeting with clients, conducting a few interviews, and becoming acquainted with the caseload. All in all, not such a tough week."

"Did I mention how happy I am that you're planning on taking the Maryland bar and joining your brother?"

"Once or twice."

"Is that all?" He chuckled. "Somehow I lost count."

Sophie watched him slowly lower into his favorite chair. "Pop, are you feeling okay?"

"Just a little tired. I'm not used to so much festivity in one weekend." He rested his head against the back of the chair and closed his eyes.

Sophie watched from the sofa, her shoes off, her legs pulled up under her. She'd hoped to take this opportunity to talk to him about the restaurant and her plans, but now was clearly not the time. He was obviously exhausted. She'd stay until the caterers left and make sure he had dinner and headed up to bed early. She closed her own eyes, thinking about the upcoming weeks and all she would need to accomplish. She'd just finished planning her opening-day menu when the scent began to envelop her.

"Okay, how are you doing that?" She opened her eyes.

"Who are you talking to?" her grandfather asked.

"You. I'm talking to you. There's no one else here."

"Are you sure of that?" A small smile played across his lips.

"Come on, Pop. Fess up. If you're somehow making that happen, just tell me, okay?"

"Do I look as if I'm doing anything except trying to take a nap in my favorite chair?" He raised his head a few inches off the back of the chair and opened his eyes.

"Somehow you rigged something . . ." Sophie got up. "I know. It's one of those plug-in fragrance things. You found one that smells like gardenias, right?" She began to search for outlets in the room. When she failed to find what she was looking for, she went into the hallway.

"Okay, I give up." She plopped back on the sofa.

"Please do. You're upsetting your grandmother." He closed his eyes again.

"Pop . . . oh, never mind." He was never going to admit that he was behind the mysterious scent, and she was never going to accept his explanation. Why belabor the point? Besides, if it gave him comfort all these years to keep his beloved Rose close to him, what difference did it make where the scent came from? Hadn't Jason said something like that?

Sophie had to admit, though, that it was odd that, search as she might, she could not find an apparent source. Odd, too, that it seemed to come and go. One would think that if something had been rigged up to release a perfume into the air, it would be constant.

There had been times when Sophie entered a room in this house where one minute there had been no scent at all, and the next minute, it seemed to surround her. How to explain that?

Earlier in the day, she'd been chatting with her cousin Elizabeth—called Bit by her brothers, Lizzie by everyone else—and had complimented her on her choice of perfume.

"Did you wear that for Gramma Rose?" Sophie had asked.

"Wear what?"

"The gardenia perfume."

"I'm not wearing perfume," Lizzie had told her. "That *is* Gramma Rose."

"You don't believe that."

Lizzie had shrugged. "You explain it, then. I can't. After all these years, I've given up trying."

Obviously the old man had any number of people fooled.

Sophie watched her grandfather sleep, the scent fading as he began to snore softly. Her grandmother had been gone for close to twenty years, a long time to perpetuate a myth. Yet if it was in fact Rose's presence, twenty years would be a long time to linger, a long time to wait. Could love really do that, she wondered—cross time and the barriers between life and death? Could you choose between moving on alone and remaining suspended between the two dimensions until your loved one joined you?

As she curled up on the sofa, Sophie wondered how that would work. Did you get to the other side and refuse to cross until your beloved could cross with you?

Sophie sighed and closed her eyes. After being a just-the-facts-please girl all her life, it was tough for her to accept something she couldn't see without at least making an effort to understand. It seemed that over time, everyone else—even Jesse—had come to accept Rose's presence. It was tough being the lone skeptic in a family of believers.

Most puzzling of all was the nature of love. It was becoming clear to her that some loves could last through the ages—witness her grandfather's unceasing devotion. And yet she'd once thought she loved Christopher, his infidelity had destroyed the feelings she'd had for him. If she'd really loved him, would those feelings have survived regardless of what he'd done to hurt her? When she thought about Chris now, mostly what she felt was annoyed—with him, with Anita, and mostly with herself for not seeing him for what he really was.

But if she'd cared so much for him once, how could she have been so wrong? Had there been signs that she'd missed, or ignored? What, she wondered, did it feel like when you finally found "the one"? How do you know the difference between Mr. Right for Now and Mr. Right Forever?

Was it possible to find the kind of love that had existed between her grandparents—the kind of love that still bound them to each other? She thought of the look on her brother's face as he'd watched Brooke walk up the aisle toward him, and she knew the answer. Her last thought before nodding off was that maybe someday, someone would look at her the way Jesse had looked at Brooke, and that someone would be worth waiting for, no matter how long it took.

Monday morning found Sophie at the office by seven, fired up to prove herself worthy of being the "& Enright" in the firm's name. She made a pot of coffee in the kitchen—no Cuppachino for her today—poured herself a cup, and took it with her into Jesse's office. She sat in his chair at his desk and went over her game plan. There was a stack of mail a foot high that he'd left instructions for, and that would have to be taken care of before she did anything else. Not a problem. Read, make a phone call, or respond via letter or email as the situation dictates. She was determined that by the time Jesse returned from his honeymoon, all of the work he'd left for her would be completed.

She picked up the first letter in the pile and read it through. It was from the attorney for one of the co-defendants in a slip-and-fall case requesting information that he believed Jesse possessed. She'd pull the file, acquaint herself with the case, and decide whether or not he should be privy to the information he'd asked for. No big deal.

But where, she wondered, would she find the file?

She set the letter aside until Violet arrived. Her coffee was now cold, so she took the cup into the kitchen and microwaved it to reheat. Violet was just coming through the front door when Sophie stepped into the hall.

"Hey, good morning," Sophie called to her.

"Not so much," Violet grumbled. "I overslept and it made me late. I am never late."

"You're not late. It's barely eight o'clock."

"Seven has been my usual starting time for the past

sixty years." Violet bustled past her and directly to her desk. She plopped her bag on the floor and sat at her desk. "Do I smell coffee?"

Sophie nodded. "I made it when I came in. Would you like me to bring you a cup?"

"No, thank you. I make it every morning but I rarely drink it."

"If you'd rather have tea, I could—"

"I'll get it if I want it, thank you."

"Okay, then." Sophie cleared her throat. "Violet, where would I find the *Dexter v. The Copper Pot* file?"

"It should be in the second drawer in the first file cabinet to the left of the door in Jesse's office."

"Thank you." Sophie went into the office and right to the designated file drawer, but her search was unsuccessful. She looked through each of the drawers before trying the file cabinets on either side of the one Violet had suggested.

"Violet, the file isn't in the drawer. It isn't in *any* drawer." Sophie stood in the doorway.

"No surprise there," Violet muttered. "I'm afraid your brother has little or no regard for my filing system."

Sophie frowned. "Does he have his own system?"

Violet snorted. "Try the floor."

By noon, after being forced to paw through the haphazard stacks of files Jesse had left not only on his office floor, but in the conference room as well, Sophie came to the conclusion that jeans and a sweatshirt would have been more appropriate attire than the nice linen sheath she'd donned that morning. She'd thought to make a professional impression should a client pop into the office unexpectedly, but in retro-spect, it had been a bad idea.

"Violet, I give up. I can't find a thing."

"Welcome to my world."

"How can you stand it? There doesn't seem to be any rhyme or reason for the way Jesse operates."

"Your brother is a very good lawyer, but he's the most disorganized person I've ever met. The only sav-ing grace is that he has a good memory and when he dumps something onto a pile, he generally does re-member which file is in which pile. I no longer file until he's finished with a case and he hands it to me to put away."

"Well, unfortunately, my brother and I do not share a psychic connection, so I don't know one stack from the other. I'm going to go home and change my clothes. I'm tired of crawling around on the floor in one of my favorite dresses."

"It might be best to dress down this week," Violet suggested. "There's no telling what you'll be called upon to find, or where you'll have to go to look for it."

"What do you mean?"

"There are files in the attic, some on the second floor, some in your grandfather's old office, some in your uncle Mike's."

Sophie frowned. "Why would I need to go into the attic?"

"One of those letters on Jesse's desk is from Clar-ence Edelson. He's looking for a copy of his grand-father's will."

"When did his grandfather pass away?"

"Seventeen years ago."

"And he's just looking for the will now?"

"He says he did have a copy but can't find it."

"Why would he want it after all these years?"

Violet shrugged. "It's not our place to question, dear. The client wants something from the file, we provide it."

"I may leave that one for Jesse. Meanwhile, I'm going to go home and change." Sophie grabbed her bag off the back of her chair. "I'll probably stop in town and pick up something for lunch. Can I bring you anything?"

"No, thank you. I brought something from home."

Sophie's gaze lingered on the pile of mail and the stacked files that covered the floor.

"I won't be long," she told Violet as she headed for the front door.

"Take your time, dear. None of *that*," she nodded in the direction of Jesse's office, "is going anywhere."

There'd been no provision in her game plan for taking her time. Sophie drove to the house, changed into work clothes, and was on her way back to the office when she realized the sound she'd been hearing over and over was her stomach growling. She remembered someone mentioning a place called The Checkered Cloth that was said to have really good take out. She'd yet to go food shopping, so take out sounded pretty good. She parked on a side street off Charles and went into the small storefront. The specials were on a chalkboard inside the door, and she studied it for a moment before making her selection.

"I'll have the Mandarin salad with grilled chicken," she told the girl behind the counter. "Dressing on the side, please."

"And to drink?" the girl asked.

"A bottle of water, thanks."

While she waited, Sophie picked up a folded menu from a stack that sat inside a basket on the counter and studied the offerings. Lots of sandwiches—some basic, a few more creative—and soups and salads that changed daily. Covered cake stands on the counter held layer cakes, brownies, and bar cookies. Figuring this would be her competition in the center of town, Sophie took it all in, from the light hardwood floor to the benches that stood along one wall. Not many seats, she realized, but since this was strictly a take-out establishment, the lack of seating wasn't an issue. She watched the food being prepared, noting how everything was packaged to travel, then placed in a white paper bag stamped with a picnic spread out on a red-and-white checkered tablecloth.

Cute, she thought. *Nice presentation.* She'd have to do better.

Maybe box lunches, she thought as she paid for her lunch and walked back to her car. White boxes with the name of the restaurant—she was still working on that—maybe tied up with plain white string. Something that the film people would find visually appealing, since she was going to have to depend on them if her restaurant was going to be a success. And of course, the food was going to have to be exceptional. She'd have to find someone who cooked at least as well as she did.

"What do you get when you cross the godfather with a lawyer?"

Sophie glanced over her shoulder, then smiled. "An offer you can't understand."

Jason walked toward her in dusty jeans that had a

rip here and there, a short-sleeved gray T-shirt, dark glasses, and a Phillies ball cap.

He does the suit-and-tie thing really well, she thought, remembering Saturday night, *but casual? Outstanding.*

Sophie unlocked the driver's-side door. "What else ya' got?"

"Depends. Can I use my cheat sheet?"

"Sorry, but no."

"Then I'll have to get back to you on that." He leaned against her car. "So how's your first official day as a St. Dennis lawyer going?"

"It will be going better once I finish cleaning up my brother's mess so that I can actually do legal work."

"What kind of work are you doing?"

"Trying to get things organized so that I can do the work he left for me. Then I need to set up my office. Move some stuff around." She pulled at the front of her baggy faded red sweatshirt. "Stuff you wear old clothes to do."

His phone buzzed and he hesitated. She could see he was trying to decide whether or not to answer it.

"Go ahead and take that," she told him. "I need to get back anyway. See you later."

"Okay. Sure." He nodded and took the phone from his pocket and answered the call.

She turned on the radio and found her new favorite satellite station that played '90s music, the songs from her high school days. She drove back to the office mouthing the words to "Smooth" and thinking back on the crush she'd had on Kevin Russo her junior year. He was the cutest guy on the baseball team and he drove a Jeep Wrangler, which was the designated cool car back in the day. They'd gone to the movies together three weekends in a row and she could still remember every one of those films: *Saving Private Ryan, Armageddon,* and *Lethal Weapon 4.* No one was surprised when he joined the Marines right after graduation. Their romance was short-lived— the day after *Armageddon* he dumped her for Carrie Maloney, who was rumored to be fast and easy—but for a few short weeks, Sophie had been the envy of every girl in the school. She remembered how it felt to have the cute guy pass her notes in class and wait at her locker for her at the end of the day.

It was a silly memory, she knew—she was long out of high school—but somehow it buoyed her spirits, and she went back into the office singing another song from that time—Sting's "Brand New Day"— and trying to relate the memory to life as she knew it.

She critiqued the salad as she ate at the small kitchen table: the romaine was fresh and the dressing citrusy, which she liked, but the oranges were tasteless and the chicken just a little on the dry side. Not bad, but all in all, she could do better. Maybe she should put something like this on her menu as a one-day-a-week salad special. She asked Violet for her opinion, but she claimed not to have one.

"I'm a silent partner, Sophie," Violet reminded her. "I'm not getting involved in the food or the day-to-day."

"But you can still have an opinion."

"No, I can't. One opinion will lead to another, and the next you know, I'll be bringing in my mother's recipe for lemon meringue pie."

"You have your mother's recipe for lemon meringue pie?"

"I might." Violet focused on opening the mail.

"Well, you would share that, though, wouldn't you?"

"We'll see."

Sophie smiled. The recipe was as good as hers. She went into Jesse's office and stared at the files, then poked her head back into the reception area.

"Violet, what is your filing system?"

"It's very simple. Alphabetical starting from the first file cabinet there." She pointed to the tall wooden cabinets directly across from her desk. "It picks up in Jesse's office because we ran out of room in here."

"All the files in all the cabinets are open cases?"

"I'm afraid not. I used to pack away the closed files to store in the attic, but I stopped doing that years ago because it was too hard for me to climb the steps."

"So you wouldn't mind if I weeded out the closed ones now and put them elsewhere?"

"Not at all. I'd welcome it, actually."

"Then that's what I'll do."

For the rest of the afternoon, Sophie emptied filing cabinets and sorted files. She made the decision to use one of the two small unoccupied offices on the first floor as a file room and proceeded to move the closed files into there. It seemed she'd barely gotten started when Violet called to her from the front hall.

"Sophie, I'll be leaving now unless you need me for something."

"What time is it?" Sophie pulled up a sleeve to look at her watch. "Really? Six fifteen already?"

"I'd stay and help you, but I have dinner every Monday night with some old schoolmates. I hate to miss that. There aren't so many of us left."

"I wouldn't dream of having you stay. Go. Have a great dinner. I'll see you in the morning."

Sophie continued emptying file drawers and boxing up files, all the while thinking about her restaurant. In eight more days it would be hers, and then the real work would begin. Violet's mention of her mother's pie recipe had sparked an idea. Sophie had wanted to make the restaurant reflective of the St. Dennis community in a unique way. What if she had other recipes that had been passed down through the generations there in town? Heirloom recipes, she'd call them, and she'd feature a different one every week. There'd be a special little blurb on the menu noting who'd contributed it, maybe something about that family that might be interesting or noteworthy.

So much more fun than plastic blue claw crabs and fish nets on the walls.

But what to put on those walls? she pondered while she pushed a box of files down the hall. She'd just pulled the box into the file room when she heard the front door open.

"Hello?" she called and stepped into the hall.

"How do you get a lawyer out of a tree?"

"Cut the rope."

"Damn it." He snapped his fingers. "I'm going to have to find a better website."

"I told you, I've heard them all." Her nose caught the scent of something that caused her mouth to water. "What's in the box?"

"Pizza from Dominic's. Best on the Eastern Shore. I

ordered a medium, but they made a mistake and made me a large. I was driving home and passed by and saw your car here and the lights still on, and thought I'd take a chance that maybe you hadn't eaten yet either."

"I haven't, but you don't have to . . ."

"Where do you want it?" He held up the box.

"I guess the kitchen." She led the way. "I hope paper plates are okay?"

"Since I usually eat mine right out of the box, that would be an upgrade." He put the box on the table.

"Sit." She motioned to one of the chairs before opening the refrigerator. "We only have water to drink, as far as I can see."

"Water's fine. I have beer at the house, if you'd rather. I could run home and . . ."

"No, no. Water's pretty much my beverage of choice these days anyway." She got two paper plates and a stack of napkins and placed them on the table.

He took a seat, then opened the box, and the steamy aroma filled the room.

"I had no idea I was this hungry." She sat across from him at the small table and peered into the open box. "Veggie pizza? Really?"

"What?" Jason frowned. "What's wrong with veggie pizza?"

"I had you pegged for a pepperoni kind of guy. Maybe sausage and peppers. Eggplant, purple onions, dried cherries, and arugula seems a stretch." She picked up a slice and sniffed. "Is that goat cheese?"

"I thought you might like this better than pepperoni."

She put the slice on her plate. "I thought you picked

it up, then drove by and stopped because you saw my car."

"I may have had that slightly out of order. I may have driven past first." He took a bite, chewed, then nodded. "It's better than I expected it to be."

Sophie laughed. "You ordered a pizza you didn't think you'd like because you thought I'd like it?"

"Okay, so I saw your car and figured you were working late. I called Dominic's and asked him to make something a little out of the ordinary. This is what he made."

Sophie grinned. "And if I'd been gone by the time you got back here?"

"I'd be at home, picking off the dried cherries by myself."

Still smiling, Sophie passed her plate to him. "I'll take them. You want my eggplant?"

"Nah, I'm good, but thanks."

"This was really nice," she told him. "Thank you. I'm really glad you stopped by."

"So am I."

"Oh, water." Sophie got up and took two bottles of spring water from the fridge and handed one to Jason.

"Thanks. Now, how was the family reunion yesterday?"

"Oh, it was a lot of fun. It's so interesting how people who are related can be so much alike, even if they didn't know each other growing up."

"Give me a for instance." He finished his first slice and went back for a second.

"Well, Zoey works for one of the shopping networks on TV, and she does a lot of the cooking shows. She's apparently become quite the gourmet."

"Is that your way of telling me you're a gourmet cook?"

"Actually, I am. If you're nice to me, I might even cook something special for you sometime."

"I *am* nice to you." He pointed to the pizza box.

"So you are. As soon as I get my stuff unpacked, I'll prove just how good I am."

"You're on."

"Seriously. I'm really a very good cook. I'm going to open a restaurant."

"I'll be your first customer."

"That would be my mother."

"Ah, your mother . . . fascinating woman. We had quite an interesting chat the other night."

"What exactly did she say?"

"Just stuff." His lips curved into a smile.

"What kind of stuff?"

"Just stuff like how happy she is that you're moving here, stuff like that."

"Not 'I hope my girl meets a nice young man so she can settle down like her brother has'?"

"Maybe a little."

"*Arrgghhh.*" Sophie covered her face with her hands.

"It wasn't too bad." Jason laughed. "Really. And she was charming about it."

"I'm sure she was. Mom can ooze charm when she wants to, which makes her quite the formidable courtroom opponent. I'd hate to have to go up against her."

"Well, you can't blame her for wanting you to be happy. She did say she was glad that you and Jesse have gotten close to your grandfather, though."

"Speaking of whom, did you see him today?"

"No, I was working on something else." He picked up his water bottle, then hesitated before he took a sip. "Is something wrong?"

"No, no. I was just wondering. Both he and I all but passed out yesterday after everyone left, he in his chair and me on the sofa. If the caterer hadn't made so much noise leaving, I might still be there."

"I'll be there tomorrow for a while. I'm having some shrubs delivered and will get them planted."

"How do you know where to put things? How do you know what it will look like in another year? Or in five or ten years?"

"You learn by studying, just like you learn anything else. With plants, you study their growth patterns and you know what they'll look like at different stages, how big they'll get, how their needs for sun or shade and water will change as they grow." He took a long drink of water. "I was lucky that after Eric went into the service, I was hired by a guy in Florida who did a lot of restoration work. He taught me a lot, encouraged me to go to school. The local community college had courses in landscaping, so I signed up for those. So I had both the theoretical and the hands-on education going for me when my boss retired and I went into business for myself." He put the cap back on the bottle. "Well, for Eric and me. He was going to partner with me when he got home, put up half the money for the start-up. After he died, I felt obligated to pay Brooke back for Eric's investment, so I sold the company and came here to pay her in person."

"And you stayed."

"Yes, I stayed. Logan's here," he said simply. "I saw

a need for the kind of work that I do, so I decided that St. Dennis was as good a place as any to start over."

"I'm glad you did," she heard herself say.

"So am I." He reached across the table to touch her fingers with his. "So what's your story? Why did you decide to pick up and move here?"

"Family guilt, for one, but it was more than that. Jesse was in over his head with work and really did need me. I've been a prosecutor for eight years and I was ready for a change." She was tempted to tell him about Chris, then decided against it. Lately, Chris hadn't seemed quite as important as he once had.

"So is this the change you were looking for?"

"I've only been here for a few days, but I think it's going to be fine. I like the town, I like the people I've met. I like the vibe here." She smiled. "And I think I'll like the work once I get this place organized. Speaking of which, I should get back to it."

"Is there anything I can help you with?"

"No, thanks. I'd think you'd be tired by . . ." She glanced at her watch. "Is it really eight o'clock?"

"Ten after," he told her.

She stood and cleared away the plates and the empty pizza box. "Thanks so much, Jason. I think I probably would have just kept on going and wouldn't have stopped until I passed out from hunger."

"Way to give Violet a heart attack in the morning." He pushed back his chair. "Do you have much else to do tonight?"

"I do, but I think I'm going to let it go. There were some boxes I was going to bring back, but my arms are starting to feel like noodles." She let them hang straight down. "I'm afraid I'm out of shape."

"Your shape looks just fine to me."

"Two compliments in three days," she mused. "Keep it up and I might start forgetting that I'm a lawyer."

"Speaking of which . . . how many lawyers does it take to screw in a lightbulb?"

"Please." She rolled her eyes. "Three. One to climb the ladder, one to shake it, and one to sue the ladder company. Old as the hills."

"I gotta find some better material," Jason muttered. "So where are the boxes you need moved?"

"In Jesse's office, but you don't have to . . ." Too late. Jason was out the door, down the hall, and into Jesse's office.

"These on the floor?" he called back to her.

"Yes. The ones . . ."

"Where do you want them?" He was carrying them, one on top of the other.

"In here." She showed him into the new file room. "Anyplace is fine. Thank you."

"Two more. Be right back."

She liked the way he moved, all easy saunter, like he had all night.

"This should do it." He returned with the remaining boxes and put them down on the floor next to the others.

"Thank you so much. I'd been reduced to pushing them all the way from the front of the office and it was taking me forever." She leaned back against the filing cabinet. "You've saved me about a half hour, not to mention my back and my arms."

He took two steps toward her, took her hands and drew them upward until they rested on his neck, then lowered his mouth to hers and kissed her. As kissers went, she thought, Jason was an A-plus. The tickle she felt whenever he got too close was more like an electric charge that went straight to her gut. By the time she caught her breath, he'd eased away from her, but her face still felt the brush of his five o'clock shadow and her heart was still racing.

"How 'bout I help you lock up?" His hands had slid to her waist as if they belonged there.

"You don't have to . . ."

"It's dark, and there doesn't seem to be anyone else around."

He planted one soft kiss on her forehead, then took her by the hand. On their way out of the room, Sophie turned off the light.

"I just have Jesse's room and the kitchen to close up," she said.

"I'll take care of the kitchen."

He let go of her hand and walked to the back of the hall while she went to the front. She restacked a pile she'd knocked over earlier, picked up three files she'd decided she'd need to read through before acting on the most recent correspondence, and swung the strap of her bag over her shoulder. Then she snapped off the office light, as well as the overhead in the reception area, and took the key from her bag.

"Got everything?" Jason asked, and she nodded.

She locked the door behind them and he followed her to her car, opening the door for her so she could drop the files on the backseat.

"Thanks again for everything," Sophie said. "For dinner, for helping move stuff . . ."

"Any time." He brushed a strand of hair back from

her face. "Let me know if there's anything else I can do. I usually knock off work around six thirty or seven."

"Will do." She got into her car and he closed the door. "I'll let you know when I get my kitchen stuff unpacked so I can show off my skills. I promise you'll be knocked out."

He leaned in through the car window and kissed her on the lips. "I already am."

Chapter 17 ⌒

"D ID you have a pizza delivered last night?" was the first thing Violet asked when she came into the office on Tuesday morning.

"Sort of." Sophie looked up from the file she was reading. "Jason stopped by on his way home from picking one up and he offered to share it with me."

"That was nice of him." Violet stood in the doorway for a moment.

Sophie assumed she was waiting for her to say something, so she did. "Yes, very nice."

"He's a nice boy," Violet added.

Was there any point in reminding Violet that Jason was thirtysomething and no longer qualified for boy status? Probably not. Besides, everything was relative.

"Yes, he is. Very nice."

"I know your grandfather is very fond of him, too," Violet persisted.

"I assumed. Jason's doing a lot of work at Pop's."

"And doing quite a fine job. Your grandfather is very pleased."

"Good. I want him to be happy." Sophie went into

Jesse's office and surveyed the floor. She selected a stack of case files at random and carried them to her office. The light in her small room in the back was better, she told herself, softer, and the chair was more comfortable. Then, too, there was the matter of Jesse's desk being too cluttered to spread out another file.

She read through the case, found the information she was looking for, made the calls Jesse had wanted her to make, then jotted down a few notes for the file. She worked her way through the stack, then took a five-minute break to take a call from Cameron.

"Hey, Ellie tells me you're buying the old Walsh place. Cool."

"It *is* pretty cool." Sophie smiled. "We go to settlement one week from today."

"And you think it might need some work?"

"I know it does. It's just a matter of how much and what it will cost. I was hoping you could help me out on both counts."

"Absolutely. When can we get in to take a look?"

"At your earliest convenience. I have a key," she explained.

"How about tomorrow afternoon around four?"

"Perfect. I'll meet you there. You know where it is, right?"

"Sure. Everyone knows Walsh's."

Sophie tapped her pen on the blotter after they ended the call, thinking she'd have to come up with a name for the place, and soon. She couldn't keep calling it "the old Walsh's" or "the restaurant."

At one, she ate the lunch she'd brought from home, changed her clothes, and resumed the task of sorting through files and putting closed cases in the new file room. Violet left at five, and at five thirty, she started to glance out the front window every fifteen minutes. It wasn't until seven that she admitted she'd been watching for Jason, and it took her another twenty minutes to own up to the fact that she'd been hoping he'd stop in. His help aside—if not for him, she'd probably be in traction from lugging all those heavy files from one end of the office to the other—she found that the more time she spent with him, the more she liked him. She liked the fact that he was thoughtful of not only her, but her grandfather and his nephew as well. That family meant a lot to him. That he made her smile, made her laugh . . . and oh, yes, made her heart race and her knees weak. Made her want more when he kissed her.

Funny, she thought, as she prepared to close the office for the night, but when she broke up with Christopher, the last thing she wanted was another relationship. He'd burned her so badly, she'd thought it would be forever before she'd be able to trust anyone again—before she'd even *want* to trust another man again, before she'd want another man to touch her. And yet here she was, a mere three months later, watching the street and watching the time, disappointed that Jason hadn't stopped in again tonight. Not that he was obligated to, of course, but still . . . it would have been nice to see him again tonight.

She gathered her things and went through the office, turning off the lights. *Maybe tomorrow night,* she thought as she locked the front door.

A girl could hope.

Jason stood at the take-out counter of the new Thai restaurant and scanned the menu for what seemed like the fiftieth time. Thai Gardens was a new place, located on the highway just outside of town, but a woman he'd chatted with at Walt's last Friday night mentioned that the food was really good there. At the time, he doubted she'd talked it up so that he could buy dinner for someone else, since she'd clearly been wrangling for a dinner date, but the obvious type had never interested him. Actually, Jason had no type. He'd dated women of different sizes and shapes and hair coloring, athletic women and couch potatoes, smart women and women who were . . . well, endowed in other ways.

There were times when he almost wished he did have a type: it might have made it easier to know what he was looking for. Up until recently, he hadn't really been aware that he was looking. But it occurred to him that he was over thirty, a small business owner—and now a property owner—so he'd crossed a lot off his "to do" list, and maybe it just followed that meeting the right woman should be next.

But lately, it seemed he'd been interested in only one woman, and he wasn't sure how to go about pursuing her. For one thing, she was his friend's younger sister, and he'd learned back in high school that dating a friend's little sister could have repercussions. For another, Jason and the grandfather of the lady in question had a relationship that he'd hate to see ruined if, for example, he was dating the granddaughter and things turned out badly. Still, there really wasn't anyone else who'd caught his eye the way Sophie Enright had, and while he wasn't much of a gambler, there was something about her that made him believe it was worth a try.

So here he stood, trying to decide between the Panang Curry, the Pad Thai, and the Kao Pad Saparod. The last sounded the most exotic—chicken with jasmine rice stir-fried with pineapple—but he didn't know Sophie well enough to know if it would appeal to her. It sounded good, though, so he ordered it and the Pad Thai, which he'd had once before and liked. He took a seat and waited for the food to be prepared, and twenty-five minutes later, he walked out with a brown bag of aromatic goodies in the crook of his arm.

He drove into town and headed straight for the office on the corner of Old St. Mary's Church Road. He came to a stop in front of the building, his heart sinking when he realized the office was dark. He got out of his car and checked around the side, just in case Sophie was working in her office toward the back, but there were no lights on. He could have kicked himself for having wasted so much time scrutinizing the menu and deliberating—his mother would have said "dillydallying"—over what to order. He walked back to his truck and thought about driving past Sophie's house, but he wondered if that might seem too much like stalking.

Either way, he'd struck out. He got back into the cab of the pickup and drove home, hoping he liked what he bought, because it looked like he'd be eating Thai for the rest of the week.

∽∾

Sophie could barely contain herself on Wednesday morning, knowing that she'd be meeting with Cam and Ellie to go through the restaurant that afternoon.

She tried to play down her excitement when she mentioned it to Violet, who was fixing her morning tea in the kitchen.

"Oh, by the way," Sophie said with all the nonchalance she could muster, "Cameron is looking at the building this afternoon. You know, checking it out to see what repairs it needs."

"That's nice, dear." Violet dunked a tea bag into a cup of steaming water.

"So I guess we should know pretty soon how much it's going to cost to fix up."

"He'd be the one to talk to about that." Violet nodded. "Have you seen the box of stevia that I brought in last week? I thought I put it in this cabinet."

"Next one over." Sophie tried again to engage Violet, hoping she'd show some enthusiasm. "So I guess I'll bring in Cam's estimate as soon as I get it, so we can go over it together and you can decide what you want to invest."

"You'll make the decisions on what you need for the renovations and for your start-up costs, and that's what I'll invest. It's as simple as that." She looked up from her cup, glared at Sophie in the way only Violet could, and added, "Please keep in mind the silent part of 'silent investor.'"

"Got it." Sophie nodded and took her coffee into her office.

Sophie read the correspondence on the first file, then started reading through the case itself, but she was having a hard time concentrating. She was excited about the walk-through this afternoon and wished there were someone she could talk to who shared her enthusiasm.

That person obviously wasn't Violet, who had felt inclined to remind her that any interest she might have was strictly financial. And, of course, silent.

Forcing herself to focus, Sophie somehow managed to put all thoughts of her new venture aside while she read, made notes, and fielded phone calls, but by two thirty, she'd had enough. She changed into work clothes and turned off her office lights.

"Violet, I'm going to head over to River Road and get the place opened up as much as I can for Cameron."

"I'll close up if you're not back by five or so," Violet told her without looking up from her computer screen.

Sophie was almost out the door when Violet called to her.

"Good luck. I know how much this means to you. I hope the damage isn't too terribly bad."

"Thanks, Violet. I hope so, too."

Sophie's stomach churned with anxiety all the way to River Road. What if there was real structural damage? Or a roof that was totally rotted underneath? Or termites? Or . . . well, something else that she couldn't think of right at that moment that would be equally disastrous? Why hadn't she asked Cameron to go over the place before things had gone this far? Settlement was now less than a week away. Was it still possible to back out if he uncovered insurmountable problems? And even if he did, would she want to?

Even the beauty of the afternoon didn't brighten her mood. Between leaving the office and arriving at the property, she'd thought of everything that could possibly go wrong today. But once she'd parked her

car and opened the building, all the negativity had
melted away. This was her place; she knew it. It was
meant to be hers. When she heard Cam's truck, she
eagerly walked outside to greet him and Ellie.

"Cool building." Ellie jumped out of the passenger
side with a smile on her face. "I love that it's stone.
There aren't too many stone buildings in St. Dennis,
so this is unique. I like it."

"Thanks. So do I." Sophie held the door open.
"Come on in and take a look at the inside."

"The outside looks great." Cameron stopped for a
moment and studied the façade. With a penknife he
took from his pocket, he poked at the wooden windowsills. "Solid, no rot. Nice. Needs paint, some new
windows. These aren't very efficient and the screens
are pretty much destroyed, but the rest of the place
looks solid." He walked around the front. "The mor-
tar between the stones looks pretty tight. That's a real
plus. There might be a few places that could use a
little touch-up, but for the most part, it's looking
pretty good."

Sophie let out a deep breath.

"Let's see what you think of the inside." Sophie
ushered them in. "I hope you remembered flashlights."

"Biggest ones I could find." He held up two huge
lights.

"That should do it." Leaving the front door open,
Sophie showed them around. "This is obviously the
dining room . . ."

Without comment, Cameron began his inspection,
shining the light over every inch of the room before
disappearing into the kitchen.

"This is his thing," Ellie told Sophie. "If there are problems, he'll find them. But while he's doing that, show me what you have in mind here . . ."

Sophie went over her plans for the interior and the furniture, but hesitated when it came to décor.

"I still don't know for sure what I want it to look like in here. I want it to reflect St. Dennis, but I don't want kitschy-beachy." She mentioned her idea of borrowing recipes from old St. Dennis families to include on the menu. "I'm trying to get Violet to cough up her mother's lemon meringue pie recipe."

"Oh, I have lots of recipes from my great-aunt Lilly," Ellie told her. "Maybe you'd like to look through them, see if there's something that you could use in the restaurant."

"I'd love to do that. And I did think of asking my grandfather if my grandmother was known for anything in particular—you know, a dish that she always served."

"Pound cake," Ellie told her.

"What about it?"

"Rose Enright was known for her pound cakes. She made several flavors. Lemon, poppy seed, coconut . . ."

"How would you know that?"

"Lilly wrote about it in one of her journals. She and Violet and Rose had tea together once a week on Friday afternoons, alternating houses. Rose always made pound cake and Violet made pie. Lilly made chicken salad and chocolate soufflé."

"And you have the recipes?"

"Of course." Ellie grinned. "Lilly made notes on just about everything. She had a little notebook where she kept recipes that she borrowed from her friends.

On the front page, she wrote 'The Blossoms Cook.' How cute is that?"

"The Blossoms Cook," Sophie repeated thoughtfully.

"Oh, and I have some photographs, like I promised. I left them in my bag. Be right back." Ellie took off for the truck.

Cam came into the dining room.

"How's it look so far?" Sophie asked anxiously.

"Better than I thought in some areas, not so great in others," he told her. "Is there a key for the second floor? I want to check something up there, and then I'll need to look at the attic."

"I have the key." Sophie handed it over.

"Thanks." He started for the door.

"Cam, do you know anyone who does signs?" she asked.

"You mean, for here?"

She nodded.

"What did you have in mind?"

"I like the sign that's out there. I like the size and the shape, but of course, I'll be changing the name."

He stepped outside and looked up. "You could reuse it. Just repaint it. What did you have in mind?"

Sophie took a piece of paper from a notebook in her bag and wrote the name she'd just decided on and handed it over to Cam.

"That's it? That's what you're calling your place?"

"Yes. It just came to me."

"I like it. Very nice." He handed the slip back to her.

"I can do the lettering myself, but I need to have someone take the sign down for me."

"I'll do that before I leave today. It should only take a minute. Meanwhile," he said, "there's another floor to look over before we talk about what it's going to take to make this a working restaurant again."

Sophie heard his footsteps on the stairs, then overhead as he went from room to room. She took a deep breath and hoped the second floor didn't need much. She planned on moving in as soon as it was livable. If she was paying the mortgage here, she didn't want to be paying rent somewhere else for any longer than necessary.

"Sophie, come out into the light," Ellie called from the doorway. "These old photos are pretty dark, and you're going to want to see them."

Sophie stepped outside, the bright sunlight causing her to blink and squint.

Ellie laughed. "I did the same thing when I came into the light after being in there. I bet you'll be happy once you have electricity."

"That's the first thing I want after closing next week. The second will be water."

"Here's a picture of my great-aunt, your grandmother, and Violet Finneran." Ellie turned the picture over. "First Families Day, 1944. Do you love the hats? And the dresses?"

Ellie held out the photo and Sophie took it.

"Oh, God, yes. I love the dresses, and the hats . . . and look, they're wearing white gloves. No one dresses like this anymore, I'm afraid." She studied the photo for a moment, an idea forming in her mind. "Could I see the others?"

"Sure." Ellie handed over the photos one by one,

along with a running commentary including the date and the place as nearly as she could tell for each one.

"Ellie, could I have a few of these to enlarge? I think a wall of photos of old St. Dennis would be just the thing." She stepped back inside and pointed to the wall next to the kitchen door. "Can you see it? Right there . . ."

"That's perfect. And of course, take whichever pictures you'd like."

"I promise, I'll get them back to you." Sophie went through the stack again, pulling out several that she thought captured the spirit of the three girls. "What's this, here, in the background?" She held up a photo.

"That's the carriage house at Lilly's. My house, now. That's the building the historic society is restoring. The one Grace recruited you to work on?"

"Oh, right. Saturday morning."

"Cam and I are stoked to see what's inside, as is half the town."

"You haven't gone inside?"

"Can't get the lock off. Grace said she didn't think the chain had come off the door since my uncle Ted died. Hence the raffle to guess what's inside. I understand they've already sold a lot of tickets."

"Sounds like we'll all be surprised when the lock and chain come off that door." Sophie held up one of the pictures. "This is a great shot of the three girls. Croquet?"

Ellie nodded. "Apparently a favorite of Lilly's. There are several photos of the girls—well, the ladies—

playing. Even a few of my mom playing with them when she was younger."

"Your mother was from St. Dennis?"

"She stayed with my great-aunt a lot when she was younger, then from what I've heard, made trips back when she was ill, before she died."

"I'm sorry for your loss. Maybe we could use a few pictures of your mother, if you have any."

Ellie laughed. "There are thousands of pictures of my mother. She was Lynley Sebastian."

"The model? Like, one of the first-ever super-models?"

"That was her." Ellie nodded.

"We'll definitely have to have some pictures of her on the wall, and maybe a recipe or two that she liked?"

"She didn't really like to cook so much, and I don't recall she had favorites, but I'll see what I can come up with."

"Great. Boy, you never know about these small towns. Lynley Sebastian. Dallas MacGregor. Berry Eberle." Sophie handed back the photos she had not selected. "Thanks. I'll take good care of them."

"I bet your grandfather has some great shots of Rose," Ellie noted. "I bet he'd love to have you use some of them."

"First I have to tell him I bought this place."

"You didn't tell him?"

"I didn't tell anyone. Well, you and Cam, and Jesse, but that's about it." *Tonight,* Sophie told herself. *I'm going to have to talk to Pop tonight.*

Cam came around the side of the building.

"Should I be sitting down?" Sophie said when she saw him.

"All in all, the building's not in bad shape." He leaned back against the fender of his truck. "I'll have to go over my notes and figure out what it's going to cost. I know that's your concern."

Sophie nodded.

"The wiring needs some updating. The electrical box in the kitchen notes that the last updates were in 1982, so while we're not talking about knob and tube here, there are some new requirements that will have to be met to bring the system up to code. The plumbing looks good—no sign of old leaks that I could see—but we'll need the water turned on to know for sure, so that's a question mark for now. The fixtures in the two restrooms should be updated, by the way. Now, I found no evidence of roof leaks, so I'd leave it alone."

"I'm not hearing anything that I didn't expect," Sophie said.

"Well, structurally, you're okay, and that's a good thing. But you will need an exterminator before you do anything in there. Insects and rodents—you probably already know that. And it looks like something . . . raccoon or squirrel . . . made a nest under the eaves at one time. You want to get rid of that mess. We'll take care of that for you when we start working."

"How did it get in, and is it out?"

"Looks like there was some loose clapboard at one time, but someone nailed it back down. So whatever was in there is gone, but it left a mess."

"But nothing really bad so far," Ellie noted. "That's good, Sophie."

"There's a lot of cosmetic work that needs to be done, and you are going to have to find someone who can test and repair those old appliances should they need it," Cam told her. "Once the place has been cleaned out, you're going to have a lot of work on your hands. Some of it, I'm guessing, you're going to want to do yourself."

"The painting, yes. But the refinishing—the floors, the counter—and of course, the wiring and the plumbing, I'll want you to do all that."

"I'll call my subs and get some prices worked up for you. I can get whatever permits you're going to need, but you're going to have to call the electric company, have the service put in your name, and tell them you'll want service to begin on Tuesday. Someone from the water company is going to have to come out, locate the connection, and turn the water back on. You let me know when that's scheduled and I'll run the system and check the pipes the next day."

"Okay."

"As far as the apartment is concerned, same thing. We'll check it out once you have water here and see if there's any problem we need to address. Otherwise, you'll probably want new fixtures in the bathroom and you'll need appliances in the kitchen, and there's a lot of peeling paper in the bedroom and the living area. That's cosmetic, though, too. And we talked about needing the windows replaced. That goes for upstairs, too."

"Could be worse," she reminded herself.

"I'll get back to you by the end of the week with

some prices on what we've talked about so far. I'll stop back later with a ladder and take that sign down for you." Cam walked around the cab to the driver's side and opened the door. "In the meantime, if you think of anything else, give me a call."

"I will. Thanks, Cam." Sophie walked Ellie to the pickup. "And thanks, Ellie, for the photos and for the information. You've given me a lot to think about."

"You're welcome. I'm really intrigued now—can't wait to see what you're going to do with the place."

Sophie stood in front of what would soon be her business and watched the pickup pull away, then went back inside. She stared at the big blank wall and tried to envision the photos, enlarged and framed, telling the story of friendships that had lasted for so many years, and still did, if you considered that Violet was still alive and still cherished Rose's memory.

There were other stories in St. Dennis, she thought as she locked up. Maybe she could beg a few other photos for her walls. Grace Sinclair must have some early pictures of the inn, and wouldn't photos of a young Berry Eberle—Beryl Townsend to movie buffs—be fabulous? Maybe pictures of Dallas as a teenager, and Lynley Sebastian as a schoolgirl.

She tucked the photos Ellie had given her into her bag and started the drive home, but somehow she found herself making the turn at Old St. Mary's Church Road. *Time to talk to Pop,* she told herself. *Time to let him know what's going on.*

She parked out front and rang the doorbell, then waited patiently for her grandfather to arrive at the door and open it.

"Hi, Pop. Can I come in?"

"What kind of a question is that? Of course you can come in." He held the door for her, then closed it behind her once she was inside. "Can we give you some dinner? Mrs. Anderson reheated some of the leftovers from Sunday before she left. There's plenty of ham, and . . ."

"I'm sorry. I didn't realize it was so late. I can stop back."

"Don't be silly." He took her arm. "Come in and tell me what's on your mind."

He led her into the kitchen and, always the gentleman, held a chair out for her at the old square table.

"Let me fix you something." He tottered to the cabinets and took down a plate.

"No, Pop, really. I'm not hungry." The thought of putting food into her stomach made her feel even more queasy than she already was. "I just need to talk to you about something."

He turned and looked at her for a long moment, then returned the plate to the cupboard.

"Some tea, then, perhaps. Or coffee. Jesse had Clay drop off some beer after the reception. You know, the bottles with Jesse and Brooke's picture on them?"

"Nothing, Pop. Really. Just . . . I just want to talk."

"All right, then." He took the seat next to hers. "Now, tell me what's bothering you."

"I know how happy you are that I'm here in St. Dennis, and that I'm going to be working with Jesse at the office," she began. "I know how important it is to you that the firm remains in the family."

"Of course." He nodded. "Of course, it's important. Enright and Enright is a tradition in this town, and in this family. It matters. And yes, I'm delighted that you're part of it. Makes up for other disappointments I've had over the years, if you follow."

She swallowed hard. "I'm just hoping that after you hear what I have to say, you won't think of me as another disappointment."

He turned to her with puzzled eyes that studied her face for a very long moment.

"What's this all about, Sophie? Have you changed your mind about working with Jess?"

"No, no. Well, not completely." She took a deep breath. "Okay, here it is: I bought a piece of property here in St. Dennis. The old Walsh restaurant out on River Road."

He nodded. "I know the place, of course. Used to be one of the only places in town to get a decent crab cake. Your grandmother loved them. Nice investment, Sophie. You'll turn a pretty profit on that land in another year or so when you sell it. I approve."

"I don't think you'll approve of the rest," she said. "I'm not buying it as an investment, and I'm not planning on selling it. I'm planning on fixing it up and reopening it as a restaurant."

Silence followed. Lots and lots of silence. Finally, Curtis said, "Run that past me again. I couldn't have heard you correctly."

"You heard right, Pop. I want to reopen the restaurant."

"What about your law career?" The frown deepened his brow. "What about the firm? Where did all this crazy nonsense come from, anyway?"

"I've wanted my own restaurant since I worked at one back when I was in school. Every summer for years. I really loved it." She forced her voice to remain calm. "And as far as the firm is concerned, I'll still be working with Jesse, but only in the afternoons."

"How can you possibly give your all to both?" He pushed away from the table. "How can you expect to run a restaurant and give your clients the time and attention they deserve?"

"I'll work it out, Pop, even if I have to work until midnight every night. Mostly, I'll be doing legwork, research, and writing briefs for Jesse's cases. Those are things that I do very well and that he—well, he's terrific in court, in front of a jury, but he hates the detail work, hates the research. He'll still be the trial guy and I'll do much of the work behind the scenes."

"This is just crazy, Sophie." Curtis stood unsteadily, one hand resting on the table.

"Pop, sit back down and let me talk to you." When he didn't move, she tugged at his hand. "Please. Let me tell you what I want to do there. Please hear me out."

He sat back down, his face unreadable, then nodded to her to begin. She did.

Over the next hour, Sophie told him everything, about how she liked being a prosecutor but didn't feel complete. How she'd dreamed of having her own restaurant since she first put on the apron at Shelby's when she was sixteen. How when her mother went back to law school, she took over the cooking duties. How nothing had ever seemed as creative or as interesting or as much fun as cooking.

"Fun?" he said flatly. "It's hard work."

"Yes, it is. But so is law if you don't love it. I like

being a lawyer, Pop, but I don't love it." Before he could comment, she told him about her plans for the new restaurant, how she wanted it to reflect the best of St. Dennis, past and present. How she wanted to honor her grandmother and her friends and others who had come before her in the community. "I want it to be a special place, a place that people will talk about when they visit the town, a place that the locals will embrace because it reflects so much of who they are."

She told him everything she'd dreamed of doing there.

"Ellie told me that Gramma Rose was known for her pound cake," she added. "She said her great-aunt wrote about it in a journal."

He nodded slowly. "Pound cake with berries in early summer, with peaches in August. Some sweet apple and caramel sauce in the fall. Chocolate with cherries in the winter." Unexpectedly, he smiled at the memory. "And sour cherry cobbler. We used to have sour cherry trees out back. They died out around the same time she left us." He fell silent for a moment before adding, "Rose was quite the baker, back in the day. Yessir, she surely was."

"I hope I do her memory justice, Pop."

"No doubt you will," he said softly. "When is all this going to happen?"

"I settle on the property on Tuesday."

"And I'm just finding out about this now?" His eyes narrowed as his anger flashed.

"I was afraid to tell you." Even to herself, she sounded weak.

"Does Jesse know?"

"Yes, but . . ."

"But you weren't afraid to tell him?" His voice rose.

"I had to tell him; he was counting on me." As soon as the words were out of her mouth, she winced. "What I mean is . . ."

"*I* was counting on you." Her grandfather pushed away from the table again, preparing to stand.

"I know that, but I couldn't think of the right way to tell you. I'd just gotten to know you again after so many years of being separated from you." Tears filled Sophie's eyes. "I knew you'd be disappointed with what I was doing, and I didn't want you to be angry with me for letting you down. I didn't want you to think I was just like my . . ." The words stuck in her throat.

"Like your father?" Curtis asked softly.

She nodded.

"Dear girl, you are nothing like your father." He sighed deeply. "And you could never disappoint me the way he did, Sophie. Craig let us down in a hundred ways. It wasn't just his not joining the firm. Frankly, by the time he'd gotten through law school and by some miracle managed to pass the bar, I'd already given up any thoughts of him working with me and his brother. It would have been a disaster."

"I'm sorry," she whispered.

"Oh, my dear, I'm the one who's sorry." He shook his head. "Your grandmother and I spent many, many hours wondering what we had done to have made our son turn out the way he did, but we never did figure it out." He took one of her hands. "Somehow all the good of this family skipped right past him and went straight to his children. You and Jesse are a blessing to me."

"You're not angry?"

"I didn't say that." He hesitated. "I'm not going to lie, Sophie. I'm not happy about this. I don't see how you'll be able to do justice to both the firm and your restaurant. I think you're overestimating yourself."

"I'll manage."

"We'll see." He cleared his throat. "So who else knows about this? Besides Jesse."

"Cam and Ellie." When his eyebrows rose, she hastened to add, "Cam went through the building to make sure it wasn't about to fall down. I need to know what it's going to take to renovate it. And Ellie was there with Cam. She gave me some photos of Lilly and Violet and Gramma Rose. I'm going to enlarge them and frame them, hang them on the walls. I was hoping you'd have some photos I could use as well."

"How are you paying for this venture of yours?"

"I sold my condo, and I have some savings."

"And that's going to be enough to do everything you need to do? Have you had to take out a loan?"

She nodded. The less said about that, the better.

"It wasn't a loan from the bank here in St. Dennis. I'm on the board, and I see how much is loaned out and to whom."

"I have a private loan."

"Mind telling me who?"

"I'd rather not say." She squirmed under his scrutiny.

"And why is that?"

"My investor prefers to remain anonymous."

"I see."

He probably does, Sophie thought.

"What will you do if we find that you're not carrying your weight at the office, or if you realize that your business needs you one hundred percent of the time?"

"I'll deal with that if it happens, but I believe in myself, Pop. I wish you could, too."

"I wish you success, Sophie," he said stiffly. "On both fronts. But now, I'd like to watch my news program, if you don't mind."

"Oh. Of course." She stood at the same time he rose from his chair. Before he could protest, she leaned over and kissed him on the cheek. "I love you, Pop. I don't want to do anything that would hurt you or upset you. But I have to do this for myself. If I'm wrong and I bungle it, I'll have to live with that. But I have to try." One last deep breath. "I'm proud to be an Enright, and I'm proud that you think I'm worthy to work in the family firm. I did a lot of good work back in Ohio, and I'm proud of that, too. But if I don't do this now, I probably never will, and I know I'll regret it. Please try to understand."

He nodded and walked her to the door, then opened it and stepped aside for her to leave.

" 'Night, Pop."

"I love you, too, child," he whispered as he closed the door behind her. He stood and watched until her car pulled away from the curb and disappeared down the street.

He walked slowly into his study and turned on the light, then plunked down in one of two rocking chairs and reached for the remote. Before he could turn on the TV, the scent began to surround him, and he sighed.

"I know you're there, Rose, and I know you have something to say.

"I do want her to be happy. And I understand this is her dream. But I have a dream, too. I dreamed my family's firm would outlast me by at least another generation."

He tried to ignore the voice that whispered in his head, the voice that only he could hear.

"And don't think I can't figure out who loaned Sophie the money. An anonymous source, indeed. Oh, don't worry, I won't . . . of course I won't yell at her. I am not yelling now."

He lowered his voice an octave or two anyway.

"I don't want Sophie to be disappointed, either. I don't think she realizes how hard it's going to be to make a success of this project of hers. Only open for breakfast and lunch! Hmmmph. Who ever heard of such a thing? How does she expect to make any real money if she doesn't open for dinner?"

The other chair began to rock slowly. Curtis knew Rose meant business when the chair rocked.

"She was afraid she was disappointing me the way Craig did, Rose. Can you imagine?" His voice softened. "I told her she isn't anything like her father. Yes, of course I think about him." He paused. "Too late for that, my love . . . I don't see a reconciliation in this lifetime. It's been too many years. I don't know him anymore. I suspect Craig most likely feels the same way about me."

He rocked slowly.

"His girl is a lot like you, yes. Yes, she is. And I do

respect her for wanting to do her own thing. I just wish her doing *her* thing didn't interfere with her doing *my* thing," he grumbled.

A few more minutes of rocking. "Why does everyone think they have to keep things from me? I wish Sophie had told me sooner. I wish she'd come to me instead of Violet. And I wish that Violet hadn't gone behind my back. And yes, I wish Jesse had told me when he found out. Seems like everyone I love best is hiding things from me, like they don't trust me."

The rocker stopped abruptly.

"Interfere? Why would they think I'd interfere?" He snorted. "When did I ever interfere in someone else's business? Rose?"

As the scent began to fade from the room, Curtis muttered, "Ah, nuts," turned up the volume on the TV, and tried to lose himself in the day's affairs.

Chapter 18 ⤳

Some people turned to alcohol in times of stress. Sophie, however, required fat and sugar to bring her back down from the high level of anxiety she'd achieved.

"Ice cream." She drove past her house and made a right at Cherry Street. "A double."

She'd had no way to anticipate her grandfather's reaction to her news, never having tangled with him before. He obviously had been displeased, but he hadn't yelled or lectured, and he hadn't disowned her, so as far as Sophie was concerned, it was all good. Still, the anxiety demanded to be assuaged.

She parked in the municipal lot across from the police station, waved to Beck, the chief of police, who was backing out of his reserved spot in front of the building, and walked to One Scoop or Two.

Ice cream and maybe some gossip, she was thinking as she walked past the open window. There appeared to be quite a crowd inside, not surprising as the temperatures had been steadily climbing over the past few days. The bell chimed when Sophie opened the door, and Steffie, the owner and ice-cream maker, glanced up from behind the counter where she was filling an order.

"Hey, Sophie." Steffie gave a wave with the hand that held the scoop right before dipping it into the case and coming out with a perfectly round ball of something darkly chocolate. "Great wedding last weekend. What do you hear from Jesse and Brooke?"

"Nothing," Sophie called back and got in line behind a woman who had a toddler in each hand. "Which is as it should be, since they're on their honeymoon. They'll be back soon enough."

"True." Steffie handed over the cone she'd been building and directed the customer to the cash register, where a girl with long, light-pink braids rang up the sale.

Sophie studied that day's selections, which were written on a chalkboard hanging behind the cash register. So many flavors, so little time . . .

"What can I get you, Sophie?" Steffie asked.

"I don't know what I want. Everything sounds fabulous."

"Of course everything is fabulous." Steffie grinned. "But you want the coconut pineapple mango medley."

"I do?"

"You do. Just made it this morning and there's only a little bit left. It's divine, if I do say so myself."

"Sold. Two scoops on a sugar cone, please."

"Might only be enough for one generous scoop," Steffie told her. "Does it have to be two?"

Sophie nodded. "It's been that kind of day."

"Well, in that case, we'll put a scoop of chocolate ecstasy on the bottom—it has little bits of bitter chocolate and fresh coconut in an extra-dark chocolate base. We'll put the fruity flavor on top."

"Great. Thanks."

When she'd finished scooping and declared the cone a masterpiece, Steffie handed it over.

"This looks like sin on a sugar cone." Sophie sampled as she proceeded to the cash register.

"Only if your idea of sin is eating an entire day's worth of calories at dessert." Steffie turned to the girl at the cash register. "Paige, this is my friend Sophie. She's Jesse's sister." To Sophie, she said, "Paige is my niece, my brother Grant's daughter. I make her work for me after school to keep her out of trouble."

The girl with the pink braids crossed her eyes and made a face at Steffie.

"Darling girl." Steffie smiled sweetly. "Dallas is her stepmama. She keeps threatening to put Paige in one of her movies. Of course, it would have to be a horror film . . ."

Paige stuck her tongue out behind Steffie's back, and Steffie laughed as if she'd known it was coming.

Sophie paid for her ice cream, said goodbye to Steffie and her niece, and walked out into the warmth of an early evening in late spring. She strolled along the boardwalk that led to the marina. The long dock jutted into the Bay and boats bobbed up and down on the gentle waves. It was peaceful and helped restore her after the tension leading up to the conversation with her grandfather. All in all, that had not gone badly, and while she was grateful, she was still drained by the self-inflicted drama that preceded the conversation.

There were benches every ten feet or so along the

Bay, most of them empty at this time of day. She selected one near the end of the dock, sat, and nibbled at her ice cream. Seabirds landed and took off, some on the water, some on the wooden pilings. It was like a scene from a magazine, with the sun setting across the Bay and the birds swooping around, and she was happy to be part of it. Two young men in their early twenties hopped from the deck of a boat to the dock, carrying a large cooler between them. From the way they were struggling, she surmised that they must have made one heck of a catch. Crabs or fish, she wondered, and was about to ask when she heard someone calling her name.

"I thought that was you." Jason sauntered along the pier, a ball cap backward on his head, his dark glasses dangling from the neck of his shirt, and that bit of facial scruff she'd decided was adorable.

"Where were you?" She scooted over on the bench to make room for him.

"On my way to Walt's for dinner. I'd ask you to join me, but it appears you've already moved on to dessert."

"It's Dessert First Wednesday," she told him. When he raised an eyebrow, she added, "I've had *A Day*, but it's all good now."

"Anything you want to talk about?"

She thought it over: did she want to share all that drama with Jason? Maybe.

"I had to tell my grandfather something I knew he wasn't going to like. I was a bundle of nerves going in, but it worked out okay." She shifted on the bench so that she could face him. "I wasn't sure how he'd react. I've never been in a situation with him where I knew I was going to incur his disapproval, and I didn't know what he'd do."

"I've always found your grandfather to be a pretty reasonable guy."

"Your relationship with him is different."

"I'm sure it is." Jason settled against the back of the bench, one arm draped casually behind Sophie. "But I know him pretty well, and I know how much he cares about you, so I can't imagine him being anything but supportive of you."

"I'm sure he loved my dad once, too, but look what happened there." Sophie explained, "They haven't spoken in years. For most of our lives—Jesse's and mine—we never saw our grandparents. It's just been the past couple of years that we've reconnected."

"What brought you back together with him?"

"Jesse decided it was time. We knew that there was a family law firm in St. Dennis, and one day, Jesse just decided he wanted to be part of it. So he came here and made an appointment with Pop . . ."

"He had to make an appointment to see his own grandfather?"

"Yes, and from what Jesse told me, that didn't go so well at first. Somehow, he convinced Pop to give him a chance—to give him one year at the firm—and Pop agreed." Sophie smiled. "My brother's a very good lawyer, and he showed 'em just how good. He and Pop sort of worked their way into an understanding, and their relationship grew from there. Ours, too— mine and Pop's. But it's just another thing I'll never really be able to forgive my dad for."

"For keeping you from your grandparents?"

She nodded. "I wish I could have known my grand-mother while she was still here."

"Hey, it's never too late. According to Curtis, she never left."

"Don't start that again." Sophie laughed.

"I'm glad to see you laugh. For a moment there, you almost looked like you were going to cry."

"For a moment, I almost did," she admitted. "My grandfather means a lot to me, and knowing he wasn't going to be happy with me upset me a lot."

"How'd you leave it with him?"

"He's okay. He's not happy, but he didn't slam the door in my face, either. I guess it's one of those situations where he knows that he's going to have to accept something he doesn't like, and that probably isn't easy for him."

"I don't see him staying mad at you for too long."

"I hope he doesn't."

"Would it be prying if I asked what you did?"

"I told him I was going to buy a restaurant."

"You mentioned that the other day, but I didn't think you were serious."

"Oh, I'm very serious. I bought a place . . ."

"Already? Where?"

"Here. In St. Dennis."

"Great. That means you're definitely planning on staying around for more than just a little while. Good news for me." Jason grinned. "So tell me about your restaurant. Would I know it? Have I been there?"

"I doubt it. It's not really a restaurant yet. It'll be awhile before it's up and running, but I'll let you know when."

"Are you going to tell me where it is?"

She paused. "I'd rather show you. And I will, on Tuesday. That's when I go to settlement. After Tuesday, it'll be all mine."

"It's a date." He tugged at a strand of her hair. "And speaking of dates, since you're not interested in having dinner with me tonight, how 'bout Friday night?"

"I'd love to. Sure." She licked ice cream from her fingers. "What time?"

"Seven work for you?"

She nodded.

"Want me to pick you up at the office?"

"No. I'll be sweaty and disgusting from moving boxes around. I'll need to go home and shower and change."

"You're staying in Jesse's old place on Hudson Street, right?"

"I am. Do you know the address?"

"Sure. We played poker there a few times."

Sophie made a face. "Poker? At Jesse's? I didn't know he played."

"He shouldn't."

"That bad, eh?"

"I don't remember him ever winning a hand."

"Slow learner." She wiped her hands on the last of the clean napkins and balled them up in her hand. "I guess I'll see you on Friday."

"I guess you will."

Jason stood and offered her a hand. As he pulled her up, her gaze lingered on his fingers. She hadn't noticed until then how big his hands were. They were hands with character, not particularly smooth, given the nature of his work, but not rough, either. She had a momentary flash of those hands on her skin, and she averted her eyes.

"Where are you parked?" he asked.

"Just down there in the lot."

"Want me to walk you?"

"No. Go eat your dinner. I'll see you soon."

"Right." He leaned down and planted a quick kiss on the side of her mouth, then started to walk away. He'd gone about ten feet, then stopped and called to her. "Hey, did you hear about the lawyer who witnessed a car accident?"

"Yeah, yeah. He handed out business cards and said, 'I saw the whole thing. I'll take either side,'" she replied. "I told you, I've heard them all."

"How 'bout this one, then . . ."

"Save it for Friday." Sophie laughed and kept on walking. "And get some new material."

Friday started out rainy and cool, but by five o'clock the clouds had lifted and the sun was shining.

"Lots of tourists coming into town this weekend. Place is going to be mobbed," Violet grumbled as she straightened up the office kitchen, something she did every Friday before she left for the weekend. Sophie had offered to help, but Violet brushed her off. "I've been taking care of this office for sixty years. I think I can manage."

"Okay, then." Sophie swung her bag over her shoulder. "So why will there be a lot of tourists this weekend?"

"The nice weather brings them out like swarms of bees. Come Saturday noon, the sidewalks will be crowded and you'll be hard-pressed to get so much as a cup of coffee at Cuppachino."

"Then I guess I'll have to get my coffee early," Sophie said. "Violet, I'm taking off now, so I'll see you on Monday."

Violet continued wiping down the counter. "Early for you, isn't it? Big date tonight?"

"Actually, I'm having dinner with Jason Bowers tonight."

"In my day, that would have counted as a date."

"It still does." Sophie smiled.

She flipped off the light in Jesse's office as she passed by, paused to consider taking a file or two home, then decided against it. Jesse would be back tomorrow afternoon, and she suspected his first stop after his home would be the office. Sophie decided to leave things just as they were.

The air smelled so fresh and clean when she stepped outside that she paused on her way to the car just to take a deep breath. She could smell the magnolias across the road and the tulips at the library on the opposite corner. Everything felt new and happy, and that suited her mood just fine. She drove off looking forward to dinner with Jason.

It was her first real date in months, her first dinner date since the last time she and Christopher had gone to Ethan's two nights before she discovered him in the backseat of his car with Anita the Skank, as Gwen still referred to the woman in texts, emails, and phone conversations. Anita was welcome to him. Eventually, he'd probably cheat on her, too.

Thinking back over their relationship, it occurred to Sophie that Anita might not have been Chris's first indiscretion. There'd been times when he'd broken dates at the last minute, begging off because of work. In retrospect, she knew there was a good chance he'd been "frying other fish," as her mother once said about her father.

Sophie sighed as she pulled into her driveway. What was the point in getting involved with anyone if you were just going to be disappointed? How do you know when to trust, and when to run? There should be something, some sign, she was thinking while she unlocked the front door, something you could rely on to know the good guys from the bad guys. She said as much to Gwen, who called forty minutes later, just as Sophie emerged from the shower.

"What brought that on?" Gwen asked.

"I have a date for dinner and I was thinking about how nice it would be if we knew right off the bat who was going to mess with our minds, as opposed to the guys you could trust." She tucked the phone between her shoulder and the side of her face. "Think of how much time and aggravation that would save."

"You mean, like maybe a little red dot in the middle of the guy's forehead that sort of pulses when he's lying?"

"I hadn't thought of anything quite that specific, but I like it. That would work."

"So who's the guy?"

"Jason Bowers."

"Jason, your grandfather's landscaper? Friend of your brother's? That Jason?"

"That Jason."

"I doubt he's a game player."

"Why would you say that? You've never met him."

"I don't have to meet him. He's Jesse's friend. Most guys don't mess around with their friends' sisters. Unless, of course, they're A-holes and just don't care."

"Point well taken," Sophie said thoughtfully. "He and Jesse are friends, but he's even closer to my grandfather. He'd never do anything to jeopardize that relationship."

"There you go, then," Gwen said cheerily. "He could be one of the good guys."

"He *is* a good guy."

"Just be careful. You haven't gone out with anyone since he-who-shall-never-be-named-again. Rebound relationships are tough on everyone." She paused. "On the other hand, rebound sex can be very good. Then again, of course, it can be very terrible." She paused again. "Most of the time, it's terrible."

"Who's talking about rebound sex?"

"No one. But you were thinking about it, right?"

"Not in those terms," Sophie said dryly. "At least, I wasn't. Until now . . ."

"You look great." Jason stood in the doorway. "I'll be the envy of every guy in Walt's."

Sophie could feel his eyes from the top of her head to the tips of her toes. She'd chosen her favorite dress, a long, lean gray knit, sleeveless with a deep cowl collar. She'd belted it with a wide swath of multicolored leather that hung loosely on her hips, stacked a row of bangles on her left wrist, and slipped into her favorite red heels. She wore round moonstone earrings set in silver and a wide silver band on the middle finger of her right hand. Aside from the wedding, it had been months since she'd been this dressed up—this decked out—and it put her in a happy frame of mind.

"Thanks. So do you." He *did* look good, she mused as she grabbed a cardigan to throw over her shoulders and a black clutch. Khakis and a lightweight brown sweater suited him.

"Another beautiful night on the Eastern Shore," Jason commented while she locked the front door behind them. "Warm temps, starry sky, light breezes. I could do without the humidity, though."

"I'd think you'd be used to it, having lived in Florida."

"That's why I could do without it. It's not as oppressive here, but still." He paused in front of the pickup. "I hope you don't mind the truck. It's my only ride, unless you'd rather take the dump truck or the Bobcat."

"Of course I don't mind." She walked to the passenger-side door. "The Bobcat might have been fun, though."

"It's only a one-seater. You'd have to sit on my lap." He opened the door for her and watched her slide in. "Of course, as small as the 'cat is, finding a parking spot would be easy."

He walked around the front of the truck. "Captain Walt's okay with you? I should have asked first."

"I love Walt's."

"Good. I heard that soft-shells from the lower Bay are in this week." Jason climbed into the cab and started the engine.

"Soft-shell what?"

"Soft-shell crabs. What kind of a St. Denniser are you?"

"The new kind. I've only been here for a week, re-member."

"I'd think it was in your DNA."

"To listen to you, one might think you're a native."

"I eat out a lot, and when you eat out in a Bay town, you get to know what's local and what's in sea-son, and you learn how to eat like a native."

"So what's the deal with soft-shell crabs?"

"They're crabs that are caught after they've molted their shells but before they've grown new ones, so they're soft," he explained. "You eat the whole crab."

"What do you mean, the whole crab?" She frowned.

"Claws, appendages, legs, torso . . ."

"That's the most disgusting thing I've ever heard." She grimaced.

Jason laughed. "Your brother loves them."

"My brother will eat anything. Surely they'll have something else on the menu."

"You just missed the oysters by a couple of weeks. The season's over for this year, but they were awe-some."

"You do realize that you're bragging on the oysters like a native."

"Gotta call 'em as I see 'em."

"So what's in season now? Besides naked crabs."

"There's always rockfish." He glanced over at her. "Striped bass. Excellent fish."

"I've had that, and I liked it."

"It's always on the menu at Walt's. And clams. Hardshells. Also good."

The truck turned onto Kelly's Point Road, which led to the municipal building, Scoop, the marina, and at the end of the dock, Captain Walt's, where thirty-seven years ago Walt brought his bride, Rexana, and his dream of having a first-class seafood restaurant right on the Bay.

"This place started out as a waterman's shack," Jason told her after they'd parked and walked the length of the dock to the door. "Walt's added on to it over the years."

"That would account for the funky way the building kind of rambles along, half on the dock, half on the shore. I think that haphazard look gives it character."

They stepped inside and waited for the hostess. Jason had made reservations, and had requested a bayside table.

"This is so pretty," Sophie said once they'd been seated. "I love looking out at the Bay."

"It'll be even prettier once the moon rises," he told her. "It sort of flows right across the water."

They studied their menus for a moment before giving their orders to the seasoned waitress. Wine was ordered and poured.

"Here's to the first of what I'm hoping will be more dinners in the moonlight." Jason raised his glass and touched the edge to Sophie's.

She met his eyes over the top of the glass, smiled, and wished she'd never thought of that red-dot-on-the-forehead thing. If such a thing existed, would it be pulsing now? And would she be willing to take a chance if it were?

"You know, right out there," he nodded in the direction of the Bay, "about one hundred and fifty or so years ago, pirates used to drop anchor, row ashore in the dead of night, and terrorize the townspeople.

They'd kidnap a group of women, put them in a makeshift pen, then ransom them back to their families. They reenacted it last year on First Families Day to raise money for the historic society."

"What do you mean, they reenacted?"

"Some of the guys dressed up in pirate gear, grabbed some women out of the crowd, and carried them to the pen, which was a roped-off area in front of the library. Then the mayor auctioned them off." Jason smirked. "Your brother got hit with a big ticket. He bid on Brooke, but she thought she was worth more and refused to leave the pen until he upped the ante."

"Wish I'd been here for that." She smiled up at the waitress who was serving her salad. "They do that every year?"

"They do something different every year. I'm not a member, so I don't know what they're doing this year."

"Did you dress up and play pirate?"

"Sure. What guy hasn't wanted to be a pirate at least once in his life? Oh, sure, he was probably eight or nine at the time, but delayed satisfaction is still satisfaction."

"Who did you kidnap?"

"What?" He frowned. The question was obviously unexpected. "Oh. Mary Beth Sykes, I think."

"I don't think I know her."

"Probably not." Head down, he took a few bites of salad.

"Looks like I have a lot to learn about my new home."

"There's always something going on here. Even in the winter. It's been really good for the merchants. The tourists have done a lot for St. Dennis. Even I've benefited."

"In what way?"

"Everyone spruces up their properties before the tourist season begins. Shops, office buildings, private homes, the B and Bs, restaurants—everyone puts on their best face to impress the day-trippers and the weekenders, hoping they'll come back, maybe even to rent one of the cottages or book rooms at the inn or one of the B and Bs for their next weeklong vacation. I'm super-busy by the first of March and running right through the fall. I had time to work on your grandfather's place because we could start early, before the big push."

"It's stunning, what you did there."

"Thanks. It was an interesting project because of its scope, but also because I had to do a lot of research before I began."

"How did you go about doing that?"

"We started with some old photos that your grandfather had. Then, once he decided which era he wanted the garden to reflect, it was just a matter of determining which plants—trees, shrubs, flowers— would have been growing here at that time. The photos helped a lot, but it wasn't always possible to identify some of the plants because of the quality of the pictures."

"You like your work."

"I love my work. There's nothing else I'd rather do."

"That's how I feel about opening my restaurant."

"Ahh, yes, the mysterious restaurant."

Sophie laughed. "Nothing mysterious about it. I'll happily show it off to you as soon as it's mine."

"Tuesday, right?"

"Right. Meet me at the office around one, and I'll take you there. That is, if the time works for you."

"I'll make it work for me."

Their entrées were served, and Sophie tried not to stare at his plate.

"Soft-shell crabs," he told her. "Don't judge."

"They just look like little aliens that have been . . ." She shook her head. "Never mind. I won't say another word. I'll just sit here quietly and eat my beautiful rockfish, and you can have at those . . . things. Enjoy."

He caught the sarcasm and smiled. "I will."

The waiter returned to their table and refilled their glasses.

"Damn, two glasses of wine with dinner," Sophie mused. "I usually limit myself to one."

"Any particular reason?"

"Several. I have a low tolerance for alcohol, it seems, so it doesn't take much to make me silly. And also because as a prosecutor for the past eight years, I worked closely with the local and state police. I would have been mortified if I'd ever been stopped for a suspicion of DUI and later had to face the same officer in court, not to mention any of the judges that I dealt with on a daily basis." She toyed with her glass for a moment. "Besides, I handled several cases where driving under the influence caused serious accidents. It's not something I'd ever do."

"Well, tonight you're not driving, so you have nothing to worry about. And since my tolerance is apparently a little better than yours, I think we're good."

They finished their entrées, passed on dessert, and wandered hand in hand to the end of the pier. The moon spread golden shadows across the water, along the marina, and onto the dock.

"It's so pretty here and it smells so good." Sophie took a deep breath of the night that was a curious mix of magnolia and salt air. "I keep telling myself that I need to see more of the town. There are so many streets I haven't driven down yet, so many shops I haven't poked into. It seems as if I travel between my house and the office and Pop's, and that's about all."

"Come Tuesday you'll have your restaurant. Or is that on the aforementioned route?"

"Not on the route, no. But I'll still be working for Jess part time. I came here to help him out, and I'm not going to leave him in the lurch."

"How are you going to swing that? Restaurant, law office?"

"I'll work it out."

"I don't know anyone like you, Sophie." He turned her around to face him. "I've never known anyone like you."

"I hope that's a good thing."

"It's a wonderful thing." He lowered his lips to hers and kissed her. There was nothing tentative about this kiss. It was direct and demanding and filled with need. Sophie pressed into him and parted her lips, inviting his tongue to explore. Her heart raced and her breath quickened, and heat spread through her body as if she'd been set on fire.

"My place or yours?" she managed to ask. Before he could respond, she said, "My place."

They walked back to his truck at a quicker pace, and as she strapped into her seat belt, Jason asked, "You sure?"

"Positive."

She watched his beautiful hands grasp the steering wheel, imagined them caressing every inch of skin on her body, and had to bite her lip to keep from making a sound that might prove embarrassing, given the fact that they were still a few blocks from her house. He pulled the truck into her driveway and before he turned off the engine, asked again, "You're sure you want to . . ."

She leaned across the console, took his face in her hands, and kissed him, her tongue teasing his, assuring him without words that she knew exactly what she was doing. His hands were at her waist, pulling her closer, and her arms wrapped around his neck. She ached for him to touch her with those hands and sighed deeply when they found their way to her breasts. She wanted out of her dress, out of everything, wanted him out of those khakis and that sweater. She pulled away and unhooked her seat belt, while his mouth found its way down the side of her throat and his hands were sliding up her thighs.

"Inside," she gasped. "We can't . . . not here . . . driveway. Neighbors . . ."

"Right. Neighbors . . ." Jason jumped out of the truck at the same time she did and followed her to the path that led to the front door. His hands were on her as she fumbled with the key, scrambling her brain to the point where she had to ask herself if the key turned to the right or to the left.

Finally, the door was open, and they were inside,

though barely, before she was on her tiptoes to reach his mouth. She kissed him hungrily, and he responded by lifting her up to trap her body between his and the nearest wall. She eased her dress up to her hips and unhooked her belt, dropping it to the floor with a clang. He pressed his body hard against hers, and she pressed back with her hips to grind against him. His lips trailed to her neck and her collarbone, and she urged him lower, but her dress was in the way. She struggled to pull it over her head and tossed it. She slipped the straps of her bra lower, pressing his mouth to her flesh with one hand and tugging on his belt with the other. He hoisted her a little higher in his arms to take her breast in his mouth, and she gasped at the shot of heat that followed.

"My room . . . ," she managed the few words.

"Where?" he gasped.

She pointed down the hall to the right and he followed, his mouth and tongue still working their magic. He pushed the door open with his foot and placed her gently on the side of the bed. She inched back toward the pillows and removed her underwear while he shed his clothes, then lay back with open arms to welcome him. Her legs encircled his hips and she moved under him to guide him and to urge him closer, then lifted herself to allow him inside her. She moaned when he entered her, arching her back and giving herself to him as completely as she could. They moved together wordlessly, an occasional sigh of pleasure the only sound they made. The rhythm picked up, increasing in tempo and the need for release. When that release finally came, it shattered her body and left her mind reeling. When she finally found her voice, it was to utter one word.

"Crap," she said softly.

"Crap?" Jason lifted his head. "Did you say 'crap'?"

"I meant, as in 'holy crap, that was amazing.'"

"Not 'holy crap, what the hell did I just do and God please keep me from doing it again'?"

"Not on your life." She pulled him back to her so that his head rested against her shoulder and chest.

Her arms around him, Sophie closed her eyes and tried to remember the last time she'd felt such a powerful connection. She searched her memory hard but couldn't recall ever having felt such a hard slam of emotion, a slam that hit her on every level. Her breathing easing almost to normal, she felt him stir. His lips kissed the hollow of her throat before starting a very slow inching downward.

"Let's see if there's anything beyond 'oh crap,'" he whispered.

She arched her back to help him find his way, leaned her head back, closed her yes, and tried to come up with a more articulate way of expressing her satisfaction.

Chapter 19 ☙

SOPHIE stretched her arms and legs, then reached over to the other side of the bed, where she felt . . . nothing but sheet. Opening her eyes and sitting up, she looked around the room. From the bathroom, she could hear whistling, soft and low, and recognizing the tune, she grinned from ear to ear. She lay back and listened. The guy was not only handsome, buff, smart, and cool, he was incredibly sweet.

When he came out of the bathroom, fully dressed, she felt a momentary stab of disappointment.

"Sorry. I have a meeting in ten minutes with a client." He leaned over to kiss her. "I should have told you I'd have to leave early."

"What time is it?"

"Almost nine."

"Not so very early," she noted. "That song you were whistling . . ."

"I looked it up on the Internet, downloaded it to my iPad. You were right. Very romantic. 'The Twelfth of Never.' A long, long time, indeed." He kissed her again. "Speaking of time—when is Jesse due in?"

"Sometime this afternoon. I'm supposed to meet

him at the office at some point, but I have no idea when."

"You're going over to Ellie's this morning, though, right?"

"Oh, the historical society thing. Yes, I was recruited."

"You know how to get there?"

She shook her head, and he gave her directions.

"Thanks. That's easy enough to find." She plumped the pillow up behind her. "What's the attire at these things?"

"Formal. Definitely. That slinky little thing you wore to the wedding would be just right."

"You remember what I wore last weekend?" She was intrigued. Christopher had never really seemed to notice what she wore.

"Couldn't take my eyes off you, babe. Could barely keep my hands to myself."

"Good to know."

"I'll see you at Ellie's." One more tiny smooch on the tip of her nose, and he was gone.

Sophie rose onto her elbows and listened as Jason's footsteps trailed down the hall, heard the front door open, then close. Had she even locked it last night? That could have proved embarrassing, had someone decided to break in. Smiling at the chaos that could have ensued, Hollywood-style, she plunked her head back against the pillow and sighed deeply. Contrary to whatever Gwen might have thought, that had *not* been rebound sex. That had been simply spectacular sex.

Christopher Lemaster, you should be so lucky.

She got out of bed, pushed the curtain aside, and

watched the black pickup back out of the driveway. Humming, she headed for the shower.

Jason left his truck halfway down Bay View Road and had to walk the rest of the way to number one, Ellie's house at the very end, where the dunes met the macadam. He surveyed the gathering crowd for Sophie, and when he couldn't locate her, he walked to the table where the raffle tickets were being sold.

"You ready to guess what's behind those doors?" asked Hamilton Forbes, who served as one of the directors of the historical society. "Ten dollars a guess."

"I'll guess twice." Jason handed him a twenty, and he was handed two large numbered cards in return.

"Make 'em count, son," Ham told him.

Jason scratched the back of his neck. He had no way of knowing what might be inside that building. He didn't know the people who lived here before Ellie did. Hell, Ellie didn't know the people who lived there, and she was related to them. He guessed a workbench on one card, and a lawn mower on the other.

"Lawn mower's been guessed about eighteen times already," Ham noted.

"Best I could come up with in a pinch." Jason shrugged. "What happens if we're all right?"

"Then you all get to split half of what we take in." Ham snagged the next person to walk by and sold a few more tickets.

Jason waved to Grace, who was deep in conversation with a woman he didn't recognize, and walked the perimeter of the group. He'd just reached the tree line when he saw Sophie out of the corner of his eye. He could pick her out in any crowd, he thought. He knew how she moved. He stood back and just watched her for a moment, taking pleasure in the way she smiled at people, the friendly way she touched this person's arm or the small of that person's back as she passed through the throng. She was so natural, her manner so easy and unaffected, and so beautiful he could barely believe that last night hadn't been the best dream he'd ever had. Could have been, but there she was, raising a few fingers in greeting and making her way to him.

Jason couldn't say at that moment where or how far this thing between them would go, but he was all in until the last living second.

"Hi," she said.

"Hi." He looped his thumbs through his waistband lest those hands reach out for her. He wasn't sure such a PDA would be appreciated. He had to settle for one of her smiles, and just for a moment, they were back at her little rented house, alone in their own little world. "You're on time."

"Barely. I had a phone call."

"Anything wrong?"

"What? Oh, no. Just a friend I worked with back in Ohio."

"Did you buy a ticket?"

"Sure. I bought two."

"What did you guess?"

"A lawn mower on one."

"So did I, and apparently so did half the people here."

"It seemed logical."

"What about the second one?"

"I guessed a carriage." She looked up and smiled,

and his heart thumped an extra few beats. "Makes sense, right? Carriage house? Carriage?"

"Well, there go Cameron and Grant with some serious-looking tools to cut off the chain, so I guess we'll know soon enough."

"Looks like Grace is going to say a few words first," Sophie noted.

"I'm so pleased to see so many of you here this morning." Grace spoke from the back porch, where she leaned against the top rail. "As you know, we pick one building to renovate as best we can with the funds we raise, and this year, we've chosen the Ryder-Cavanaugh carriage house. Ellie hasn't been able to get the lock off, so today, we're bringing out the big guns. Cam has some cutter thing that he thinks might be able to work through the chain, so we'll see."

"If he can't get it open or if the place is empty, do we get our raffle money back?" someone from the crowd called.

"Sorry, but no. As you can see, Ham Forbes is holding all the cash, and we all know he's never voluntarily given up a dime he didn't have to." She smiled. "We knew what we were doing when we put him in charge of the raffle."

Ham laughed good-naturedly along with the crowd.

"Now, I think most of us know that the original house on this property was built by the keeper of the lighthouse that was just beyond those trees." Grace pointed off to her left. "If you know your local history, you'll recall that *that* house actually stood where the carriage house stands now, the house that was burned by the pirates that used to terrorize St. Dennis, but that's another story. It's said that the foundation of the original house can be seen inside the carriage house, but I don't know anyone who's actually seen it, so we all might be in on a big discovery today. The lighthouse, of course, has been gone for many years now, though the base is still standing."

"So if I guessed that we'd find the foundation in there, and it's there, I win, right?" a woman in the front of the crowd asked.

"Sadly, no, since that's common knowledge." Grace glanced toward the carriage house. "Cameron, you and Grant ready to begin?"

"We are." Cam held up a bolt cutter. The handles were three feet long, and the cutting end looked deadly.

"Go for it," Ellie urged him.

Grant held the thick, rusted links in his hands, and Cam proceeded to cut away. When the chain finally fell to the ground, releasing the lock, Cam pushed open the high, wide double doors and the crowd cheered.

"I guess I could have done that months ago," Cam acknowledged.

"But look at all the fun we'd have missed." Grace came down from the porch. "Not to mention the fact that the historical society will benefit." She turned and gestured to Ham, as president of the organization, to follow her inside. "Here we go, people."

With Grace and Ham leading the way, the crowd pressed forward. The air inside was stale and musty, and cobwebs hung from the ceilings. The windows of the old structure had been painted black at some point in the past, so those with flashlights turned them on. There was some light chatter, then silence.

"Would you look at that!"

"I'm looking, but I don't know what I'm looking at!"

"What do you suppose that is?"

Fifty-two pairs of eyes stared at the great glass object in the middle of the floor.

"It's the lamp and the lens from the old lighthouse," an awed Grace told them.

"It's a Fresnel lens." Jason knelt down to inspect the glass.

"How would you know that?" Sophie asked.

"I did some work on the grounds at a lighthouse in Florida that was being restored. The engineers showed me how the whole thing worked. The lens surrounds the lamp sort of the way a lamp shade surrounds a lightbulb. This one was probably fixed, showed a steady stream of light. There was also a revolving lens that made a flashing light."

"Cool," someone in the back said.

"Very cool," agreed Cam. He looked over his shoulder at Ellie. "Any idea what you might want to do with it?"

She shook her head. "None whatsoever. I mean, what *does* one do with a giant glass lamp shade?"

"Sell it to a lighthouse somewhere?" someone suggested.

"This one's cracked—see there?" He pointed to deep within the lens. "Besides, I don't think any of these are still operational," Jason told them. "Most modern lighthouses use aerobeacons, some have gone to LED. I don't think there's a market for Fresnel lenses. I could be wrong, but it's doubtful. I guess maybe the Coast Guard might know."

"Maybe we should move it to the historical society's building," Ellie said.

"The building's too small." Grace appeared thoughtful. "Maybe we could put it on display somewhere, though, if Ellie agreed."

"My lens is your lens." Ellie shrugged. "If you want to move it, be my guest."

"I suppose for now, this is as good a place for it as any, until someone comes up with a plan for it." Cam stood, his hands on his hips, still staring at their find.

"Anyone have 'lens for the old lighthouse' on their raffle card?" Grace glanced around. No hands shot up.

"Then I thank you all for your donations to the organization. Now, let's put those flashlights to work and see if we can locate the foundation of the old house that's supposed to be in here."

Several dozen flashlights sent beams of light around the darkened structure. Finally, Cameron called out from the left side of the building.

"I think this is it." He knelt down and moved some dirt away from a line of random stones. "Looks like it started here and went across the back of the building."

"I believe you're right." Grace came closer to inspect the rubble. "It's always gratifying when reality proves a legend to be true."

She whipped out her camera and began to take pictures. "Story and photos in Thursday's edition of the *St. Dennis Gazette*," she told everyone. "This is an exciting day. Ellie, thank you for allowing us to break into your carriage house."

"Thank you for suggesting it," Ellie said. "I've been wondering what was in this place for months. I just found my great-aunt's croquet set in the corner, and I'm not sure what all else we might find."

"I found some empty paint cans." Grant held one up. "There are a few old tires, some garden tools, and a rusty bicycle along the back wall."

"There's an old pair of rubber boots under the window," Gabby, Ellie's fourteen-year-old half sister, piped up.

"Stick your foot in one and see if there's anything inside," Cameron teased.

"Ewwww!" Gabby and her friend—who Sophie recognized as Steffie's niece, Paige of the pink braids—both looked appalled.

"Now, let's see if we can figure out what needs to be done to restore this fine old building." Grace was still beaming with the thrill of discovery. "My thought was that we break into teams, and that each team would adopt a different part of the building to work on. Try to keep your experience in mind when you sign up. Cameron, since you're acting as our general contractor, you don't need to sign up for anything specific, but I'd like everyone else to commit to a portion of the work, however small." She glanced around the crowd. "Look around, see what you'd like to do, then meet me out at the table where Ham was selling the raffle tickets and we'll sign you up. First workday will be next Saturday. But please, please don't sign up to do a job if you aren't sure you're going to follow through. If you say you're going to work, you're going to have to work. We'd like to include Ellie's house and the carriage house on the next Independence Day tour, so we need to get the job done quickly."

"Want to be on my team?" Jason's hand was on the small of Sophie's back. Through her T-shirt he could feel her warmth, and it took him back to last night, and this morning, and the smoothness of her skin.

"Sure. What shall we sign up for?"

"I'm thinking maybe the windows—paint and repair—then maybe restore the old window boxes for the exterior."

Sophie followed Jason to one of the five small windows in the structure.

"I'd like Cam's opinion," he continued, "but I think we'll need to scrape the paint from the panes and from the mullions, then maybe regrout the glass." He inspected the first window, then went on to the second. "The window boxes won't be a problem. They look solid enough. I think we'll just paint and rehang them, then plant them up." He moved on to the next window and Sophie followed. "You in?"

She hesitated, and for a moment, he thought she was going to decline.

"Sure. I can spare a little time on a few Saturdays. You don't think it will take too long, do you?"

"Why? You going somewhere?"

"No. But . . ." She appeared thoughtful. "If it goes more than three weeks, do you think we could work on Sundays instead of Saturdays?"

"I don't see why not." He looked over his shoulder and asked, "You got some hot Saturday dates coming up?"

She shook her head and started to say something, when Cameron walked over.

"So, are we all set for Tuesday?" Cam asked Sophie.

"I'm all set. You've got everyone lined up?"

Cameron nodded. "One o'clock."

"I'll be there."

"See you then."

Jason listened, but didn't ask. He didn't have to. Obviously, Sophie had hired Cam to work on her new building. Later, as Sophie signed up for her work project, Jason managed to take a few steps back to where Cam stood.

"So, you're doing work on Sophie's new place," he said as if he knew all about it.

"Yup. Putting a rush on it for her, pulling guys from another job, bringing my best subs in so she can open in time to cash in on some of the early tourist traffic."

"Nice of you. By the way," he asked, trying to appear nonchalant, "where is it?"

"Didn't she tell you?" Cam asked.

"No."

"Then you're going to have to ask her. My lips are sealed."

"Oh, come on. Don't be a jerk." Though he'd have been hard pressed to admit it, it bugged him just a little that she wouldn't tell him but she'd already shared her new place—her dreams—with Cam.

"I'm not trying to be a jerk. She made us promise not to tell anyone about the place. Since she hasn't released us from that promise . . ." Cam shrugged.

Sophie and Ellie, deep in conversation, walked in their direction. Jason tried, but he couldn't look away from Sophie. He liked the way she walked, the intensity of her expression as she chatted with Ellie.

"I'm going to go out on a limb and guess that look of lust isn't being inspired by my fiancée." Cam lowered his voice. "Otherwise, if you were looking at Ellie like that, I'd have to hurt you."

Jason took a stick of gum from his pocket and unwrapped it, folding it into his mouth while pointedly ignoring Cam's remark.

"So what's going on?" Cam asked. "And since when?"

"Don't know what you're talking about." Jason jammed his hands into his pockets.

"Oh, please. It's written all over your face." Cam smirked. "So the questions remain. Since when, and does Jesse know?"

"Does Jesse know what?" Sophie asked as she and Ellie joined them.

"Does Jesse know about the project." Jason shot Cam a conspiratorial look. "You know, in case he and Brooke want to participate."

"I'll see him in a few hours. We're having dinner with Pop. Maybe you could join us."

Sophie smiled at him and Jason couldn't help himself. He had to smile back. She brought out something in him that he couldn't put a finger on, except to know it was something he'd never felt before.

"I have Logan tonight," he recalled.

"Maybe Brooke will want Logan to come with us, since she's been away for a week."

"I mentioned that to Logan, but he said he'd see her when she got home and he didn't have to see her all night." Jason shrugged. "Brooke, on the other hand, might have other plans."

"Let me know if that changes." Sophie glanced at her watch. "I should go. I want to get a few things put away at the office before Jesse gets back."

"We're done here anyway." Jason looked around at the dispersing crowd. "Most everyone's leaving now."

"What's on your schedule for tomorrow?" She started to walk toward the street, and he walked along with her.

"I'm hoping to put the finishing touches on your grandfather's garden."

"All day?"

"Probably."

"Well, I guess I won't see you until Tuesday." Sophie looked genuinely disappointed.

"I'll be at your office at one."

"Make it twelve forty-five," she told him. "I'm supposed to meet Cameron at one at the property."

"I can't wait to see this place." Jason stopped at the front fender of her car. He really wanted to kiss her, but thought twice of it. There were lots of folks mulling around, and he suspected it would make her uncomfortable. It was still too new, whatever this was that was between them. There'd be other times, he reminded himself. Like Tuesday. "How 'bout we go out to dinner on Tuesday night to celebrate?"

"I'd love that. Yes, let's celebrate." Her eyes were shining, and he could barely stand it.

"It's a date, then." He opened her car door for her, then closed it when she got inside. She started the car and pulled away from the side of the road, passing him after she turned around in Ellie's driveway.

" 'Bye," she mouthed the word, and for a moment, he thought she might have blown a subtle kiss in his direction.

Jason watched the car disappear, then made his way down the road to his pickup. This night wasn't going to be anything like last night, but he had Tuesday to look forward to, and who knew how many nights would follow after that?

⌒⌒

Early Tuesday morning, singing along with the radio at the top of her lungs to Elton John's "Candle in the Wind"—the original version—Sophie drove to River Road for her last look around before the closing later that morning. She'd stopped at Cuppachino for her morning coffee, but at eight thirty, most of the regulars had already come and gone. Just as well, she reminded herself. She was a bundle of nerves and probably would be until the closing was over and she had the deed to her property in her hands. She didn't want to discuss it with anyone, didn't want to explain what she was doing until it was done, because if something went wrong at the last minute, she'd have to be explaining over and over why her restaurant wasn't going to happen after all. There were times, such as this, when her maternal grandmother's favorite adage—"The less said, the better"—definitely applied.

The words died in her throat as she approached her destination. Her foot on the brake, she all but stopped dead in the middle of the road. There, in the property next to hers, stood a mountain—*three* mountains—of something that looked horrible and smelled even worse, and a dump truck that was backing in through the opened gates appeared to be about to dump yet another load of whatever it was onto the ground, right next to the fence between the restaurant and what had been a vacant lot next door.

She flew onto the parking area in front of her place and jumped out of her car.

"Hey!" she called as she ran along the fence, waving to the driver to get his attention. When that failed, she ran past the gate and onto the freshly blacktopped yard. "Hey, stop!"

The closer she got, the worse the smell.

She ran up to the cab of the truck and banged on the window.

"Stop! What do you think you're doing?" she demanded.

The driver leisurely rolled down the window. "Huh?"

"You can't dump that . . . that stuff here," she panted.

The driver—identified as Lennie by the flap on his shirt pocket—appeared confused.

"You're going to have to dump this . . . *stuff* someplace else." She looked around and spotted an empty spot across the parking lot. "Like over there." She pointed across the yard. "Move all this over to there."

"My orders were to dump it here." Lennie pointed to the stinking, steaming pile that he'd already dumped next to the fence.

"Well, that must have been a mistake. I'm asking you nicely to please . . ."

"Take it up with the boss, lady."

And with that, Lennie began to back up the truck.

"Fine. Fine." She waved for his attention. "Where can I find him?"

"Right there." Lennie pointed to the black pickup that was just pulling in through the gate.

Sophie walked around the back of the dump truck prepared to give someone a piece of her mind. Who dumps huge—gigantic, really—piles of stinking soil next to someone else's property? She rounded the cab in time to see Jason hop out of the pickup.

"Hey," he said, obviously pleased to see her. "What are you doing here?"

"She's giving me shit, that's what she's doing!" Lennie yelled through the open window. "Wants me to move the mulch, but I told her . . ."

"You . . . you . . . this place . . . ?" Sophie stammered.

"Is mine, yeah. But what are *you* doing here?" Jason repeated.

"Jason, you have to tell him to put all that stuff back onto his truck and move it over there." She again pointed to the place she'd determined would be the farthest from the fence.

"Why would I do that?"

"Because it stinks, that's why."

"Yeah, it does. But what difference does it make where he puts it?"

"You can smell it from next door."

"So what?" He looked over at the old restaurant. "It's vacant."

"Not for long."

"What do you mean, not for long?" Jason's eyes began to narrow. "Oh, please tell me that you did not . . ."

"I did. I bought it."

"You bought . . . ? It was *you*?"

"What was me?"

"You're the one who bought that place?"

"Yes." It was her turn to be confused. "What's the problem?"

"The problem is that I've been trying to buy it for the past six months. The woman who owned it . . ."

"Enid Walsh."

"Whoever. She was supposed to let me know when she decided to sell it. How'd you get her to sell?"

"What difference does it make now?"

"I just want to know how you managed to buy it out from under me."

"I didn't buy it out from under you. I bought it because I want to reopen the restaurant." She took a step back away from him, her hands on her hips.

"I don't suppose you could have done that somewhere else?"

"I wanted this place."

"So did I." He blew out a long breath. "You didn't think to tell me this?"

"Was I obligated to?"

"Not obligated, but under the circumstances . . . I mean, I thought we were, you know . . . a thing. It would have been nice if you'd told me your plans."

"I was going to tell you, but things . . . took off in a different direction the other night, and you were in a hurry in the morning. Besides, I thought it would be fun to surprise you."

"I had an appointment. I told you that. And for the record, I hate surprises."

She sighed. "Look, the bottom line is that it's done. I'm going to open a restaurant there, so you have to move those piles. The odor will turn away customers."

"What customers? Doesn't look to me like you're ready to open for business."

"No, but I will be." She tried to stare him down. Jason didn't blink. "So how long do you think that"— she pointed to the mulch piles—"will be there?"

He turned to calculate. "I ordered what I thought I'd need for at least the next month. So I'd say, oh, four weeks maybe."

"And it's going to continue to stink like this?"

"Well, it is getting warmer," he told her. "That last pile he dumped, that's mushroom soil."

"What's mushroom soil?"

"It's what comes out of the mushroom houses after the mushrooms have been harvested." He stared down at her. "You do know what mushrooms grow in, right?"

"Not exactly."

"It's basically a mixture of hay and grass and horse manure. It arrives smelly—the hay and the grass ferment, and the horse manure, well, you know, is *manure*. So it pretty much stays that way for a while. The warmer it gets, the stronger the smell."

She grimaced. "That's disgusting."

"It makes a great soil enhancer. People like it for their gardens because their plants grow better."

"Yeah, well, it won't do much to enhance my customers' dining experience."

"Sorry, but it is what it is."

"Great." She exhaled loudly. "This is just great."

"When do you figure on opening?" He studied the

building for a long moment. "It must need a lot of work."

"It does, but Cameron has a schedule. He thinks he and his crew will need no more than three weeks, start to finish."

"How come they haven't started already?"

"I don't officially own it for another . . ." She glanced at her watch. "Another forty-five minutes. Closing's this morning."

"So you don't actually own it yet."

She shook her head.

"So you haven't made any investment yet."

"Not financially, but emotionally . . ."

"Sell it to me." He grabbed her hands. "I'll give you five thousand dollars more than what you paid for it."

"No."

"Ten."

"Are you crazy? No. This is going to be my restaurant." She pulled her hands from his. "And what would you do with it? Knock it down so you can stash more piles of stinky, dirty soil stuff?"

"Of course not. That was going to be my shop. Retail. I plan to have a full nursery here. Trees, flowers, pots . . ."

"Wind chimes and garden gnomes?" she scoffed.

"If my customers want them, yes. Sophie, I've been dreaming about this for months. I started making plans to buy this vacant lot the first time I saw it. My plan all along was to buy the adjoining parcel and have my business go retail."

"Why can't you build a place on your own land?"

"Because this is where I'll be growing things and

parking my equipment. Backhoes and trucks and tractors. There's no room for a shop here."

"I'm sorry that I threw a wrench into your dream, but I have dreams, too. And my dream is to renovate that place next door and open my own restaurant."

"What's wrong with being a lawyer?" he asked. "I thought you liked it."

"I do like it. I'll like owning my own restaurant better."

"Why can't you find another place for your restaurant?" he persisted.

"Because this is where I want to be. Why can't you find another place for your shop?"

"Because my business is already here." He ran a hand through his hair. "Look, if you took my offer, you could find another place. You could make a nice little profit without even lifting a finger."

"I don't want to sell, and I don't want to look for another place. I've found my place, and that"—she pointed across the fence—"is it. I'm planning to put tables outside. I can't have people sitting down to eat with that stench in the air. You're going to have to move that stuff."

"What do you propose I do, Sophie? That's several tons of mulch and topsoil, and yes, mushroom soil. It's not exactly a shovel-and-wheelbarrow job. Sorry, but it stays where it is until it's sold." He paused. "Besides, what difference do you think it would make if I move it another hundred or so feet away? It's still going to smell."

At a standoff, they stared at each other.

Finally, he just shook his head, muttered something about someone having unrealistic expectations, then turned and walked away, right to his pickup. He got in and drove off without looking back.

"Fine. Just . . . fine." She walked through the gate and across the broken macadam on her side of the fence.

"Fine," she repeated as she got into her car and turned the key.

She was still muttering to herself when she arrived at the Realtor's office for the closing. She forced a cheeriness she genuinely would have felt if not for her argument with Jason. He could move that pile of stinky mess if he really wanted to. And he could build a little something over there on his own property if he really wanted a small shop. He didn't need her place to sell his plants and his pots and his damned garden gnomes. Why couldn't he be happy growing his plants and designing landscapes for his customers? And why did he need a shop, anyway? From everything that she could see, he was plenty busy enough as it was.

Sophie signed her name where she was supposed to and made polite chatter with the lawyer for the seller and the Realtor, but as soon as she received her packet of documents, she was out the door. Cameron was bringing his electrician and his plumber at one, and she intended to have the place open and ready for their inspection at twelve fifty. Jason Bowers could go sulk until he grew up and accepted the fact that she was as entitled to buy that building as he was, that her dreams were just as important as his. It wasn't her fault that she got to Enid Walsh before he did—okay, so maybe she had a little help with that, but still, she had no way of knowing that he'd had his eye on the place all this time. How could she have?

Too late now, she thought. *What's done is done.* Jason was just going to have to come around or live with the consequences.

And so, a little voice inside her whispered, would she.

Chapter 20 ⌣

THE electricity in the former Walsh's restaurant had been turned on as per Sophie's request, and Cameron had removed the boards from the window, so in spite of the gray clouds that blocked the sun, there was ample light inside. Sophie had dusted off a few chairs and a table, and now Cameron sat across from her, his clipboard in one hand.

"So we already talked about the windows. I'm suggesting we go for the most energy-efficient ones you can afford. I've listed prices for several different grades on the estimate, and you can look them over, make your decision, and let me know so I can order them right away. We might even want to put a rush on them. Now, the floors are going to have to be refinished—I have a guy I use who does a terrific job, I can bring him in if you want—you're going to want to use a really durable finish, like a bar top, or the stuff they use on basketball floors." He glanced up at her. "Feel free to stop me at any point if you have any questions."

"What?" She tuned back in. For a moment, activity on the other side of the fence had distracted her, and for just a split second, she'd thought that the pile of mulch was being removed. It was, but only as much as filled the pickup, which then drove through the gates and sped away.

"I asked if you had any questions so far."

Yes. Why are men such jerks?

She paused to consider that someone as well educated as she should be able to express herself more articulately. But seeing that fetid pile of mulch rising like Vesuvius on the other side of the fence seemed to bring out the worst in her, so under the circumstances, *jerk* was the best she could come up with.

"Not so far." Sophie made an effort to sound pleasant. It wasn't Cam's fault that Jason was being so hardheaded about his stupid, reeking piles of rank soil. What had he called it? *Mushroom* soil. As if giving it a name made it less offensive.

"Okay, then." Cam continued. "The plumber's coming back tomorrow after the water's been turned on. I think the pipes look fine, but you'll want him to check it out, and the municipal code changed within the last six years, so we'll have to make some changes in the plumbing and the electrical systems to bring everything up to code. You need new fixtures in the bathrooms, so make a trip out to Snyder's on the highway and pick out what you need. Doesn't have to be fancy, but you want things to look nice and to be serviceable. I'll call out there before you go and let them know to give you my discount."

He looked up at her again, waiting for her to say something.

"Sophie?"

"Oh. Okay." She nodded.

"Okay, what?"

"Okay, what you said."

"Nice try." Cameron repeated what he'd just said, then asked, "Where are you, anyway? Just so excited about buying this place that you can't focus on the nitty-gritty?"

"I guess." She nodded. "I am pretty excited."

"Want me to go over the rest of this later?"

"No, let's finish up. I guess I need the bottom line on the renovations sooner rather than later."

"I won't have final numbers until after the plumber finishes his inspection tomorrow, but this is how it's shaping up so far."

"Seriously?" She blinked. "I thought it would be a lot more than that."

"The structure's good and the roof is good, two big items right there. There is work outside—painting and the windows—but most of the work is going to be confined to the kitchen. I won't start that until after the exterminator's done his thing." Cam paused. "You did call the exterminator, right?"

"He'll be here in about an hour."

"And remember that none of this," he tapped the clipboard, "reflects any repairs or replacements you might have to make on the appliances."

"The repair guy's coming tomorrow. I couldn't find anyone local, so I called the manufacturer and they gave me some names. I did find a repairman from Annapolis who was able to fit me in tomorrow afternoon. As far as the refrigerator and the freezer are concerned, I called the refrigeration guy you recommended. He'll be here on Thursday morning."

"Sounds like you're all set, then." He removed a

copy of his estimate from the clipboard and passed it over to her. "Call me after the exterminator is finished and we'll go from there."

"Thanks, Cam." She stood at the same time he did, then walked with him to the door. "I really appreciate all your help."

"Oh, you wanted that sign taken down." He went out to his truck and returned with a ladder, which he set up under the sign. Five minutes later, he brought the large wooden oval into the restaurant and asked Sophie, "Where do you want this? It's pretty heavy."

"Over there is fine." She pointed to a space along the wall. "Thanks, Cam."

"Anything else you need while I'm here?" he asked from the doorway.

"No, I'm good. Thanks. For everything." She walked outside.

"Call me if you think of something you want done."

"Will do."

Sophie watched Cam jump into his truck and waved as he turned around before driving onto the roadway. She glanced over at Jason's lot while pretending to ignore it, but his truck wasn't there, and neither, she assumed, was he. She went back inside, her emotions still a jumble. She wished she could leave the doors open to air the place out, but the smell from the other side of the fence was too strong. She made the decision right then and there that the mess on the other side of the fence wasn't going to ruin this day for her.

Sophie was delighted to have this place, to have an opportunity to prove to everyone—as well as to herself—that she could make this restaurant work. She touched each chair as she passed by and turned on every light switch. With a broom that she found in the ladies' room, she swept the dining room floor to pass the time while she waited for the exterminator. When she finished that chore, she sat at a table and read over Cameron's preliminary estimate. She got a bottle of water from her car and took a long drink, standing next to the SUV and pretending not to be watching for activity on the other side of the fence.

It was so annoying that he wasn't there to see her ignoring him.

The exterminator arrived on time, and she declined his invitation to follow him around to view his findings.

"That's okay, but thanks." She forced a smile. "You just go on and do your thing, and I'll just sit here and do mine until you're finished."

She sat at the window table with a pad of paper in her hand and wrote out the menus for opening week. Breakfasts would be just as Shelby had suggested, hearty fare to entice the early risers who made their living on the water, lighter fare after eight A.M. The watermen could expect a simple menu: eggs scrambled or over easy, bacon or sausage, home-fried potatoes, toast. She wondered if anyone local had homemade jam for sale.

Saturday night at dinner, after Pop had announced to Jesse and Brooke that she was going to be a part-time lawyer and a part-time cook, Brooke told her to call Clay ASAP and make sure he'd have enough eggs from the flock of chickens he and Lucy were raising to supply her on a daily basis. Maybe if needed, he could buy some extra hens. Sophie had caught up with him at Cuppachino yesterday, and he promised to meet with her to go over what organic vegetables she thought she'd need. He gave her the name of another local farmer to contact in the event he couldn't supply her with everything in sufficient quantity, but promised if her place did well, he'd plant with her in mind next year. As a brand-new business, she didn't anticipate much in the way of customers for the first few weeks, but it was gratifying to know that someone thought she might do so well that one supplier wouldn't be able to keep up with her demands.

She doodled a few daisy-like flowers, then started the breakfast list she'd start serving around eight. A different specialty omelet each day, maybe crepes occasionally. Breakfast meats might not be a big item with the film people, though turkey sausage might work out, and definitely the fruit and yogurt she'd previously thought about. Somewhere she had a fabulous recipe for granola, if she could remember where she'd put it. Muffins, of course, but she'd buy them from Brooke. Maybe pancakes or waffles in the cooler months.

The lunch menu would be more extensive, but still simple: a signature soup—she'd have to work on that—plus a soup of the day in season: corn and crab in the summer, pumpkin or butternut squash, clam chowder, or oyster stew in the fall and winter. For a moment, it crossed her mind that if things didn't go well this summer, she might not be here to see the winter, but she dismissed the thought immediately. No point in inviting negativity into her new little world.

Salads would vary with whatever was fresh and

available: strawberries, goat cheese, and candied walnuts with spring mix in early summer, a Cobb or tossed salad at the height of summer to take advantage of all the fresh produce, and Waldorf late in the season when apples would be plentiful.

Sandwiches, of course. Burgers were a necessity, but if she could buy crab locally she could do crab cakes as well. BLTs made from garden lettuce, applewood-smoked bacon from that farm over in Ballard, and heirloom tomatoes from Clay. Maybe a grilled or roasted vegetable wrap. Chicken salad from that recipe her aunt Libby gave her.

Desserts would be as simple as Shelby had suggested: brownies, and cupcakes from Brooke's shop, plus a dessert of the day, like that lemon meringue pie Violet mentioned, and a pound cake from Gramma Rose's recipe, and something from Lilly Cavanaugh. Ellie had promised she'd drop off a bunch of recipes. Sophie knew she'd find something that she could make ahead of time.

And that would be it for the menu, other than beverages. Coffee, tea, sparkling water, iced tea. Maybe a few sodas, though she didn't drink them herself and wasn't sure they fit in with her plan to serve mostly local and natural. There wasn't much natural about any soda she'd ever had, but she'd think about that.

She sketched out an ad she'd place in the *St. Dennis Gazette* on the Thursday before she opened. How big an ad could she afford? She'd have to talk to Grace to see what she suggested.

She heard tires on the gravel out front and raised her head hopefully, but it was just a Jeep that was using her parking lot to turn around. A few minutes later, a red truck stopped in front of the mulch yard and an older man hopped out, opened the gate, then drove through. How long before she stopped looking up every time she heard a noise outside?

Until Jason found his way over to apologize.

Would that happen? She sighed, realizing that she didn't know him well enough to know if his sense of fairness was stronger than his ego. And it *was* a matter of fairness, she insisted. She had every right to pursue this property, as much right as he did. Still, she understood that he was disappointed—wouldn't she have been, if somehow he'd beaten her to the punch and purchased the restaurant while she was back in Ohio?

Of course she would. The real question was whether or not she'd have thrown a tantrum over it. All right, perhaps *tantrum* was too strong a word. And whether or not she'd have done something that would impact the success of his business. She'd planned on alfresco dining this summer, but how could she seat patrons outside to dine with that gross smell drifting over the fence? How appetizing was that?

The exterminator, Ed Sellers, came out of the kitchen.

"Is there a key to the second floor?" he asked.

She took it from her bag and handed it to him. "What's the bad news?"

"You got ants. Mice, a'course, and a boatload of stink bugs. Little bastards are everywhere this year." He took the key and went upstairs.

It could be worse, she told herself, and it didn't sound like anything that couldn't be taken care of.

She crossed her fingers and waited until Ed reappeared.

"Same visitors upstairs as down. Basement?"

She shook her head—no, the building didn't have one.

"Okay, then, here's what I can do." For the next fifteen minutes, Ed outlined his plan for ridding the building of every living thing. "Now, you're going to want to keep the place closed up for a night, but after that, you'll be good to go."

"I can live with that."

"Good. How 'bout I come in first thing on Friday morning? You'll have the place back on Saturday afternoon."

"Perfect. I'll see you on Friday."

He handed her his estimate and she folded it to put aside for later review. After he left, she took a peek. The number circled at the bottom wasn't nearly as much as she'd feared, and she breathed a sigh of relief. So far, so good, as far as the expenditures were concerned.

Jesse had agreed to give her the afternoon off, since she'd done so much to organize his office in his absence. She'd been amused to find that it made no difference to her brother if he had to search his floor for a file or if he found it neatly filed away.

"As long as I know where to find it when I need it, what difference does it make where you put it?" he'd asked after she showed him the new file room she'd set up.

"Sometimes someone other than you might need the case." She fought back a smile. The remark was so typical of his haphazard, devil-may-care attitude.

But in the end, he'd admitted that he was impressed with the work she'd done, and offered her the afternoon to take care of her business.

"But I expect you here tomorrow at two P.M.," he'd told her.

"I'll be here," she promised, and she would be. Hopefully by then her head would have stopped spinning. Her brain was threatening to go on overdrive with all she had to do, now that she owned the building she'd coveted. What was the saying about being careful what you wished for?

She made a list of all she had to do, in order of priority. When everything had been written down, she felt a rare migraine coming on. She decided to break the list down into sections—the dining room, the kitchen, the restrooms, the exterior. It looked more manageable to her once those lists were on separate pieces of paper. A mind game, to be sure, but right then, her mind was a churning mess.

Today she could wipe down all the tables and chairs, clean the dining room floor, and wash the windows. The kitchen would remain off-limits until the appliances had been dealt with and Ed had finished doing his thing. Satisfied she had a workable plan, she locked the door and drove home to pick up some cleaning supplies. She grabbed a quick take-out lunch from The Checkered Cloth and took it back to River Road.

The black pickup was in the middle of the lot when she returned. She slowed as she drove by, and took her sweet time gathering her things and getting out of the car and unlocking the front door, giving Jason ample opportunity to see her, but he was nowhere in sight. She went inside, carrying her lunch and a bucket filled with cloths and bottles of heavy-duty cleaners. She went back out to the car once for the vacuum, but there was still no sign of Jason.

Annoyed that she couldn't have annoyed him by her presence, she plugged in the vacuum and went to work. When she was finished, she scrubbed every table and chair. Several were a bit wobbly; those she set aside for repair while she finished the task of cleaning the big room. When she was done, the place smelled like Lysol, but the dust and cobwebs were gone and she could see out the windows. Her arms and her back ached and she was exhausted, but it was one day down and counting, and she felt pretty damned good about that. She locked up for the day and took her take-out lunch, which, in her cleaning frenzy, she'd forgotten to eat.

She was dead on her feet when she arrived at her house and barely could stand in the shower. She'd discovered muscles she'd forgotten that she had, and none of them were happy about having been reawakened. She dried her hair, pulled a long T-shirt over her head, and collapsed onto her bed. Tomorrow would be her first day of double duty—restaurant in the morning, the law office at two. She fell asleep wondering if perhaps she'd been a tad cocky about her ability to balance both.

On Wednesday morning, Jason drove through the gates of his yard slowly, his eyes fixed on the old stone building on the other side of the fence. Sophie's car was parked by the door, the lights were on, and rock music was drifting across the lot. He could see a form moving about behind the front window. If things were different between them, he'd park next to her and go inside, help her out with anything she might be doing.

Funny how things can go from zero to sixty in the blink of an eye. One minute you're at the start of something big; the next, you're chopped meat. He was still trying to figure out how that conversation had escalated so damned quickly.

Sophie bossing around the guy who'd been trying to deliver mulch was probably a good place to start. Jason accusing her of buying the property out from under him would probably be right up there on the list. As if he had any right to it in the first place. As soon as the words were out of his mouth, he regretted the accusatory tone, but there was no taking it back. She'd been on a verbal tear, and there'd been no way to stop her at that point.

He'd wanted to explain that he'd had the mulch piles dumped near the fence because his heavy equipment was parked on the other side of the lot. Until recently, he'd had no reason to expect that someone else—least of all Sophie—had bought the building next door. It never occurred to him that anyone else would be interested. He'd just assumed that the building would, in time, belong to him.

He reminded himself of what happened when one assumed.

He did, in fact, feel like an ass.

All of which did nothing to resolve the situation. If he hadn't been so pissed off, he would have told her that moving those tons of soil and mulch wasn't as easy as picking up a shovel. He'd paid to have them dumped there, and he'd have to pay someone to move them. If he'd had time to cool off—and if she hadn't stomped away—he'd have explained that sooner or later those piles would be gone, because he'd have sold and delivered it to his clients. Hell, some of that mulch would be spread around her grandfather's garden by the end of the week.

That she had actually purchased that place was still gnawing at him. Yes, she'd told him that she bought a restaurant, but it had never occurred to him that she meant the place next door. He didn't think of it as a restaurant. To him, it was a stone building that would make a great retail shop. All along, he thought she'd been talking about some other place, some other place that he didn't know about. There was still a lot about St. Dennis that he didn't know.

He parked the pickup and got out, the day's work schedule in his hands. His crews were already there, waiting for their assignments. He tried to put the argument with Sophie behind him while he walked across the lot.

"Hey, boss, did you see someone's in that place next door?" Kevin, one of his foremen, asked.

Jason nodded and started to go over the assignments.

"What do you suppose is going in there?"

"It used to be a restaurant," someone said. "Nice place. We used to go there when I was a kid."

"Be nice if it was a restaurant again. We could stop in, pick up lunch. Convenient," another of the guys chimed in.

"Wonder who bought it?"

"If you girls are finished gossiping, I have the schedule for today." Jason held up the clipboard. The last thing he wanted to hear was how great it would be to have a restaurant right next door. As if that were a good idea.

Fifteen minutes later, he was back in the cab of his truck, his work crews settled and the scope of each job reviewed. He'd turned the key in the ignition, but he was having a hard time driving away when he could see Sophie through the glass. He wanted to talk to her, but what would he say? He was sorry that she was upset over the mulch piles, but he couldn't just wave a magic wand and have them disappear. He couldn't apologize for being upset that she beat him to the property, because he'd be lying. What good was an insincere apology? He hadn't been exaggerating when he told her that he'd planned his business expansion around that property.

Besides, didn't she owe him an apology as well? How was anyone supposed to have known that she was opening a restaurant there? Lennie the delivery guy hadn't known, but she'd yelled at the man as if he should have. For that matter, she'd yelled at Jason as if somehow he'd known and had made the decision to store the mulches and soils in that particular spot just to irritate her.

He was having a real hard time reconciling the crazy woman who'd been yelling like a banshee in his yard just the day before with the woman who'd brought him into her bed just a few days earlier. That woman, *that* was a woman he was starting to think of as the one who could be worth staying with. The unreasonable harpy? Not so much. Which one, he wondered, was the real Sophie? How to get through to the former without reawakening the latter?

And how was he supposed to go about making things right when he really hadn't done anything wrong?

Chapter 21 ⌒

SOPHIE hit the ground running at six A.M. By seven she was in the hardware store picking out the paint for the chairs and tables and carrying her newly purchased supplies to her car. She'd slept so soundly that when the alarm sounded that morning, she'd bolted upright as if she'd been shot. Aching and tired, she'd dragged herself downstairs for coffee and drank her first cup hanging over the railing on the small back porch, telling herself that by the time she finished the work at the restaurant, she'd be in shape and feeling fine. Somehow her back and her arms weren't getting the message.

The sun had already warmed the dining area when she arrived on River Road and she carried the boxes of paint, rollers, and brushes into the building. She wished she could leave the door and windows open, but the smell from next door was still too strong. She wondered if there was something that could be sprayed on those piles, like the stuff she saw advertised on TV that refreshed fabrics.

She moved all of the furniture to the perimeter of the room before spreading a newly purchased drop cloth on the floor. She lined up the chairs, opened the first can of black paint, and went to work. She painted the first chair, then stood back to assess the completed job. The paint she'd chosen was a semigloss, and even as it was drying, she knew she'd made the right choice. Sophie liked the way the paint accentuated the lines of the chair. She moved on to the next chair, and the one after that. Her arm was getting a little tired, but determined to stick to her schedule, she kept going.

The sound of car tires out front drew her attention. Sophie straightened up, hoping to see a black pickup parked next to her SUV, but instead of the truck, there were two sedans, one on either side of her car. She opened the door and stepped out just as Brooke, Steffie, and Vanessa hopped out of one and Lucy Sinclair Madison and Ellie hopped out of the other.

"We came to help," Brooke told her. "Jesse said you could probably use a few extra hands this morning, so we thought we'd come over to see what you need."

Ellie handed her a cardboard container of coffee and a small white bag. "We thought we'd bring you a little something from Cuppachino. There's a strawberry pecan muffin in the bag. Brooke made them this morning, and I for one can attest to their deliciousness."

"Thanks so much," Sophie said, one hand on her heart. She'd never expected anyone to offer help, not even Jesse. That the women she was still getting to know wanted to pitch in touched her. "I appreciate the coffee and the muffin, but really, you don't need to . . ."

"Of course we don't. But we're happy to," Vanessa

assured her. "We all own our own businesses and we all know how hard it is to pull everything together, especially if you're on your own, the way most of us were when we first started."

"Besides, we heard this was going to be the new 'in' place in St. Dennis, and we wanted to be able to say we knew it when," Lucy added.

"Guys, this is so nice of you."

"Then invite us in and show us around." Brooke took Sophie's arm, and the others followed them into the dining room.

"I was just starting to paint the chairs," Sophie explained.

"They look fabulous. So much better in black," Ellie noted, and the others nodded their agreement. "Good call."

"I'm debating on whether to paint the tables to match or some other color," Sophie said.

"The lines are very clean and simple," Steffie noted. "I'd think maybe white. Two coats of the most durable white you can find."

"I think maybe you're right," Sophie agreed. "I'll need a trip back to the hardware store. I only bought black."

"What color for the walls? And what kind of artwork? Window treatments?" Lucy grilled her.

The questions continued as Sophie showed them around the kitchen.

"These dishes aren't bad at all." Brooke opened a cabinet and took out a plate. "I think under all the dust, they're all plain white."

"White plates on a white table?" Ellie asked.

"Black place mats," Lucy said.

"Could work." Ellie turned to Sophie. "Didn't you say you wanted some photos to enlarge to hang in the dining room?"

"I thought old photos of my grandmother and her friends would be just the thing, since I want to showcase St. Dennis here."

"Black-and-white photos on that big wall out there would be awesome." Brooke nodded. "We have some photos of the farm from back in the 1940s when my grandparents had it, if you're interested in seeing those."

"I'd love to. Especially since I'll be buying eggs and some produce from Clay."

"My mom has lots of photos from the inn over the years," Lucy said.

"The Inn at Sinclair's Point is a St. Dennis landmark," Sophie noted. "I'd love to include a few of those if your mother doesn't mind."

"She won't mind," Lucy told her. "Just don't be surprised when she shows up with her notebook and camera in hand. When I told her what you were doing, she got so excited. You know she's going to want to write about it for her paper."

"Anytime." Sophie thought about all the free publicity a well-timed article might generate. "I'd love to have her come after we're finished with the renovations."

"Maybe we can have Mom do before-and-after articles. That would certainly draw interest to your place."

"Thanks for your ideas, guys. I appreciate it."

"Now, what can we do?" Ellie asked. "Put us to work."

"Jesse said you'd be in the office this afternoon by two, so let's get on with it. We can talk décor while we work," Brooke said.

"I'll take the dishes out of the cupboards and wash them," Lucy volunteered. "I'll stack them out here on the counter and you can sort through them and see what you can use and what you need to replace."

"That would be great, Lucy. Thanks."

"I can help Lucy." Steffie followed Lucy into the kitchen.

"I can help paint," Brooke told her.

"Me, too." Vanessa stepped up.

"What can I do?" Ellie asked.

Sophie stopped to consider what else needed to be done right away.

"What are you calling the restaurant?" Ellie knelt to look at the sign Cameron had stood against the wall the day before.

"Blossoms," Sophie told them.

"Blossoms." Ellie turned to her. "After your grandmother, my great-aunt, and Violet?"

Sophie nodded.

"I love it! Does Violet know?" Ellie stood, her hands clapped together.

"Not yet."

"I won't let on, then." Ellie promised. "But we need to scrape *Walsh's* off that front window and paint the new name on. I can do that. I'll just need a razor blade to get the old paint off. What color do you want to use for the new name?"

"I hadn't thought about it. I wanted to repaint the old sign, and I had a new logo in mind."

"Let me see."

Sophie pulled her notebook from her bag.

"Just the three stems of flowers, tied together with a ribbon." Sophie held up her sketch. "Not very artistically done, but I think you get the idea."

"I like it." Ellie nodded. "I like it a lot. Mind if I play with the design? It would look great on the sign and on the window, and you could use it on the menus as well. I did some design work when I worked in PR."

"Ellie's great-grandmother was a famous artist." Vanessa had been leaning over the counter, listening. "Her mother was a painter, too."

"I had no idea," Sophie said.

"My mother actually did have a lot of talent, much more than I, though she didn't pursue it as much as she should have. Time ran out on her, I guess. She stopped painting when she got sick. I can paint a little, but I'm not in her league, nor that of my great-grandmother." Ellie handed the notebook back to Sophie. "But I'd love to work on that design for you."

"Be my guest." Sophie tucked the notebook away. "Did your great-grandmother live in St. Dennis?"

"Most of her life. She had to use her maiden name on her work because my great-grandfather thought it was scandalous that she would sell her paintings and make money from them." Ellie smiled. "She left a fortune in artwork in that house on Bay View Drive. Fortunately, my best friend knows art—she owns galleries here and in Europe—and she knew the work right away. Carly—my friend—has them all now, and she's cleaning them and preparing them for exhibit."

"So are you going to let your friend sell all those

Carolina Ellis paintings that you found?" Vanessa asked.

"I have mixed feelings," Ellie admitted. "On the one hand, Carly tells me that the money those paintings could fetch would be phenomenal, especially if someone wanted the entire collection. On the other hand, I didn't know my great-grandmother, and all I have of her are those paintings and her journals, so I don't know. Fortunately, I don't have to make a decision now. I told Carly she could display them after they've been restored. She's been a really good friend to me, and for her to have an exclusive would be good for her business. But sometimes I think maybe the paintings should stay in St. Dennis." Ellie shrugged. "Cam and I are doing okay with his contracting business, so I don't feel inclined to make an immediate decision on selling them." She slapped her hands together. "But right now, we have other work to do. I'm going to run out to the hardware store and see if I can find some good razor blades to start on those windows. I can pick up the white paint for the tables while I'm there."

Over the next few hours, the women worked at their tasks, interrupted only when someone thought of a funny story to share, or when a song came on the radio that they all chimed in on. Occasionally a song would play that enticed them all to momentarily abandon their work and dance fever would break out. By the end of the morning, the chairs were all painted and the dishes sorted into piles of "stay" and "go." The previous owner's name had been scraped from the front window, and Ellie had begun to sketch the new design onto the glass.

"If you'll trust me with the sign, I'd like to take it home with me to work on," she told Sophie.

"Sure. Go for it."

"Just promise me that if you don't like the way it looks, or if you don't like the way I've interpreted your design, you'll say so. I swear, you won't hurt my feelings," Ellie told her.

"I promise. I'm excited to see what you'll come up with."

"It's ten minutes till one," Brooke announced from the kitchen doorway. "If Sophie's going to be at work by two—and trust me, Jesse will notice—I think we should knock off, drive into town, and grab some lunch."

"Great idea," everyone agreed.

"Who's minding your businesses?" Sophie asked.

"My mother is at the bakery, and Vanessa and Steffie both have full-time employees," Lucy told her. "I don't have another wedding at the inn until next weekend, so I was able to take a day off. And Cam gave Ellie the day."

"I appreciate all the help, I really do. Please give my thanks to everyone who made this possible." Sophie felt almost overwhelmed by the gestures of friendship that had been offered that morning.

"It's the least we can do," Steffie told her as they all gathered their bags and Sophie turned off the lights. "We can't wait till you open. We've been needing a nice place to meet for lunch. I just know that Blossoms is going to be just the thing."

Agreeing to meet up with the others for a quick bite at the Crab Claw just outside of town, Sophie locked the doors and got into her SUV, then fell into line behind Vanessa and Lucy. Having something to take her mind off her disagreement with Jason had been welcomed, but as she passed by his property she felt the pang in her chest return. She hated not talking to him, but at the same time, she wasn't sure how to resolve the problem, or if there even was a resolution. Of course, he did have every right to put whatever he wanted on his property, whether she liked it or not. So far, it appeared he wanted those piles of dirt to stay right where they were.

She sighed heavily as she stopped for the stop sign. Who'd have thought that her new romance would be derailed by a pile of mushroom soil?

Jason watched the women stream out of the building next door and disappear into the cars that were parked out front. A moment later, Sophie came out and locked the front door before getting into her SUV and falling in line with the small caravan that exited her side of the parking lot. It seemed that half the women in St. Dennis had shown up at Sophie's place and they'd all come to work. Nice that she had such support from her friends.

He called to the workman who was loading mulch onto a truck to meet him at the Enright property on Old St. Mary's Church Road, then peeled out of the parking lot. He was running late and hated to keep Curtis waiting. Of course, thinking about Curtis only made him think about Sophie. As if he needed something else to call her to mind. It seemed he couldn't think of much else lately.

Curtis was at the end of the drive, not bothering to

hide the fact that he was waiting for Jason's truck to pull in.

"Someone dropped off a load of trees," Curtis said by way of a greeting. He pointed toward the middle of the yard. "I don't think they're the trees we talked about."

"Well, then, let's take a look." Jason dropped out of the cab and accompanied Curtis across the lawn. The mole tunnels were gone, he noticed, making a mental note to remind the contractor to send in his bill.

"See, we asked for pines." Curtis stood in front of the stand of balled and burlapped evergreens. "These don't look like pines to me."

"They're not pines," Jason told him. "These are blue spruce, and these taller ones are cryptomeria."

"I thought we ordered all pines," Curtis insisted.

"No, you decided you didn't want pines. You wanted something different, you said."

"I did?" The old man looked momentarily confused.

"You did," Jason assured him. "But if you've changed your mind, and you just want pine trees here, I can send these back and put in another order."

"What do you think?"

"I think these are going to look just fine. Especially the cryptomeria. They grow really tall and will provide nice privacy."

"Why do I need privacy?"

"Well, you said you wanted to block the view from the river."

"Oh. Well, I suppose those tall trees will do that."

"They will." Jason nodded, trying to conceal his

alarm. Curtis was usually really sharp, not at all confused the way he appeared now. It wasn't just that he claimed to not remember having ordered those particular trees, it was the look of bewilderment that gave Jason pause.

"I should keep them, then."

"Let's look over the bed where they're going to be planted, and you can tell me where you'd like each of the trees to go. Why don't we go into the house, and we'll draw up a plan?"

"All right." They'd taken a half-dozen steps toward the house when Curtis grabbed Jason by the arm and said, "Say, did you tell me that you bought a lot from Hal Garrity down on River Road?"

"I did. That's home base for my business now."

"Did you know that my Sophie is buying the old Walsh place?"

"I believe she already has."

"Well, then, that makes you neighbors." Curtis was beaming, as if that were a good thing. Jason supposed that under other circumstances, it would be.

"Yes, it does."

"I suppose it would be an imposition of me to ask you to keep an eye on her."

"Excuse me?"

"Young girl out there in that damn-near-abandoned building all by herself. Anything could happen."

"I think Sophie can take care of herself, Curtis."

"She thinks she can. Thinks she wants to run a damned restaurant. A restaurant! Wants to be a cook, for all that's holy! She's a lawyer, damn it. An Enright lawyer in St. Dennis. That means something. What the hell does it mean to be a cook?"

"I guess you need to ask her that question."

"I already did. Know what she said? She said that cooking made her happy. I told her that she didn't know happy until she brought her toughest case before the toughest judge in the state and went up against the nastiest opposing counsel on the Eastern Shore—and won. That's happiness, boy."

"Maybe for her, happiness means something else."

"Know what she's planning on selling in that place of hers? Quiche. Strawberry salads. Yogurt and granola. *Granola.* Who eats that stuff?" If Jason wasn't mistaken, Curtis actually huffed. "This is the Chesapeake. We eat crabs and oysters and fish. How is she going to make a living cooking stuff like that?"

"She'll do okay."

"And the place is a dump. Have you seen it? Of course you have. You're right next door there. I have to tell you, that's the only consolation I have. That you're right there if she gets into trouble." Curtis patted Jason on the back. "Now, I got Violet to drive me out there on Sunday afternoon. That place has been boarded up for years and it needs a ton of work. She's going to go broke fixing it up before she even opens for business."

Jason wasn't sure how to respond to that—the place did need a lot of work—so he made no response at all. Instead, he continued walking to the back porch and helped Curtis up the stairs. He got the man into the kitchen, where he poured them both a glass of iced tea from the pitcher Mrs. Anderson had left in the refrigerator.

"She's a stubborn cuss, that girl is. I tried to talk some sense into her, but I was just wasting my breath."

"She'll do okay, Curtis. Sophie's a smart girl, and I'm sure she has a plan. I wouldn't worry about her too much."

Jason kept Curtis talking until he was satisfied that the old man was himself again.

An hour later, the trees each having a designated destination, Jason was driving back up Old St. Mary's Church Road. At the corner across from the park, he made a left, then parked the car a few doors down from Enright & Enright's offices. He'd been disturbed by his conversation with Curtis and thought someone in the family should know. He was hoping that someone would be Sophie.

"Hello, Jason." Violet stood just outside the door of the first office when he entered. "Nice to see you."

"Hi." He gave her his best smile. She was, after all, the gatekeeper.

"Are you here to see Jesse?" Before Jason could respond, she added, "He just got back to the office."

"Ah, well, actually, I . . . ," Jason began.

"Hey, Jason." Jesse stepped into the hall. "What's up?"

"I just wanted a minute, if you have one." Disappointed, but knowing he couldn't very well bypass one Enright for the other, especially since the other probably wouldn't see him anyway, Jason followed Jesse into the office. When the door was closed behind them, Jason said, "I just came from your grandfather's place."

"I know you've been doing a lot of work there for him. We were over there on Saturday, and love what you've done so far. He's really excited, by the way, and that makes everyone happy. He doesn't have a lot to do these days, so it's good to see him interested in something."

There was no easy way to say it, so Jason put it out there straight.

"He seems a bit confused today, Jesse."

"What do you mean, confused?"

Jason repeated the conversation he'd had with Curtis about the trees, then added, "He seemed pretty much himself when I left, but I thought you should know. Maybe stop in on your way home."

"I'll do that. Thanks, Jace. We all worry about him living there by himself. If anything should happen, well, he's pretty much on his own." He looked across the table and asked, "Did you tell Sophie?"

"Ah, no. I'd just gotten here when I ran into you."

"She's in the back office there. Go on back and say hello. She's been working herself like a dog today. Brooke tells me that a bunch of them went out to give her a hand at her new place, helped her clean, wash stuff up, that sort of thing. Tired as she is, I gotta admit, she's true to her word. Showed up here at the office at two on the nose and has been working all afternoon on a bunch of cases I have coming up within the next few weeks." Jesse lowered his voice. "I just hope she can keep it up, you know? I don't think this is going to be as easy as she thought."

"I'm sure she knows what's best for her." Jason made a point of looking at his watch. "I gotta run. Got an appointment in five minutes on the other side of town, and you know what traffic is like this time of the day. I'll see you later."

Jason called goodbye to Violet on his way out the door. He'd heard Sophie's voice in the hall and couldn't leave fast enough. The last thing he wanted was a confrontation with her in front of her brother.

He sat in the cab of his truck for a few moments. This was such a small town, there was no way to avoid running in to her, and no way to avoid having everyone in town find out about their . . . what to call it? Misunderstanding? Falling out? That would do, he supposed.

He drove home without thinking where he was going. Normally he'd have picked up something for dinner on the way home, but tonight he forgot. It was still early, though. He could call in someplace, maybe have something delivered. There was a stack of take-out menus in a kitchen drawer. He went through them all twice, but nothing appealed to him.

He wished things had gone differently with Sophie, but he couldn't turn back the clock. He wished he'd been able to be happy for her that she got what she wanted, wished that he hadn't wanted the same thing. He wished he could call her and meet her for dinner to celebrate her new venture. Wished he could bring her back here and talk her into staying the night. Wished he could wake up in the morning and spend a little time watching her sleep.

Wished he knew how to take things back to the way they were just one short week ago.

Chapter 22 ⤳

THOUGH the alarm, shrill and loud, rang inches from Sophie's head, it took several minutes for the sound to pierce through her deep slumber. She raised a groggy hand and slapped at the offending clock until she hit the snooze button. Four days of rising at six, working in the restaurant until one, making a quick change for the office by two, and working there until seven or eight had totally worn her to a frazzle. When the alarm went off the second time, she pulled herself up, her pillow behind her, and tried to focus.

Why, she asked herself, had she ever thought this would be a good idea?

She ambled into the bathroom, then into the kitchen, where she made coffee and counted the minutes until it was ready. Through the kitchen window she could see the making of a beautiful day. She took her coffee out onto the back porch to listen to the birds. In her bare feet, she went down the steps and into the garden to see what might be growing there. Not much, she realized. A few daylilies that had yet to bloom, a few Shasta daisies that appeared to be overgrown, and a rosebush that had a lot of black spots on the few leaves that remained on its thorny branches. She made a mental note to ask Violet if she knew anything about roses, then sat on the back step to drink her coffee in the sunshine that was just making its way across the backyard.

She was still sitting and sipping when she realized it was Saturday and she couldn't go into the restaurant until the afternoon. The exterminator had told her to keep the building closed up for at least twenty-four hours, and then, if she had to go inside, to open all the doors and windows and allow the pesticides to clear out before she spent too much time in there. She could go back to bed for a few more hours of much-needed sleep. Of course, having caffeinated herself, sleep might be hard to come by. She could go into the office early and get a leg up on the research that Jesse needed her to do for an upcoming criminal trial.

Or she could sit here and drink coffee and watch the day unfold, which seemed to be the best immediate option. It had been days since she'd been able to just sit and not think of work or Blossoms or Jason. Thinking about Jason gave her a monumental headache. She'd never been in a situation like this one. She and Christopher had never argued, had never disagreed. They were both headed in the same direction, wanted the same things, or so she'd thought. Relationships were either wrong or they were right. Most of the time, she had to admit in retrospect, they'd been wrong. If he'd been Mr. Right, wouldn't things have worked out? Everything in her past told her that when it came to relationships, there was black and there was white, but never gray.

This situation, however, confused her. It seemed . . .

gray. As a prosecutor whose job it had been to ferret out the truth, she was now at a bit of a loss. She tried to weigh the facts.

Jason had dumped several loads of smelly crap next to the fence that separated their properties.

Sophie had not told Jason that she'd bought the property next door; therefore he had no way of knowing that she was planning on opening a restaurant there.

Okay, she'd give him that. Score one for Jason.

However, when she told him of her plans and asked him to move the piles, he refused.

He should have moved them, shouldn't he?

She sighed, unable to answer with any confidence.

Which left the question remaining: had she been unreasonable in expecting him to move the mulch piles?

Gray, she told herself. Totally gray.

Right now, gray was better than black or white. Gray meant maybe there was room for compromise, something else she'd learned as a prosecutor. You didn't always get your way in court, either from the judge or from the jury. When the evidence could go either way, when she wasn't totally convinced of a defendant's guilt, it often made more sense to offer a plea. She'd found it harder to compromise when she was certain they had the guilty party but the evidence might not have been there to support a conviction. She preferred things to be either/or, but it didn't always work out that way. It was puzzling that this time, she wasn't sure who was right.

Of course he had every right to run his business from his own property—as much right as she had.

But she couldn't sacrifice her restaurant so that he could open a plant shop. Did he think that if he left those smelly old piles there long enough, she'd give in and slap a sale sign on the building?

The only sign that was going to be hung was the one that Ellie was painting with the name, Blossoms, on it.

So, stalemate.

How annoying that their individual dreams had gotten in the way of what might have been! Being with Jason had felt so right, so magically, fairy-tale right, that it felt wrong that things had turned out the way they had. Where, she wondered, had the magic gone? Why couldn't he have been Mr. Right? It had started to seem as if he might very well be.

Sophie took a sip of coffee, found it had long since gone cold, and poured it over the side of the step into the grass.

Interesting, she thought, that she hadn't deliberated this much when her relationship with Christopher ended. That, to her, had been an easy call. He cheated on her. Off with his head. Yes, it had hurt, but there, the boundaries had been clear. She'd cut that tie and never looked back. Never wondered if there'd been room for compromise, or if she'd done the right thing; never asked herself, *What if . . . ?*

So why, she asked herself now, had it been easier to walk away from Chris—after they'd been together for almost two years—than it was to walk away from Jason, after so short a time?

It had never occurred to her to fight for Chris. She'd let Anita have him without hesitation. So why was she replaying the scene with Jason over and over in her mind?

Maybe, a small voice inside her whispered, because Chris hadn't been worth fighting for, and maybe Jason was.

She thought back to last Saturday morning, when she woke to find he'd risen before her, that moment when she reached for him and found only empty space, the sudden sense of loss she'd felt when she thought he'd gone, left her bed without even saying goodbye. The smile she'd felt welling up inside when he'd walked out of the bathroom to kiss her and tell her he'd see her later at . . .

Oh, shit. Ellie's carriage house. The historical society. Saturday.

Today was Saturday.

Sophie scrambled to get into the house and upstairs, where she threw on a pair of cropped pants and a worn-thin short-sleeved sweatshirt. She grabbed a bottle of water from the fridge on her way out the door. A glance at the clock told her she was already late. Where had the time gone?

She had to park three houses down from Ellie's on Bay View Road, but was relieved to see a few others arriving late as well. She tried to slip unnoticed into the crowd that was milling around the carriage house, and she thought she'd succeeded until Jason looked up from the window he was working on and said, "I didn't think you'd be here."

"I'm not a quitter," she told him.

"Good. How 'bout washing the panes in the windows so I can paint them? Paper towels and window cleaner are on the table over by Grace."

"Fine." She winced when the word came out of her mouth. She hadn't meant it to sound so strident. She took a deep breath. "Aren't the panes loose? I don't want to knock them out of the frames."

"Just go easy. I've already secured them with joint compound but it may still be setting up on the two side windows, so do them last."

"All right."

She gathered up the paper towels and the bottle of cleaner and tried to get away from Grace with only a polite exchange. But Grace being Grace, she wanted the details of Sophie's plans for the restaurant. After promising to meet later in the week for photos and an article for Grace's paper, Sophie moved on to her task.

Going from one window to the next, she sprayed the panes and rubbed until the glass was clear. When she finished, she picked up the discarded paper towels and tossed them into a trash can just outside the carriage house.

She turned in the doorway to look back at Jason, who was leaning over, pouring pale green paint into a tray. The gray tank top he wore stretched across the muscles of his shoulders and when he stood and raised the paintbrush, his biceps seemed to ripple. She remembered those arms and the way they'd wrapped around her, remembered how those shoulders had felt when she ran her hands over them. The bolt of heat that flashed through her weakened her knees.

Maybe things weren't so gray after all.

His eyes on his granddaughter, Curtis stepped into the carriage house and followed her line of sight. Ah, yes. There was Jason. Pleased by what he perceived to be a sign that things were developing nicely between them, as he'd hoped, he called to Sophie.

"There you are." He walked toward her, leaning heavily on his cane. "How's your project coming along?"

"It's . . . I guess it's all right." She seemed surprised—and perhaps not particularly pleased—to see him.

"Good, good."

"Hey, Curtis," Jason greeted him. "You sign up to help yet?"

"I doubt anyone would want my help," Curtis replied. "I just stopped in to see this lamp lens that I've been hearing about."

Jason turned and pointed to the huge glass lens that still sat in the middle of the carriage house floor. "There it is."

"Well, now, would you look at that? How did that work, do you suppose?" Curtis walked around the lens as if inspecting it.

Jason explained the process to him as he had explained it the weekend before.

"Fancy that." Curtis looked directly at Sophie, hoping to pull her into the conversation. "I remember when the lighthouse stood out there, almost right on the beach. I remember when a storm back in, oh, I think it might have been 'forty-six, brought it crashing down. Heard it all the way over on Bancock Street."

"1846?" Jason asked.

Curtis laughed and slapped him on the back good-naturedly.

"Funny guy here, right, Sophie?"

"He's a riot, Pop."

Curtis was beginning to pick up a tension between the two of them. Something in the way they pointedly were not looking at each other, smiling with no trace of humor or warmth. Something, Curtis decided, was not right.

He chatted with them for a few more minutes, and failing at his attempts to include both of them in the same conversation, excused himself to chat with Grace, all the while watching his granddaughter and Jason work around each other.

This simply would not do.

Disturbed, Curtis said his goodbyes, kissing Sophie and reminding Jason that he was to stop over later that afternoon to pick up a check for the work he'd been doing. Then, feigning fatigue, he asked Violet, whom he'd accompanied, if they could leave.

"Of course, Curtis." Violet waved to Sophie, then said goodbye to the group of volunteers she'd been regaling with tales of the previous occupants of Ellie's house and the fun they'd had when they were younger.

"It always makes me so nostalgic, coming here," she told Curtis as they walked to her car. "It reminds me of when I was young, and Lilly and Rose were still alive. Such times we had . . ."

"You were always fun to be around, Violet. I know how close you and Rose, in particular, were all through your school days."

"That we were, Curtis."

Violet's car was parked at the end of Ellie's driveway, a privilege Violet assumed because of her age.

The pair got into the car and began the drive back to Old St. Mary's Church Road in silence, Curtis distracted by the apparent coolness between Sophie and Jason, and Violet accustomed to a quiet car.

When they made the turn onto Charles Street, Curtis asked, "Do you suppose it's true what they say about Grace Sinclair?"

"What on earth are you talking about? What do they say about Grace?" Violet's eyes narrowed, but she never took them from the road.

"Oh, that she knows . . . spells, or something like that," he mumbled.

"They still say that, do they?"

"It used to be the talk of the town, how Grace and Alice Ridgeway and a few others dabbled in . . . whatever it was they dabbled in . . ." He sighed. "You know what I mean, Violet."

"Yes, I certainly do." Was that a half smile of amusement on her face?

"So, does she?"

"Does she what, dear?"

"Does Grace Sinclair still do that stuff?" He wondered if he sounded as silly as he felt, but it was for a good cause, wasn't it? "Spells."

"What kind of spell did you have in mind, Curtis?"

"Something like a . . . like a . . ." He lowered his voice. "A love spell."

At first, Violet appeared not to have heard, but finally, she said, "I'm trying to figure out why a man whose next big birthday will be ninety would be interested in a love spell."

"It's certainly not for me."

"Why, I do believe you're blushing, Curtis Enright."
Violet seemed to be having a little too much fun with
the conversation.

"Don't be ridiculous. I don't blush," he grumbled.

"I'm assuming that if it's not for you, the spell you
have in mind has something to do with Sophie."

Curtis nodded.

"Don't you think Sophie is old enough and smart
enough to take care of things in her own time?"

"Maybe in her time, but perhaps not in mine. And
I want to see the girl settled before my time is up."

"I see." Violet slowed as she approached his house
and stopped at the curb. "The young man you have in
mind would be . . . ?"

"Jason."

"Of course. I should have guessed."

"He's the right one for her, Violet. Rose and I both
agreed."

"And Sophie? How does she feel about Jason?"

"I haven't asked her."

"And he . . . ?"

"Haven't asked him either."

"Then why on earth would you want to interfere?"

"Because I know what I know, that's why," he
snapped, then softened. "Sorry, Violet. It's just that,
it's one of those things you just know."

She nodded. Apparently there were things she just
knew, too.

"So?" he asked pointedly.

"Sometimes it's best not to meddle," she said. "Sometimes it's best to just let nature take its course."

"This isn't one of them."

"All right." She seemed resigned. "I'll see what I can do. But don't blame me if things don't go well."

"Thank you, Violet. I thank you, and Rose thanks you." He touched her arm briefly, then opened the car door. "And someday, Sophie will thank you, too . . ."

"I certainly hope you're right," she said as she drove away.

He stood on the sidewalk while she turned around in his driveway, then raised a hand to wave as she passed by on her way home. He was grateful that not only had she agreed to help him—whatever form that help might take, he hadn't asked—but that she hadn't made him feel any more foolish than he already did. He was so grateful that he decided right then and there that he'd never bring up the fact that he knew she'd loaned Sophie the money to open her restaurant.

"Well, I guess we'll see if there's any truth to all those stories people used to tell about Grace and Alice and the others," he said aloud as he unlocked the front door.

He leaned his walking stick next to the hall table and paused as it occurred to him that Violet seemed to know an awful lot about that whole spell thing. Had she said she'd see what *she* could do, or that she'd see what could be done? He couldn't remember which it had been.

"Rose, you don't suppose that Violet . . ." He shook his head, dismissing the thought. Violet was much too sensible a woman to ever be involved in such nonsense.

Of course, *he* thought it was nonsense. But the way things were going, he figured it couldn't hurt.

Feeling that the situation was under control, Curtis went into his study and plopped in his favorite chair, picked up the new thriller that had arrived in the morning mail, and began to read.

And that was where, several hours later, Jason found him, slumped over the arm of the chair.

Chapter 23 ⌒

J ESSE, Brooke, and Sophie sat quietly in the waiting room at Bay Memorial Hospital, where Curtis had been taken following Jason's call to 911. When a tall, thin doctor stepped into the room and asked, "Enright family?" they all stood at the same time.

"How is he?" three voices asked at once.

"You're Mr. Enright's . . . ?"

"Grandchildren."

"Which one of you is Jason?"

"Ah, none of us. He's the one who called me," Jesse said. "Is he here?"

"He was. He followed the ambulance when Mr. Enright was brought in and helped with the admission process. I assumed he was family."

"He's a friend of the family," Jesse told him. "What can you tell us about our grandfather? Is he all right?"

"Can we see him?" Sophie asked.

"Right now, we're running some tests, and until we have the results, we won't be able to tell you much of anything. It appears he's had some sort of spell, but we're not sure what caused it. He's still unresponsive." The doctor looked up from his notes. "Does anyone know if he has a DNR?"

"What's a DNR?" Brooke asked.

"Do not resuscitate," Sophie replied. "Is it that serious?"

"I'm just covering the bases. Do you know if he had a living will?"

"He does," Jesse said softly. "I saw a copy at the office."

The doctor nodded. "Why don't you all go on home. We'll call you if he comes around, or when we know something definitive."

"I want to stay," Jesse said. "I think someone should be here when he wakes up."

"I'd stay with you, but I need to drop Logan off at Jason's," Brooke said as she stood. "It's Saturday."

Guys' night out, Sophie recalled.

"I'll do it," Sophie told them. "You guys stay here with Pop, and I'll go pick up Logan and take him to Jason's. Besides, we need to thank him for getting Pop to the hospital and for calling Jesse." She stood and grabbed her bag from the back of the hard plastic chair she'd been seated on. "Call me if there's a change."

"Will do. Thanks, Sophie." Brooke gave her a quick hug. "I'll call Logan and tell him you're on your way so he can meet you outside."

Sophie's running shoes made an odd muffled squeak on the vinyl tiled floor as she hurried to the elevator, her thoughts jumbled, her prayers disjointed. It was difficult to think rationally, she discovered, in panic mode. The thought of losing her grandfather overrode everything else. He'd become so dear to her, so important in her life over the past year, that she couldn't imagine what it would be like without him.

"Please hang on, Pop," she whispered as she got into her SUV. "Don't give up."

She wondered if sometimes one had a choice: stay or go? Given the chance to choose, she was pretty sure which her grandfather would take. How many times had he spoken wistfully of Rose, how much he missed her, how he was only marking time until they could be together again? Was it wrong for her to pray that he not get his wish just yet so they might keep him with them a little longer?

Of course, she knew the outcome wasn't in her hands. Whatever was to happen was in accordance with a plan of someone else's design, and they would all have to accept that, whatever it was.

Still, she would miss him. It hurt her heart to think how much.

She stopped at the end of the driveway leading to the Madison farm to compose herself. When she felt she had it together, she parked the car, and she'd just gotten out when she saw Logan headed down the path from the house where he lived with his mother and Jesse on Brooke's family farm.

"Hi, Sophie!" Logan waved and broke into a trot. "Mom said for me to watch for you, so I did."

"Good thinking on your mom's part." Sophie got back into the car. Had Brooke told Logan about Pop? The boy had gotten pretty close to Curtis and would surely be upset if he thought his great-grandfather by marriage was in peril. Sophie decided not to mention it unless Logan did.

"So what's on the agenda for tonight?" she asked.

"Pizza!" He chortled. "Uncle Jace said I could pick what kind tonight since it was just him and me. Cody had to go somewhere with his mom and dad, so he can't come with us. We're going to go out to a movie."

"What are you going to see?"

"Uncle Jace said it's going to be a surprise." Logan sat with his overnight bag on his lap. "Do you know where my uncle lives?"

"Ahhh . . . no. Actually, I don't. What a silly thing for me not to ask." Sophie felt more than silly, she felt incredibly foolish. Her mind was so focused on her grandfather's condition that she forgot she hadn't been to Jason's home before.

"I figured you didn't," Logan said, "because you're going the wrong way."

"Why don't you tell me which way?"

"Turn around here and then go back to Doyle Street and turn that way." He pointed to the right.

"Then what?"

"Then you go on that street till you get to his house."

"Sounds easy enough. I'm sure you know what his house looks like, right?"

Logan rolled his eyes at her. "Duh. I stay there every weekend."

"Right. I forgot." Sophie followed Logan's directions, turning where he said to turn, stopping in front of the house he pointed to.

"There. That's my uncle's house." Logan barely waited for the car to come to a stop before jumping out.

Sophie debated on whether or not to go up to the door, when Jason appeared in the driveway. He and Logan greeted each other with high-fives; then after a few words, Logan took off for the front door and Jason walked over to Sophie's car.

"How's your granddad?" he asked with obvious concern.

"The same, I guess. He's still not awake." She tried to look away from his gaze but could not. "The doctor said you called 911 and went to the hospital with him."

"I followed the ambulance in my car so he wouldn't be alone if he came to. I called Jesse from the car on the way over."

He leaned on the driver's-side door. His hair was still damp from the shower he'd obviously just taken and his T-shirt clung to his chest. It was hard not to stare.

"He was out when you found him?"

Jason nodded. "I was supposed to meet with him at four, and I got there a little early. When he didn't answer the door, I wasn't concerned at first, because I knew he'd been out with Violet and thought maybe they went someplace and were a little late getting back. But when it got to be four fifteen and there was no sign of him—you know how he is about being punctual—I went back to the house and rang the doorbell. No answer out front, so I went around back. The door was open, so I knew he was there. I went in, called his name, but there was no answer. He wasn't in the kitchen or the living room, so I figured he'd be in the library, which he was, in that big, old green leather chair he likes so much. He had a pulse but it was faint, and I couldn't rouse him. That's when I called 911."

"We can't thank you enough. If you hadn't found

him when you did, he might be gone by now. He still might not . . ." She couldn't bring herself to finish the sentence. Her eyes spilled over with tears, and Jason squeezed her arm.

"If I can do anything . . . *any*thing . . . call me."

"We will. Thanks, Jason."

"Look, I'm taking Logan to the movies. You're welcome to come with us. It might take your mind off things for a while."

"Thanks, but I should get back to the hospital with my brother and Brooke."

He straightened up and backed away from the car. "Keep in touch, okay? I mean, about Curtis."

"Right. I will."

She turned around in his driveway and went back the way she came. She reached the stop sign on the corner before she realized that he was still standing in front of his house, and that she had no idea what that house looked like. All she'd seen when she pulled up in front had been Jason.

She was a block away from the hospital when her phone rang. The caller ID told her it was Jesse.

"Soph, you on your way back yet?" Jesse's voice was tense.

"Yes. I'm almost there. Has something happened? Is he . . ."

"No. I wanted you to stop and pick up Violet on your way, but if you're that close . . ."

"I'll go back for her. I know it's important for her to be there. Did you call anyone else?"

"I called Uncle Mike and left a message—he's in Florida, but he could probably get a flight up tomorrow morning if he gets the message in time to make arrangements. I called Nick; he's going to call Zoey and Georgia. And I called Mom, because I thought she'd like to know."

After a long silence, she asked, "Did you call Dad?"

"I'm thinking about it," was all he said.

"Maybe you should run that past Uncle Mike, see how he feels about it."

"That was the plan."

She turned around in a convenience store parking lot and drove back to St. Dennis. She hated not being there with Jesse and Brooke, but at the same time was grateful to be moving, to have something specific to do. Sitting and waiting was too stressful. She turned on the radio and sang her way to Violet's. She didn't want to think about losing her grandfather and she didn't want to think about having lost Jason. So much easier to focus on remembering the words to "Stairway to Heaven" on the classic rock station. So much easier to be making conversation with Violet on the drive back to the hospital.

Sophie dropped Violet off at the front door and went to park her car. By the time she found a spot and returned to the place she'd left Violet, the older woman had gone on ahead to the third-floor waiting room. When Sophie arrived, she could tell by the look on her brother's face that things were not going well.

"There's been no change, but the doctor said we could go in two at a time." Jesse turned to Violet. "Why don't you go in now with Sophie for a few minutes."

"Oh, but don't you think you'd rather . . . ," Violet began to protest.

"You and Pop have been friends for what, a hundred years?" Jesse made a lame attempt to tease.

"One hundred and seventeen, I believe." She tried to force a smile.

"I think you should be there with him now, for a while, anyway." Jesse turned to Sophie. "He's in room 357. First bed."

"Have you seen him?" Sophie asked.

Jesse nodded. "I sat with him while you were gone. I don't know if he knew I was there, but I talked to him as if he could hear me. Maybe he could . . ."

Sophie hugged her brother for a long moment, then took Violet by the arm, and together they found room 357. She was shocked at her grandfather's appearance. Where earlier in the day he'd been completely himself, now he looked as if he'd aged ten years in a matter of hours. His skin was gray, his eyes remained closed, and his breathing was shallow.

She stood next to the hospital bed and pulled a chair close for Violet, who sat immediately and took one of Curtis's hands.

"Well, it's been a long journey, hasn't it, old friend?" Violet whispered. "If this is where it's supposed to end, go peacefully. Rose has been waiting a long time." She patted his hand for a minute or two. "On the other hand, should you decide to stay, perhaps you'll agree that you should probably not remain in that big house all by yourself. You can move in with me or you can go into a home, but your days of living in that mansion are over, my friend."

Curtis's lips moved, slowly at first, but Sophie couldn't make out any words. Violet stood and leaned over him and appeared to be listening. Sophie thought she heard him utter the word "spell"—but wouldn't swear to it—to which Violet assured him, "It's been taken care of." He then sighed deeply and seemed to slip back away to wherever he'd been.

"What was that he said, about spelling . . . ?" Sophie whispered.

"Just something he'd asked me to look up for him, dear," Violet said without taking her eyes from her old friend's face. "There are so few of us left, you know, from that time. My husband's long gone—Rose, too—so many of our friends." She shook her head. "It's hard to see another leave this place."

"Do you think he's really going to . . . ?" Sophie couldn't bring herself to say the word.

"It's not for me to say."

Sophie sat on the side of the bed and watched her grandfather's labored breathing. "Do you believe all that stuff about my grandmother? You know, about her being in the house, just waiting for him . . . ?"

Violet nodded. "I do."

"Even though you couldn't see her?"

"I'm not so sure that sometimes I didn't." Violet smiled. "Though that's neither here nor there. We can't see love or friendship, but we know those things are real."

"That's not the same as seeing ghosts."

"*Ghost* is just a word, and a misunderstood concept at best. Who's to say what form we'll take, or what we'll find when we pass from this world to the next?"

"So you believe . . ."

"Oh, in so many things, dear. Perhaps someday, you will, too, if you live long enough." Violet glanced at the figure on the bed, then looked up at Sophie. "Perhaps you should get your brother now."

Sophie sent a text to Jesse, telling him to come to Curtis's room. She waited for him in the hall outside the room, wanting to give Violet a few moments alone with her old friend. Jesse and Brooke were there in a flash, but when they entered the room, they were shocked to find Curtis's eyes wide open.

"Tell me the truth, Vi," he was saying, "were you one of the ones who dabbled?"

Before she could respond, Sophie and Jesse descended upon him.

"Pop! You're awake!"

"Oh, my God," Sophie exclaimed, "you're awake!" She tried to grab the buzzer to summon the nurse, but her grandfather took it from her hand.

"Don't be calling people to come in here, now. They'll start poking and prodding again," he grumbled. He glanced up at Sophie and saw the tears on her face. "What's all that about?"

"Pop, we were afraid we were going to lose you," she told him.

"I thought I was going," he told them, "but apparently I've more to do here before I go for good. Damn it. Thought I was going to make it this time, but something sent me back."

"We're all glad you're here, Pop," Jesse said.

"I'll bet you called Mike, didn't you?" Curtis tried to sit up.

"I did." Jesse nodded. "Nick and the others, too."

"Well, call 'em all back and tell them not to bother. I just saw everyone a month or so ago. Especially Mike. He'll be fussing, trying to bully someone into letting him get on a plane tonight. Tell him to save his energy." Curtis fumbled with the controls for the bed, trying to sit upright.

"Maybe you shouldn't sit up until the nurse comes in," Brooke said.

Curtis responded with a dirty look while he continued to adjust the bed.

"He's back to normal," Violet announced.

"Apparently," Jesse agreed.

"Now, if you'll all go away, I want to talk to Jesse alone."

"Not until I have my say." Violet drew herself up in the chair. "You gave us a damned hard scare, Curtis. Took a few years off me, and I don't know that I have that many to spare. I think it's high time you moved out of that big house. You can't continue to live on your own anymore."

When Curtis started to protest, she shut him down.

"It's not an option. Had it not been for Jason's quick thinking, you might have gotten your wish and we'd be making funeral arrangements right now. It's time to give it up, Curtis."

"I am not moving to a home," he said indignantly. "Never."

"You can move to *my* home," Violet told him. "You can stay with me."

"Are you suggesting we *cohabitate*, Vi?"

"Call it what you will." She sniffed.

"We'll be the talk of the town. Why, I can hear the gossip mill starting to grind already."

"I'd think that at your age, you'd be flattered."

Violet stood, then turned to Jesse. "You make him understand that he cannot continue to live alone."

"I'm not deaf, and I'm not stupid," Curtis grumbled.

"Then act like it."

"What's wrong with my house? Why don't you move in with me, you're so set on us living together."

"Your house is too big. Mine is just right."

"What about Rose?" His voice softened. "I can't leave Rose behind."

"She'll know where to find you."

Violet walked out the door and waited for Sophie in the hallway.

Sophie caught up with her a few moments later. "Guess you told him." She grinned.

"What do you suppose he'll do?" Violet's concern was evident.

"He'll go to your place when he leaves here," Sophie assured her. "Jesse just told him he wasn't going to go back to the house, and he could choose to go along with your suggestion, or he could go to Florida to live with Mike, or he could go to an assisted living facility. I think we all know which of the three he'll choose. But are you sure you want to take him on? He can be a handful, not to mention that he's a grumpy old man at times."

Violet laughed. "I've known that grumpy old man for seventysome years, worked for him for sixty. I can handle Curtis Enright. His bluster never bothered me." She sobered for a moment. "It's the least I can do for him and for Rose."

"I think that your plan is the best," Sophie assured her.

"Well, then, I think I'd like to go home now, if you wouldn't mind taking me. I think this old lady has had enough excitement for one night." Violet reached for Sophie's arm and leaned on it.

It occurred to Sophie that she'd never known Violet to need assistance before, but she wasn't sure if it was physical or emotional fatigue that caused the older woman to want to lean on someone else.

"Oh, wait one second." Sophie ducked back into the room. "Jess, I'll make the phone calls to Nick and Mike, but I'll need their numbers."

Jesse, already deep in conversation with their grandfather, handed her his phone. "You can get the numbers from there, then leave it with Brooke."

"I was just on my way back to the waiting room," Brooke told her. "Let's do this outside."

Once in the hall, Brooke whispered, "Your grandfather isn't taking this as lightly as he tried to make us all think."

"Good. He shouldn't take it lightly." Sophie opened Jesse's phone directory and began adding the numbers she needed to her phone. When she finished, she handed the phone back to Brooke.

"Are you sure you don't want me to make some of the calls?" Brooke offered.

"No, I'm good. Thanks."

"Someone should call Jason. He should know."

Sophie held up her phone. "I've got his number. I'll call."

"Okay." Brooke hugged Sophie, then walked toward the elevator where Violet was waiting, and hugged her, too.

Sophie pushed the down button, and a moment later, the elevator pinged and the doors slid open. She waved goodbye to Brooke, then helped Violet into the car, where two men and a woman with a small child waited patiently for the doors to close.

On the way home, Sophie asked, "Violet, what did my grandfather mean when he asked if you dabbled?"

"Oh, that." She chuckled. "He meant painting, dear. He wanted to know if I still painted."

"Do you?"

"On occasion."

"Are you working on anything now?"

"Actually, I dabbled a bit this afternoon."

"I'd like to see some of your work sometime."

"Perhaps you shall, dear." In the darkened front seat, Violet smiled. "Perhaps you shall . . ."

Chapter 24 ⌒

AFTER she dropped off Violet, Sophie made the calls to Nick and to Mike, both of whom were relieved to hear that not only was Curtis apparently recovering, but he wouldn't be returning to the house where he'd lived alone for so many years. It was, everyone agreed, time.

She saved the call to Jason for last. When his voice mail picked up, she left a simple message: "My grand-dad rallied. It looks as if he's going to be all right." She hesitated. "We just wanted you to know and we wanted to thank you again."

She couldn't think of anything else to say that would be appropriate, so she disconnected the call. She wanted to say, "Call me. Can we please talk?" But she was afraid that maybe he was okay with the way things ended. Maybe he didn't want to talk. Maybe he was still angry that she'd bought the prop-erty he'd set his heart on.

She changed into short sweatpants and a tee when she got home, then heated up some soup she had in the refrigerator. She was sitting on the back porch eating when her doorbell rang. Two quick rings. Her brother.

She went inside and let him in.

"I was hoping you hadn't gone to bed yet." Jesse looked tired from the long day at the hospital.

"Not for a while. Want some soup?"

"Yeah. I didn't get dinner and I'm starving." He walked past her to the kitchen.

"Help yourself."

He did.

"So what's up?" She took a seat at the table, and after filling a bowl from a pot on the stove, Jesse sat across from her.

"I just wanted to go over a few things with you." He took a few spoonfuls of soup before continuing. "Pop wants to write a new will."

"Go on."

"Aside from the usual bequests—you, me, Nick, Zoey and Georgia, Uncle Mike and his kids—he wanted to make sure that stuff that's been in the family for a long time stays in the family. Some pieces of furniture and some of Gramma's stuff, jewelry and silver and stuff like that. He had a list of who gets what. It's fair, and I could tell he's been giving it a lot of thought. I think everyone will be happy with the way he's distributing things." He paused to eat a little more.

"It's good of him to think of all of us."

"You know how he is about family."

"He mention Dad?"

Jesse shook his head. "It's sad, isn't it? I hope my kids and I never have that kind of distance between us."

"You'll make sure that you don't. You know too

well what it's like not to have a normal relationship with your father."

"Do I ever," he muttered. "Anyway, back to the will. He's made a few other bequests—to Violet, of course, and to Mrs. Anderson. Oh, and to Jason. He was very particular about what he was leaving Jason."

Surprised, Sophie put her spoon down. "What's he giving Jason?"

"Apparently, Pop has some first editions of some plant books that Jason was interested in. He gave me a list of the titles. And he wants Jason to have the greenhouse."

"That might be a bit strange, once the house is sold and someone else is living there."

"He wants the estate to pay to move the greenhouse to Jason's place out on River Road."

Good, Sophie thought. *I know just the spot for it.*

"And anyway, the house isn't being sold," he went on. "He's giving the house to St. Dennis."

Sophie frowned. "How's that going to work?"

"He's got it all spelled out. He's leaving money for maintenance and upkeep, but he'd like the house to be used for tours and for education, maybe to showcase local art or something."

"What if the town doesn't want it?"

Jesse grinned. "There's no provision for that."

"It could be used as a moneymaker," she said. "Weddings and meetings and such."

"Well, that will be up to the town council. By the way, Pop's doctor came in while I was there, checked him out, ran another EKG. Says he can go home in a few days, once they get him hydrated. Apparently he was dehydrated when they brought him in."

"I was really afraid we were going to lose him," Sophie confessed.

"So was I." Jesse finished his soup, rinsed the bowl and the spoon, and set them on the counter. "Thanks for the snack."

"You're welcome."

She walked him to the door. "You weren't breaching any confidentiality by telling me about Pop's will, were you?"

"No, he said I could share it with you. Oh, and he also told me to give you the next two weeks off. He said you were looking gaunt—his word—and that I should give you some time to get things set up at the restaurant. So there you go. Bonus weeks. Use them well." Jesse stepped outside.

"Shocking," she laughed. "We both know that he hates the idea, but two weeks off would be awesome. I could really use the time, and frankly, it's harder than I thought it would be," she admitted.

"I'm trying really hard not to say 'told you so.' "

"I'll be fine, once all the physical work is done. It's just that right now, it's all a bit overwhelming. Trying to get the place organized and figure out what I can keep and what I should toss and what I need to order and what I can make over."

"Take the weeks. Get your shit together." Jesse headed down the sidewalk.

She nodded and leaned on the door frame. "Thanks."

"Oh, and call me if you need help." Jesse got into his car, waved, and gave one quick toot on his horn as he drove away.

Sophie watched the taillights disappear, then stood in the doorway for a few minutes, watching the stars wink overhead. She made a wish on the first one she saw, then closed the door behind her, turned off the lights, and went to bed, thinking that maybe the star didn't exist that could make her wish come true.

Cameron was waiting for her at the restaurant the next morning, a checklist in his hand.

"I heard about Curtis," he said. "Is everything all right?"

"He's good. How'd you hear about it so fast?" Sophie unlocked the front door.

"Ellie saw Brooke picking up take-out from the Thai place last night."

"He'll be fine. I'll tell him that you were asking for him." She turned on the lights. "Thanks for putting the bulbs in so we can see what we're doing."

"Yeah, it was pretty dim in here." He handed her an envelope. "Copies of all your permits, estimates, and my contract are in there. Take some time to look everything over and sign it when you get a chance. Ask if you have any questions. You don't have to do it right now. I can see you're antsy to get to work."

"I just want it all done. Jesse gave me the next two weeks off to try to get ready to open, but I don't know if even that's going to be enough time."

"You won't need more than that. My guys will be in tomorrow and out by Thursday. You'll have new windows, nice shiny floors, new bathrooms, and new lighting fixtures and ceiling fans. What's the story with the appliances?"

"The guy who inspected the cooler and the refrigerator said they both need new compressors, which he can install on Tuesday. Said other than dust on the coils, things looked pretty good. The stove is okay, just needed some cleaning out of a mouse nest in the oven and a lot of spiders around the burners. The exterminator got rid of everything that had been living in here for the past six years, so right now, I'm the sole occupant."

"What else do you have to do?"

"I need to order some dishes and some utensils, get my final menu worked out, order supplies, and oh, yes. I'll need to hire some people. Two waitresses to start, a dishwasher, another cook. Someone to help prep."

"That going to be enough?"

"We'll see. I don't know that business will be all that brisk at first."

"You might be surprised. A lot of people are talking about it."

"Let's hope they do more than talk."

Cameron left with the promise to return in the morning with a crew to tackle the bathrooms and the new windows. Sophie put a drop cloth on the floor next to the largest wall and opened a can of paint. By four in the afternoon, the entire dining room had been freshly painted and Sophie was envisioning how the enlarged photos in their black frames would look against the pale yellow walls. She washed her brushes off in the deep stainless-steel sink in the kitchen and set them on the counter to dry. Then she walked down to the dock behind the trees and sat on the edge, dangling her feet in the water and watching the swans on the other side. She leaned her head back to catch the sun, and when her hair got too hot, she stood up.

"Break's over."

She made a call to Grace Sinclair to place ads in the paper for the employees she thought she'd need to start, and to set up an interview for Wednesday. The preopening publicity would be good to generate interest that, according to Cam, was already starting to build. She made a shopping list of items she'd need for the kitchen and her first week's food requirements. She called Clay Madison and discussed the amount of eggs and produce he could supply. Then she called three other farmers and sketched out her first week's menu.

She had almost finished with the lunch specials when she heard activity next door. She went to the window and looked out across the fence. For the first time, she noticed that the smelly piles had gotten smaller. How much smaller might they be by next week, she wondered. If Cameron's crews were as good as he claimed they were, she could target Friday of the following week as her opening day.

Of course, by then, Jason would probably have had another delivery. The thought of a new pile of stinking mushroom soil a stone's throw from her side window made her want to cry.

She stepped outside and walked around her building, taking note of the work she still had to do out there. Weeds to pull, volunteer saplings to be cut down, flowers to plant. She walked to the front and was considering how she'd manage to have something growing and blooming by the front door in a week, when a car pulled in behind hers. She turned to look just as a man in dark glasses hopped out of a black BMW.

"Hey! Sophie!" he called merrily.

Christopher? She blinked.

"Chris?"

"How are you?" He put his arms out as if to hug her, and she took a few steps back.

"What are you doing here?" She ignored both his question and his attempt to touch her.

The thought of him touching her made her cringe.

"I came to see you, to talk to you. I've missed you. I can't stop thinking about you." He looked around, first at her restaurant, then at the lot next door. "They told me at that coffee place in town that you'd probably be out here. What's with this place, anyway?" He looked around, obviously unimpressed. "You giving up a legal career to open a café? Here?"

"It's really none of your business." She took another step back. "I'm sorry you made the trip, sorry you felt compelled to see me. I can't imagine what would have possessed you to come all the way out here without even calling. If you had called, I would have saved you from making the drive. I don't want to see you, I don't miss you, and I don't want you here. Please go."

"Sophie, let's talk this out. We were good together . . ."

"No. In retrospect, we weren't. If we'd been all that good, you wouldn't have been sleeping with Anita. So I don't have anything more to say to you. Please leave."

"At least show me around your new place." He pointed to the restaurant with no real interest.

"No, Chris, I really, really want you to go."

"Look, Sophie, just give me a chance . . ."

Sophie studied his face and the desperate sound of his voice. A gleeful expression spread across her face.

"She dumped you, didn't she?"

"What? No. Of course not," Christopher protested. "I just got to thinking . . ."

"Anita dumped you and you thought you could sweet-talk me into taking you back."

"Look, Sophie, we had a good thing . . ."

"Which you screwed up by screwing around. But I don't hold a grudge. Actually, I should thank you. This"—she pointed to the building behind her—"is the best thing that ever happened to me."

"So does that mean . . . ?"

"It means I want you to leave. Now, Chris."

"If we could just sit and talk for a few minutes, if you could let me apologize again. I'll do anything . . ."

"Buddy, are you deaf, or are you just stupid?" Jason walked around the fence.

Chris frowned. "Who's that?" he asked Sophie.

Jason put an arm around Sophie. "Want me to pick him up and toss him into the mulch, babe?"

"That would be nice." She nodded calmly. "Yes, I think I'd like that."

Chris looked from Sophie to Jason and back again.

"Seriously, Sophie? You and this . . . goon . . . ?"

Sophie smiled. "He may be a goon, but he's my goon."

"You couldn't seriously prefer . . ." Chris pointed to Jason as if he couldn't bring himself to finish the sentence.

"Any day of the week, Chris," Sophie assured him.

Chris looked momentarily stunned. "If that's what you want . . ."

"It's exactly what I want."

Chris shook his head and backed toward his car as if afraid to turn his back on Jason. He got in, revved the engine, and peeled out of the parking lot.

"Thanks," Sophie said. "I was afraid I wasn't going to be able to get rid of him."

"I wasn't trying to eavesdrop," Jason told her. "But I was right there on the other side of the fence, and it sounded like he was getting pushy, and not in a good way."

"He was. I'm glad you stepped in."

"Who *was* that guy?" Jason asked.

"My ex."

"Pardon me for saying this, but he seemed like an asshole."

"He is."

There was silence for a long moment.

Later, Sophie tried to remember who laughed first. All she could recall was that one minute they were staring at each other, the next, laughing their heads off.

"Sorry about the goon thing." She tried to catch her breath but couldn't.

"I've been called worse."

They watched the black sedan speed down River Road and blow the stop sign. Seconds later, they heard the *whoop-whoop-whoop* of the police siren.

"Oh, my God, that's so perfect!" Sophie dissolved into new peals of laughter.

"Is gloating appropriate right about now?" Jason asked.

"Totally." She laughed so hard she began to hiccough. "I hope Beck throws the book at him."

"Speeding in a thirty-five-mile-an-hour zone plus ignoring a stop sign should equal a hefty fine," Jason pointed out.

"Good. That's what he gets for just showing up here out of the blue like that." Sophie shook her head. "I don't know what he was thinking."

"You really had no clue? He hasn't called?"

"I haven't spoken to him since that night of Logan's science fair." She sobered. "He called to give me some bad news on a case he knew I cared a lot about, then used that as an opportunity to apologize for his extremely bad behavior."

"Am I allowed to ask what he did?"

"Caught him doing the deed with a co-worker." Sophie paused, then added, "In the backseat of that very car, by the way."

"I'm sorry."

"Don't be. I meant it when I told him that breaking up with him was the best thing that ever happened to me." She watched his face and could tell he thought she was rationalizing. "If I'd stayed in Ohio, I'd never have gotten this." She pointed to the building, then remembered his interest in it. "Sorry. You're probably wishing I hadn't . . ."

"I'm okay with it now."

"Really?"

"I wanted to tell you that before you open here, I'll have gone through all the mulch. Next delivery, I'll have it dumped over on the other side of the lot and down closer to the river. I'm having some trees cleared off tomorrow to make room." He added, "I skipped the mushroom soil this time around."

"What about your shop? Your retail shop?"

"I'll think of something else."

She watched his eyes watching her, and she couldn't resist. "Want to come in and see what we're doing?"

"I'd love to." He followed her inside and she closed the door. "I've never seen the inside."

He looked around the dining room. "Not too big, not too small. Manageable, I'd think."

"I hope so."

"You still planning on working here and with Jess?"

She nodded. "He gave me two weeks off, though. At the insistence of our grandfather, but still."

"Nice of him. What are you calling it, by the way?" His gesture encompassed the building.

"Blossoms." Sophie smiled. "That's what they used to call my grandmother Rose, Ellie's great-aunt Lilly, and Violet."

"Nice tribute. It suits." He smiled. "I wish you all the luck, Sophie. I hope your place is a huge success."

"Thanks. I hope you mean that."

"I do." He started toward the door. "Thanks, by the way, for the phone call last night. I appreciate that you thought to call me."

"Of course."

"And he's all right? Curtis?"

"He seems to be. He is one tough old bird."

"True enough. Well . . ." He was at the door, his hand on the knob.

She had the sudden feeling that if he left, he'd never be back, and the thought made her panic. If there was ever a chance for them, she had to make it happen now.

"What movie did you see?" She took a step in his direction.

"What?" He paused in the doorway.

"The movie you and Logan saw last night. What was it?" She took another step.

"Oh, some animated car thing. Logan's into animation."

"Sorry I missed it." Another step closer.

"Maybe next time."

"When?"

"When what?" He appeared momentarily puzzled.

"When's the next time?"

"When would you like it to be?" He stepped forward to meet her halfway.

"Now. Right now." She opened her arms and he pulled her close, nuzzled the side of her face, then kissed her hungrily.

"God, I missed you," he murmured.

"Me, too," she said between kisses. "I wanted to tell you that I was sorry that I got pissy, sorry that I yelled at your guy in the truck, sorry that I hadn't told you sooner that this was the place . . ."

"I'm sorry that I wasn't a more gracious loser. Sorry that I tried to make you feel guilty about having bought this place. Sorry that I dumped mulch so close to your property."

"I'm sorry that . . ."

He placed a finger over her lips.

"We're done being sorry," he told her. "Let's let it go."

"I was so afraid we were over." She rested her head on his chest. "I didn't want us to be over."

"We're not over," he whispered. "We're not over, Sophie . . ."

"Let's lock up." She pulled away from him.

"Your place or mine?"

"Your place this time." She was smiling as she turned off the lights and grabbed her keys from the table where she'd tossed them earlier.

"We're not over," she repeated aloud while she drove to his house on Doyle Street. There was still a chance they could find the magic again, and maybe even make it last.

On Monday night, back at Sophie's, just before she fell asleep, she heard Jason whisper, "Just want you to know that sometimes I have nightmares. They can be disconcerting, I would think, if you're not aware that it happens."

"Same nightmare?" She twisted slightly to look up into his face.

"Pretty much."

"Want to tell me about it?"

He fell silent, and she thought he'd decided against sharing that part of himself, which was okay as far as she was concerned. When—if—he was ready, he'd talk about it.

"You know my parents died in a car accident," he said long after she'd assumed he'd fallen asleep.

"I remember you said that, yes."

"Did I mention that the accident was my fault?"

"You were driving?"

"No, my dad was."

"Then how was it your fault?"

"I sneaked out one night after my parents were

asleep, took my dad's car, and picked up a few of my buddies and went joyriding. I'd just dropped off the last of the guys and was headed home, thinking how clever I was to have gotten away with it, when I got pulled over because one of the headlights was out. When the cop realized that I was under age and had no license, he took me into the station and called my parents to come pick me up. By this time it was almost five in the morning. They got Eric out of bed to drive them to get me."

Sophie had a bad feeling that she knew where this was going, but she sat back and let him tell it in his own time.

"My mom came into the station for me, never said a word, just pointed to the door. My dad had gotten the car back and was waiting outside. Neither of them spoke on the drive home. It was obvious that they were really angry, super disappointed in me. I knew I was in for it when we got home. Two blocks from our house, a drunk driver wiped out on a deep curve and crossed into the opposing lane of traffic."

"Your lane."

"Yeah. Hit us head-on. My dad and my mom both died instantly. I walked away with only a few broken bones."

"So you're saying if you hadn't taken the car that night that your parents would still be alive."

"That's what it came down to, yeah."

"Jason, the person responsible for that accident was the guy who was driving drunk."

"But if I hadn't . . ."

"That wasn't the cause of the accident." She took his face in both her hands. "Believe me, as a prosecutor, I've seen more than my share of fatal accidents caused by drunk drivers. Drunk drivers cause accidents."

He lay back against the pillow, and it was a long time before she heard his breathing relax and knew he'd finally fallen asleep.

Much to Sophie's surprise, the next morning, Jason had a flatbed truck deliver a dozen pine trees, which he lined up along his side of the fence that separated his property from hers. Until he'd actually gotten inside the restaurant, he told her later, he hadn't realized how noisy his trucks sounded inside those stone walls. On Wednesday, a crew of guys with chain saws began clearing the far side of his lot, cutting down the saplings and sending them through a wood chipper.

"The chips are pretty green, but they'll age," Jason told her. "Eventually, I'll be able to sell them. In the meantime, they're making way for a delivery of topsoil."

"And mulch." She grimaced.

"Usually people are looking for mulch when they're putting in their gardens and their planting beds early in the season. That time is pretty much past now."

"So, in other words, I don't have to worry about the stench driving my customers away until next year?"

"*Stench* is such a harsh word."

"Not if you'd smelled it from inside my place."

"Well, that's one thing you don't have to worry about next week when you open."

"Yeah, I just have to worry about a lot of empty tables."

"I think that idea you had to invite people in the night before so they can sample the menu is terrific."

"Let's hope they'll like what they see."

"I like what I see."

"I hope so." She laughed and went into the kitchen, returning with a plate piled with slices of pound cake.

"Here. Take these over and pass them around to your guys—see what they think."

"Those guys will eat anything. I don't think they're the critics you should be courting."

"Go. Get out of my hair. I have a dozen more recipes to test today."

"Great." Jason took the plate and headed for the door. "I'll be back for lunch . . ."

Every day for the following week, Sophie crossed something else off her list of must-dos. When she finally got around to the outside of the building, she asked Jason if he had a pair of snips she could borrow, and maybe a shovel.

"What do you have in mind?" he asked.

"I want to get rid of the weeds that are growing around the building—you know, make it look tidier. And I want to cut out that viney stuff around the front door so I can plant some flowers out there."

"What kind of flowers?"

"Lilies, roses, and violets."

"Lilies we can do, and roses we can do. Violets are out of season right now."

"Is there something I can plant that's sort of violet-colored?"

"Let me take care of the outside. You go back to whatever you were doing."

"I was thinking about working out here."

"I've got it covered."

True to his word, by the end of the week the grounds had been cleared of all the trash, trees, weeds, and vines, and at the door, newly planted red Knock Out roses, yellow daylilies, and purple salvia grew. Ellie had talked Sophie into letting her paint not only the sign that would hang over the door, but the front window as well. The small bouquet of the three flowers, loosely tied together with a trailing blue ribbon, was exactly what Sophie had in mind, and, as she told Ellie, much better than anything she might have drawn. The bouquet would be Blossoms' logo and would appear on the menus and the sign out front, as well as all the ads she'd run in the local paper.

On Saturday, Jason and Sophie arrived early at Ellie's to complete their contribution to the restoration of the carriage house, and on Sunday, she invited Jesse, Brooke, Curtis, and Violet to Blossoms to test a meal.

"I thought you were going to invite a lot of people the night before you open," Jason said.

"I am. This is the test before the test."

Curtis had been a bit cranky about the whole thing until he arrived and saw the name on the window.

"Blossoms," he read softly, but he made no comment.

Once inside, however, he stood transfixed in front of the wall of photographs.

"Oh, for pity's sake, where'd you get that picture of me in that rowboat?" he asked. At first, Sophie thought he was annoyed, until he turned and she could see the laughter in his eyes. "I must have been all of about eleven. Took on the big boys in the annual boat race."

"You win?" Jason asked.

"Came in dead last."

"And look, Pop, here's Gramma Rose . . . ," Sophie began.

". . . in her wedding dress." His eyes misted over. "Never saw a more beautiful sight in all my life."

"She was very beautiful." Sophie slipped her hand through his arm. "See, here she is as a girl. With Lilly and Violet."

"Let me see that." Violet left her purse on a table and adjusted her glasses. "Oh, my word. Look at that. We were so young. Hard to believe we were ever that young."

"Here's a picture of Lilly and Lynley Sebastian," Curtis pointed out. He turned to Jason and said, "Did you know one of the first supermodels grew up right here in St. Dennis?"

"No, I didn't." Jason stepped closer to take a look. "I remember her. All the guys had this poster of her on their bedroom walls."

"Did you?" Sophie asked.

"Absolutely."

"You know that's Ellie's mother, right?" Jesse walked over to inspect the wall.

"What? No." Jason's eyes widened. "I had no idea."

"That's where Ellie gets her good looks," Curtis told them. "Not that scoundrel of a father of hers. Lost a bundle to that son of a bitch."

"Okay, Pop, water over the dam." Sophie steered him to a table, pleased that her photo wall was proving to be such a success.

She and Jason had pushed several tables together to make one long enough to accommodate everyone.

"Sit, please," Sophie announced. "I want to start serving."

"You're cooking *and* serving?" Brooke frowned. "How's that going to work?"

"I won't have a waitress until Thursday, so Jason offered to fill in today." Sophie went through the swinging door into the kitchen.

"Really?" Curtis turned to Violet and smiled. "Did you hear that, Vi? Jason is helping Sophie in the restaurant today."

"Nice of him." She smiled back.

"Indeed." He mouthed the words *thank you*.

"You're welcome," she whispered.

Sophie came out of the kitchen with several small bowls on a tray.

"Okay, these are roasted chickpeas. I want to serve these to every table while people are looking at their menus." She proceeded to place a bowl on the table in front of every other person.

"Chickpeas for breakfast?" Jesse made a face.

"On the lunch tables." She smacked his arm lightly as she walked by.

"These are yummy," Brooke told her. "It's a great idea. Inexpensive yet innovative. I like it."

"Thanks." Sophie hustled into the kitchen for the next tray, which she gave to Jason to carry.

"Here's a sampling of the lunch selections. If something doesn't work, please say so now, or it goes on the menu that I take to the printer this week."

Jason stood on her left as she reeled off the contents of the tray, from the BLTs to the chicken-avocado-bacon on a croissant. Everything was met with approval, so she went on to the desserts.

Again, Jason appeared with a tray.

"I was lucky to have been able to cull some recipes from several St. Dennis residents. Violet, here's your mother's lemon meringue pie. I hope it serves her memory well." She pointed to another plate. "Here's Gramma Rose's pound cake, Pop. You'll have to let me know if it lives up to hers. And Lilly Cavanaugh's cherry tarts." Jason passed out samples of each. "Some days I'll have brownies, some days crème brûlée— Grace Sinclair gave me her recipe—and India Devlin emailed me her great-aunt Nola's recipe for coconut cake, which she swears is the best on the planet. I haven't tested that one yet, but it looks amazing."

"My grandmother used to make an apple pie that kicked butt," Brooke told her. "Maybe my mom would cough it up if you ask nicely."

"Thanks. I'll give her a call."

When the meal was over, Sophie asked for suggestions, criticisms, and critiques.

"I can't think of one thing," Brooke told her. "Everything was awesome. If this is what you're going to offer, Blossoms is going to be around for a long, long time."

"God, I hope so." Sophie sank into a nearby chair. "I've dreamed about a place just like this since I was seventeen. I can't believe it's really happening."

"You should be very proud of yourself, Sophie." She was at a loss to hear those words come from her grandfather's lips. "You've worked very hard, and you're earning all the success I know you're going to have."

"Yeah, me too," Jesse conceded. "I hate to admit it, but I don't think you're going to fall on your face." He raised his water glass. "Here's to dreams coming true, little sister."

"Thanks, Jess." She fought back a lump in her throat.

"Now, you sit, and we'll do the cleanup." Brooke stood and began gathering up the plates. "Come on, Jess."

"What?" Jesse turned to her in mock horror.

"You heard me. Up." Brooke took him by the arm and he pretended to resist, but he cleared the table.

Sophie tried, but she couldn't sit still. She ended up in the kitchen putting things away and reorganizing a cupboard in the process. By the time everyone had left, she was buoyed by their praise but dead on her feet. She slumped onto a counter stool, her face in her hands.

"What's wrong?" Jason came up behind her and massaged her shoulders.

"I can't believe it's really going to happen," she whispered. "What if . . ."

"Uh, no. No what-ifs. You're going to knock 'em dead at your preview party and on opening day, this place is going to be packed. You'll see."

She reached back to touch one of his hands. "Thank you."

"For . . . ?"

"For helping me today. For encouraging me. For letting go of this place so that I could do this."

"That whole week when we weren't speaking, I was miserable." He wrapped his arms around her from behind. "I realized that I could give up part of my dream if it meant yours would come true."

"Aww, Jason . . ." She turned around in the chair.

"I have a business that's doing very well, and I have eighty-five percent of what I wanted. So I don't have a shop. I'll think of something when the time comes. I wasn't ready for it this year, anyway."

"Well, if we're confessing, I have to admit that I was pretty miserable, too. All I could think about was how happy I am when I'm with you. I hadn't been happy like that in . . . maybe forever."

"Not even with BMW guy?"

"Not for a moment."

"Come with me." He lifted her off the chair.

"Where are we going?"

"Down to the river."

She locked the front door, and they went out the back. Three steps out the door, he stopped and snapped his fingers. "Wait here. I forgot something."

He was back in a minute with a brown paper bag in one hand and two juice glasses in the other. "Sorry. I don't have champagne glasses."

"You bought champagne?"

He nodded and took her hand. "I figured this would be a night to celebrate."

They walked to the end of the old dock and sat, just as Sophie had the other day. This time was better, she thought. This time, she was with Jason.

"Nice evening," he said.

"Beautiful," she agreed, and it was. The sun had set over the water and touched the river with color. The first of the lightning bugs had come out and the air was tinged with fragrance.

Jason popped the cork and poured bubbly into each glass, then raised his.

"Here's to new beginnings, to dreams."

"To dreams coming true," she added.

They clinked their glasses.

"I will never forget this night, Jason. I will always remember how special it was, having you with me when I could show off my dream to my family, to prove it could work."

"My mom always said that life is made up of memories. That your memories are the story of your past." He kissed the side of her face. "Someday this will be part of our past, too. A memory we made together."

"I like the sound of that." She took a sip of champagne and stood, pulling him up by his hand. "Since this is a night for making memories, let's go back to my place and make a few more . . ."

Diary ~

So many pleasant surprises this summer—so many wonderful things to look forward to. The latest here in St. Dennis is the opening of a new restaurant out on River Road. I'm talking about the total remake of the old Walsh place. Sophie Enright purchased the building and has renovated it completely, and what a makeover she's done! You'd never recognize it as the same place. And my goodness, the food she's serving—breakfast and lunch only, don't you know—delicious. Deliciously different, Brooke calls it. I personally love the way she's allowed our town to take center stage. Aside from the fact that almost everything she serves is locally sourced—let's hear it for keeping our farmers in the black!—she's decorated the dining room to reflect the history of St. Dennis. How clever is that? She has photos on the walls of people who lived here, past and present—especially her grandmother, Rose Enright, and Rose's friends, Lilly Cavanaugh and Violet Finneran. Their photos are everywhere, delightful shots from years past. It's most charming. I could spend hours in there, just looking at the pictures and reminiscing. There's even a picture of my Dan and me in front of the inn, the year we were married. My, how the inn has changed since then! And here's something fun that she's done: she's borrowed recipes from some of us old-timers and has specials on the menu made from those old recipes. I wish I'd thought of that for the inn, I don't mind saying. I offered her my crème brûlée recipe, and she's promised to let me know when she's going to make it.

She's a clever girl, that Sophie. She invited a group of people from town to a pre—grand opening taste test of her menu, and it had everyone buzzing for the past week. Everything she served was excellent, I must say, and I know I for one will be stopping in often for her lunch specials. Dallas MacGregor was especially pleased to have such a fine place right down the road from her new studio, which opens in three weeks. She tells me she's almost fully staffed, and she's preparing to start work on <u>Pretty Maids,</u> her first film. Sophie promised to make special box lunches for Dallas's people. She is doing a very early breakfast for the watermen, but she tells me they apparently haven't gotten the memo, because she isn't doing the early morning business she expected. I told her to be patient—once word spreads, she'll have people standing at the counter waiting for one of her delicious breakfast sandwiches, which, she said, were a late addition to the menu.

I love when our young people show such respect for our past, and love that she's honored her grandmother in such a lovely way. Did I mention that she's named her place Blossoms, after Rose, Lilly, and Violet?

As previously reported—you can't take the newswoman out of the girl, you know—Sophie and Jason are becoming quite the item. Lucy says they're fixing up the apartment over Blossoms, and that she wouldn't be surprised if they decided to share it once it's finished. I can't help but wonder if somehow Vi's sudden request for some very particular herbs didn't have something to do with that.

And now, for the best news ever. EVER. Ford is coming home! Yes, my baby is coming home! I can hardly believe it myself. No, I don't know the exact date, or the reason, only that he's told his sister that he thought it was time (if he'd asked me, I'd have told him it was long past time). Frankly, I don't care why. I just want him home and safe. It's the answer to my every prayer for the past five or six years, and finally, I will be able to lay my head on my pillow at night and sleep peacefully through the night, knowing exactly where all my children are, and that they're safe from harm. I bless that boy of mine for his selfless devotion to others, for his concern for his fellow man, but as his mother, most of all, I bless him for coming home.

~ Grace ~

Rose Enright's
Perfect Pound Cake

½ pound (2 sticks) unsalted butter, softened
3 cups sugar
1 cup plain yogurt (Greek works best) thinned with
    3 tablespoons heavy cream or milk
½ teaspoon baking powder
3 cups all-purpose flour
6 large eggs at room temperature
2 teaspoons vanilla
½ teaspoon almond extract
Powdered sugar, optional

Preheat oven to 325°F.

In a large mixing bowl, cream the butter and sugar together.

Add the yogurt and mix until incorporated.

Sift the baking powder and flour together.

Add the flour mixture to the creamed mixture, alternating with eggs, one at a time, beating after each addition.

Add the vanilla and almond extracts and pour the mixture into a greased and floured 10-inch tube pan. Bake for 1 hour, 20 minutes, until tester comes out clean—start testing at 1 hour, 10 minutes.

Turn onto a cake plate when slightly cooled and dust with powdered sugar.

India Devlin's
Great-Aunt Nola's
Coconut Cake

½ teaspoon vanilla
½ teaspoon coconut extract
¾ cup flaked coconut (soak in 2 tablespoons milk)
2½ cups plus 2 tablespoons flour
3 teaspoons baking powder
½ teaspoon salt
¾ cup butter, softened
1½ cups sugar
3 eggs, separated
¾ cup milk

Preheat oven to 350°F and prepare two 8-inch round or square cake pans or a 13×9×2 pan (grease and flour). Add the vanilla and coconut extracts to the milk and set aside.

Sift the flour, baking powder, and salt together. Set aside.

Cream the butter with a mixer for 30 seconds, then gradually add the sugar and mix on medium speed for 5 minutes. Beat the egg yolks and add to the butter mixture.

Add flour and milk alternately to the butter mixture, stirring after each addition, until smooth.

Stir in the coconut.

With clean, dry beaters, beat the egg whites until stiff but not dry. Gently fold into batter.

Turn into pans, baking for 25 minutes.

Cool in pans 10 minutes, then invert onto racks and cool completely before frosting.

FROSTING
2 tablespoons coconut
4 tablespoons milk
½ cup butter, softened
1-pound box of confectioners' sugar, sifted
½ teaspoon coconut extract
½ teaspoon vanilla extract

Soak the coconut in the milk. Beat the butter with a mixer on medium speed for 30 seconds. Add ½ of the sugar and beat well. Drain the coconut and add the milk to the butter mixture, beating well. Gradually add remaining sugar until desired consistency. Blend in the extracts and coconut.

Frost cake and cover with as much coconut as the cake will hold.

CRAB CAKES À LA BLOSSOMS

¾ *cup plain breadcrumbs*
1 *pound fresh crabmeat, drained well, picked over*
¼ *cup mayonnaise*
3 *tablespoons chopped fresh chives*
1 *tablespoon Worcestershire sauce*
1 *tablespoon Dijon mustard*
1 *teaspoon lemon juice*
Zest of one lemon
Salt and pepper
1 *large egg, beaten to blend*
Paprika
¼ *cup olive oil*

Place ½ cup of the breadcrumbs in a shallow dish. Mix the crabmeat, mayonnaise, chives, Worcestershire sauce, mustard, lemon juice and zest, and remaining ¼ cup breadcrumbs in a medium bowl to blend. Season with salt and pepper. Mix in the egg.

Form crab cakes into several rounds—the number of crab cakes depends on the size you want them to be. Coat them with the breadcrumbs in the dish, then sprinkle with paprika.

Transfer crab cakes to a baking sheet, cover, and refrigerate for 1 hour.

Heat the oil in a heavy large skillet over medium heat. Working in batches, add crab cakes to skillet and cook until golden brown and heated through. Time will be determined by the thickness of the cakes.

Transfer crab cakes to a paper towel lined plate and let rest for a moment before serving.

Lilly Cavanaugh's Curried Chicken Salad

2 cups diced cooked chicken
1 apple, peeled and diced
1 cup diced pineapple
¼ cup raisins
½ cup shredded coconut

Combine all ingredients.
Add the prepared dressing.
Refrigerate at least one hour before serving.

Dressing
1 tablespoon curry powder
2 tablespoons chicken broth
1 cup mayonnaise
2 tablespoons chutney, including syrup

Add the curry powder to the broth and simmer for about 30 seconds to one minute (don't let it burn), making a paste. Add the paste to the mayonnaise. Stir in the chutney.

Violet Finneran's Mother's Lemon Meringue Pie

Pastry for one 9-inch pie (store-bought or homemade)

Pie Filling
1 cup sugar
¼ cup plus 1 tablespoon cornstarch
¼ teaspoon salt
4 large egg yolks
¾ cup fresh lemon juice
2 cups cold water
1½ teaspoons finely grated lemon zest
6 tablespoons unsalted butter, cut into tablespoons

Meringue Topping
4 large egg whites at room temperature
¼ teaspoon cream of tartar
¼ teaspoon salt
½ cup sugar

To make the filling, in a medium saucepan, combine the sugar with the cornstarch, salt, egg yolks, and lemon juice. Whisk in the cold water and cook over moderate heat, whisking constantly, until the mixture comes to a boil. Boil, stirring, for 1 minute. Remove from the heat and add the lemon zest and butter, stirring until the butter is melted.

Pour the filling into the pie shell, cover with wax paper, and let cool to room temperature.

Preheat oven to 350°F and position a rack in the upper third.

To make the topping, in a large stainless-steel bowl,

add the cream of tartar to the egg whites, then beat with the salt until soft peaks form. Gradually add the sugar and beat until stiff and glossy peaks form.

Remove the wax paper from the filling. Scrape the meringue onto the pie and gently spread it over the filling all the way to the crimped edge of the piecrust. Make swirls with the back of a spoon.

Bake the pie for about 7 minutes, or until the meringue is golden brown. Transfer to a wire rack and let cool to room temperature, then refrigerate until chilled and set, at least 3 hours. Cut the pie with a sharp knife dipped into hot water and serve.

MAKE AHEAD: The recipe can be made through step 4 and refrigerated overnight. Top with the meringue and bake, then let cool before serving.

SOPHIE ENRIGHT'S
ROASTED CHICKPEAS

2 (15-ounce) cans chickpeas (garbanzo beans), thoroughly drained and rinsed
2 tablespoons olive oil
½ teaspoon of spice of your choice—ground cumin, curry, ground chili pepper, or cayenne pepper
1 tablespoon minced garlic
½ teaspoon sea salt

Preheat oven to 400°F and arrange a rack in the middle.

Place the chickpeas in a large bowl and toss with the remaining ingredients until evenly coated. Spread the chickpeas in an even layer on a rimmed baking sheet and bake until crisp, about 25 minutes.

Read on for a preview of book eight from the

CHESAPEAKE DIARIES SERIES

ON SUNSET BEACH

Available from Ballantine Books in Spring 2014.

Ford Sinclair eased his rental car onto the approach to the Chesapeake Bay Bridge-Tunnel in Virginia Beach and reduced his speed. It had been several years since he'd made this crossing, and he wanted to savor it. The bridge—named one of the Seven Engineering Marvels of the Modern World—had been a favorite destination when he was a young boy and his father was alive. Some days, they would sneak away from the family's inn, just the two of them, and head south in the old Bayrider down through Virginia's Pocomoke Sound. His father would drop anchor off Raccoon Island where they'd sit for a while and watch the cars over the north-bound span of the bridge-tunnel—which was still new back then, and attracted attention like a shiny new toy—then they'd head back into Maryland waters where they'd spend the rest of the day fishing. They'd go home, more often than not sporting a farmer's tan along with a cooler of whatever had been running that day, rockfish or sea bass or croakers. Once, his dad had helped him bring in a tuna that had given him—at ten—the fight of his life. The memory was so vivid that whenever Ford dreamed of that day, he still felt the rod biting into his hands as he struggled to hold it.

The bridge-tunnel itself was, in fact, a marvel. A little over seventeen miles long from shore to shore, it was exactly what the name implied: a series of bridges and tunnels that crossed the Chesapeake Bay where it joined the Atlantic Ocean, connecting Virginia Beach to Virginia's Eastern Shore.

Ford stopped at the first of the four bridges and pulled over into the parking area. He walked to the rail overlooking the water from which he could see for miles. Below, where the Chesapeake and the Atlantic met, the water was still dark and disturbed from last night's storm. In the distance, a large Navy vessel headed into port at Virginia Beach, and far out in the ocean, another made its way toward the bridge. Noisy gulls circled overhead, hoping for a handout from the sightseers on the pier, while others swooped and soared over both sides of the bridge. Ford closed his eyes and inhaled the scent of salt water, and held it in his lungs for a few seconds before letting it out in a *whoosh*. Chesapeake Bay born and bred, he hadn't realized how much he had missed its scent until this moment. Suddenly, he couldn't wait to be home. He climbed back into the car and continued his trek north.

After two mile-long tunnels and three more low- and high-level bridges, Ford reached Route 13 and headed for Salisbury, Maryland. There he'd pick up Route 50, the road that led west to his home town on the Eastern Shore. The radio reception was spotty through here—some things, he thought, never changed—so he could only pick up a country station.

He'd been away too long to know who was singing, only caught enough to know it was a girl with a pretty voice singing about vandalizing the SUV that belonged to her cheating boyfriend. He turned it off when the static drowned her out, and drove in silence, the windows up and the air conditioner blasting against the heat and humidity of the late-summer afternoon.

Before he knew it, Ford was crossing the bridge over the Choptank River and was halfway to Trappe, where he and his buddies had proven their manhood by spending the night in the haunted White Marsh Cemetery and living to tell about it. Even now, memories of that night made him grin. They'd been so cocky, all five of them, until they heard the faint tinkling of a tiny bell borne on a breeze around three in the morning. They spent the rest of the night wide awake, huddled in the car, windows closed and the doors locked, but still bragged that they'd lasted the night because they didn't drive back out through the cemetery gates until dawn.

Ford's smile faded when he recalled how far he'd come from that cheeky kid whose most terrifying moments had been spent in a dark cemetery with his friends telling ghost stories. Back then, he'd never imagined what real terrors this world held. The innocent boy—brash though he may have been—would never have understood the things he'd come to see as a man. Even now, Ford was at a loss to really understand what motivated a man to commit atrocities such as those he'd witnessed over the past six years.

He was close to home now. One left turn off Route 50 and he was almost there. He cruised along just under the speed limit so he could take it all in.

If there hadn't been another car behind him, he'd have slowed even more as he passed the Madison farm. Ford had learned to ice skate on the pond that lay beyond the corn field. It had been Clay Madison—now married to Ford's sister Lucy—who'd taught him to skate. Clay had always been sweet on Lucy—even as a small kid, Ford had known that. An old pickup was parked near the back of the farmhouse, and he thought briefly about stopping to say hello, but he knew if his mother caught wind of him stopping somewhere other than home first, he'd be in for an earful. And somehow, his mother had always known what he was up to. He'd never really figured out how she knew things, but she did. He thought she must have had a pretty darned good spy network, though she never seemed to keep track of Dan or Lucy the way she'd kept track of him.

Ford hoped that hadn't held true these past few years. He hated to think she might have somehow picked up on exactly where he'd been and what he'd seen and done.

Though his mother's phone calls and letters had kept him abreast of the changes in St. Dennis, the development of the town's center still surprised him. He wasn't sure what he'd been expecting, but it wasn't the upscale shops he passed by. The supermarket was still in the same place, but its previously dingy façade had had a significant facelift. When he left, most of the current storefronts had been boarded up or were still single-family homes. Now the shops he passed told a story of increased prosperity—Cupcake, Book 'Em, Bling, Sips, and on the opposite side of the street, Lola's

Café, Cuppachino, Petals and Posies. Only Lola's and the flower shop had been there before he left.

A new sign at the corner of Kelly's Point Road pointed toward the Bay, and listed the attractions one would find by following the arrow: public parking, the municipal building, the marina, Walt's Seafood—Ford was pleased to see that the St. Dennis landmark restaurant was still open—and something called One Scoop or Two.

His mother hadn't been kidding when she said there'd been a lot of changes in a very short period of time.

Farther down Charles Street was the right turn for home. He turned onto the drive that led to the inn and stopped the car. A very large, handsome sign pointed the way to the Inn at Sinclair Point. The drive itself had been recently black-topped, some of the trees on either side had been cut back, and it was now, he realized, two full lanes wide where, for as long as he remembered, it had been one.

What next? Ford wondered as he drove around the bend and got his first view of the inn that had been his family home and business for generations.

The large, sprawling main building had been painted since he left, the fading white walls now rejuvenated. The cabins that faced the bay had been painted as well, and he noted that the front of each now sported a window box that overflowed with summer flowers. He parked his car in the very full visitors' lot and sat for a moment, trying to take it all in. There were new tennis courts, a fenced-in playground, and if he wasn't mistaken, jutting out into the Bay was a new dock—longer and wider—to which several boats were tied. Kayaks and canoes lined the lush lawn that stretched toward the water like a carpet of smooth green Christmas velvet.

And everywhere, it seemed, people were engaged in one activity or another.

"Damn." Ford whistled under his breath. "Mom wasn't kidding when she said they'd made a lot of changes."

He got out of the car and looked around. While so much was different, the inn still somehow felt the same. Of course, he reminded himself as he gathered his bags out of the trunk of the car, it was still home.

Home. He stared at the building that loomed before him, where a seemingly endless stream of people came and went through the door to the back lobby. No amount of paint or landscaping or added features could change the way he felt when his feet touched ground at Sinclair's Point. The restlessness he'd experienced when his plane landed that morning began to fade, but it was still there, under the surface. He knew that the sense of peace he felt would be fleeting, and could not be trusted.

He barely made it across the parking lot when his sister flew out from the back door.

"You're late, you bugger! We've been pacing for hours!" Lucy threw her arms around his neck and hugged him.

"My plane was late." He dropped his bags and returned the hug for a moment, then held her at arm's length. "But look at you. You're all tan and your hair's long again." He tugged on her pony tail. "When I left, you had that short 'do and you were working your tail off out in L.A., and now you're . . ."

"Working my tail off in St. Dennis." She laughed.

"Business is good?"

"Business is great. If we were any busier, we'd be double-booking dates and holding weddings in the parking lot."

"Well, you must be doing something right, because you look a million times better than you did the last time I saw you. I'm guessing marriage agrees with you."

"Totally. Work is good, home life is fantastic. I never thought I'd come back to St. Dennis to live— and me, live on a farm? Ha! But I guess it just goes to show, never say never."

"I'm glad you're happy, sis."

"Never happier." Lucy took his arm. "Let's go inside. Mom has been pacing like you wouldn't believe."

"I would believe. Mom never changes."

"I hope not. She's amazing, with all she does here at the inn, and she still keeps the newspaper going. Of course, that's her baby." Lucy chatted away as they walked to the inn. "She still does the features and most of the photographs—though sometimes someone in town will have a great shot of something or other and she'll use it. She did hire someone to do the ads, though, and someone to handle the books. And of course, the printing and mailing . . ."

Ford frowned. "Mailing? Since when has she mailed out the paper? Who's she mailing it to?"

"You *have* been away awhile. Gone are the days when you could only pick up a copy at the grocery store or Sips." Lucy grinned. "The *St. Dennis Gazette* now has out-of-town subscribers, mostly summer people who want to keep up with what's going on in town so they'll know when to plan to come back. She mails the paper every week to places as far away as Maine, Illinois, and Nebraska. In your absence, little brother, the family business has become the go-to spot on the Chesapeake. We're big doin's, kiddo."

He paused and looked around. "The place looks amazing. And busy! I don't remember ever seeing so many people here, especially this late in the summer. And I see there's been a lot of work done on the grounds. I don't remember a gazebo there." He nodded toward the structure that sat between colorful flowerbeds and the water.

"We had a professional landscaper in last summer and he suggested the new gazebo and designed the new gardens at my request," Lucy explained. "I had a big-ticket wedding here, and the bride wanted the ceremony out on the lawn overlooking the Bay. Since she was dropping a bundle, we did what we had to do to make the area as gorgeous as we could."

"Well, you succeeded. It's really beautiful." He took one more look around before reaching for the door. "Who'd have ever thought the old place could look like this?"

"Dan, that's who. That brother of ours was determined to make the inn shine, and he did."

Ford opened the door and held it for his sister. Once inside, he gazed around the lobby, then whistled.

"Nice."

"Pretty cool, huh?" Lucy grinned. "Not fancy, but just . . . upscale and cool."

"Like me." Dan emerged from behind the reception desk. "Hey, buddy . . ."

Ford dropped his bags and hugged his older brother. "I can't believe what I've seen here so far. You've done a great job. Dad would be so proud."

"I like to think so." Dan gave Ford one last pat on the back before releasing him. "But the inn's old news to us. How are you? Glad to be home?"

"I'm dazzled by the changes, but yeah, glad to be here."

"I hope you can stay for a while." Dan picked up his brother's bags.

"I don't have any plans right now. I'm just glad to be back in the States, glad to see you guys again." Ford glanced around the lobby. "Where's Ma?"

"She's in her office. She's been pacing like an expectant father since dawn. Come on." Dan headed across the lobby, Ford and Lucy following behind.

"Ma has an office here?"

Lucy nodded. "She still has the newspaper office, but she likes to work here sometimes. Says she likes to keep an eye on things, likes to see the comings and goings."

"There sure seems to be a lot of that going on," Ford observed.

"Never been busier." Dan rapped his knuckles on a half-opened door, then pushed it open. "Mom, look who's here."

Grace was out of her chair, arms around her son, in the blink of an eye. She held him for a very long moment.

"Well, then," she said as she stepped back to hold him at arm's length, "let me have a good look at you." Grace's eyes narrowed. "You've lost so much weight. Your face is so thin. Are you feeling all right?" She looked around him to address Dan. "Tell the chef he's going to be working overtime until we put a few pounds back on your brother."

Ford laughed. "Ma, I'm fine. I might have lost a few pounds, but you know, where I've been, fine dining was only a dim memory. A *very* dim memory."

"And where have you been?" Grace forced him to look into her eyes.

"Here and there," he told her. "Africa, mostly."

"That covers a lot of ground, son," she said softly.

Ford nodded. He knew she was fishing for details, but right now, he wanted nothing more than to savor the experience of being home. He knew there'd be questions to answer, but the longer he could leave the past behind him, the better off he'd be.

"Well, we can get the whole story from Ford over dinner." Dan stood in the doorway. "Right now, let's get you settled in, then we can get together in the dining room and have a great dinner. We managed to snag a phenomenal chef from a fine D.C. restaurant last year. He's part of the reason we're such a hot destination venue for parties and weddings."

"Ahem." Lucy coughed.

"You didn't let me finish." Dan smiled at his sister. "Lucy's skills as an event planner are what really made our name, but the chef has turned out some pretty spectacular meals."

"We gave him the menu for tonight." Grace took Ford's arm as they walked into the lobby. "All of your favorites."

"That's great, Ma. Thanks."

"How 'bout you and I go out to your car and get the rest of your bags?" Dan offered.

Ford held up the two bags he'd brought with him. "This is it. Been living in tents or huts for the past six years, so I don't own very much."

Their expressions said it all.

"Really," he told them. "It wasn't always that bad."

They walked toward the stairwell in silence and Ford could only imagine what they were thinking. When they got to the bottom of the steps, his mother said, "Oh. Dan's son D.J.'s been using your old room, dear, so we moved you to another suite. I hope it's all right."

"It's fine, Ma. Any room that has a bed and a bathroom with a working shower is more than fine," he assured her.

"There really isn't another room in the family wing, since Diana has Lucy's old room. We needed to keep Dan's children together, and . . ."

"Ma, don't worry about it."

"I saved a special room for you." Dan took Ford's bags from his brother's hands. "Overlooks the bay, has a sitting room and a bedroom. Nice fireplace, one of the few rooms that has its own balcony . . ."

"Captain Tom's old room?" Ford paused on the step.

"Yup."

Ford grinned. "I always wanted to sleep in that room."

"I thought you'd like it." Dan grinned back.

"Dan, don't you think the room just around the

corner from our suite might be more appropriate?" Grace frowned and gave her eldest son a look of clear disapproval.

"Nah. You heard Ford. He wants that room." Dan continued up the steps.

"Ford," Grace called from the bottom of the steps. When he turned, she said, "That room might have a few"—she cleared her throat—"cold spots. You might be more comfortable sleeping in a different room."

"'Cold spots' is Mom's shorthand for 'uninvited guests,' if you get my drift," Dan whispered loud enough for their mother to hear.

"Daniel, you know there have been reports . . ." Grace waved her hands in defeat. "Oh, never mind."

"Ma, you still think that the old captain is hanging around?" Ford laughed. "Dan used to try to scare me with that old tale about how the old man never left the building and how he haunts his old room." He winked at Grace. "I don't scare quite as easily anymore. But I'll tell you what. If Tom shows up, I'll be sure to get an interview for the *Gazette*. Can't promise a photo, though . . ."

He took the steps two at a time to catch up to Dan, who'd already reached the second-floor landing.

"You remember the way?" Dan asked.

"Sure. End of this hall, take a right and go to the end. Last door on the left. I used to sneak in there every chance I got. Never did see the captain, though."

"I think that was something Mom made up to keep us from going out onto that balcony and falling off." Dan made the turn onto the side corridor and Ford followed.

"It wouldn't surprise me. She and Dad had any number of crazy stories about their ancestors. Tom was, what, Great-granny Hunt's maternal grandfather?"

"Something like that. I know he went back about four generations." Dan handed one of the bags off to Ford so he could search his pockets for the key to the room. "Sea captain, had a whole fleet of ships at one time. Rumored to have been a Union spy during the Civil War. Smuggled slaves north in his ships."

"That's his portrait downstairs in the library, isn't it?" Ford asked.

"Used to be. Now he's hanging right over the fireplace in here." Dan fitted the key into the lock and gave the door knob a good twist. The door swung open silently.

The two men entered the suite through a short hall that led to a sitting room with a brick fireplace over which hung the ancestor in question.

"Ah, there's the old guy." Ford stood with his hands on his hips. "Good to see you again, old man."

The portrait's dark eyes seemed to be looking back at them as they entered the room.

"I'm sure he's happy to see you again, too." Dan went past him into the bedroom. "There's only a light blanket on the bed, but if you need something else, just let housekeeping know. It's been pretty hot lately, and even though we have central air these days, this part of the building doesn't seem to cool off quite as well as some of the others."

"Central air, huh? So much for Ma's cold spots." Ford followed Dan into the bedroom where an old poster bed stood directly opposite a pair of French doors. Ford crossed the room to open them, stepped out onto the balcony, and inhaled deeply. "Ah, the Chesapeake. Nothing smells quite like it."

"Be grateful we had this end of the marsh dredged last year, or you'd be smelling something else entirely."

Ford laughed. "Hey, that marshy smell is a big part of one of my fondest childhood memories."

"Yeah, you and that buddy of yours . . ."

"Luke Boyer."

"Yeah, him. I remember the two of you used to spend hours out there and come home covered in mud and mosquito bites."

"Tracking nutrias. Never caught any—never really wanted to. The fun was all in the hunt."

"You'd find the hunting not as good these days. Nutrias have been mostly eradicated in this area. I'd like to get my hands on the guy who thought it would be a good idea to raise those nasty little things." Dan stood in the doorway, his hands on his hips.

"I don't think anyone expected them to get loose. I think it was someone's get-rich-quick scheme. Raise the animals, sell them for their pelts. Just didn't turn out that way."

"They created chaos in the marsh here a few years ago before the town found a way to control them. Furry little bastards ate through large sections of the wetlands, cleared out whole areas of bulrush, cordgrass, cattails—you name it, they ate it. Big loss of habitat for a lot of wildlife. You take out the native grasses, the sediment erodes, and the native plant populations suffer."

Ford walked to the end of the balcony and looked

across the vast lawn to the wetlands his brother was going on and on about. He knew all about the nutria and the damage the population had done in changing the face of the wetlands. He was well acquainted with the many ways that outside forces could change a place.

He could have told Dan how the long bloody wars had changed the face of emerging African nations, but what, he asked himself, would be the point? Besides, the last thing he wanted to do right at that moment was to look back at the devastation he'd left behind when he'd boarded the helicopter outside Bangui in the Central African Republic. There were so many rebel groups battling the government forces—rebel groups themselves—it had become impossible to know for certain who was shooting at whom. As the member of a small, covert team whose job it was to protect remote villages from being preyed upon by any of the rebel militias, Ford had witnessed the kind of horrors that were the stuff of nightmares. Being here, in this peaceful place, was almost jarring to his senses.

"So, you ready to head downstairs and see if we've exaggerated about our chef?" Dan asked from the doorway.

"Think I could grab a quick shower and change my clothes first?" After having traveled nonstop for the past forty-eight hours—including a debriefing in McLean, Virginia, just that morning—Ford was a little road weary.

"Sure thing. Just come down to the lobby when you're ready." Dan started toward the door. He glanced back over his shoulder and said, "I guess it must be great to be back after all those years living in those foreign places."

"Yeah. It's great to be back."

"I'll see you downstairs." Dan closed the door behind him.

Ford stood in the middle of the small sitting room, taking in the papered walls that surrounded him and the cushy carpet under his feet, the comfortable-looking sofa and chairs. He went into the bathroom and stared at the clean white tiles and the gleaming glass shower. There were fluffy towels on a chrome shelf and a new bar of soap in a porcelain dish on the counter next to the sink. He picked up the soap and inhaled its light pine scent. The everyday things he'd once taken for granted were now luxuries that he'd only dreamed about. He turned on the hot water and let it run through his fingertips.

After where he'd been, home seemed like the most foreign place of all.